GYPSY MOVED CLOSER TO ELISABETH'S HOSPITAL BED.

She made herself look down. "Oh God." She closed her eyes. "Elisabeth?" Her voice cracked.

She was talking to herself. The woman in the bed was her, or the person she'd been. Every hair, every inch of pale skin was absolutely familiar. This was her. Once upon a time.

Elisabeth looked like she was asleep. Her blond hair was neatly brushed and fanned across the pillow, and she wore a dark green silk kimono that had always been one of her favorites.

Her favorites . . .

Gypsy edged a little closer. "Elisabeth." She took Elisabeth's hand, then dropped it when she realized what she was doing. She was holding her own hand.

"Oh, God! Who am I!"

She was so unnerved she didn't hear the door open.

"Gypsy Dugan!" Elisabeth's husband said the name like a curse.

And what could she answer? *Hello, dearest. Look who's here?*

Once More with Feeling

EMILIE RICHARDS

AVON BOOKS ◆ NEW YORK

ONCE MORE WITH FEELING is an original publication of Avon Books. This work has never before appeared in book form. This work is a novel. Any similarity to actual persons or events is purely coincidental.

AVON BOOKS
A division of
The Hearst Corporation
1350 Avenue of the Americas
New York, New York 10019

Copyright © 1996 by Emilie Richards McGee
Inside cover author photo by Best Photography
Published by arrangement with the author
Library of Congress Catalog Card Number: 96-96026
ISBN: 0-380-78363-0

First Avon Books Printing: August 1996

AVON TRADEMARK REG. U.S. PAT. OFF. AND IN OTHER COUNTRIES, MARCA REGISTRADA, HECHO EN U.S.A.

Printed in the U.S.A.

RA 10 9 8 7 6 5 4 3 2 1

SOMETIME DURING THE RESTLESS ETERNITY of Thursday night, Elisabeth Whitfield dreamed that Owen, her husband of twenty-five years, was having an affair. She woke up Friday morning, as she had every morning for the past month, afraid it wasn't a dream at all. As Friday afternoon waned she completed preparations for the dinner party that might give her the proof she needed.

Elisabeth's parties were always elegant, tasteful, and ultimately forgettable, too much like their hostess to be truly memorable. She had learned to give a party from her mother, Katherine Brookshire Vanderhoff, who had insisted that God and the American flag came in a poor third and fourth behind an eternally pleasant expression and a flair with canapés. She had learned to choose wines and menus, caterers and florists. She had learned how to set a congenial atmosphere.

But she had never learned to like any of it.

This afternoon Elisabeth was enjoying the fine art of hostessing even less than usual. Weeks before, when she had seen the party only as a chance to socialize with old friends, she had rashly decided to hire younger, fashionable, and totally unfamiliar help. Now, with her enthusiasm at an historically low ebb, she was paying the price.

The new caterer, a sleek young redhead in Ralph Lauren khaki, had furtively examined every visible room of the Whitfield residence as she and her assistant marched in and out carrying platters and equipment—Elisabeth's own kitchen had not yielded the proper number of copper bowls and marble pastry slabs. She had carefully evaluated the neoclassical furniture, Owen's prized collection of Barbizon landscapes, the octagonal skylights and the white granite floor of the entrance hall.

"You have an absolutely spectacular home," the caterer pronounced at last, when Elisabeth's kitchen no longer looked as if it belonged to her.

Elisabeth acknowledged the compliment with the smile she had learned from her mother. "It's kind of you to say so."

"I've catered parties all over the Gold Coast, and I've never seen anything quite like this. Everything's . . . perfect." The young woman dragged out the last word like a feline with an exceptional vocabulary.

"My husband is the architect."

"I know."

Elisabeth suspected that the caterer also knew what clients Owen had designed for, the international competitions he had won, and his income to the nearest hundred thousand. She obviously had her sights set on more than the kitchens of Long Island.

The florist was new, as well. The old man who had faithfully provided Elisabeth with pastel tulips in the spring and pastel chrysanthemums in the fall had died quietly at Christmas, knee deep in pink and white poinsettias. Rick With-No-Last Name, his ponytailed and fashionable replacement, was a different breed entirely.

Elisabeth found the young man in the first floor powder room, assembling an arrangement of leafless twigs and excrement-hued cinnamon fern in three upturned rolls of toilet paper. As she watched he stood back to observe what he'd done, then leaned forward and artistically unwound a foot of one of the rolls and draped it over the edge of the counter.

It was good toilet paper. Elisabeth had to give him that much. A squeezable roll of ecological white. He turned and grinned infectiously. "Sm...oking!"

Blinded by white teeth and shining expectations, she lowered her eyes and found an arrangement of brightly colored bowl brushes in a stainless steel urinal on the floor beside the commode. The brushes were interspersed with long stems of bottlebrush buckeye.

"I can't wait to see what you'll do in the dining room." She added a gentle, vaguely regretful warning. "Just remember, there are going to be some terribly staid old fogies here tonight. And there are only so many Nassau County paramedics on call at any given moment."

He laughed conspiratorially. "I thought an aquatic theme since you're serving fish . . ."

She pictured mermaids impaled on skewers and belly-up dolphins with arugula and radicchio in what passed for their navels. "Remember the first arrangement you did as a very young man. That's what I want."

"Can't do it. I didn't bring my skulls today."

Elisabeth could see that this conversation, like too many aspects of her life, had spun out of control. Rick had quickly guessed the truth about the woman who had hired him. She was the eternal peacemaker, a doormat who would always back down rather than cause a fight. She was so nauseatingly gracious, so intrinsically diplomatic, that at one time or another every charity on Long Island had asked her to oversee a fund-raiser.

She was a woman on whom a man could easily cheat, assured that she would be too dignified to call the matter to his attention.

She swept methodically through the rest of the house to consult with the cleaning crew, examine the linens, and reprimand Owen's bookend golden retrievers, who lolled on a Savonnerie carpet and refused to move as much as a tail for Georgina, the gray-haired matron in a fifties housedress, who was attempting to vacuum around them.

Today Elisabeth found no comfort in familiar rituals. She probably needed hormones. She definitely needed a drink.

Instead, upstairs in the master suite bath she fished aspirin from a plastic vial and swallowed it without water. In the mirror with a museum-quality gilded frame, she saw an ash-blond, forty-something woman with a serene expression and pale blue eyes that were as untroubled as the May sky.

Behind the eyes was a fishwife clawing her way to freedom.

She washed her hands and automatically massaged lotion over them. At thirty she had been able to pretend that she would age gracefully. She had dieted and exercised, and the flat plane of her abdomen had fueled the lie. But now, at forty-eight, the truth was always in view. Hands with prominent veins, hips that had blossomed to their full genetic potential, feet in shoes that were designed primarily for comfort.

The telephone rang, but she ignored it. It would be Owen's secretary Marsha, checking to see if Elisabeth needed any last-minute assistance before the party. If there were errands, Owen wouldn't do them himself, of course. His staff was motivated to help by personal loyalty and generous salaries. Owen would smile his warmest smile and extend his hands in a little-boy-lost gesture. They would respond with whatever was needed. *Scottish salmon from Fraser Morris? Consider it done, Mr. Whitfield. Three bottles of Chateau Haut-Brion? I'll make the calls.*

Owen could design and oversee every detail of the

construction of award-winning houses or entire developments, but he could not locate a case of Bordeaux if he were standing in a Paris wine cellar. Everyone understood that.

She had understood it once upon a time.

Elisabeth had one blessed hour before she had to reassemble the worst of the florist's masterpieces, an hour before she had to give last-minute instructions to the caterer. She forced everything out of her mind: the fact that she was growing older with nothing substantial to show for it, the fact that she was married to a man who looked at her and didn't see her anymore, the fact that she was giving an intimate dinner party for her closest friends and was no longer looking forward to being with any of them.

The fact that one of her guests might well be sleeping with her husband.

She did what she had been doing for more than a year to forget the shackles that bound her to her outwardly enviable life.

She turned on the television.

On her bed, snuggled against Irish lace pillows, she watched a familiar crystal globe materialize on the screen. Once she had counted the globe's facets by taping the opening of the show, then pausing frame by frame as the globe turned full circle. There were twenty-four, each with a different scene reflected on its surface. She knew each image, although the effect was meant to be subliminal. A soaring eagle, the convertible that had carried Jack and Jackie Kennedy on their final ride together, the mushroom cloud of a nuclear bomb, Hopi kachina dancers, Bill and Hillary.

That scene dissolved into the next. A gavel fell against a polished wood surface, once, twice, three times. And before the sound could die away, a man began to speak.

"What you are about to hear is the truth, the whole

truth, and nothing but the truth." Elisabeth mouthed the words in sync with the announcer. As the final truth was uttered, a woman appeared on the screen.

"Hello. This is 'The Whole Truth,' and I'm Gypsy Dugan."

Before she had married Owen, in the days when she was still young and filled with confidence and spirit, Elisabeth had worked in television news, too. She had briefly tasted the joys that Gypsy probably took for granted, and she had relished them.

Elisabeth didn't know when Gypsy Dugan had become her alterego. She didn't know when the sexy news anchor had begun to represent all the things that were missing in her own life. She did know that no one suspected her fascination with the woman or the show, and that she intended to keep it that way.

She was Elisabeth Whitfield, scion of a family as old as the thirteen colonies, wife of the revered Owen Whitfield, mother of a grown, beloved son. She appeared to have everything, but she was only just discovering how little she had settled for.

On the screen Gypsy Dugan shook back her short dark hair. There was nothing warm or sympathetic about her smile. It was as erotic as an X-rated film and every bit as cynical. She was Scarlett O'Hara with a mission. No matter how maudlin the subject matter, how shocking the feature story of the day, her dimples flirted dangerously with her ripe, full lips. She was every man's fantasy and every woman's nightmare. She was Gypsy Dugan.

And she was a living reminder that Elisabeth Whitfield might have been somebody, too, if she had just tried harder.

Gypsy waited for the final signal, then she leaned back in her chair and half listened to the familiar bustle that characterized the end of another taping. An assistant came to unhook her mike, someone else gathered the props on the semicircular desk. No one tried to start a conversation, although she hardly noticed. Her gaze was riveted on the man standing just outside the studio lights. If she'd been anyone else, she might have licked her lips in anticipation. Instead she allowed one corner of her mouth to turn up. Just the tiniest bit.

He waited until the path was clear, then he moved toward her, a twentieth century pirate in a Davide Cenci suit. Charles Casey, dark-haired, dark-eyed, and perpetually in need of a closer shave. He was "The Whole Truth's" star reporter and the hottest lover Gypsy had taken in a decade.

"You could have manufactured a tear or two for the lead-in to the Williston story," he said when he was towering over her. "I mined the pathos in that one for all it was worth. Even Gypsy Dugan should squeeze out a tear for the death of a homeless mother and her two little angels."

Gypsy examined her nails, a supremely clichéd but nonetheless effective signal—besides, she wasn't at all happy with her latest manicure. "We've got Nan for the teary segments. She could cry buckets at the grand opening of a shopping mall."

"But that wasn't Nan's segment."

"No one wants to see me cry, Casey. You know that's not why they watch the show." She glanced up. "Did you come here to critique my work? Or did you have something better in mind?"

"Like?"

"An early dinner."

"Where?"

She tapped her disappointing nails. "Aureole," she said at last, choosing a place where he would have to mortgage his soul for a last-minute dinner reservation. She studied him from under her lashes. "*If* you have the clout to get us a table. But then I have to be back here to go over tomorrow's script. I'm not at all happy with the new writers Desmond hired."

Something blacker than sin glistened in his eyes.

"You're sure you don't have time to come to my place instead? We could send out for something."

"I am absolutely sure." She stood up slowly. A strict Catholic upbringing provided the inspiration for this particular exhibition. As a young teen she had learned to rise from her chair one inch at a time, so slowly that the nuns at St. Mary's had grown impatient and passed over the fact that her skirt was rolled at the waist and just a foot short of paradise.

Those years of practice served her well now. Casey's weight shifted to his heels and his gaze shifted, too. There wasn't a man anywhere who could resist Gypsy Dugan's legs. She ignored the fashion mavens—just as she had ignored the nuns—and wore her hems where she wanted them: smack dab in the middle of her thigh.

Casey's gaze drifted downward as slowly as she unfurled. From his pained expression she knew that he disliked this particular performance, but he was helpless not to become a one-man audience. "What about after you've finished here?" he asked.

"It will be very, very late." She placed her index finger against his lips. "Too late. But don't let that stifle your creativity."

He didn't kiss her finger; he sucked it into his mouth and nipped it with his sharp pirate's teeth. Then he blended back into the shadows.

Gypsy's dressing room was her sanctuary. The temperature was exactly seventy-two degrees year-round, and there was always fruit juice and mineral water waiting on ice. Tito Callahan, the media mogul for whom "The Whole Truth" was just one juicy tidbit in a banquet of television and newspaper holdings, had commissioned his personal decorator to redo the dressing room as a surprise bonus after the negotiations on her last contract. The walls were aubergine satin, and the Persian rug was fine enough to adorn a sultan's harem.

Today, after taking care of the thousand and one

details that signaled the official end of her working day, Gypsy closed the door behind her and went straight to her dressing table.

The clothes she wore were on loan to the show from a Trump Tower boutique, and she stripped them off and left them exactly where they landed. She considered changing into a black dress that she kept for such moments, a sleek, form-fitting tube with crisscross straps that left little to the imagination. But Casey thought entirely too much of himself, and she didn't want him to believe she was dressing up to please him. Instead she slipped into her street clothes, unfastening two of the buttons on her red silk blouse and replacing the simple pearl studs in her earlobes with a spray of faux rubies that would have glared like searchlights on camera.

She had thrown a towel over her shoulders and was creaming her face when someone knocked. The sound was too hesitant to be Casey's, but it was familiar, all the same. "It's not locked." She attacked the cream with a wad of tissues.

The door opened a crack. "Are you decent?"

"I'm never decent."

Desmond Weber, the show's executive producer, closed the door behind him and stood with his back against it. He was a man in his mid-fifties with the sturdy build of a linebacker carried incongruously on a jockey's short legs. His wiry gray hair was clipped and contoured with poodle precision; his nose was a classic pug, and his eyes were as soulful as a cocker spaniel's. Gypsy glanced at him, then turned back to the mirror. "I'm a work in progress here, so you don't have to blockade the door. I'm not going to run."

Desmond moved farther into the room. "I thought the taping went well."

"You know what? It would have gone better if you'd given me some stories with meat on them. Christ, Desmond, how many more segments are we going to do on that poor homeless woman from North Carolina? Don't you think digging up her date for the senior prom was a bit much? She's dead. Does anyone care whether she got roses or carnations that night?"

"Yeah. Our audience cares."

"Then they're bigger assholes than I thought."

"Hey, aren't we in a charming mood?"

"*We* certainly are not." She stroked concealer under her eyes. These days it had become her first line of defense. She might not be sleeping worth a damn anymore, but she wasn't going to tell the world.

"Have you noticed that everyone's tiptoeing around like you're an unclaimed suitcase ticking sixty beats to the minute?"

"They're just doing their jobs quietly, the way they're supposed to."

"You're never jumpy. And suddenly, you're jumpy as hell. Everybody's noticed. Everybody's worried."

"Everybody's wondering how they can use it to scramble up the old career ladder!"

"Come on, Gyps. Not everyone's as motivated by misfortune as you are."

She was silent, because he was right. She knew she had a gold-plated reputation for ruthlessness, although everyone agreed it was never personal. Gypsy wasn't unkind. She was simply obsessed with herself.

"Is it your . . . security problem?" Desmond asked.

She abandoned the concealer for custom-blended foundation. "At least you didn't say my *imaginary* security problem."

"Come on. I know you think it's real."

"Why yes, now that you mention it. Nearly spilling one's guts on a Fifth Avenue sidewalk can give a person those kinds of fantasies."

"Look, I know it was hard, traumatic even, to watch somebody you knew and respected drop dead right beside you—"

"Yeah. Particularly when you think that the gunman who killed him was taking aim at you, too." Gypsy glanced at Desmond again. "And don't tell me that none of the witnesses believe anyone besides Mark was the target. I've read the police report myself. I know what it says. But I was standing right beside him."

"Look, we're taking your fears seriously. If there's any chance that the man who shot Mark wants to take you out as well, then we have to protect you. You're being watched twenty-four hours a day."

"Right. And the only thing I can be sure of is that next time, if *I'm* the victim, I'll go to my glory with an audience."

"We've hired the best men out there."

"And not a one of them could have kept Mark from getting shot." Usually Gypsy saved her reminiscences of that moment for the middle of the night when her Xanax wore off, but now the whole scene flashed through her mind.

Mark Santini had been hired the previous fall as "The Whole Truth's" newest director. A promising young man with energy and ideas to spare, he had taken Gypsy to lunch several weeks before Christmas to discuss a new concept for the show, and they had chosen a restaurant some blocks from the studio. The day was unseasonably warm, and afterward Mark suggested that they walk along Fifth Avenue to see the holiday windows. Half a block from St. Patrick's Cathedral a man stepped out in front of them and blasted a hole through Mark's cashmere overcoat. Gypsy watched in horror as Mark slumped to the ground. Then the man lifted the gun in her direction.

And he smiled.

"He didn't shoot you," Desmond reminded her. As he spoke the door opened behind him, but despite the subject under discussion he didn't even turn to see who it was. Security at the studio was high-tech and impenetrable. There were too many competitors in the lucrative world of investigative news to risk media espionage.

Gypsy's gaze strayed to the man at the door. Her

voice changed subtly. Now she sounded bored. "We'll
never know why Mark's killer didn't pull the trigger
again, will we? Maybe the gun jammed. Maybe he
realized he didn't have time to get off another shot.
He was gone before anyone could ask for an explanation."

"Or maybe he just didn't have any reason to kill
you," Casey said from the doorway. "The cops have a
pretty good idea why this guy might have wanted
Mark dead, and it doesn't have anything to do with
you."

Gypsy knew the prevailing theory. Mark's extended
family was rumored to have murky ties to organized
crime. His death had all the traits of a Mafia hit, a
lesson, perhaps, to some distant uncle or cousin who
had gotten out of line.

She shrugged carelessly and uncapped her mascara.
As far as she was concerned, the conversation had
ended. Desmond was the only person to whom she
admitted her worst fears. Casey was another matter.

"No more of this tonight," she said. "I'm sure your
watchdogs will keep me safe, Des. Besides, when I'm
in Casey's hands, I never have anything to worry
about except Casey's hands." She redid her lipstick,
then reached for a bottle and spritzed her cleavage
with a new fragrance that claimed to contain synthe-
sized human pheromones.

"Try to lighten up a little, will you?" Desmond
asked. "Especially on Nan."

She wrinkled her brow in mock sympathy. "Poor
little Nannie-poo. Has the wicked Gypsy woman hurt
her teensy-weensy feelings again?"

"Just ease up on everybody, Gyps. It'll make my life
easier, and in the long run, that's good for you."

She waved Desmond out the door. "Go tell whatever watchdog is lurking in the shadows tonight to take
his dinner break. Casey will take over my care and
feeding for a while, won't you, Casey?"

"With something like pleasure." Casey waited until

the door closed before he crossed the room. Gypsy rose to greet him, but he didn't embrace her until she rested her forearms on his shoulders. The game was hers to call, and she had made certain that Casey realized it from the start.

He was a tall man, but she was a tall woman. It was just as well, since she couldn't imagine gazing up at him with adoring eyes. She liked her lovers nearly nose to nose; she never wore anything lower than three-inch heels.

He lowered his head, and she smelled the spicy essence of Joop. Casey's lips were warm against hers, but the kiss was not all that she had expected. There was nothing rakish or demanding about it. It was almost . . . gentle.

She pulled away and her eyes narrowed. "What's that about?"

He didn't answer for a moment. She could see something like a struggle behind his perpetually cynical expression. "I know you're scared," he said finally.

"Do you?" She stepped back, one perfectly arched eyebrow sailing high above the other. "Well, you're wrong. I'm angry. I just don't like the fact that my daily life's been affected by all of this. But I'm not scared. I've never been scared of anything in my whole life."

"Everybody's scared of something."

"Bullshit." She paused a heartbeat or two to recover. "Gypsy Dugan's not like everybody else. She's in a class all by herself."

"Even Gypsy Dugan's afraid of dying."

"Gypsy Dugan isn't going to die. She's planning to live forever." She said the words, and for the moment they lingered in the air, they were true. She had no intention of meeting her maker. In spite of the fears she had voiced to Desmond, it was simply inconceivable.

"We're all going to die. Even the reigning sexpot of the television tabloids. We'll just have to do everything we can to make sure it happens later rather than sooner."

One corner of her lips turned up provocatively, and she wiped her lipstick off his mouth with her thumb. "Don't worry about me, Casey. I've got an incentive to stay alive. I hear they've reserved a place down below for women like me. If I want heat, I'll wait out eternity on a yacht in the Mediterranean."

2

THERE WAS NO SURE WAY TO TELL IF A MAN was sleeping with another woman other than to catch him in the act. Elisabeth had never followed Owen to his paramour's apartment or hired a private detective to snap photographs through discreetly veiled hotel windows. She hadn't detected the scent of unfamiliar perfume on his perfectly tailored suit jackets or discovered lipstick stains on his shirt collars. In the past weeks, as the possibility of Owen's infidelity had nagged at her one long lonely night after the other, she had watched and waited. She hadn't snooped, and she hadn't interrogated.

But she was almost sure she knew who the woman was.

"I'm glad you scheduled an evening for me at home." Owen came out of his bathroom freshly showered and wrapped insecurely in a towel. "I've been gone so much recently that I had to stop in the village to get directions to our house."

She was surprised he would so casually go right to the heart of her suspicions. In the past two months Owen had been home not more than a dozen nights. Theoretically he kept an apartment in Manhattan just for those occasions when he had to work late or entertain clients. These days Elisabeth suspected a different kind of entertaining altogether.

"All those meetings. I just don't know how you keep it up." Elisabeth didn't even blink at her own double entendre. Her tone was sympathetic. She sat on the bed in his bedroom and resisted twisting the bedspread into a noose.

He honored her with his most charming smile. "Well, I'd never be able to do any of it without you. If you didn't see to our social life, I'd probably be a hermit and somebody else's assistant to boot."

She accepted the praise with a gracious nod. Owen's ultimate success was due to his unmistakable brilliance and little else. But he had achieved success faster because of her family background and contacts. He was the poor son of Polish immigrants with an American name that was only three generations old. Their marriage had assured immediate access to some of New York's finest families. On her darkest days she wondered if that had been his major reason for proposing to her.

"Tell me the guest list again?" Owen dropped his towel in the middle of the floor and strolled stark naked into his state-of-the-art closet, which was equipped with everything except a live valet.

Owen naked, even when Elisabeth's mood was grim, made her swallow involuntarily. "The Molnars. The Adamsons. I ousted Tipper and Al Gore to make room for Grant . . . and Anna." For a moment she didn't think he'd heard her, then his head popped out of the closet. He flashed her the same grin that twenty-six years ago had sent her heart plummeting straight to her toes.

"I *was* listening," he said. "Who else?"

"Just the O'Keefes."

He rolled his eyes and disappeared again.

"*I* like them," Elisabeth said—and despite his pretended disapproval, she knew Owen did, too. "Marg is so 'old money' she can say or do anything she wants."

"Is that why she showed up at our last dinner party

in bedroom slippers? Her money's so old no one would take it at the shoe store?"

"One slipper. She'd just had her toe operated on."

"And since when does Grant get invitations to our parties?"

Since she had decided to watch Owen with Anna Jacquard and see if her suspicions had any foundation. Elisabeth kept her voice light. "Since Anna did. She and Grant are last-minute substitutions for the Considines, who had to leave town unexpectedly. I called them both at the beginning of the week. Anna was only too glad to help out, but I had to bribe Grant."

"With what?"

"The keys to the beach house next weekend for God knows what reason." She absolutely adored her son and refused to think what he might be planning to do at their Amagansett summer cottage—and with whom.

Owen stepped out of the closet with dark suit pants unzipped low on his hips and his white shirt unbuttoned. He was fumbling with a gold cuff link. "Are we having this party because you want to, Bess? Or is it a check on the social scorecard?"

She was surprised he had asked. Owen was usually oblivious to those kinds of subtleties. "A bit of both. I thought it might be a pleasant way to take care of some of our obligations."

"Thought? Past tense?"

"It should be fun."

He raised a brow, but he fumbled on in silence. Elisabeth didn't volunteer to help him. That past weekend she had heard a well-known psychologist lecture on the dangers of codependency. The psychologist had described his patients at length. They had all sounded entirely too much like her.

Owen fastened the cuff link at last and started on the opposite wrist. They had been married so long that Elisabeth could chart every mole and scar on his body. She knew the number of hairs on his chest and the precise way he clipped his toenails. He liked his shirts with starch—he claimed that in a former life he had been a particularly penitent monk—and he favored ties that the upwardly mobile dared not wear. Nothing about Owen Whitfield was surprising, but everything was seductive.

He caught her staring at him. His eyes gleamed brighter. "Well, do you like what you see?"

What she saw was a middle-aged man with the rawboned build of his Slavic peasant ancestors and dark hair that was fast turning silver. The skin around his brown eyes was crinkled from too many squints and too many smiles, but he would no more visit a plastic surgeon than live out the last of his days on a Palm Springs golf course.

So far Owen had avoided the curses of too many men his age. His hair was still thick, his waistline trim. He had yet to consider that his charms might have diminished, and he was right. He was still so attractive, in fact, that Elisabeth suspected that even her closest friends might be tempted to have an affair with him if he crooked his little finger. To her knowledge, he had never crooked for any of them.

But he may very well have crooked for Anna.

She didn't allow that thought to show. "I've always liked looking at you. Show me a woman who doesn't."

He smiled, but didn't deny it. "We should spend more time together. I've been neglecting you."

"Dogs and children can be neglected. Not adults. You're not responsible to me for a certain number of hours a year."

"What if I'd like to be?"

She was anything but flattered. As usual lately, he had missed the point. "I'd rather not be an entry in your appointment book." She slid off the bed. "I've got to finish dressing."

They kept separate bedrooms for those nights when he arrived home late and didn't want to disturb her, but more and more often, even on the rare occasions when he was home, they slept apart. He had moved his clothes into this room a year ago. Now there was a bookcase beside the bed packed with Tom Clancy novels, architectural tomes, and volumes of obscure Polish poetry. Her clothes—and life—were across the hall.

He stopped her before she got to the door. "Let me rephrase. I miss you."

His brown eyes seemed sincere, but she wondered how many seconds it would be before his thoughts turned back to the thousand and one details of a successful man's day and away from his undemanding wife.

"I'm delighted," she said. "We'll have to see what we can do about it."

He stroked one practiced finger along her cheek-bone to the corner of her mouth. "There'll be time after the party to make a start. Just don't encourage Grant to stay around."

She didn't quite meet his eyes. "I'll boot him out the door."

She thought about their exchange as she stepped into a navy dress with a crisp white Chanel jacket and later, when she adjusted the downstairs lighting so that it was subtle enough to complement the women's makeup. Owen was an enthusiastic, inventive lover, and sex had held their marriage together in the early days when they were learning to live together. They had even managed to find time for each other when Grant was a baby and Owen's future was anything but assured. But if they made love tonight, it would be the first time in a month.

At least for her.

"What shall I do?"

Owen's words startled her. Elisabeth had grown so used to his absence that his presence in the house, in her *life,* was almost a surprise.

She continued fiddling with a table lamp and didn't

turn. "There's nothing, really. I thought we'd have coffee in here after dinner. Be sure nobody bunches up over in that corner." She waved toward a small, private conversational grouping of wing chairs at the opposite end of the living room.

"And how do I stop them?"

"Open the closest window. Create a draft."

He rested his hands on her shoulders. "Is that one of those things the blue-blooded instinctively know?"

She couldn't pretend she was something she was not. As a child Elisabeth had learned the fine art of fitting into society. She could gracefully wend her way through a party tent on the lawn of any East Hampton mansion. She could converse at length with the Four Hundred's brightest butterflies and never utter a meaningful word. She was known in the exclusive circles in which she moved to be a "brick," or a "rock," ironically suitable for a woman who had allowed her architect husband to design her narrow world.

"It's one of those things the wives of successful men learn by paying close attention to the wives of other successful men," she said with inbred tact.

"You've never needed to pay attention to anyone. You were born for this."

"I'd like to think I was born for a bit more." Her words were clipped. The sentiment behind them was lengthy.

His thumbs began a slow massage, exactly where tension had tied her shoulder muscles into knots. "Don't disparage yourself. You make everyone comfortable. You have such a knack for it. I've never met anyone who so completely puts others at ease. You're a sensational hostess."

She didn't know how to tell Owen that he was making everything worse. There had to be more to life than knowing what wines to serve and how loud to set the volume on the sound system. Gypsy Dugan came to mind. Gypsy could probably entertain the entire

United Nations in a South Bronx tenement, serve root beer with prime rib, play Nine Inch Nails at top volume, and by the next day no one would remember.

But they would remember her.

The doorbell rang and the comforting fingers stilled. "Georgina stayed for the evening. She'll get it," she reminded Owen.

"I guess I'm supposed to station myself somewhere and wait."

"Mom?" Grant's voice drifted in just ahead of him. He appeared in the doorway. "Bet you're spraying the lightbulbs with White Linen."

Owen corralled their son in a huge bear hug before Elisabeth could move. At twenty-four Grant was six-foot, slender but solid, with shoulders that were broad enough to take his father's playful abuse. His hair was the pale brown of his eyes, and the strong slash of his cheekbones were a carbon copy of Owen's.

Grant broke away from his father, embraced Elisabeth, and kissed her cheek. "The house looks wonderful. I like what you did in the entrance hall."

She squeezed her eyelids shut in resignation. "Oh God. That was the florist. I forgot to look. What did he do?"

"You'll see. Am I the first one here?"

"You are," Owen said. "Were you hoping to get an early start on the hors d'oeuvres?"

Grant manufactured a waif's pathetic smile. "I live on a teacher's salary, remember? Unless I'm invited to the homes of the rich and famous, I can only eat dinner on alternate Wednesdays."

Owen slung his arm over Grant's shoulders. "Careful what you say or your mother will package up every bite the guests and the dogs don't eat and send it home with you."

"This is my baby you're talking about," Elisabeth said. "No gallows humor, please."

Although Owen and Grant were both joking, there was a kernel of truth to their exchange. Grant's existence was hardly hand-to-mouth, but he rarely had money to spare. He taught English in a public high school in the Bronx, where security guards routinely roamed the hallways and the only poetry his students were familiar with was spray-painted on subway walls. In his second year on staff he had moved into the neighborhood so that he could be available to his students after classes.

"Hi, am I too early?"

Elisabeth looked up to see Anna. Georgina had obviously let her in before she rang the bell. Elisabeth's welcoming smile was as automatic as the stab of betrayal she felt. "Of course not."

She watched Owen abandon his son and move toward Anna.

Anna Jacquard had begun working for Owen one year ago. She was thirty-two, with dark hair and eyes, a milkmaid complexion, and a restless, artistic temperament that drew men to her like honeybees to the lone lily in a field of daisies. Tonight she was dressed in velvet leggings and a silk tunic she had probably dyed herself. Her hair hung in an unfashionably long braid that was so perfect a choice, strangers stopped her on the street and warned her not to cut it.

Owen took her hands in his. There was a pause before they greeted each other, as if they were assessing changes, accumulating memories—despite the fact that they had seen each other only hours ago at the office. Owen bent his head and brushed his lips against her cheeks. Her eyelids lowered in something longer than a blink. She seemed to hold her breath, to savor . . .

"Elisabeth . . ."

Elisabeth realized that Anna was coming toward her now. Owen's greeting, which had probably taken only seconds, had ended. But Elisabeth still felt it like a tangled knot inside her. Anna extended her hands to Elisabeth as she had to Owen, but the expression in her eyes wasn't nearly as warm. "The house looks lovely. And the flowers in the entrance are inspired. Is that your handiwork?"

"It's most decidedly not." Elisabeth squeezed Anna's hands, then dropped them quickly. "Thank you for coming on such short notice. We're always glad to have you here."

The last was a lie. Once upon a time Elisabeth *had* been happy to have Anna here. Hiring Anna Jacquard had been a coup for Owen. She was a supremely talented architect who had begun the career climb in a prestigious Dallas firm. But Owen had seen one of Anna's designs at a convention, and he had been completely enchanted. There was a similarity in the way that they thought about space, about light and angles and working in harmony with nature. He had made a point of seeking her out, and, just a month later, of making her an offer that was too good to pass up.

And one month ago Elisabeth had begun to wonder what other offers Owen had made her.

"I love coming here." Anna had a subtle smile, one that didn't light up her face so much as highlight its finer points. "You are the perfect hostess."

Elisabeth had a vision of those words as her epitaph, chiseled on a white granite crypt that looked astonishingly like this house. She murmured some properly insincere words of gratitude.

The doorbell rang again, and the remainder of the guests arrived in closely spaced groups of two. Anna and Grant wandered toward the library, where drinks were going to be served. Elisabeth and Owen went to the entrance hall, where Rick had filled a corner with calla lilies and oddly sculpted coral under tulle that billowed convincingly each time the door opened.

She tried to put the intimacy of Owen and Anna's greeting out of her mind as she greeted Marguerite and Seamus O'Keefe.

"We are obviously having something that swims for dinner," Marguerite said, pointing to the arrangement.

Elisabeth kissed Marguerite's cheek. "I'd hate to think what he might have done if I'd been serving venison. I'm afraid he would have given us his personal rendition of the death scene from *Bambi*."

"I gave a dinner party the week that Berlin was reunited. The florist built a wall of flowers across the dining room table and it collapsed spectacularly when the first course was set on the table. I have grown fond of rose petals in my consomme."

"Tell me his name wasn't Rick."

Marguerite gave a sly wink. "However did you know?"

Marguerite, tall, blond, and horsey, had been Elisabeth's friend since infancy. She could ride to hounds in the morning and picket Madison Avenue furriers the same afternoon without a thought for the irony. She had blood ties to the Vanderbilts, the Roosevelts, and other historic three-syllable names too numerous to mention, but she had married apple-cheeked Seamus O'Keefe, who called himself a landscape architect and was really just a gardener. Seamus had made it his life's work to dig up every inch of Birch Haven, their Litchfield County estate, and replant it with tropical plant life that required constant vigilance. In private Owen called him Exotic Compost O'Keefe in honor of Seamus's never-ending supply of Zone 10 plants that hadn't made the adjustment to Connecticut's Zone 5 winters.

The Adamsons arrived next. Missy Adamson—who once had debated excising the "i" in her first name to make it more politically correct—was a steel magnolia from the heart of Dixie. Behind the Confederate cotillion smile, the stiffly sprayed dark hair, and the sorghum-sweet accent was a woman with graduate degrees in three languages and the canny ability to use them in furthering her husband's career. Richard

Adamson, with a smile as powerful as Owen's and sandy hair that hadn't yet turned gray, was a former congressman who was busily positioning himself to become the next Democratic governor of New York.

Richard kissed Elisabeth on the lips, a chaste, political kiss that was only slightly more intimate than a handshake at a crowded rally. Elisabeth had dated Richard when she was an English Literature major at Mt. Holyoke and he was prelaw at Yale. Even then he had been intent on running for office someday, and he had limited himself to girls with pristine, proper backgrounds. On the third date she had begun to understand that behind Richard's quick wit and sincere desire to change the world dwelled a man who was capable of marrying her solely because her bland patrician beauty was an ideal complement to his. They had remained friends despite the fact that she had refused to go out with him again.

"Every time I come here I realize Owen didn't do his best work for me." He turned up the wattage on his smile to be certain Elisabeth knew he was teasing. "This house is spectacular. Ours is merely magnificent."

Richard and Missy had hired Owen's firm to design and build a "country house" in another North Shore community. Their home stood on six acres overlooking Long Island Sound, and three years ago it had garnered Owen a prize from the American Institute of Architects.

"I'll consider a trade," Elisabeth said. "Our view of Manhattan isn't nearly as perfect as yours." In reality, the Whitfields had no view of Manhattan.

"I'll warn you, you can't take a thing with you. I want it exactly as it is."

"The weeds in my flower garden and the lint in my dryer?"

He laughed. "Sorry, the deal's off."

Owen ushered the O'Keefes and Adamsons into the library, where a fire roared and the caterer had begged to serve hors d'oeuvres. Before Elisabeth could make certain the first tray was on its way, the doorbell rang again. She waved away Georgina and answered the door herself.

Atilla Molnar smothered her in an expansive hug, followed closely by his wife Lorraine. They were similarly dumpy and good-humored, but Atilla was a shrewd businessman who had expanded his father's tiny Hungarian language newspaper into a chain of tiny English language newspapers that stretched from sea to shining sea.

"Got a story for you," he told Elisabeth as the three of them walked, arms around each others' waists, toward the library.

She murmured her interest. Attila was the editor of the *Paumanok Sentinel,* the paper for which Elisabeth wrote an occasional feature story. Several years ago, after turning over management of the syndicate to his oldest son, Attila had taken over the *Sentinel* as a hedge against retirement. Then he had patiently convinced Elisabeth to write for him whenever time permitted. It was the one thing she did that had absolutely nothing to do with her role as Owen Whitfield's wife.

Elisabeth untangled herself from the Molnars and led them into the library, where greetings were exchanged. She got them drinks and made sure everyone else was comfortable before she drifted back to Atilla's side. The conversation centered around the room itself, with its dual Palladian windows looking over the terrace and formal garden, and the white marble fireplace with a fanciful curved mantel that echoed the arch of the windows. It was Owen's favorite room, one where he sometimes sat for hours with papers and books strewn over the mahogany table.

"I have never seen a house with such perfect views . . . except maybe ours," Missy said. "It's like you frame every one of them before you even break ground. Do you, Owen? Is that what you do? Is there a window in any house you design that looks out over a driveway?"

"Oh, even his driveways are spectacular," Marguerite said. "Most of us would consider ourselves lucky to gaze at one."

"So when are you going to let me renovate Birch Haven?" Owen asked Marguerite.

"Birch Haven would suffer tremendously if so much as a tile were pried loose."

"I can't even get her to replace the slipcovers," Seamus said. "Marg says that only the nouveau riche care if their slipcovers are frayed."

Marguerite slipped her arm through his. "The newly rich will not stay that way if they throw away their money."

As the conversation drifted to people they all knew, Elisabeth forced herself to relax an inch at a time. She reminded herself that except for Anna, the people assembled in the library were ones she really cared about. The fire was warm; the caterer's rumaki was memorable. And Anna and Owen hadn't exchanged any new soulful glances in the minutes since Anna's arrival.

"Then, of course, there was that horrible story about her on one of those news shows that really aren't. You know the ones I mean. The kind that do reenactments and interviews with the pet groomers of celebrity murderers."

Elisabeth looked up at Marguerite's words. She knew everyone had been discussing the fate of a former New York congresswoman who had been drummed out of office after a titillating scandal, but she had lost the thread of the conversation. "What show is that?"

"I'm sure I don't know the name of it. 'The Whole World,' or something like that."

"'The Whole Truth,'" Lorraine said. Attila's wife never apologized for her working-class roots, her tastes, or her nasal Bronx accent. "I watch it all the time. I'm gonna slim down to a size three one of these days and dye my hair. I think I'd look just like that Gypsy Dugan."

"You really watch it?" For once Marguerite was stunned.

"Sure I do. I sit there with a box of Kleenex, and I get a good cry almost every day. Cheaper than a psychiatrist and I pick up fashion tips by watching what that Gypsy wears."

Attila turned to Elisabeth. "Remember I told you I had a story for you?"

"Absolutely."

"Well, it was Lorraine's idea. Gypsy Dugan's coming to a symposium at Stony Brook as a guest lecturer, and I managed to get a ticket. I want you to do a feature about her for next week's paper."

Elisabeth couldn't think of a thing to say. For a moment she wondered if Attila suspected her peculiar fascination with Gypsy Dugan.

"Oh, Attila, I've read every article Elisabeth's written for you," Missy said. "They're all completely tasteful. What on earth could she say about this Gypsy person?"

"That's the whole point," Attila said. "The meeting of the princess and the fifty-dollar hooker. Elisabeth's observations will make a great story."

"Meeting?" Elisabeth said.

"Yeah, I got you an interview right afterward. You get ten minutes alone with her, so you'll have to do some fast talking."

Richard turned to Elisabeth. "I've met Gypsy Dugan."

She was moving beyond surprise. "Have you?"

"When I was in Congress. She started out as the political reporter on one of the local affiliates, covering events in the Capitol from time to time. Fifty-dollar hooker gives her too much credit. Even then she had a reputation as someone who was sleeping her way up the ladder instead of putting in her time."

Elisabeth felt instantly defensive, but tried to keep it from her voice. "I've seen the show. She may be what you say, but she lights up the screen."

"You've seen the show, Bess?" Owen asked. "You don't watch anything except Jim Lehrer on public television."

"How would you know what I watch when you're not at home?"

"After all these years I think I know your tastes."

"Maybe not as well as you think."

"Mother's much earthier than you give her credit for," Grant told his father. "I suspect she has an entire secret life that the rest of us have never suspected."

"You make me sound far more interesting than I am," Elisabeth said.

Marguerite's gaze flashed to Anna, who was taking in this conversation with her lips softly parted in disbelief. "I think there are unplumbed depths to our Elisabeth," Marguerite said. She looked straight at Owen. "And were I you, Owen, renowned architect or no, this is one plumbing job I'd do myself . . ."

"Trust me, I could discuss Elisabeth's plumbing with the best of them," he said.

Elisabeth had seen Marguerite assessing Anna. Elisabeth had never discussed her fears about Anna with Marguerite, but now she knew intuitively that they were shared. The warmth she'd begun to feel died a swift, icy death. She forced a response. "I think I'd rather discuss this Gypsy Dugan. I have to say the madonna-whore angle doesn't excite me."

"Princess-whore," Attila said.

"As bad. Let's not assume that because my family's in the Blue Book I don't have all the normal instincts of any other woman. Even a woman like Gypsy Dugan."

There was a hiccup in the conversation. "Are we back to plumbing?" Marguerite asked when no one else spoke.

This time Elisabeth forced a smile. "No. We're back to giving every woman her due, even a celebrity like Gypsy Dugan. She strikes me as intelligent and witty. And the few times I've caught the show"—she didn't even flinch at the lie—"she's impressed me with her honesty. Maybe you need a box of tissues when you watch, Lorraine, but it's clear that Gypsy Dugan doesn't, and she doesn't pretend to. What you get is what you see, and the viewers know they can trust her. I'd guess that's why she's made it to the top."

"The top?" Missy shrieked like a Mississippi riverboat calliope. "Elisabeth, that show can't possibly be the top! Not tabloid trash like that. Diane Sawyer and Barbara Walters are the top."

"The latest Q scores say that Gypsy Dugan is the most recognized female anchorwoman in America." Attila turned up his hands. "And it looks like Elisabeth's the only one here who understands why."

"I know you have more than a passing acquaintance with television news," Richard said to Elisabeth. "I know you used to work in a television newsroom before you married Owen. But take my word for it. We don't want to encourage these kinds of shows or these kinds of people. This country has enough problems with deceit and ignorance. Maybe a woman of your background and intelligence can find something to admire about Gypsy Dugan, but think about the average American. Is he or she capable of sorting the truth from the rest of the trash?"

"Why Richard, how unegalitarian of you," Marguerite said. "I thought you were the champion of the average American. Have you changed political parties right along with everybody else?"

Elisabeth watched Richard's aristocratic nostrils curl. She balanced her desire to continue the argument with her duties as hostess. Duty won out. "I'm sure if my article provokes even half as much interest in the subject as we've shown tonight, the *Sentinel*'s circulation will double. When is this lecture scheduled, Attila?"

"Friday at two."

"Friday?" Owen caught Elisabeth's eye and shook his head.

For a moment Elisabeth didn't understand. Owen had never interfered with her freelancing before. Of course there had never been a reason to. She had made certain to put everything else first.

"The Caswells," he said.

Her heart sank. Lee Caswell was a North Carolina developer who was interested in having Owen's firm design a prestigious oceanfront complex of hotels and condominiums. He was coming to town for negotiations and Elisabeth had agreed to take his wife shopping on Friday morning. They were to join the men in the afternoon for lunch.

Owen waited expectantly. She knew what he assumed she would do. She even opened her mouth to do it. Then she shook her head. "I'll be there, Attila," she said. "I can change my plans."

"You're sure? Because it's a story I don't want to lose."

"I'm absolutely sure." Her gaze flicked back to Owen's face. He was angry, although she doubted that anyone else could tell. But he wasn't looking at her. He was looking at Anna, and she at him. His expression didn't change, but his eyes said everything. Lee Caswell was an important man. So was Owen Whitfield.

And Elisabeth was just his wife.

Elisabeth lifted her chin and smiled at the others. "Missy, let me get you another drink."

"I'm heartily sick of pasta, Casey. I can't imagine what made you choose that place or this cab." Gypsy leaned against the backseat of the battered gypsy cab without making enough room for Casey. As horns bellowed behind them he squirmed in beside her, squeezing his lithe body into position like the last piece of a complicated jigsaw puzzle.

"I chose it because your expectations were ridiculous. If you want to eat at a place like Aureole, give me a month's notice. Without it you'll get pasta in the Village."

"Bad pasta!"

"Mine was excellent."

"You have no taste. You're still a poor mick-spick from Hell's Kitchen. If it's got meat in it, you think it's gourmet."

He snuggled in tighter. "So speaks the girl from the wrong side of Cleveland. Pierogis more your style, Gypsy?" He laughed as she punched him. "Kielbasa? Sauerkraut?"

"I'm as Irish as you are, you jerk!"

"Which is only half-Irish, as you've neatly pointed out. What's your other half? Slovak? Polish? You're sure as hell no WASP."

"I'm half–Rumanian Gypsy. And if you don't show some respect immediately, I'll put a curse on you!"

"You already have. I must be cursed to want to spend time with you." He grabbed her flailing fists and held them tightly.

"Mister," the driver said, turning in his seat with the world weariness that even a week of driving the streets of New York could produce. "Gotta have number and street. You never gimme it. Number. Street."

"Sure, I know," Casey said. He gave the address of the studio. "And remember, go by way of Brooklyn, okay?"

"What?" The cab driver's English wasn't up to complicated instructions. Gypsy made a practiced guess that the man hadn't lived outside of Latin America for more than a year.

"I told you before. I want you to take half an hour to get us there." Casey clasped Gypsy's flailing hands together in one of his and fished in his pocket with the other.

"What are you talking about? And why are we in this, this . . . jalopy?" Gypsy tried to wriggle from his grasp. The cab was an old gray Ford that had seen better days and never seen official licensing. It had been waiting for them when they emerged, and Casey had told her it was a gypsy cab for his Gypsy woman.

Casey managed to free his wallet. He plucked two bills from it and handed them over the front seat. A volley of fluent Spanish followed. "*Comprende* now?" he finished.

"Yeah," the driver said.

"And remember just drive. No free shows."

"Yeah."

"Casey, I have to get back to the studio!"

"Didn't you hear my instructions?" Casey slipped Gypsy's arms over his head. He forced her back against the worn plush seat. "We're headed there right now."

"What in the hell do you think you're doing?"

"Showing some creativity."

"You're showing some balls, that's what!"

"Not yet, but very, very soon."

She tried to kick him, but it was a weak attempt.

"It's getting dark and the windows are tinted. I made sure nobody's going to see us," he assured her. As if to make his point he drew his trenchcoat over them so that the driver's view was blocked, as well.

"Do you think I care about that?"

He smiled grimly. "That's right. Stupid me."

"You take way the hell too much for granted!"

He released her hands. They stayed where they were.

His didn't. He lifted her skirt, and she smiled a little. She knew what he'd find. Her thighs were warm, smooth, and bare. He slid his hands up to her hips and found them bare, too. Some of the thrill seemed to go out of the seduction. "You slut, you knew, didn't you?"

"Knew what?"

"Knew we were going back by way of Brooklyn. Either that, or you forgot your underwear this morning."

Her smile widened provocatively. "What makes you think I own any underwear?"

"What's a man got to do to surprise you, Gypsy?"

She ran her tongue slowly along her bottom lip. Then she pulled his face down and did the same to his. "There's not a man alive who could," she whispered against his mouth. "But if you want to die trying, that's all right with me."

By midnight the Whitfield house was empty again. Even the caterer had gone home.

Elisabeth supposed Owen had gone to bed, too. His bed. In his room.

She turned off the last light. The Roman temple atmosphere of the house was most pronounced when nothing but moonlight filtered in through the tall windows. She had argued with Owen when he showed her the drawings. She had wanted something more casual, an English country house with tasteful clutter. Laura Ashley had lived to design for women like Elisabeth. But Owen had won, and now, of course, she was glad. The house was extraordinary.

Even if it no longer felt like home.

She hugged herself since there was no one else there to do it. The terrace with its silver moonlight puddles and strange beckoning shadows was a temptation. But the night was cool, although the spring day had been warm. She didn't want her flesh as chilled as her heart.

It was funny how quickly a life could change. She had conceived tonight's party as a chance to relax with close friends, then she had poisoned that innocent impulse by inviting Anna.

"Bess?" Owen's voice whispered from the shadows behind her. "Are you coming to bed?"

"I don't know. Am I?"

"What's wrong with you tonight? You're a million miles away."

She felt his arms come around her. Her own hug had felt warmer. "I don't know."

"I doubt that."

She had her opportunity to confront him now. The moment had arrived to tell him what she suspected— no, what she knew. Because now she did know. An evening of watching Owen exchange intimate glances with Anna had strengthened her suspicions.

One stolen moment at the evening's end had confirmed them.

The time for confrontation ticked slowly away. She had been trained from infancy to contain her feelings, and she could not articulate them now. She could not tell him that she had seen him embracing Anna on the walk to Anna's car, that she had seen him pull Anna into the shadows and hold her as close as he held his own wife now. She could not admit that she had spied on them, that she had abandoned her ethics and stalked them like a pulp fiction gumshoe. She wasn't sure how immersed Owen was in this affair or what was left of their marriage. She was only sure that somehow she had to retain her dignity.

"I don't understand why you told Attila you'd do that story," he said, when she didn't respond.

Anger flashed through her. Anger that he would so badly misunderstand her silence. Anger that he expected her to be at his beck and call while he was falling in love with another woman. "You're angry because I said I'd go to the lecture at Stony Brook instead of shopping with Didi Caswell?"

"I was counting on you. It's not like you to back out of a commitment."

"I like writing for Attila, Owen. I know it's a little job, not an important job like yours. But it's all mine."

He was silent, but he tightened his arms around her. As apologies went, it was the most she would receive.

She wasn't ready to pull the plug on their marriage. A part of her still hoped that whatever Owen had found with Anna would fade and die with time. And she knew she had to be here waiting for him when it did. "I can still take Didi shopping in the morning," she said, reluctantly offering an olive branch. "But I'll have to skip lunch. Can we take them to dinner that night, instead? Or a show?"

"I've already confirmed the plans."

"Are you trying to tell me that you never make changes in your schedule?"

He was silent for too long. "I'll explain about lunch and see if we can do something in the evening," he said at last.

"Fine."

"Why don't you come up to bed now?"

She wanted to refuse. She wanted to laugh. After what she had witnessed she was no more interested in sex than in giving another dinner party with Anna as a guest. But far too often these days there was a good excuse not to make love with Owen. How long until their marriage was nothing but excuses? And how long after that before she was a single woman again, reading about Anna Jacquard Whitfield on the pages of *Town and Country*?

"I'll be up in a minute," she said. "Where will I find you?"

"In our bed."

That seemed significant. Owen had a room. His room. But the bedroom she slept in each night was their room. And where was her room? Or her life?

She wandered the house for a few minutes, although there was nothing to check or do. She wandered, hoping for a miraculous end to her anger or her fears. She told herself that Owen was waiting and that lovemaking might breach the wall that was fast going up between them. She had to try to win him back, because if she didn't, she would have no marriage, no life at all.

But in the end, it didn't matter, because by the time she climbed the stairs and slipped in beside him, Owen was already asleep.

3

THERE WERE WORSE WAYS TO TRAVEL THAN the studio's limo. Not too many years before, Gypsy had considered herself lucky to have subway fare. At age eighteen she had thumbed her way to New York after discovering that her parents planned to commit her to two years of community college and a continued life of squalor in the Dugan insane asylum. Her mother had broken the news with her usual tact. If Gypsy wanted a college education, she could damned well work for it by living at home and taking care of the rest of the Dugan brats who had followed right behind her with rhythm method precision.

Instead she had come to New York with nothing in her pocket except the money she'd gotten from selling her stereo. Actually she'd sold her parent's portable television, too. They still hadn't forgiven her for it, even though she'd presented them with a complete home entertainment system on their last anniversary.

Outside the limo's tinted windows, the Nassau County vista was as monotonous as only suburbia could be. There was little of interest here, but Gypsy could smell money somewhere off in the distance, along the Sound where the Great Gatsby and his society pals had partied the nights away. She had partied there herself, and would again. And last week she had said "yes" to a June houseparty in the Hamptons. As her star rose, so did her invitations.

She had come a long way from an overcrowded Cleveland hovel where scenic meant a day when pollution from neighborhood smokestacks blew west instead of east. She had no gypsy blood. She had been born plain old Mary Agnes Dugan, and she was the offspring of every insipid immigrant group that had grubbed and plodded through Cleveland's factories and mills. But she shared with the gypsies their disdain for the ordinary and their unconventional methods of getting what they wanted. After years of listening to her mother scream the word at her, Gypsy had proudly taken the name as her own.

The glass pane separating her from the limo driver slid from view. "Miss Dugan?"

The young man at the wheel was one of the countless rent-a-bodyguards who materialized in and out of her life on eight-hour shifts. He was the best-looking of the lot, with a blond crew cut and baby blue eyes. More than once Gypsy had toyed with the idea of asking him to guard her body in the most intimate ways, just to see what he'd say.

She dimpled appropriately and leaned forward. "What is it, Randy?" She took her time with his name, caressing it slowly with her vocal cords.

Color rose in his clean-shaven cheeks. "I just wanted you to know that we'll be there before too long, ma'am."

"That's just fine. I'm enjoying the ride."

The glass slid back into place. She *was* enjoying the ride. She never let on, but she still got a thrill from the luxuries that were now hers to enjoy. The limo was larger than her first New York efficiency. And she had shared that with a man until she found a job sorting mail at NBC. She wasn't a whore, despite the opinion of the right-wingers who regularly bombarded the show with mail. She was merely a woman who knew what she had to trade and traded it wisely.

The landscape outside the tinted windows grew less jumbled as they neared the Suffolk County border. Now there were occasional glimpses of fields and woods. To one side of the expressway they passed a shopping mall that sprawled like a small city.

Gypsy wished there had been a spectacular shoot-out in the food court or a celebrity kidnapping at Sterns or IKEA so that the mall could have been her destination. Lecturing to a crowd of graduate students and professors sounded as dull as the missionary position, but it shored up her image as a serious television journalist. The studio had prepared a talk for her that made "The Whole Truth" sound like the last bastion against the erosion of free speech.

The limo slowed, although there didn't seem to be a tie-up in traffic. The glass slid away once more. "Miss Dugan, I need you to put your head down."

"What?"

"Head down. Now."

She obeyed, falling limply across the leather seat like a wounded bird. "What's going on?"

Randy didn't answer. The limo gathered speed again. There was nothing better to hold on to, so she gripped the edge of the seat and dug her fingernails into the soft leather. She was wearing a conservative—albeit short—linen suit, and she pictured what it would look like when she sat up again. She was about to meet her public looking like Peter Falk in "Columbo."

"What in the hell's going on?" she screamed.

"Someone's following us."

"Oh." She didn't know what else to say. Then the absurdity hit her. "Randy, you shithead, we're on the Long Island Expressway! Of course somebody's following us!"

He didn't answer, a skill he had polished to perfection.

The limo lurched to one side, then the other. He was driving like a maniac. Maybe he was a maniac.

For all she knew, the sexiest bodyguard among a choice selection of big hulking men could be Charles Manson's first cousin. Nobody at the studio took her fears seriously. Desmond probably hadn't even checked out the security service he had hired.

She rolled from side to side until her grip on the seat was no longer a match for Randy's driving. She made a spectacular three-point landing on the floor and slammed her head against the well-stocked bar. She sprawled there gracelessly and passed the time with a recital of four-letter words.

The limo gradually slowed, then it stopped its frantic weaving. Gypsy's heart was thundering so fast that for moments it was just one long beat. Finally, she found the strength to sit up, although not to climb back up on the seat. "Well?"

"I guess I was wrong."

"You were wrong?"

"They turned off."

She was shaking so hard she was forced to stay where she was. "Just like that? They turned off?"

"I'm sorry, ma'am. I'm really sorry. Look, I'll pull off so you can have a chance to pull yourself together."

"No!" She struggled to push herself up to the seat and finally succeeded. "Don't you dare stop this thing. You take me right to the university, and you park this monstrosity where everybody can see us. Do you understand?"

"I really thought we were being followed. There was a dark car with two big guys in the front. Every time I switched lanes, they did, too. I sped up, so did they. I couldn't take any chances."

"I've got a lump on my head as big as one of your erections, you little prick! And a suit that looks like I had sex in it!" She looked down at the damage. "And a run in my hose!"

He didn't answer, which was wise. She took care of the hose by stripping them off. She carried a spare in her briefcase, and she managed to wriggle into them as Randy took an exit ramp. Her mirror showed no sign of a lump on her forehead—she suspected that would emerge right in the middle of her lecture. She combed her hair, freshened her makeup, and did her best to smooth her skirt and jacket.

Neither of them spoke for the rest of the trip, although Gypsy could see Randy's eyes repeatedly darting to the rearview mirror. She didn't know if he was spying on her or looking for the two big guys. Whatever he saw or didn't, he seemed calm again. She was anything but.

The university was a tree-shaded oasis after the long drive and the car-chase-that-wasn't. Close to the hall where she was to speak they slowed to a crawl as students crossed the road at odd moments and angles.

"I'll park and check the area. You stay locked inside until I come back to open your door," Randy said. "We've been promised the university will have a couple of campus cops waiting in front and more inside."

"Sure," she said acidly. "We can't be too careful. A dark car might drive right up the center aisle of the auditorium while I'm speaking."

He parked the limo between two red traffic cones at the curb, a job not unlike docking the *QE2*. After he turned off the engine he didn't speak . . . or move.

"Look, I don't want to be late," she said. "Can't you get *this* part of it right, at least?"

"I don't see . . . the cops." He sounded far away, but before she could ask what was going on, he pushed his door open and got out, closing and locking it behind him. She watched as he passed in front of the windshield, then she looked down to gather up her purse and briefcase.

When she looked up again, Randy was lying face-down in the middle of the sidewalk twenty yards away.

"Shit!" Gypsy was out of the limo before she could

think about it, sprinting, then diving at his prostrate body. "Randy!" She grabbed his shoulders and shook him hard, banging his chest against the sidewalk. People began to close in on her.

She could feel her new hose rip to shreds and ping like tiny slingshots against her calves. "Randy!" She shook him again. Then she grabbed one muscular arm and tried to turn him over.

"Let me help." A young man wearing a black leather jacket knelt beside her, and together they managed to get Randy to his back.

Randy's eyes were wide-open and staring at heaven's gates.

Gypsy slapped her hands over her mouth.

The man in black leather felt Randy's neck for a pulse. He moved his hand, then again. "Jesus, I can't find a pulse. Does anybody here know CPR?" Another student, a woman with long, straight hair pushed her way through the gathering crowd and knelt at Randy's other side. She placed her ear against his chest.

"Cops. There are supposed to be cops!" Gypsy got to her feet to look for help. Somebody had to call an ambulance, and the cops were an obvious first choice. But the hall entrance was the only view that wasn't blocked. There were no cops there or anywhere in sight.

Gypsy's fears for Randy died under the crushing weight of new fears for her own safety. Randy was dead. There were no cops.

And a dark car had tailed them on the Long Island Expressway.

She dived at Randy again, frantic this time to get to him. There was no visible evidence of a gunshot wound, but she wasn't going to take the time to investigate further. He was dead, and that was good enough for her. She pushed the young woman to one side and searched for Randy's pockets, methodically patting down all the parts of his anatomy that had appealed to her just an hour ago. She found the keys and jerked them free.

The crowd parted as she darted toward the limo. She unlocked the door and slid into the driver's seat. Gypsy hadn't driven in years; she hadn't needed to. But the powerful motor roared as she pulled out into the narrow lane and took off the way she and Randy had just come.

"Damn." Elisabeth looked at the dashboard clock again, although only seconds had passed since the last time. After leaving the city she had gotten behind every slow driver on the Expressway. And once again, the traffic was too thick to change lanes easily.

She was going to be late for Gypsy Dugan's lecture. She had gauged her time too closely, placating Didi Caswell with one more stop at Cartier's.

Elisabeth managed to pull into the fast lane, and this time she stayed there. She was a careful driver, so considerate that Owen refused to drive with her. But today, she was Mario Andretti in a tan Mercedes. She was Elisabeth Whitfield, about to make a close examination of the woman who had nearly become her obsession.

And why had Gypsy Dugan assumed such monumental proportions in her mind? Elisabeth concentrated on her driving, but the question was such a familiar one that she could consider it, as well.

The answer was just as familiar. Gypsy Dugan was the road Elisabeth hadn't taken. She could watch Gypsy staring back at her from the television screen, and she could see the life she might have led if her decisions had been different.

She switched lanes again and pressed down harder on the accelerator.

Gypsy Dugan was twenty-eight. Elisabeth had made it a point some time ago to piece together the anchorwoman's life story. At twenty-eight Elisabeth had turned men's heads, too. The breasts that sagged now without an underwire bra had been taut and lush. She had never had a model's figure; hers had been womanly and inviting. And men had noticed and approved.

That was only one tiny similarity, of course. Hardly enough to consider. But there were others. Straight out of college Elisabeth had gotten a job at a small White Plains television station. For the first six months she had been nothing more than a glorified gofer, but she had loved everything about her work. She had a deep, abiding interest in the news, and she knew she would have a flair for presenting it, when she was given the chance.

She moved up to writing next, and her forte was human interest stories. Her bosses were so impressed with her ability to ferret out interesting material that they rewarded her by giving her a short spot every Wednesday at noon during the local newscast. Then, as the spots drew attention, they were increased to twice a week and finally, to twice a week during the evening telecast.

She photographed well; everyone had agreed about that. She had a pleasant voice and a perfect oval face. Her hair was a soft silver-gold that looked almost platinum under studio lights, and she mined that asset by wearing it long enough to touch her shoulders. Her warm smile—and a lifetime supply of social small talk—put her subjects at ease. Consequently they told her things that they had never told anyone before.

Her connections hadn't hurt, either. Her family was only moderately wealthy, but their roots extended deep into some of America's richest soil. As a child she had played tennis in the Hamptons, skied at St. Moritz, and sunned her pale skin in Cap d'Antibes. Better yet she knew a host of people who had lived just as she had—and she knew how to use them. She quickly graduated from spots at the local dog pound to spots interviewing the occasional celebrity who wandered through White Plains. She sensed what names to drop in order to get interviews, and only rarely was she turned down.

There were few anchorwomen in the early seventies. Elisabeth aspired to be one of them someday. As part of her career climb, at the beginning of her third year out of college she moved to a more prestigious station in Manhattan.

Then she met Owen Whitfield.

The driver of a rusty sedan leaned on his horn as she cut in front of him to get to her exit. She glanced at the clock again as she braked on the ramp. Despite a valiant effort, she was still going to be late.

Suddenly she was furious at Owen in a way she never had been before—or perhaps had never acknowledged. She had given up everything for him. Theirs had been a whirlwind courtship, even though her parents had disapproved of the match. One night at a neighbor's party she had fallen in love with the poor young architect with the delicious smile and the collar-length dark hair. He had promised that he would never tie her down or hold her back, and she had believed him. She had worked for two months after their marriage. Then she had gotten pregnant with Grant.

Even then she believed she could still have it all. But after Grant's birth, she discovered just how wrong she was. Owen was awarded a fellowship in Rome, but he refused to go without her. It was a simple choice between her needy little family and the television station where she still spent far too much time getting coffee for less-talented men. On the evening of her last day at work Owen expressed heartfelt regrets that she'd had to give up so much. But it was the last time he ever did.

Today, Owen and the demands of their life together had kept her from her job, her pitiful, inconsequential job, once more.

Elisabeth understood her strange affinity with Gypsy Dugan. She looked behind the anchorwoman's desk at "The Whole Truth," and she saw the woman she might have been. A better-bred, less-obvious version, perhaps, but even that might have been different. As Owen's wife she had stayed in the social circles in which she had grown up. Had she stayed at her job and fought her way through the ranks, she might have learned to value different things. She might have dared more, compromised less. She might have been less concerned with doing the right thing and more concerned with her own happiness.

Gypsy Dugan was a woman who put herself first. If Elisabeth had put herself first, perhaps she would not be a dissatisfied, premenopausal society matron married to an unfaithful man who looked straight through her and never even realized he was doing it.

She sped down the ramp so fast that she nearly ran the stoplight at the bottom. When the light turned green she forced herself to drive slower, but once she was out of the worst of the traffic, she clamped her foot down on the accelerator again. She might miss Gypsy's opening remarks, but she'd be damned if she was going to miss more than that. She had a lecture to attend and an interview to do. This time the whims of Owen Whitfield would not defeat her.

She glimpsed the university before she saw the limo. She was gloating about the minutes she had gained since leaving the Expressway. Getting to the lecture had assumed mythic proportions in her mind, and she reveled in the thrill of conquest. If she could do this, despite all the obstacles, life still held possibilities. The crisp institutional architecture was as welcome to her as her first sight of London as a schoolgirl.

She was going to make it.

The limo bore down on her before she could act to evade it. It was as dark and imposing as a hearse, and the irony didn't elude her, not even as she desperately spun the steering wheel. The Mercedes fishtailed, in perfect obedience to her panicked commands, but the limo driver couldn't change course. As the limo sped directly toward Elisabeth, she realized she was going to die.

Even as her eyes squeezed shut in acceptance, she wondered who would take her place at dinner with the Caswells that night.

There was pain, such extreme pain in Elisabeth's chest and torso that smothering was preferable to drawing a breath. The pain only lasted for an instant. Then there was darkness, a lush midnight black abyss that was so profound, so enveloping, that as she sank into it she knew it was the velvet arms of death.

She didn't know how long she rocked there, suspended and content like a nursling snuggled against a mother's breasts. Her next moment of awareness was triggered by an explosion of light and demons tearing at her lungs.

Somewhere nearby a male voice shouted. "This one's back, but we're going to lose her again if we don't get her there soon!"

She wondered who was back, and where they had gone in the first place.

"Well, the other one's still breathing, but that's the most I can say!"

She preferred the darkness and sought it again. This time it was less comforting and more intriguing. As a child she had dreamed of flying, wildly colorful dreams where she had drifted above the earth, weightless and free. She was drifting now, as if she had misplaced her body, only to find that she had never needed it in the first place.

She was still surrounded by the abyss, but there was a subtle air current, as pleasant as the first gentle breeze of evening after a torrid summer day. The breeze wafted around her, but it didn't carry her forward. She rode it like a ship at anchor.

Time did not matter here. The abyss mattered, and

the gentle currents. Her inability to move forward mattered, but only as an intellectual exercise. She could stay here, suspended forever, and not feel cheated. Her sense of peace was complete.

The darkness was split by light again. Her eyelids flew open involuntarily, and the light doubled in intensity. It was circular, and so painful to behold that she wanted to reach out and shut it off. But she was paralyzed. She was no longer weightless, but heavy and stiff.

There were human shapes above her.

"BP fifty over zero," someone shouted. "We're going to lose her again."

She wanted to tell them she wasn't lost. She knew who she was, if not where.

A woman bent over her as other voices shouted orders in the background. "You're at the emergency room. Hold on, honey. We've called your family. Now don't you leave us again."

"I don't know why you bother," a male voice said. Elisabeth could feel hands moving over her body, and she knew the voice must belong to the hands. "She can't hear a thing."

"Hold on," the woman said, bending over her again. "I know you can hear me. Just hold on."

A new voice spoke. "Maybe you should tell the other one to hold on, Kathy. That's Gypsy Dugan, lying over there."

"Never heard of her."

"You sure as hell will if they lose her. And they're about to."

"Damn!"

As suddenly as she had left it, Elisabeth was back in the abyss. She was no longer tethered, but moving with the currents. The feeling was delicious, like floating in an ocean with no fear of sharks or undertow.

The darkness was less than complete now. There was light in the distance, a light so radiant it defied comparison to anything she had seen before. And the instant she experienced it, she realized she was no longer inside her human form.

Her human form lay on a stretcher where voices and hands labored to keep her alive as they simultaneously discussed the vital signs of Gypsy Dugan.

The accident was suddenly clear. She remembered the impact of the limousine, the shattering of glass, the screaming of metal. And she had screamed, too. She had realized she was going to die. She had thought briefly of Owen and their plans for the evening. Now, that seemed remarkably foolish. Her life hadn't even flashed in front of her eyes.

Or perhaps it had. She had spent the greatest portion of her own life living Owen's. If her last thought was of his schedule, then that was symbolic of the woman she had been at the moment of her death.

Except that Owen and dinner with the Caswells hadn't been her final thought. Not quite. Just as her eyes closed, and just as she'd thought of Owen, she had caught one final glimpse of the limo. And she had realized that the limo driver was a woman.

Gypsy Dugan.

Suddenly Elisabeth understood the discussion in the emergency room. For some reason, known only to herself, Gypsy Dugan had been tearing down the road toward the Expressway in a black limousine. And she hadn't been sitting where celebrities sit. She had been behind the wheel, aiming straight for Elisabeth's Mercedes.

But not on purpose. Gypsy hadn't tried to hit her. Elisabeth remembered an intersection just ahead, and another car edging out. Gypsy had swerved to avoid the car, and the limo had spun out of control. The panic in Gypsy's eyes was the same panic Elisabeth had felt. For that moment they had been sisters, bonded by the knowledge of what was about to happen.

Perhaps Gypsy was hovering in this twilight world with her.

The feeling of peace vanished, and she no longer drifted. She became a swimmer struggling against the current. Immediately she was back in the emergency room, but she didn't need her eyes to see. She wasn't even on the stretcher anymore, where two men and three women worked frantically over her body. She was floating above it all, like a sentimental life-after-death reenactment on "The Whole Truth." She could see everything without turning or focusing. In less than a moment, less than the blink of an eye—if she'd had an eye to blink—she understood everything that had happened.

No one was willing to give up on her. They were possessed. Her death was an insult and, as yet, an unacknowledged one.

They had lost one patient today. They would not lose another.

Elisabeth saw the sheet that covered Gypsy. Someone had just pulled it up to her shoulders, although no one had yet shown the courage to cover her face. There were two men and a woman in a circle around her, but although they appeared shaken; no one was trying to help her. Clearly, Gypsy was beyond help.

This was particularly clear to Elisabeth because she knew that Gypsy was in another place in the room. There was just the briefest moment of contact, an impression, a whisper. Now the essence that was Gypsy had no body, but Elisabeth could sense her anyway. This was still the Gypsy she had seen so often on the television screen. Sassy, courageous, and amazingly—considering everything—seductive.

There were no words, but Elisabeth understood that Gypsy was moving toward the abyss, and with characteristic panache, she embraced the experience. Gypsy Dugan was on her way to the biggest scoop of all.

Then Gypsy was gone and Elisabeth was acutely aware that the emergency room team just below was still struggling.

"If you bring her back again, God knows what we'll have on our hands," one of the men warned another.

"She has a name," one of the women said. "Her name's Elisabeth Whitfield."

The abyss beckoned, and darkness blotted out the bright lights, one by one.

It was time.

But it wasn't. The velvet arms of death had never seemed so comforting or conversely, so terrifying. Elisabeth wanted to live. Gypsy might be ready to move ahead to whatever awaited her, but Elisabeth was not. The abyss had taught her that there was no reason to fear dying, that whatever waited after death was as pure, as perfect, as indisputably glorious as heaven—and not one bit like hell. There was no judgment there, but only an assessment she was to make herself.

Her assessment was that she had not lived long or well enough. She had not accomplished all that she could have. Time after time she had taken the easy way out, choosing comfort and tradition over risk.

She couldn't die. She wouldn't. Gypsy had lived exactly as she had wanted to. If nothing else could be said about her, that much could. Elisabeth didn't even have that to show for her life.

She would not die.

The lights faded completely, but this time there were no velvet arms to comfort her. She was suspended in time and space, and there was no sensation. Then consciousness vanished completely, and Elisabeth was no more.

⌒ 4

A BIRD TRILLED RELENTLESSLY, SO RELENT-
lessly that Elisabeth wished a hawk would emerge
from the thick clouds that surrounded her and carry it
away. She thought she was fond of birds, had even
tramped through forests and swamps with a notebook
in one hand and binoculars in the other. Somewhere
along the way she had learned to distinguish a wax-
wing's chirp from a redstart's warble. But this bird's
song was unfamiliar. Worse than unfamiliar.

She considered retreating again. She was exception-
ally good at that by now. She could judge the exact
moment when pain would swoop down, like the hawk
in her imaginings, and tear her flesh into ragged
strips. Just as the agony became unbearable, she could
burrow inside herself, hide deeper in the clouds of
total oblivion until she forgot the pain that was
waiting for her every time she emerged.

But even as she perched on the edge of uncon-
sciousness, she realized that something had changed.
The pain was fierce, but it wasn't growing stronger.
The thick clouds were dispersing, along with her
possibility of escape. She felt only gratitude that the
sky was turning an unadulterated blue once more.

The bird wasn't a bird at all.

Elisabeth opened her eyes and peered at white
acoustical tile. For a moment she thought the clouds

53

had descended, then as her eyes focused, the pattern of tiny holes in identical squares began to make sense. She was gazing at a ceiling. And the bird was the tinny sound of a portable radio. A portable radio blasting rap music.

She opened her mouth to protest, and fire streaked across her face. Her lips felt swollen and cracked. She tried to run her tongue across them, but her brain refused the command. She tried again, only to realize that something blocked her progress.

"Not the worst job I've ever had." The voice of a young woman competed with the aggressively rhythmic patter from the radio. Elisabeth couldn't place the direction of the sound.

"She doesn't need a lot of care. Just lies there. Food goes in, food comes out. I check her vital signs, check the monitors. Check the action on the daytime dramas when I get too bored."

The voice that responded was deep and masculine. "Then there's been no improvement?"

"How'd you get up here, anyway? S'not supposed to be anybody in this room but hospital personnel."

"I bribed the security guard."

The woman laughed. "With what, sugarplum? Your autograph?"

"Do you think she's going to wake up?"

"You have to ask the doctors that."

"I've asked."

"And you don't like what they say?"

"They don't say anything worth listening to."

"There've been times . . ." The woman paused. "Sometimes I'm encouraged."

"Can I see her?"

"Nah. Something happened and somebody found you here, I'd be the one in trouble. You'd better get on, now."

"Look, if I give you my card, will you call me if something changes?"

"I don't know . . ."

"It would mean a lot."

"You're hard to say no to, you know that?"

"I depend on it."

Elisabeth didn't know where she was or why, but she knew the man's voice was somehow familiar. The woman's was not. And the music that was pouring from the radio was something she'd only heard from the stereo systems of passing cars. Everything, the room, the woman, the music was alien. Everything except the man's voice.

Owen. Even as she pulled Owen's name out of the clouds, she discarded it. Owen's voice was deeper, and there was a guttural quality to his "r's," just the faintest husky rumble that betrayed the fact that he had grown up speaking another language. The voice wasn't Grant's, either. Grant's was higher, a resonant tenor, and his enunciation, like hers, was prep school perfect, as if his thoughts were carefully divided into syllables and spelled out in phonetics.

She knew other men, although she couldn't recall their names just now. But the man speaking was not one of them. Of this she was sure. Still, she knew him somehow. She knew him.

Something cool ran down her cheek. It took her a long time to realize that she was crying.

The conversation was over now, and someone was stomping relentlessly. The stomping grew louder and louder.

"Awake again, huh? I wonder what you're thinking about when you stare at the ceiling that way. Are you thinking at all? Or are you still way off in dreamland?"

Elisabeth tried to turn her head toward the woman's voice, but she found she was immobilized. Frustration filled her, and the tears fell harder.

"Well, look at that."

A hand brushed the tears away. A soft, gentle hand. "Honeypot, can you actually hear me this time?"

Elisabeth tried to answer, but the same impediment

that had stopped her from licking her lips kept her from speaking.

"No, don't try to talk." The same soft hand linked fingers with Elisabeth's. "Look, if you can hear me, if you know what I'm saying, squeeze. Just a little will be fine."

Elisabeth tried. The wrong hand clenched spasmodically.

The woman sighed. "Damn. Thought we had something this time." She started to unweave her fingers, one by one.

Elisabeth squeezed again.

"Whoa . . ." The fingers wove back into place. "Try that again, sweetcakes."

Elisabeth squeezed.

"Once for yes, two for no."

Elisabeth squeezed once.

"Do you know where you are?"

Elisabeth squeezed twice. She had never done anything more exhausting.

"You really do understand, don't you?" The woman laughed. She sounded absolutely delighted. "Look, I'm going to bend over the bed so you can see just who you're talking to. My name's Perry, and I'm your day nurse. You're in the hospital, and you're as safe as a bug in a rug."

A face appeared where ceiling tile had been. The face was pale brown and unlined, with arching eyebrows and a spectacular smile. The whole picture was framed in shoulder-length dreadlocks. "I'm going to call your doctor now. Dr. James Roney is treating you. You'll like old Jimbo well enough. I ever get in an accident, I'd want him making all the decisions. Course, I couldn't afford Jimbo myself. Uh-uh. I'd probably get some intern who'd never seen blood before."

Elisabeth was reluctant to let go of Perry's hand. It was a connection to a world she still didn't comprehend. It was an anchor.

Perry seemed to understand. "You ought to see all the flowers people have sent you. Couldn't keep them in here. Too many machines, so we've been taking them around to people who didn't have anything to look at themselves. Kept all the cards, though, so you could see those when you came to. They'll keep you busy for a while."

Elisabeth wanted to respond. She opened her mouth, but the same restrictions existed.

"No, you can't talk yet," Perry said. "They've got you hooked up to stuff that looks like it could blast you straight to the moon if that's where they wanted to send you. You've got tubes going everywhere, and some of them are strapped across your face. But all this junk's kept you alive, and now you're awake. Before long they'll wean you off of it, machine by machine. Meantime, you just lie there and let us fuss over you. Understand?"

Elisabeth squeezed once.

"Good girl." Perry withdrew her hand. "And now I've got to get somebody to call Jimbo. But I'll be back."

Footsteps pattered across the floor, then the sound disappeared and Elisabeth was left alone with a driving beat and a face still wet with tears.

Hard rock blasted from the radio the next time she drifted out of the clouds. Someone insisted over and over that they weren't getting any satisfaction. She had an instant impression of a dingy Manhattan apartment and a man with long dark hair dancing across a worn linoleum floor, his arms outstretched.

Owen.

"My guess is that she'll be waking up on and off for a couple more days, just for a brief period each time. Then, she'll become more and more lucid. Eventually, she'll be back in the land of the living."

It was a man's voice, not Owen's. This man was soft-spoken, almost lyrical in the way he stroked and lingered over words. Elisabeth had to strain to hear him clearly because the music on the radio was so loud.

Another man spoke. His voice was high-pitched and anxious. "You're sure about that?"

"I'm never sure about the human brain."

"But you think she's on her way back?"

"She is, and with luck there won't be too much damage."

"Damage. Sheesh! Give it to me straight, Roney. What kind of damage are we talking about here?"

"That's not a question I can answer with any certainty."

"Look, give me some idea. What could we be facing?"

"Anything from minor headaches to paralysis. But more likely we can expect something in between. Memory loss that may or may not abate. Disorientation. Some problems with speech or hearing, perhaps. I've seen patients with similar injuries who've forgotten the simplest things, like how to chew and swallow or blink their eyes. Some of them never get any better. Others head right back to work after a little physical therapy, and there are no residual effects."

"And you think Gypsy might be one of those?"

"I wish I could say."

The voices trailed off, but Elisabeth fought to make sure that her thoughts didn't. Horror had filled her as the men discussed her prognosis. She had imagined herself paralyzed for life, her memory destroyed, the most natural and normal reactions beyond her abilities. The doctor hadn't sounded particularly hopeful.

But the two men hadn't been talking about her. They had been talking about someone named Gypsy.

The name tugged at her. She knew her own name. And she remembered Owen and Grant. But so much was unclear. How had she gotten here? And how long had she been like this? She knew there were people around, but no one seemed familiar. She knew there had been a nurse named Perry, then another who hadn't bothered to introduce herself. Now there was a doctor, too, but he was discussing another case with yet another man whose voice was unfamiliar.

Who was Gypsy? And where was Owen? The last question seemed the more important of the two. She was lying in a hospital somewhere, and neither her husband nor son was here with her.

Her cheeks were wet again. This time she understood why.

"Well, I was just about to call Perry a liar."

A man smiled down at her, replacing the bleak view of ceiling tile. The smile was soothing, the smile of a father for his favorite recalcitrant toddler. The face was plain, with nothing to particularly recommend it except kind gray eyes.

"I'm Dr. Roney."

Elisabeth felt her hand being lifted and held warmly in his.

"Where's . . . Owen?" The voice that emerged was huskier and lower in pitch than what she'd expected. At first she was confused, than she realized her throat had probably been damaged.

He bent closer. "Don't worry. You probably don't owe a thing. I'll bet you've got a Cadillac of an insurance policy. You're in great hands here, and the only thing you have to do is recover."

She tried again. "Where—"

"You're in a private room. You were in an accident about three weeks ago."

"Three . . ."

"You've been in and out of a coma. It's the body's way of gearing down all unnecessary systems for a while to speed recovery. Let's just say you've been hibernating."

"Let's . . . not."

He laughed. "You've retained a sense of humor. That's a very good sign."

Elisabeth wanted to close her eyes and forget this man and conversation, but she was afraid if she did, she would be lost in the clouds again. "I want . . . I want to see—"

"No visitors yet." He shook his graying head. "Not for a while. Look, I'll be honest. You've just come through a really tough time. My guess is that you're going to make a great recovery. But we might very well delay it if we move too fast. This conversation is all the stimulation you need today."

"When?"

"Soon, I promise. But let me decide. That's what I'm paid to do."

She didn't have the strength to argue with him, but she'd never heard of medical treatment that excluded family so completely. Didn't love and encouragement speed the healing process?

He squeezed her hand. "Do you have any more questions? Is there anything I can tell you before we let you rest again?"

"Owen . . ."

"Now, I told you not to worry about that. I'm sure you have all the insurance coverage you need."

"Go . . . away."

He laughed, squeezed her hand again, then dropped it. His face disappeared from view and she was left staring at tile again.

She wondered where Owen was at this moment. Was he sitting outside the hospital room with Grant, waiting for word on her condition while Jimbo Roney made bad jokes about his name? He had been with her the night that Grant was born, and he had refused—absolutely refused in that ancient era before fathers in the delivery room were a normal occurrence—to leave. He had held her hand, skirted angry nurses, and tolerated a doctor who had lectured him on hospital policy throughout the entire delivery. All because he loved her.

Where was Owen now? She couldn't believe he had let Dr. James Roney keep him away.

Perhaps Owen had better things to do with his time.

Elisabeth had grown accustomed to her own tears. She supposed some tears were in order now that she was lying immobilized in a hospital bed and her husband was nowhere in sight. She wondered if Anna Jacquard was comforting him. Or perhaps the reality was even worse. Perhaps he and Anna were sitting outside this room together, waiting to hear about their future. She couldn't make herself believe that Owen wished her dead. But she wondered exactly how sad he would have been if she had died in the accident. A wife recovering from a near-fatal car crash was a tough wife to divorce, and Owen had a reputation to protect.

Car crash.

For a moment her thoughts squealed like the sounds of two sets of brakes and collided like a limo and a Mercedes bent on total destruction.

She had been in a car crash. A hideous, head-on car crash. And the driver of the other vehicle had been none other than Gypsy Dugan.

She moaned. The accident was suddenly clear to her. She had been speeding. There had been no opportunity to steer clear of the limo because she had been going too fast. At the last possible moment she had thrown up her arms to protect her face. She had blacked out when the steering wheel slammed against her chest.

She had heard two men talking about Gypsy, and now she knew why. So Gypsy was still alive, but her prognosis was unclear. Elisabeth had nearly killed her. And if Gypsy didn't recover . . .

"Oh, God . . ."

There was no comforting response from anyone in the room. She was alone.

And what about her own injuries? Elisabeth could

recall the moment of impact and the terrible, crushing pain. She was still in pain, but she hadn't asked the doctor what injuries she had suffered. She had asked about Owen. That seemed remarkably foolish now.

"Perry . . ."

There was no answer. If Perry was on duty, she had probably gone out into the hall with the doctor, and Elisabeth was alone with her fears.

She had to know how badly she'd been injured. She tried to focus on her own pain. What hurt, and how badly? Her head throbbed unmercifully, but she ignored that. She already knew her head had been injured, probably from contact with the windshield.

She stared at her feet and tried to pinpoint the worst of the pain. One hip—she couldn't remember what to call that side of her body—felt as if it were aimed in an entirely new direction. The leg below it felt as if it had been wrenched from the socket, then jammed in place backwards. She tried to wiggle her foot and found she couldn't.

She told herself not to panic. The foot was still there. It had to be. She forced herself to concentrate on the rest of her body. A shoulder and an elbow hurt, and so did her neck. She had the oddest feeling that someone had been using her abdomen as a trampoline, and her chest for target practice. Everything felt different, as if the body was a stranger's, but she had been too protected and too careful as a child to have a frame of reference.

She had to see for herself. That was only one way to quiet her own fears. Perry had said she was hooked up to machines, but how many? Was she still dependent on technology to keep her alive?

She turned her head, one slow inch at a time. Light washed over her in waves, but she didn't black out. She was perspiring by the time she turned her head toward the door. She couldn't see all of the room now, but she could see enough to know it was small and colorless. The door was shut, but it had a large window that looked out on a hallway. There was one fluorescent bulb above a sink and mirror. She couldn't see anything else.

She hadn't passed out. She had moved her head, and she was still conscious. Slowly, carefully, she turned back to her original position, and when she was finished she was staring at the ceiling again.

She had passed the first test, and there was no one to stop her from attempting the second. There were tubes in her arms, but no restraints bound her to the bed rails. She moved each arm carefully, and pain streaked to her fingertips. Undaunted, she flattened her palms against the mattress. One hand was wrapped in gauze, but her fingers weren't restrained. She arched that hand and dug in with her fingertips. Her other hand flattened and pushed. She lifted slowly. She wasn't foolish enough to think she could sit up. All she wanted was enough height to be able to see her feet.

She pushed harder and perspiration dripped into her eyes. She was higher now, but tiring quickly. One look. She needed one look, then she could collapse back to the bed and process what she'd seen.

She gathered all her strength and pushed herself higher. The room was warm, and she wasn't covered by a sheet. Her gaze traveled down her legs. There were two feet at the end of the bed, and one was in a cast, suspended on something that looked like a complicated rope and pulley.

Strength gone, she fell back to the mattress and let relief fill her. She was still in one piece, although obviously that piece was now the worse for wear. But she was alive and on the mend. She was going to survive this.

She lay quietly and thought about the body she'd just seen. She had lost weight, but she didn't look as

bad as she'd feared. Her hips were definitely narrow-
er, and her breasts were smaller. She lifted her head a
little and peered down at them. Yes, smaller, but
perhaps that was only because she was lying down.
They made small but impressive mounds under the
plain hospital gown.

Her legs seemed longer.

She closed her eyes and tried to remember her legs.
Her eyes had traveled farther than she'd expected in
order to find her feet. But she was not in the best
condition to make accurate judgments. Her feet had
seemed very far away, but for the last three weeks, she
hadn't even remembered she had a body. What could
she expect?

Her legs seemed longer.

The thought nagged at her, despite her attempts to
put it in a proper perspective. And her breasts seemed
smaller and firmer. She had been a vegetable since the
accident, and surely that had made changes in her
physical condition. But the worst accident couldn't
replace short, sturdy legs with a chorus girl's. And
weight loss under these conditions didn't firm and
tone a body.

She looked younger.

Had she really needed to lose weight so badly that
even a near-fatal car crash had improved her appearance?

She needed proof she was imagining all the
changes, but she didn't want to risk another look. She
settled for raising her hands. Seconds passed as she
lifted them to eye level. Her nails were short and
blunt, probably to keep her from scratching herself or
one of her caretakers. But her fingers were long and
shapely, like her legs. She stared at them and tried to
analyze in what ways they seemed different. Had her
fingers always been this long? Her hands this narrow?

There was something else. Something missing. She
stared harder, even though her hands were trembling

by now. Her skin seemed darker, more an olive tint than rose. Maybe her heart wasn't pumping properly or her liver or kidneys had sustained damage.

There was something missing.

She moved her hands closer to her face and squinted at them. She stared at the hand closest to the door, and then she remembered. Her wedding ring and the solitaire diamond that Owen had given her on their tenth wedding anniversary were gone.

She dropped her hand to the bed and closed her eyes again. Of course the rings were gone. She was in a hospital where anything could disappear. On admittance they had probably taken all her jewelry and locked it in a safe. Owen probably had everything in his possession.

There was something missing.

She opened her eyes again and raised her hand one last time. She stared at her ring finger, and then she realized what was wrong. There was no white space where her wedding ring had been. She had worn the wide gold band for twenty-five years without once removing it, but there was no tan line above it. The space where her rings should have been was exactly the same color as the rest of her.

This was not her hand.

She almost laughed at her own absurd conclusion. Whose hand could it be? Had they grafted a new one after the accident? Was she some sort of female monster for a modern Dr. Frankenstein to assemble? If so, he had stolen legs from a Rockette and hands from a Jergen's model, and she should be nothing but grateful. Maybe Owen would be so intrigued he would forget Anna and remember to come home every night.

The hand in question stole its way to her abdomen. She was as flat and taut as she had been before pregnancy. She moved it slowly higher to her breasts. They were firm, young somehow, and the nipples seemed larger than she'd remembered. She examined her breasts every month like clockwork. She knew how they felt. They didn't feel like this.

Her hand stole higher, first to her shoulder, then to the side of her neck. She expected to feel her hair, but there was nothing there. She wondered if someone had cut it off or worse, shaved her head. She was too old for the Sinead O'Connor look and too young to have lost all her vanity.

Just over her ear she felt the soft brush of hair against her fingertips. They *had* cut it, then. She wondered who had done it? The ends curved over her fingers, and a deeper foray indicated it was probably cut into layers. It felt surprisingly thick and almost coarse in texture. Not like her hair at all. She had always been afraid to try a short cut because her hair was wispy and fine.

She moaned. The news was good, but she was increasingly panicked. She had survived in one piece, and she was able to think and even to move again. But nothing felt as it should. No matter how many times she tried to tell herself that this isolation from her own body was to be expected, she couldn't make herself believe it. She had not discovered one familiar thing about herself, except the fact that she was undeniably female.

She needed proof. Just one bit of proof was all it would take. Then she could go back to sleep and forget all this.

A birthmark. She was surprised the solution was so simple. She had a birthmark on the inside of one arm. It wasn't particularly large, and it had faded with the years, but as a child she had been so self-conscious about it that she had refused to wear short sleeves. She was wearing short sleeves now, and it would be a small matter to raise her arm and investigate.

She rested first and gathered her strength. She remembered the first time Owen had discovered the birthmark, and the romantic fuss he had made over it.

She had never known that a man's lips in that very spot could reduce a woman to putty. But in the early years of their marriage, Owen had reduced her to putty frequently.

She lifted her arm at last. The sleeve of her gown clung and she swatted at it with the opposite hand until it fell back toward her shoulder. She stared at her arm, her thin, firm arm, unmarred by any blemish.

"No!"

She turned to her other side, praying she had made a mistake. She had chosen the wrong arm. That was all. This sleeve fell away without fuss and she stared at another expanse of unblemished flesh.

"No!"

The door opened with a hiss. "Hey, what's going on here?"

Elisabeth recognized Perry's voice, but she was too distraught to respond. She moaned and wrapped her arms over her chest. "No . . ."

Perry came into view. "Are you in pain? Do you need a shot? It's almost time."

"No . . ."

"You poor baby doll. What can Perry do for you? Do you want me to get the doctor?"

"Please . . ." Elisabeth was sobbing, great gulping sobs that seemed to echo through her head.

"Now, I'll be right back. He's still on the floor. Don't you go anywhere, candy cane. You stay right there."

The door hissed again.

Elisabeth tried to sit up. She had to have another look, a closer look, but she was too weak. She couldn't raise herself this time. She flailed from side to side helplessly.

She heard footsteps in the hallway, then the door opened wider. "Calm down. You've got to calm down. This is going to set you back weeks."

Elisabeth recognized Dr. Roney's voice, but she

couldn't seem to obey his commands. She was panic-stricken.

She felt hands at her shoulders, holding her in place. "Please, you've got to stop this. I don't want to put you in restraints."

She turned her head toward the sound of his voice. His face loomed above her. "Please . . ."

"Can you tell me what's wrong?"

"I'm not . . . myself."

He smiled his sanctimonious, fatherly smile. "Of course you aren't. You're not going to feel like yourself or even look like yourself for a while. But you will eventually. I promise you will." He continued to hold her shoulders, but he turned his head away and said something to Perry. Then he turned back to Elisabeth. "I'm going to have Perry give you something to help you feel calmer. And when you wake up the next time, you'll be that much closer to recovery."

"I'm not . . . me!"

"But you will be. I promise. You're going to be as good as new, Miss Dugan. And you're going to be right back on television before you know it." He winked conspiratorially. "And that's the whole truth."

5

THE MAN WHO CAME INTO VIEW THE NEXT time Elisabeth opened her eyes was dark-haired and dark-eyed. She stared at his cynical pirate's smile and commanded herself not to panic.

"You look like hell," he said.

She moistened her lips, but no sound issued from her throat.

"Don't talk." He reached for her hand, but not, she suspected, to take her pulse. He linked fingers and lifted her hand to his lips to kiss her fingertips, lingering over each and every one.

When he had baptized them all he held her palm against his lips. "You know you scared us to death. Nobody can talk about anything else."

"Who . . ." The voice that emerged was husky and low. Not her voice at all.

His dark eyes narrowed. "Don't you know me?"

She had a terrible feeling that she did. The feel of his lips was far too familiar, and so was the feel of his hand holding hers. His face was familiar, too. Only the last time she'd seen it, the *only* times she'd ever seen his face, it had been framed in a nineteen-inch television screen in her bedroom.

"Charles . . ."

"Casey to you, my love. You've never called me Charles in your life."

69

"Casey . . ."

"How are you feeling? Are you in much pain?"

She had to be dreaming. There were rational explanations for everything, even the most bizarre anomalies. She believed in science, in painstaking exploration and conclusions based on logic. She was not lying in a hospital bed staring up at Charles Casey, the sexiest television reporter on the airwaves. She was dreaming of him.

When she didn't speak he went on. "They say you're making a good recovery. It can't be soon enough to suit me."

"Who . . . do you think . . . I am?"

This time he kissed her knuckles, then he rubbed them against his sandpapery cheek. "I know who you are." His voice dropped a key. "Better than almost anyone."

"What . . . do you know?"

Eyes glittering, he lifted one raven-wing eyebrow. "Do you want all the details?"

This was not real, and this raw hunk of sensuality was not standing beside her bed. But now that she was certain of that, she thought she might as well enjoy the fantasy. Owen—who was probably somewhere with Anna living his own personal fantasies—could be damned. "Every . . . bit."

His voice deepened to a husky rasp. "I know that you have a mole right between your breasts, a sweet little mole that's just visible where your bra dips . . . on those rare occasions that you wear a bra."

She lifted her unclaimed hand to her chest, which was covered by a plain blue hospital gown. "That's hardly . . . everything."

His eyes smoldered. "I know exactly where to kiss you, starting with that sweet, sexy mole and working my way in lazy, lazy circles to the peak of each breast. And I know the way you pretend it doesn't do much for you, while inside you're melting."

"You're an egotist . . . off camera, too."

He laughed, a rich, deep laugh that made her think of bittersweet chocolate and rainy Paris midnights—and she was sure he depended on it. "Ah, you understand me too well, Gyps."

"Gyps?"

"Gypsy, then. But we've never been formal with each other, have we?"

"Not you, too." She closed her eyes. Of course this was why Charles Casey had entered her dreamworld. He worked on "The Whole Truth" with Gypsy Dugan. She had been on the way to see Gypsy Dugan at Stony Brook. And she had crashed her Mercedes into Gypsy's limo.

Or she thought she had. Quite possibly that was all part of the same dream. For all she knew, she'd played double dare with a city bus or a sixteen-wheeler. Her memory of Gypsy Dugan driving the limo could be as ridiculous as the rest of this.

"Not me, what?" Casey's voice was close to her ear.

She opened her eyes, fully expecting him to have turned into someone else. But the same devilishly handsome man was smiling down at her. "Who am I?" She rotated her head a little to see if he metamorphosed into a three-headed goat or Newt Gingrich's mother.

"Have you really forgotten?"

"Enlighten . . . me."

"Your real name isn't Gypsy, but I'm not supposed to know that. You're little Mary Agnes Dugan from Cleveland, and you started calling yourself Gypsy when you ran away to New York."

"Mary Agnes . . ." She couldn't picture the woman that the world knew as Gypsy Dugan with such ordinary names.

"Mary's not too surprising. Your mother spends her life on her knees."

"My mother's . . . alive?"

"Your mother's right here in this hospital, or she was a little while ago. But we've made the staff keep her away from you. She's a woman guaranteed to send anyone back into a coma."

She congratulated herself on having such a rich dream life. Not only did she have a gorgeous man at her bedside, she had an interesting dysfunctional family, besides. She supposed if her real-life family was too busy to sit by her bedside, this was the next best thing.

Casey rubbed her knuckles against his cheek again. Something, some uninjured edge of her libido, responded with a frisson of warmth. "I can't stay much longer," he said. "They only gave me five minutes. Tell me, are you putting me on, or are you really confused about who you are?"

Elisabeth wasn't confused at all. She knew exactly who she was. And when she woke up for real, she knew she would look down at the same soft, middle-aged body and hear the same mellow, cultured tones echoing from her lips. In the meantime she really ought to be enjoying this for all it was worth. Up close, Charles Casey was a mighty fine sight indeed.

"Just a bit . . . confused." She tried a smile, and it seemed to work. He drew his brows together, and his gaze went to her lips. "Kiss me, Casey."

"With pleasure." He leaned closer. He smelled deliciously familiar, although she couldn't place his cologne. The spicy scent made her heart beat faster, as if her body had been preprogrammed to respond to him, and his scent was the cue. His lips were warm against hers and wonderfully firm. The kiss was gentle enough, but it promised myriad pleasures that wouldn't be gentle at all. He lingered, his lips still close to hers. "You can be a real bitch, Gyps, and there've been times when I wished you were out of my life for good. But not like this. I'm glad you're going to be all right."

"Am . . . I?"

"Yeah. You're going to be all right, and you're going

to come back on the show and make everyone's life hell again. We're counting on it."

"Casey . . ."

"What?"

"The accident . . . Was anyone else . . . ?

"Don't worry about that now."

"But . . . I want to know."

He hesitated, as if trying to decide what to tell her. "No one was killed, if that's what's worrying you. And no one's blaming you for what happened— although nobody can understand why you took off in the limo like that."

She felt suddenly cold. "Limo?"

"You don't remember that part?"

She reminded herself that this was her dream. Casey knew about the limo because she did, and Casey was a figment of her imagination. At least this Casey was. The real reporter was probably off somewhere interviewing child molesters or ransacking celebrity garbage cans.

"I remember." She paused, trying to get up her courage, although why she needed courage in a dream was hard to say. "Was another woman . . . hurt?"

"I've been worrying about *you*. I can't tell you what happened to anyone else, Gyps. Just concern yourself with getting well. That's what counts right now."

She knew he was lying. And why would anyone lie in a dream?

He straightened. She turned her head to follow his movements. "Casey?"

"Yeah?"

"You're better in person."

He laughed the same rich laugh. "Is that so?"

"The cameras don't . . . do you justice."

"Your brain must have been rattled pretty good. You'd never say anything that flattering if you were thinking straight."

"No?"

"And give me an advantage?"

"Maybe it's not . . . an advantage . . . if a television reporter . . . doesn't photograph . . . well."

"That's more like it. You're getting better fast. Nan's not going to be pleased."

"Nan?"

"Now I'm sure you're kidding."

She tried to remember a Nan. This Nan had to have something to do with "The Whole Truth." This entire dream had to do with the show and her own peculiar fascination with it. From somewhere she tugged out a memory of fluffy blond hair and round blue eyes. "Nan." She struggled for a last name. "Simmonds."

"Too bad. It would have been fun to tell Nan you couldn't remember her name."

"She seems . . . nice."

"Jesus, Gypsy. That's one memory you'd better work on."

"Oh. The anchor substitute . . . from hell?"

"Got it. Remember it."

"I'll . . . file it away."

He paused at the door. "File this away, too. The minute you're well enough, I'm coming over to that whorehouse you call your apartment, and I'm going to make love to you every which way except inside out. So don't take too long getting better. Because I'm not a patient man."

The door hissed shut behind him.

Charles Casey had been in her hospital room. A sexier Charles Casey than Elisabeth's perfectly healthy body had ever imagined. A man with whom her fantasy self was having a torrid affair—the likes of which Owen and Anna probably couldn't even conceive of.

She smiled softly and shut her eyes. She wasn't sure she wanted to recover.

"We're going to crank you up a little today, so you can see where you are. And there's a physical therapist coming this morning to start a new program. They got you set up for every kind of therapy they got in this place. Girl, you must have one hell of an insurance policy."

Elisabeth recognized Perry's voice. Perry was the one true constant in her life now, although she wasn't absolutely sure she wasn't imagining Perry, too.

She'd had no visitors so far. Owen might as well live on another planet; Grant seemed to have deserted her, too. And where were Marguerite and all the women with whom she had lunched and played tennis, shopped and gossiped and chaired committees? She couldn't believe that none of them were interested in visiting her.

Her only visitor had been a sexy figment of her imagination.

The room came into view as Perry cranked. She'd had a glimpse of her surroundings when the light was dim. But this morning Perry had drawn drapes and sunlight poured through a surprisingly large window. The room was more attractive than she'd realized, with peach-colored walls and floral drapes. There was a dark wooden cabinet across the room topped with a trio of flower arrangements.

Her eyes drifted down to what was revealed of her body. The chorus girl legs had to be a trick of the eye caused by her odd position. The missing birthmark was another thing entirely, but there had to be an explanation. Perhaps she'd had it removed some time ago, and just couldn't remember. She was aching for a better look at herself, but Perry, the master of the sponge bath, religiously protected her modesty. She had yet to see herself completely unclothed, not even when Perry changed her gown.

"I don't suppose you'd bring a mirror over here so I can see what I look like?" It was Gypsy Dugan's voice that emerged. She recognized it, now. It no longer even surprised her.

"Nope. No point at all in looking right now. You

wouldn't like what you see, you'd get upset, and that would make you worse. We're going to wait until more of the swelling goes down. Then you'll believe us when we tell you you're going to look exactly like your old self again."

Elisabeth fervently hoped that was true. "Who's sending . . . all the flowers?"

"Admirers, sweet pea. You must have some kind of life. There've been more than a hundred. Lots more. I should know, 'cause I'm the one that's had to get rid of them. Pediatrics was grateful at first, now when they see me coming, they bar the door."

"Admirers?"

"I'll read you some of the cards later, if you're still awake. You're staying awake longer and longer these days, though. Might just get a real conversation out of you yet."

"I'd like to . . . talk." But even as she said the words, Elisabeth wondered if they were true. Did she really want to know what was happening to her? What if Perry told her she was Gypsy Dugan? Perry seemed remarkably real. If she was part of Elisabeth's dream, was there any hope she would ever come out of this?

"First a sponge bath. Then I'm going to get you out of that gown into something of your own. Some of your friends brought clothes for you, and I've just been waiting till you were clearheaded enough to stand a little fussing."

"Friends?"

"We've been turning folks away like this was opening day at Yankee Stadium."

"Nobody's been allowed to visit?"

"Just that special somebody of yours."

So Owen had been here. Elisabeth closed her eyes and savored the sweetness of relief. Owen had been here, and either she hadn't been awake or she just didn't remember. "I wondered."

"He's been haunting these halls like the ghost of Christmas past. I tell you, that man was mine, I'd tie him to a bedpost and never let him out of my sight. That's one fine-looking human male."

"I always thought so."

"Better in person than he is on TV."

The room began to spin. "Oh, God."

"I hurt you? I didn't mean to. Had to have been a man who designed the ties on these gowns."

Elisabeth bit her lip. "TV?" The word sneaked past her teeth.

"Yeah. I always watch your show if I get off on time. Don't believe a word I hear, but I like it just the same. Never knew there were so many ways to tell a story and never tell it exactly like it happened."

"I'm not Gypsy Dugan."

Perry laughed. "Then you're sure fooling a lot of people, gumdrop."

"My name is Elisabeth . . . Whitfield."

Perry was silent.

"Did you hear me?"

"I did."

Elisabeth opened her eyes and saw that Perry was staring down at her. Her lovely brown eyes were troubled. "You've heard that name . . . haven't you?" Elisabeth asked.

"You're getting better fast. So fast I think you'll be all recovered in no time. But the brain's a funny thing. Gets rattled too much, and it sends scrambled-up messages, kind of like that telephone game we all played as kids. I whisper something to you, you whisper it to someone, pretty soon it's not the same thing at all. Your brain's having some of those problems right now. But they aren't going to last."

Elisabeth hung on to her question throughout Perry's explanation. "You've heard that name," she repeated. "Tell me . . . the truth."

"You must have heard it sometime when you were off in that coma. Signals got mixed. That's all."

Elisabeth tried to piece this together. "Why . . . would I have heard it?"

Perry sighed. "I shouldn't be getting into all this."

"Perry!"

"Elisabeth Whitfield's the name of the lady in that other car. The one you hit. She's got a room on this floor, too."

The next time Elisabeth opened her eyes, there was a woman sitting beside her bed saying the rosary. Elisabeth had plenty of time to examine her because the woman never looked up once.

"Hail Mary full of grace . . ."

Elisabeth was a Unitarian. She had a strong feeling this woman was not. Unitarianism was a religion that adorned its churches with sculpture and works of art, rarely with crosses. When prayers were said, they were most often meditations on the meaning of life or Fulghumesque anecdotes. She recognized the rosary but couldn't have chanted along with the woman if her life had depended on it.

She guessed the woman was in her mid-fifties, with silver-streaked black hair and a bulldog jaw. Her dress was steel gray with no relieving touches of color. Her only sop to vanity was a gold cross around her neck and a plain gold band on her left hand.

The woman made a complete circle of the beads before she looked up. Her eyes narrowed slightly. "How long have you been watching me?"

"A little while."

"Don't you think you could have said something?"

"I didn't . . . want to interrupt."

"That would be a first."

"Do I know you?"

The woman bit off a laugh. "Not very well. Knowing me was never much of a priority, was it, Maggie?"

So now she was Maggie, not Gypsy. Elisabeth wondered who else she would become before the day ended. Had her personality shattered into a thousand pieces at the crash site?

The woman cocked her head. "Are you lying again, or don't you really remember me?"

"I'm not . . . thinking clearly."

"Well, to my mind you never did. You were always off doing exactly what you wanted, never thinking about what it might do to the rest of us."

"The rest?"

"Your father, your brothers and sisters. You probably don't remember them at all. You've never paid them much mind."

"How many?"

The woman gave a harsh sigh. "Six."

"I guess . . . the population explosion wasn't an issue . . ."

"I had the children God intended me to have!"

Since this was just part of a dream, Elisabeth decided she could say exactly what she wanted. "And apparently, you didn't . . . like at least one of them."

"You mean you?"

"Yes."

"You're right. I don't like you. You're rude and profane, and the only reason you learned the Ten Commandments was to see how fast you could break each and every one of them."

"Did I?"

"A million times."

"Then, why are . . . you here?"

"Because I'm your mother. And you're my child."

Elisabeth fell silent. The woman's voice had cracked just the tiniest bit on her final word. Obviously there was more to her than the hard shell she presented to the world.

Was everyone in this dream some part of herself? Elisabeth knew that some psychologists believed that the purpose of dreams was to understand and integrate all the many pieces of the psyche. Was this woman some part of her? And was the mysterious Maggie a part of her, as well?

Was this her "critical parent," the sliver of her soul that would never let her feel true pride in herself? If so, then she ought to make a stab at understanding it . . . her.

She stretched out her hand. "I'm glad . . . you came."

The woman's eyes narrowed farther. "You really did get a good crack on the head, didn't you?"

"Mama . . ." The title came easily to her tongue, even though she had always called her own mother the more formal Mother. "Come on, Mama. Tell me how everyone's . . . doing."

"You've never cared before."

"Mama . . ."

The rosary dropped to the woman's lap. She took Elisabeth's hand in an uncompromising grip. "If this is some sort of con job, I'll know it. You can't fool me. Never could and never will."

"I'll . . . remember that."

"You may be a big television star now, Mary Agnes Dugan, but don't think that just because I'm a working-class nobody, I'm not every bit as smart as you."

Elisabeth drifted in and out of sleep for the rest of the day, but even when she *thought* she was awake she pretended she wasn't. She didn't want to talk to anyone until she was one hundred percent sure she was Elisabeth Whitfield once again.

But dear Lord, until that moment, what new revelations awaited in the next conversation? All roads led to Gypsy Dugan and Elisabeth's own obsession with the anchorwoman's life. She had been no different than the millions of bored housewives who settled for secondhand adventure and romance on afternoon television. She should have taken her life in her own hands and done something about it. Perhaps if she hadn't spent so many hours just comparing her choices to those Gypsy had made, she wouldn't be in this predicament. But now that she was, she had no idea how to pry herself loose.

She was living Gypsy Dugan's days, one by one. Her dreamworld was so intricate that she had invented a nurse and a mother. She had brought Charles Casey right to her bedside and decorated the pediatrics wing with hundreds of flower arrangements from her admirers. She had erased a birthmark, lengthened her legs, shortened her hair, and imagined specific injuries to a body that was only slightly to the left of magnificent.

And she was powerless to change any of it.

There was no one else in the room. Now that she seemed to be recovering, Perry stayed an eight-hour shift during the daytime, supervising therapy and coordinating treatment. But there was no full-time nurse with her at night anymore. Staff checked on her frequently, but they seemed satisfied that she could manage the call button if she needed anything.

She needed to know why she couldn't shake off this fantasy world. She was a married woman with a son and an outwardly enviable life. But no one from that enviable life seemed to care that she was lying in a hospital bed immersed in the world of one Gypsy Dugan.

"Pssst . . ."

The light was so dim that she could only make out a shadowy figure slipping in through a narrowly cracked door. She was in no mood for another confrontation about her identity.

The figure moved closer. "Are you awake?" The voice was high-pitched but masculine.

She considered pretending she was unconscious again. Under the circumstances, who would argue? But as the man moved closer, curiosity made her turn her head to see him better. "Who's there?"

"It's Des. Desmond Weber."

The name meant nothing to her. "It's a little late for . . . visitors."

"They've refused to let me see you. I had to sneak in. Don't blow the whistle, okay?"

"Why'd they refuse?"

"They've got you under lock and key. Old Roney's afraid you'll have a setback if things move too fast. I told him that's the only way you'd want them to move, but he doesn't listen to me. Asshole doctors."

"You don't look dangerous."

He leaned over her bed and grinned. Because of the darkness, his face was a blur, but she got the impression of woolly hair, middle age, and deep worry lines. "How are you doing?"

"That depends on who you think . . . I am."

The grin turned into something else. "What do you mean by that?"

"I'm *not* Gypsy Dugan."

"Come on, Gypsy. This is Des you're talking to. Do you think I don't know you better than anyone?"

"I think . . ." She licked her lips. "That's possible."

"Then where's Gypsy Dugan? Tell me that, huh?"

"Home in bed. Probably . . . with some good-looking stud." Stud? Even the words that passed her lips were words she'd never used.

Desmond laughed, and his relief was audible. "Jesus, Gypsy, you had me going there. Listen, you'll be in bed with a dozen studs soon enough. But you've got to get better fast. Our ratings are going down without you."

"Ratings?"

"Yeah. Nan just doesn't have what it takes to keep the show at fever pitch. I've got Tito on my ass. He's talking a complete change of personnel. You don't get out of here pronto, you might not have a show to come back to."

"I can see . . . why they kept you out of here."

"Gypsy." He took her hand. His fingers were stubby but warm. "Gypsy, you're breaking my heart. Nobody loves you like I do. Nobody wants better for you. But the show's going down the tubes, and that's no pun."

"Tell you what. Send me a . . . faith healer. It would be a great story. And it might . . . just work. Double your investment."

"Okay, I get it. You don't give a damn. That knock on the head rattled your brain and you just don't give a damn whether you're rich and famous anymore."

She closed her eyes, but she knew he was still there. She opened them, she closed them, it didn't matter. She had an awful feeling that nothing would make Desmond Weber or this ongoing dream go away. "Desmond, tell me about . . . Elisabeth Whitfield."

"Why the hell do you care?"

"Humor me."

"She's just some society broad you creamed with the limo. What in the hell were you doing driving the limo, anyway, for Christ's sake? You leave your bodyguard in the middle of some sidewalk, jump in the limo, and drive off into the sunset, and for what? So you can end up in the hospital with your brain scrambled?"

"Bodyguard?"

"You don't remember that part? Is this selective memory or something? Your bodyguard had a seizure. He's a diabetic. It was an insulin reaction or something. But I'm betting you thought it was some sort of conspiracy and took off because you were scared. And that's when you hit this Whitfield woman."

"Do you know . . . how she is?"

He gave a rough sigh. "Don't ask what you don't want to know."

"Tell me."

Her urgency must have communicated. He sighed again. "Not good. But nobody blames it on you. Another car pulled out illegally. You were trying to avoid it when you hit her. Both of you were going too fast. Nobody's going to be charged."

"What do you mean . . . not good?"

"They don't know if Whitfield'll make it. Didn't know if you would either, for that matter. For a while . . ." His voice trailed off.

"For a while what?"

"It doesn't matter."

"It matters."

He shrugged. "For awhile you *were* dead. They called it in the E.R. Then the next thing anybody knew, you were breathing on your own again and your heart was pumping away. They're calling it a miracle. We did a show with one of the technicians who was in the room. Doctors and nurses won't talk about it on camera." He brightened. "It was a good show. We used clips of you over the years, had a couple of charlatans come in and talk about life after death. You don't remember anything we could use for an update, do you? White lights or wind tunnels? Old boyfriends coming to greet you? It might boost ratings enough to keep us in the running while you're recovering . . . if you don't take too long."

"What if I told you . . . I am Elisabeth Whitfield."

He appeared to seriously consider her words. Then he shook his head.

"Sorry, it's a great story, but even the folks who watch the show religiously wouldn't buy it. You look like Gypsy. You sound like Gypsy. And when we've got you under the lights again, you're going to photograph like Gypsy. So you'd better come up with something more believable." He squeezed her hand. "Work on it, would you? I'm counting on you."

6

"So, DO WE KNOW WHO WE ARE TONIGHT?"
Dr. Roney looked Elisabeth straight in the eye. He
never flipped through her chart when he spoke to her,
as if direct eye contact with him could perform
miracles.

"*We* certainly do. At least I do. You'll have to speak
for yourself."

He laughed. Elisabeth suspected that every good-
natured chuckle was going to appear on her fantasy
bill. "Why don't you tell me who both of us are."

"*You* are Dr. James Roney. And for the purposes of
this dream, *I* am Gypsy Dugan."

"So you still think you're dreaming."

Elisabeth was tired of discussing her identity with
Jimbo Roney. Weeks had gone by since the day when
Perry had told him that their prize patient believed
herself to be Elisabeth Whitfield. Since then Jimbo
had made increasingly frequent visits to her bedside.
She suspected he was writing up her case for some
esoteric medical journal.

"I *am* Gypsy Dugan," she said, to short-circuit the
conversation. "Born and bred. But I still feel like I'm
living in a dream because so much is unclear."

"Good, Gypsy. Excellent. A sense of unreality is
just one of the side effects we expected after everything you've been through."

She batted her eyelashes in her best imitation of the real Gypsy Dugan. "Now, will you tell me how that poor Elisabeth creature is doing?"

His smile changed to something more suspicious. "You need to divorce yourself from Elisabeth Whitfield. It's not healthy for you to obsess about her."

By now Elisabeth knew exactly what to say. Jimbo and his staff were training her well. "It's not unhealthy to wonder how a woman I hit in a car accident is doing. I don't want her death on my conscience."

"Her condition hasn't changed."

Elisabeth had decided that Jimbo was the part of her that was in contact with reality. When he gave reports on Elisabeth's condition, she knew she was hearing the truth about herself. "Isn't anything being done to help her?"

"Everything humanly possible."

"But she's not responding?"

"No."

"Please, you're not going to take her off life support, are you?"

He seemed to be considering his answer carefully. Then he sighed. "There's still brain activity. And as long as there is, her husband won't even consider it."

"Good for Owen."

Dr. Roney frowned. "You know Mr. Whitfield?"

She hedged. "He's well-known. I've heard his name mentioned."

"Concern is appropriate. But stay away from the Whitfields, Gypsy. Your recovery is far from complete, and the mind is a tricky thing."

"I'll say," she uttered with complete sincerity.

"I understand the cast comes off today?"

"So they tell me."

"You'll need therapy for weeks yet, but I don't see any reason it has to be done as an inpatient. You'll have to promise to keep up with whatever regimen we assign, and you'll need help at home for a while. I've spoken to Perry, and she's willing to live in with you.

What would you think about getting out of this place by the end of the week if things continue to go well?"

Getting out of the hospital. For a moment the news seemed too good to be true. Could this mean that she was leaving the persona of Gypsy behind? Or could it mean she was dying? That the part of her that still functioned and communicated—even though it was trapped in another body and life—was about to abandon ship?

"Are you frightened to go home?" he asked when she didn't respond.

"I suppose it's the only way I'll find out . . ."

"You'll make it, Gypsy, I promise. I wouldn't let you out of here if there was any real doubt. You'll be confused for a while, and we both know there are some serious gaps in your memory."

"Chasms."

He smiled his most patronizing smile. "Plunging you back into your normal environment, as long as you don't overdo, will facilitate the quickest recovery. I'll continue to see you several times a week, and Perry will map out your days and monitor your progress. If there are any problems, we can have you back here in a flash."

If James Roney was her mind's objective reporter, then Elisabeth had to trust him. Perhaps plunging her back into her normal environment was psychic code for plunging her back into reality. Perhaps when Gypsy left the hospital, she would also leave Elisabeth's mind for good. Elisabeth would wake from her coma and *voilà*.

She could have her real life back.

"I'm ready," she said. "More than ready."

He lifted and squeezed her hand. "Good girl. And to celebrate, I'm lifting all restrictions on visitors. We'll have them stop by the nurses' desk first to announce themselves, but if you're feeling well enough to see them, you may."

He continued to hold her hand. His expression

changed marginally. "You've been through a lot, Gypsy. But in some ways it hasn't changed you."

"Hasn't it?"

"You're still the most attractive woman I've ever seen."

Gypsy, Elisabeth, or any female over the age of four would have recognized the gleam in Jimbo's eyes. For a few more hours her foot remained in a cast. She'd been told her face was still bruised. Her brain was the equivalent of a poorly turned omelet. But Jimbo was making a pass at her.

The old Elisabeth would have put him in his place tactfully. This fantasy Gypsy—and didn't she deserve to have some fun?—batted her eyelashes again. "I don't know how I would have gotten through these weeks without your help. You're obviously a brilliant doctor to have brought me so far."

He preened, changing from father figure to gallant lover before her eyes. "I'm just doing my job."

"I'll bet some of your cases are absolutely fascinating. Television stories in their own right."

"Now you wouldn't be trying to get me on that show of yours, would you?"

"I just might." She smiled, remembering in detail the way that Gypsy Dugan could dimple on cue.

He dropped her hand, but with obvious reluctance. "I'll be back to see you tomorrow morning."

"I'll look forward to your visit."

He turned, as light on his feet as a man half his age.

A man half his age lolled in the doorway. Dr. Roney drew himself up to his full height as Casey pushed away from the doorframe. "Don't let her get to you, Doc. She'll seduce anything in reach."

"I think you have the wrong idea."

"Sorry, but I think *you* do. Miss Dugan has the peculiar notion that she can twist any man she meets around her little finger."

Elisabeth expected to blush. She couldn't. Apparently blushing in dreams was impossible. She slipped easily into Gypsy's voice and words. "Lay off, Casey. Dr. Roney brought me good news. I can have visitors if I want them. Did you register at the desk so I'd have a choice?"

"I've always been on your approved list, Gyps."

"I can't imagine why."

"Don't tire her," Dr. Roney said. "She's still a long way from complete recovery."

"God help us all when she's cruising along at full speed again."

"That's a pretty crass metaphor for someone who's getting over a car accident, Casey. Even for you." Elisabeth pushed herself a little farther upright. In reality she was delighted to see Casey. Like Perry, he was a stabilizing influence to days that seemed unending and nights that were worse. Time had no real meaning for her. She discounted everything that happened as part of her dream life, and if she was dreaming, there were no waking or sleeping hours. But the short periods she spent with Casey seemed real to her. Although that was absurd, their conversations were a welcome break.

The door hissed quietly behind Dr. Roney. Casey strolled to her bedside. His gaze traveled slowly over her. "You're looking better."

The room seemed to heat up perceptibly. She could swear her skin sizzled as his gaze swept her. She had yet to grow accustomed to the instant sensual electricity that always entered the room with him. "I wouldn't know. They still refuse to let me see a mirror."

"I don't know why. You're a big girl. You know you got pretty banged up. You can take it."

"A plastic surgeon came by this afternoon to examine me. He doesn't think there'll be any real need for his services. Offered me a tighter chin and neck when I'm thirty-five and left his card."

"Do you want me to find a mirror?"

She nearly said "yes," then she paused to consider. She was sure she could have seen herself in the mirror by now if she'd pushed the staff to find her one. But she had been torn. Over the weeks she'd had to accept that angles and lighting tricks hadn't changed the way she perceived her body. The body was not hers. The voice certainly wasn't. It followed that the face wouldn't be, either. She would look in the mirror, and Gypsy Dugan, or a badly bruised version thereof, would stare back at her.

"We'll do it some other time," he said.

"No." She could shake her head now. She could sit up, eat by herself, complete sentences without feeling exhausted. And several days ago she had taken her first tentative steps. When the cast came off, she would take more.

She could do this, too. Because none of it was real. None of it. Seeing her face wouldn't change anything.

She took a deep breath. "Let's get this over with."

"You're sure?"

"I might as well face the inevitable."

He gave a crooked smile that looked like it ought to have a cigarette dangling out of one corner. "I'll be back."

By the time he returned she had convinced herself not to fall apart when she lifted the small hand mirror to view her face. She was dreaming, and whatever she saw couldn't change that. If she saw Gypsy, as she supposed she would, it meant nothing. If she saw Elisabeth, it might be the first step toward a return to reality.

"Before you look, just remember that you already look a lot better than you did when they brought you in here. And you're going to recover completely. Believe me, Desmond made sure of that, right from the beginning."

"Hand it over, Casey."

For a moment he looked as if he were reconsidering. Then he gave her the mirror. She lifted it slowly, until it was dead even with her face. Somewhere on the long ascent, she squeezed her eyelids shut.

"Go ahead, Gyps. You can take it."

She took a deep breath and opened her eyes. "Oh, God." The mirror dropped to her lap.

Casey picked it up. "You okay?"

Green eyes had stared back at her. Green eyes surrounded by short dark hair and separated by a sassy little nose the likes of which no Brookshire or Vanderhoff had ever produced.

He stroked her hair awkwardly, like a man who was not accustomed to giving comfort. "You should have seen yourself right after the accident. They should have made you look. Then you'd know what an improvement this is."

She couldn't care less about the swelling that still hadn't gone down, the bruises that marred one cheek, the puffiness around those green, green eyes. "Oh God, I'm Gypsy Dugan."

"Right. You are, no matter what. You're still Gypsy, and before too long, you'll look exactly the way you used to. So just remember that, and you'll be fine."

This was no dream. She knew that now. Somehow the image in the mirror was indisputable proof. "I'm living a nightmare!"

"Oh come on, Gyps, get hold of yourself. Even the plastic surgeon didn't think you needed him, for God's sake. And those guys will operate at the drop of a hat."

She was shaking. She was inside a body she'd only seen on television, behind the face of the woman she once had wished to be. She lifted her hands to her cheeks. These were not her cheekbones. They were Gypsy's. She was not going to wake up and find Owen and Grant waiting at her bedside. She would never again write articles for Attila, host dinner parties for beloved old friends, take long walks on the beach with the retrievers, or work in her garden. That life wasn't hers. It didn't even exist.

She hadn't really been prepared. No matter what she had told herself, she hadn't really been prepared!

Casey sat on the bed and captured her hands in his. "Just take a deep breath. You're going to be fine."

"That's not me!"

"Who else could it be?"

She knew exactly how far she'd get if she told him. "Casey . . ." Her voice was almost a whisper. "You've got to do something for me."

"Anything." He frowned. "I take that back."

"I want you to go down the hall and find Elisabeth Whitfield's room."

"The woman in the other car? Why in hell do you want me to go down there?"

"I have to know . . ." She took a deep breath, then another. She was in danger of hypervenilation. "I have to know if . . ."

If what? What could Casey tell her? That she was also down the hall? That she was in two places at once? Did she honestly think he could look at Elisabeth Whitfield's unconscious body and draw any sane conclusions?

Then she knew. "I want you to see if her husband is there. Or her son. Or any of her friends. Then I want you to come back here and tell me what they look like."

"Get a grip, Gyps. What possible reason could you have for that?"

"Casey, please . . ."

He kissed her hands and dropped them back in her lap. Then he stood. "You've had enough stimulation for now. It's nap time."

"Casey, can't you please do this for me?"

"I can't and I won't. You're tired. You're upset, and you're not making any sense. You need rest. Maybe I shouldn't have shown you your face."

"The hell with my face! Can't you just do this one thing for me?"

"No." He crossed his arms. "Want me to lower the bed and turn out the lights?"

"Fuck you!" The words had hardly sprung from her lips before she realized what she'd said. She put her hand to her mouth and made a fist. Tears filled her eyes.

"Well, you're sounding more like yourself," he said wryly. "Go to sleep, Gyps. Please? I'll be back tomorrow. We'll talk again." He bent over and kissed her forehead.

The door hissed as it closed behind him.

Fuck you? Where had that come from? Elisabeth Whitfield had never used the "f-word" in her entire life. Men and women made love, dogs mated, elephants copulated, even prostitutes simply screwed their clients. No one in Elisabeth's proper world fucked.

She put her head in her hands. Casey had refused her request, but now it didn't even matter. She knew what he would have found if he'd done as she asked. He would have brought back descriptions of people she'd never seen, people she wouldn't recognize if she passed them on the street.

Because this wasn't a dream and it never had been. The green eyes looking out of Gypsy Dugan's face were her eyes. She wasn't Elisabeth Whitfield at all. She was Gypsy Dugan, who had, after all, been suffering from an injury-induced delusion.

She *was* Gypsy Dugan. And Elisabeth Whitfield was nothing more than an unfortunate stranger.

Gypsy was staring at the ceiling when the door opened, and a narrow wedge of light split the darkness. "Sweet potato, you awake?"

Gypsy didn't have to turn to know who was there. "Yes."

"Good." The wedge disappeared as the door

closed, but in a moment the soft light of the bulb over the sink spread its glow through the room. Perry bustled over to the bed. "I brought you something."

"Razor blades? Sleeping pills?"

"Girl, you got it bad tonight, don't you?"

Gypsy—sometime in the hours since dinner she'd begun to think of herself by that name—didn't answer.

"Marietta called and told me you were down in the dumps."

Marietta was the head nurse. Gypsy knew all the nurses intimately, too. "Just because I asked her to put a pillow over my face and sit on it?"

"What's up? That man of yours find someone else?"

For a moment Gypsy thought Perry was referring to Owen. Then she remembered that Owen was not her man, and he never had been. Owen and everything that went with him had all been manufactured by her bruised and battered brain. Sure, there was an Owen Whitfield, any social climber who read the society news had heard of Owen Whitfield, but he was a stranger to her. And still, inconceivably, she was mourning his loss.

"You mean Casey?" Her voice sounded as if she'd been through the heavy-duty cycle of a Maytag.

Perry raised the head of the bed. "He's your main man, isn't he? Course, there's a list at the desk about as long as your arm of all the others."

"Other what?"

"Men. Nurses are keeping a roster. Got a bet going it'll top thirty before you go home."

"Thirty? Cripes, don't I do anything but . . ." She couldn't make herself say that word again, no matter who she was. ". . . screw?"

"Well, last I heard you had a successful news show. You don't need to feel too sorry for yourself, sugar babe. Most people'd die a time or two just to have what you got."

Perry had meant the words casually, but they set off sirens in Gypsy's head. The Elisabeth she had invented in her fantasies probably *would* have died a time or two to have what Gypsy did. Her life had been far from perfect.

She wanted to hear those words again. "What did you say?"

"I said most people—"

"I heard you." Gypsy sat up. She still had to struggle, but her strength was coming back.

"But maybe you don't want to hear how lucky you are. Maybe you want me to feel sorry for you. Let me see what I can dig up." Perry had been bustling around the room, but now she pulled up a chair to the bedside. "Open your mouth."

"What?"

"Open your mouth." She held up a paper plate.

"What's that?"

"You'll see."

"I can feed myself."

"Mood you're in, I'm not about to let you have a fork."

Gypsy opened her mouth. Something luscious melted against her tongue. "Cheesecake." She rolled her eyes.

"Got everything in it you're not supposed to have."

"God, that's heavenly."

"When I was a little girl and nothing was going right, my mama would take me down to the corner deli and sit me down. Then she'd order up the biggest piece of cheesecake you ever saw and we'd work on it, a bite at a time. And by the last bite, I'd spilled whatever was bothering me, she'd wiped it up good, and I was ready to face the world again."

"I wish this was that easy." She sniffed back tears.

"I was going to feel sorry for you. I'm still working out why." Perry offered another bite of cheesecake, and Gypsy took it gratefully. "I know. Kevin Costner didn't call or send flowers."

"I don't know Kevin Costner." She stopped. Maybe she did. "I don't know if I know Kevin Costner."

"Yeah, there is that. Your memory's giving you fits. Can't be fun. On the other hand, not a person out there's going to be upset if you can't remember a name or a date for a while. And there are a lot of folks willing to help you out."

"It's like somebody exploded a bomb in my head. I didn't even recognize my own mother when she visited. I don't remember her. I couldn't tell you who my father is or any of my brothers and sisters."

"You talked to your mother since the day she came?"

"No." Mrs. Dugan—Gypsy didn't even know her first name—had never returned after their brief encounter. It was as if she'd needed to be sure Gypsy was still alive, and that was all. "Something tells me we're not close."

Perry held out another bite. "She told me God brought you back from the dead for a purpose." She chuckled, started to say something, then clamped her lips shut.

"What? Tell me."

"Then she said she thought maybe God got the wrong person."

Gypsy choked. "Jesus . . ."

Perry handed her a napkin. "Too bad we don't get to choose parents, who we're going to be, stuff like that. I'd a had my eye on Whitney Houston's face, for starters."

Gypsy was silent. This conversation was going somewhere, but the destination was still just out of reach. "Was I really dead?"

"As a doornail."

"Then why am I sitting here eating cheesecake?"

"You're asking me? I haven't been to church since the day our pastor laid his hands on my head, then moved them on down to places a pastor's hands shouldn't be."

"You're kidding."

"Sometimes I find a church that's open and I just go sit there. Doesn't matter what kind it is. God doesn't care, just people with no God inside them."

"Church was always my favorite time of the week. The one time I could sit quietly and think about something besides—" She stopped. Besides Owen and their life together? Had she really almost said that?

"I didn't figure you for the churchgoing type."

Gypsy Dugan wouldn't be. Elisabeth Whitfield had been, at least the Elisabeth she had invented.

Most people'd die a time or two just to have what you got.

"I'm not Elisabeth Whitfield." She spaced the words, weighting each one.

Perry proffered another bite. "Well I'm relieved to hear you say so."

"Unless God did get the wrong person."

"Can't imagine God making mistakes. Some kind of God that'd be."

"I'm so confused."

"Sure you are, June bug. How could you help it?"

"Elisabeth's life is absolutely clear to me. But it has to be in my imagination."

"Has to be."

"But why?"

"Had a patient once who was sure he was Napoleon. You should have seen the battle plans he drew up. Wouldn't use a ballpoint pen for anything. Had to do it with a quill on parchment. He gave me one as a gift. One day I showed it to a friend who's at Columbia getting his Ph.D. in history. He said that if Napoleon had been half as brilliant, Waterloo would have been his greatest victory."

"You think I'm crazy, don't you?"

"Nah. I've got a theory."

"What?"

"Maybe you want the things you pretended Elisabeth had. Maybe that's why you made up her life like that."

"No." Gypsy didn't understand what had happened to her, but she did know that wasn't right. The Elisabeth in her imagination had not been happy with her lot. In fact, Elisabeth had wanted to be Gypsy.

Elisabeth had wanted to be Gypsy.

"Don't you want the rest of it?" Perry held out another bite.

Gypsy stared at her.

Perry lowered the fork. "Think you can sleep now?"

"Perry, when you're sitting in those churches . . ." She closed her eyes for a moment, and Owen's face was as clear to her as Perry's had just been. "Do you think about . . . an afterlife?"

"Sometimes."

Gypsy opened her eyes. "And what do you think?"

"I think I'll just wait and see. I suppose I'll know soon enough."

"What if there is an afterlife? What if decisions get made there . . ."

"You know something the rest of us don't? Something you saw when you died?"

Unfortunately, Gypsy had absolutely no memory of those moments. She shook her head. "What if . . ." The idea was too preposterous to articulate.

But what could be more preposterous than a full-blown delusion that had given her an unfaithful husband, a son, a network of friends and a life that was as clear to her as Waterford crystal?

"You're not going to figure out every bit of it tonight," Perry said. "Let me get you all tucked in, and I'll turn out the light. But no more talk about pillows or sleeping pills, you hear? I'm leaving this cheesecake in the refrigerator for you. You start feeling bad again, have Marietta get it for you. My orders."

Gypsy slid down in the bed, and Perry lowered it again.

"Thanks, Perry." Gypsy closed her eyes, but she didn't expect to sleep.

" 'Night, honeysuckle. Don't you think about anything except getting better and going home. Okay?"

But Gypsy was already locked in a silent theological discussion with an old man adorned in a long white robe and a flowing beard. She didn't even hear Perry close the door.

7

GYPSY HAD SWORN DR. RONEY TO SECRECY about the date and time of her release from the hospital. Casey knew, because he could be counted on to get her home to her apartment without a fuss. But Gypsy didn't want a crowd gathered to see her whisked away, and she didn't want publicity. She still wasn't sure she could trust herself. What would she say when she was asked how she was feeling? "Fine thanks, except I'm not completely sure this is me?"

Most of the time now she believed she was Gypsy Dugan. She was even settling comfortably into Gypsy's speech patterns, her mannerisms, and even somewhat into her personality. Perry had brought her copies of newspaper articles about the crash, most of which had a brief biography about her. She'd seen an issue of *New York Magazine* that Perry swiped from the radiology waiting room with pictures of her Manhattan apartment, and a *People* magazine retrospective published one year ago on the five-year anniversary of "The Whole Truth." She'd encouraged everyone who visited to recount the most minute details about their lives, as well as hers, in order to learn everything she could about the world she couldn't remember.

But the only world that was still clear to her was Elisabeth Whitfield's.

"You're going to do fine." Perry helped Gypsy button her blouse. Hours of physical and occupational therapy had restored much of her muscle tone, but her coordination was still less than a hundred percent. She couldn't perform the most painstaking tasks, but she was on her way.

"What if I don't remember anything?" Gypsy asked. "I walk into the apartment, and it's like I've never been there before?"

"You've seen pictures. That'll get you through the worst of it."

"Perry, these people who've been visiting . . ."

"I know. They seem like strangers."

They *were* strangers. Gypsy was convinced of it. A woman who claimed to be a former colleague had cried inconsolably about a lost lover. The woman and the lover were both lost to Gypsy; she hadn't had even the faintest quiver of recognition. Another woman with tightly permed white hair was a neighbor, another with a buzz cut claimed to be her cleaning lady. Two men with the clean-cut good looks of Mormon missionaries were her hairdresser and manicurist respectively. Another with a flamboyant red ponytail handled her business affairs.

Four men, of differing shapes, styles, and sizes had indicated they had once been more to her than friends, three had come right out and said it, and two still seemed to be vying with Casey for that honor.

And then there had been the crew of "The Whole Truth."

Gypsy shook her head. "I don't even remember the names of the people I've met since the accident, much less the others, It's all so confusing."

"It'll get better. One step at a time, gingersnap."

"Do I really have to leave the hospital in that?" Gypsy pointed to the wheelchair parked beside her bed.

"Even if it wasn't a hospital rule, you're not so

steady on your crutches yet. It'll take awhile before walking feels natural again."

Gypsy knew Perry was right. She still couldn't put weight on the foot that was taped. She had been assured of a complete recovery, but after weeks of treatment she was frustrated. Some part of her, some skeptical part that hadn't accepted the obvious truth, still believed that when she was truly well, she would wake up and find herself in Elisabeth Whitfield's body again.

She was just about to prove or disprove that theory.

"Perry, you know what would help?"

"Hmmm?" Perry was packing the remainder of Gypsy's personal items.

"If you'd run down to the gift shop and get me some new panty hose and another emery board. Mine's worn to a nub."

"You had your nails done three days ago. They have to be perfect before you can leave the hospital?"

"It would help. And take your time, would you? I need a few minutes alone to prepare myself." She practiced her Gypsy Dugan smile. She was fairly certain she didn't have it quite right, because people who claimed to know her always seemed surprised when she used it. But Perry wouldn't suspect anything; until the accident she had only known the television Gypsy.

"I guess you might need some time," Perry said.

"Do you mind too much?"

"Just let me finish up here and I'll be gone." Perry put the last nightgown in a dark leather Bottega Veneta suitcase that Desmond had brought for the trip home. She stacked up a few more odds and ends and packed them, too. Then, she vanished out the door.

Gypsy—or Elisabeth, and she was about to find out which—waited half a minute before she got up from the chair where she'd been watching Perry and hopped across the room to get her crutches. She had planned this moment carefully. For days she'd wormed information out of the hospital staff, one bit at a time, so that nobody would suspect anything.

She had discovered that Elisabeth Whitfield was still in the hospital and still on this floor. She had wheedled Elisabeth's room number from someone on the housekeeping staff who had also told her when Elisabeth was most likely to have visitors and how long they stayed. She had plotted and planned her own discharge from the hospital, making excuses when Dr. Roney had offered to let her go earlier in the day.

She wanted to catch Owen Whitfield with his wife. Because when she did, she was sure that she would learn whether her obsession with the Whitfields was a product of guilt and brain injury, or the unthinkable.

And the unthinkable was that she *was* Elisabeth Whitfield, who now dwelled in the body and the life she once had coveted.

"I must be nuts."

She swung the crutches under her armpits as she'd been taught to do and worked her way across the floor. The door was a problem, just as she'd expected, but by leaning heavily on one crutch, she was able to pull it open a crack and peer outside.

This was the part of her plan that had stumped her. She had learned a week ago that Desmond had hired security for the duration of her stay in the hospital. There was always a man, a different one at different times of day, stationed outside her door. She had questioned Desmond about it, but he had replied that she was a celebrity, and there were a lot of crazy people out there. The guards were uniformly courteous and—unfortunately—conscientious to boot. She had never practiced walking in the hallway without one trailing right behind her.

She couldn't afford to have one trailing her today.

After considering and reconsidering how to get rid of the daytime guard just long enough to make a brief escape, she'd devised a plan that might work. She planned to tell the guard that someone from his office had called her private number and wanted to speak with him. When he left to use the phone at the nurses' station, she would make her move.

But the plan remained untested. The hallway was empty, although the guard's chair was in place. Perry had reported that one of the day shift guards was enamored of one of the day shift nurses, and sneaked off to visit with her every once in a while when she had a rare break.

The timing of their courtship couldn't have been better for Gypsy's purposes.

She thumped her way through the door before it closed slowly behind her. She was out in the hallway, and the guard was still nowhere in sight.

She started down the hall to the right. The hall was nearly empty. She had purposely chosen this time of day because lunch and rounds were over, and medications were already flowing merrily into bloodstreams. Many patients were napping, and the staff was taking a break. She was banking on lethargy to keep the staff at bay. Anyone who saw her wouldn't question her too closely. They'd seen her in the halls practicing with her crutches for the last few days. They just hadn't seen her practicing in this direction.

She came to a junction and turned right. Immediately she breathed easier. Even if the guard returned right now, he wouldn't know she was gone, and even if he discovered she was, he wouldn't be sure where to look first.

"Hey, Miss Dugan." A young man in white with an appreciative glitter in his eye moved aside to let her by.

"Hey, how you doing?" she responded with a dimple.

"Got you practicing again?"

"Sure do. Just when I was getting used to being waited on."

"Well, we got to get you better, so we can watch you on that show of yours."

"I sure hope you're a fan."

"Slave." He put his hand over his heart. "Love slave."

"That's the best news I've had since they brought me to this place."

He blew her a kiss and started back down the hall.

Gypsy Dugan's life was obviously more fun than poor old Elisabeth had even imagined.

Gypsy made another turn. The hall was darker here, and there were more personnel in evidence. But no one paid her any heed. They were busy, probably overworked, and they didn't need another problem to solve. She nodded solemnly when anyone glanced at her, but she didn't dimple. She made herself look like a woman with a serious mission.

She was.

The door to Elisabeth's room was closed tight. Gypsy had hoped it would be cracked so that she could peer inside without being seen. She leaned against the wall and rested a moment. She could do one of two things now. She could go back to her own room and forget the metaphysical mumbo jumbo her poor injured brain had conjured, or she could walk through the door and solve this lulu of an identity crisis once and for all.

For a moment she seriously considered the former. Quite possibly what was waiting for her behind the door was worse than what she already knew. No one had given her a precise prognosis for Elisabeth. There seemed to be a conspiracy to keep the truth from her. If she opened the door and saw a woman—a woman she might once have been—surrounded by massive machines and space-age technology, would she learn anything except how precarious her own life might be? If Elisabeth were hovering on the verge of death, what did that say about her own survival?

At a certain point logic shut down. She could no more plot all the ramifications of this absurd delusion than she could draw a detailed map of the universe. She had to walk into that room, carefully look Elisabeth over, carefully look over any of her visitors, and then get the hell out. She would have the rest of her life, short or long as it might be, to make sense out of whatever she saw.

She took one of many deep breaths she had taken in the last long weeks and pulled the door open.

Her eyes took a moment to focus. The only light in the room came from a window beside the bed. The drapes were drawn and just a sliver of sunshine peeked between them. There was little inside the room except a bed, a nightstand cluttered with the usual hospital paraphernalia, and a small dresser. There were no hideous machines regulating Elisabeth's heart or inflating her lungs. There were only I.V.s dripping patiently and something that looked like a monitor at the head of her bed.

"Do you have permission to visit?"

Gypsy had missed the figure in a chair near the window. She swung her way closer and peered into the darkness. "I'm sorry, I didn't see you there." Gypsy was as close to Elisabeth as she ever had imagined, but she couldn't make herself look at Elisabeth's face.

The figure rose and started toward her. It materialized into a woman, tall and broad, with a Prince Valiant haircut and suspicious eyes. "We keep the room dark. We don't want to startle her if she wakes up."

The woman was a stranger. Gypsy wasn't sure whether she should feel relieved or disappointed. "Are you a friend?"

The woman looked perturbed, as if she knew *she*

should be asking the questions, but she answered politely. "No, I'm a special duty nurse, hired by Mr. Whitfield."

"Oh yes, Owen told me he'd hired special nurses," Gypsy lied.

"Then you have permission to be here?"

"Absolutely. It's just taken me awhile to get here. I injured my ankle . . . jogging. How is she?"

"I'm sorry, I'll have to check your name on my list. This is my first day."

Gypsy clamped her lips together. The nurse had moved between her and the woman lying in the bed, and now she couldn't see Elisabeth's face if she wanted to. She would either have to push the nurse aside or answer something.

"Marguerite O'Keefe," she said, before she'd thought twice. The name slid off her tongue like sun-warmed honey.

"Just a moment." The nurse moved toward the dresser where several stacks of papers lay.

Gypsy moved closer to Elisabeth. It was now or never. She made herself look down.

"Oh, God." She closed her eyes. It was like looking in a mirror. But the face looking back at her was a face she had only imagined. Or so she'd thought.

"It's all right, Mrs. O'Keefe. It's always a shock at first." The nurse's voice was solicitous now, no longer suspicious. Gypsy knew that she had found Marguerite O'Keefe's name on the list. A Marguerite O'Keefe who until this moment had only been a figment of Gypsy's imagination. *Or so she'd thought.*

"She looks dead!"

"She's certainly not dead, or I'd be out of a job." The woman put her hand on Gypsy's shoulder. "She's resting comfortably. For all we know the place where she's resting is a lot pleasanter than this one."

"What . . . are they saying about her chances . . . You know . . ."

"No one knows anything for certain, dear. All we

can do is wait and see. Go ahead and talk to her, if you want. You can take her hand. We don't know exactly what she hears or feels, if anything, but it's worth a try."

Take her own hand. Talk to herself. Gypsy bit her trembling lip.

"I think I'll take a little break," the nurse said, understanding in her voice. "I'll be back in a few minutes."

The familiar hiss signaled the woman's retreat. Gypsy didn't move. "Elisabeth?" Her voice cracked.

She was talking to herself. The woman in the bed was her, or the person she'd been. Every hair, every inch of pale skin was absolutely familiar. This was her. Once upon a time.

Elisabeth looked like she was asleep. She didn't look as if she were in pain, although she seemed smaller, shrunken somehow. Her blond hair was neatly brushed and fanned across the pillow, and she wore a dark green silk kimono that had always been one of her favorites.

Her favorites . . .

Gypsy edged a little closer. "Elisabeth." She took Elisabeth's hand, then dropped it when she realized what she was doing. She was holding her own hand.

"Oh God! Who am I?"

"I can tell you who in the hell you aren't. You aren't Marguerite O'Keefe!"

She had been so unnerved that she hadn't heard the door open again. She turned at the familiar voice and stared at Owen. Standing by his side was Anna Jacquard.

"Gypsy Dugan." Owen said the name like a curse.

And what could she answer? *Hello, dearest. Look who's here?* She stood as tall as her crutches would allow and stared back at him. For a moment she just drank in the sight. He was wearing a dark suit, one she had chosen for him, but the tie was unfamiliar. He'd had a haircut recently, an expensive, time-consuming haircut. She wondered just how many hours he had spent in the last weeks sitting by his wife's bedside.

"Wasn't it enough to nearly kill her?" Owen said. "Did you have to lie your way in here to see your handiwork?"

"Owen . . ." Anna put her hand on his arm, as if it belonged there. "Don't make a scene."

He covered her hand, as if to quiet her. But his hand stayed on top of hers for a long moment, as if the feel of it was pleasurable.

Gypsy watched the two of them and the joy she'd felt at first sight of him curled and died inside her. "I . . ." Nothing seemed appropriate.

Owen moved closer. Anna, moved with him, her hand still resting intimately on his arm. Her hips brushed his, and neither of them moved away.

He looked thinner. The few extra pounds he'd gained over the years had melted away. His face looked gaunt, but his body was the body of a younger man, as if he'd survived some life-altering crucible, and was better for the experience.

"Are you looking for a story, Miss Dugan?"

His voice dripped sarcasm. Owen was only rarely sarcastic. Like creative people everywhere, he lived deep inside himself, where the vicissitudes of life scarcely touched him. He was oblivious to much of what happened around him.

He wasn't oblivious to Gypsy Dugan.

"Do you see a camera?" she asked. "Or do you see a woman on crutches?"

See me, a voice inside her pleaded. *You know me better than anyone. Look at me and see who I really am.*

"I see the woman who nearly killed my wife. Or did kill her, if you look at it objectively. Because the woman I was married to for twenty-five years may never come out of that coma."

The woman he was married to. Not the woman he loved. Not a word about love.

"I've been told we were both at fault in the accident," she said. "But you have no idea how sorry I am that this happened." No one could possibly have any idea.

"I know enough about you to doubt anything you say!"

"You're upset. Naturally you would be." She looked him straight in the eye. "I know you must love your wife very much."

"What would you know about my feelings? This is the real world, not some absurd reenactment on your show. There's no tragic love story here for you to exploit with old home movies and interviews with our neighbors. What I feel for Elisabeth is nobody's business but my own!"

"Owen!" Anna tightened her grip, her possessive, intimate grip, on his arm. "This isn't the time."

Gypsy felt an overwhelming need to hurt him. Owen talked easily about blame, but that was all. He had always been a terrible liar. Now he couldn't even find it in himself to pretend out loud that he still loved his wife. And although she had no doubt he was truly sorry that Elisabeth was in a coma, he was still accepting solace from Anna Jacquard, as if he was used to accepting a great many things from her.

"Is this your daughter?" she asked. She turned her head and pretended sympathy. "I really don't know what to say to you, either."

"I'm an associate of Mr. Whitfield's," Anna said with dignity.

"Oh, I'm sorry . . ." Gypsy's eyes dropped to Anna's hand. "I just assumed . . ."

"What point are you trying to make, Miss Dugan?" Owen said. He moved closer.

"I came to see your wife, to make peace with her if I could." And with myself, she added silently. But there was no peace here. Her throat closed around her next words, and she could hardly utter them. "I never meant for this to happen. And neither did she. We were both victims of fate."

"You and your kind never accepts responsibility for anything, do you?"

"Me and my kind?"

"You newspeople have hounded me since the accident, tearing my life and my privacy to shreds. And now you've violated the sanctuary of this hospital room so you can whine about fate!"

"I haven't hounded anyone, Mr. Whitfield. *I've* been in a hospital bed recovering. God willing, your wife will recover, too."

God willing . . . That's exactly what she had been hoping for all along. Somehow Elisabeth would wake up, and Gypsy Dugan and her whole crazy life would disappear in a puff of smoke. For the first time she wondered if that's what she wanted after all.

Did she want the life of the woman lying in that bed? Did she want this man, and all that came with him now? The expectations, the deceits?

She looked at Anna, who was gazing adoringly up at Owen as if he were the Old Testament Jehovah spewing a wrathful justice at an erring world.

Did she want Anna Jacquard in her life? And eventually, perhaps, a messy, scandalous divorce?

"My wife has very little chance of recovery," he said.

She looked at Anna's hand, tucked reassuringly into the crook of his arm. Then she let her gaze travel back to his face. Slowly. This man had held her in his arms and made love to her a thousand times or more. He had been with her at the birth of her only child, commiserated with her when no other children were conceived, laughed with her when times were good, cried with her when times were hard.

There were no tears in Owen's eyes now.

"Perhaps your wife doesn't feel any reason to return," she said softly. Tears hovered just out of reach, but she heard them in her voice. Gypsy's husky, sexy voice. "Perhaps wherever she is now is a better place than this."

"Get out of here."

"Owen!" Anna dropped his arm and extended her hands to Gypsy. "I'm sorry. You can't know what he's been through. He's not himself."

"No?" Gypsy gathered her crutches closer. "He seems very much himself. His real self. But then I couldn't know that, could I? Because he's a stranger to me."

She turned her head and took one last look at the woman lying in the bed. When she looked back at Owen, Casey stood behind him in the doorway, with Perry beside him.

"Have you come to take me home?" She looked past Owen and addressed Casey.

"Gypsy . . ." He shook his head. "You shouldn't have come here."

"Maybe not." But she didn't mean it. Because she had needed to come. Now she knew what she had only suspected. She knew exactly who she was.

And she knew exactly who she had to become.

"Take me home, Casey," she said. She moved cautiously past Owen and Anna, but she didn't spare either of them another look.

She was finished here.

She was finished with Elisabeth's life.

Just in front of Casey, she paused. She turned and looked at the woman in the bed one more time. "Good-bye Elisabeth," she said softly. "God speed your journey wherever you were meant to go."

8

"I STILL DON'T UNDERSTAND WHY YOU'D pull a stunt like that. Did you think the Whitfield family would welcome you with open arms?" Casey picked up a particularly hideous stone fertility symbol that graced a brass and ebony side table in Gypsy's apartment and turned it around and around in his hands. He looked like a shaman performing some ancient religious ritual.

Gypsy turned away from him to stump around her living room one more time. She couldn't tell Casey the truth about why she'd gone to Elisabeth's room. Who would believe it? There was no one she could share this with. For the rest of her days she would be locked into a stranger's body, and no one would ever know.

She tried to think of something else, but there *was* nothing else. Everywhere she looked she was assaulted by the truth. The apartment was an ice-water-in-the-face kind of reminder.

She couldn't believe she actually lived here now. There was nothing hideously wrong with the building. Clustered among similar buildings on Central Park South in midtown Manhattan, it was oppressively bland but solid. Built in the thirties or later—she had been Owen's wife for too long not to immediately evaluate the architectural style and period—the building had few flourishes to compete with the treescape of the park.

She had been satisfied enough until she stepped through the door of the apartment itself. Perry's purloined issue of *New York Magazine* had obviously seen a few tough years in radiology. Sometime since then Gypsy had transformed what the magazine had portrayed as a spare, modern space into an African whorehouse.

"Casey, my memory isn't what it used to be." Gypsy stopped in front of an elephant tusk phallic symbol that projected like a great white erection from a bamboo planter. She averted her eyes.

"I had that part figured out." He reclined on her sofa, an insubstantial piece of leather furniture that looked like a cross between a slingshot and a hammock.

"I can't remember when"—*or why*—"I had it decorated this way."

"Close to a year ago."

"Do I like it?"

"You did." His brows converged. "But you don't like it now?"

"Is this your . . . taste?"

"You don't remember my place, do you?"

"Not well."

"Not at all. Come on, Gyps, you don't have to play games with me. We've all been told about your condition."

"Have you? Why don't you tell me?"

"It's going to take time for you to regain everything you lost."

"I hope to hell I don't regain whatever made me decorate this place in Early Safari."

"If you've changed your mind, all those weeks in the hospital were worth it."

She was encouraged. "This is hideous."

"We've been warned not to let you make any big

decisions for a while. Not until you're feeling like yourself again. You could clear out this place and redecorate, and next week you might wake up and mourn inconsolably for all your lost zebra skins and leopard throw pillows."

"If I did, you could have me committed." She was tiring quickly, and she lowered herself to the sofa beside him, propping her crutches at the sofa's end.

The apartment was surprisingly small. Gypsy had been able to afford a top location, but not much space to go with it. This room, which looked over the park, was the largest, ideal for a small cocktail party. But no dinner parties loomed on the horizon because the kitchen was the size of a postage stamp and poorly laid out. She doubted anyone ever did more there than warm up food.

There was a small library, filled, as one might expect, with videotapes instead of books, and a small room beside it that Perry was moving her things into while Casey kept Gypsy company. Gypsy's—*her*—bedroom looked as if it had once been two smaller rooms before remodeling. Now it was medium-sized with an opulent bath. If the rest of the apartment was *Out of Africa,* the bedroom and bath were *Arabian Nights.*

"Come here, Gyps." Casey put an arm around her shoulder and pulled her to lean against him.

She had little choice. The leather sagged with their combined weight and she slid into his arms as if the sofa had been made for this purpose alone. She was wary of being close to Casey, particularly now. Her life was in turmoil; her already questionable sanity was hanging by a thread. She had just said the oddest good-bye on record to a husband of twenty-five years.

Yet despite everything, the unmistakable sexual attraction that Casey and Gypsy had shared was still lodged somewhere in the very molecules of her youthful new body. She buzzed like a hive of hyperactive honeybees whenever Casey got within ten feet of her.

And he was much closer than that right now.

"Relax . . ." His voice was soothing—and very close to her ear. "Come on. Lean back. I don't expect anything out of you. You just got out of the hospital, and Perry's in the other room. Give me credit for a little sense."

It had never occurred to her to be worried about *him.*

She leaned; he adjusted. She relaxed one anxious inch at a time.

His breath was warm against her cheek. She was out of conversational hooks. She was out of energy, out of hope, and possibly out of her mind. *I don't feel like myself,* the words she most longed to say to him, were a masterpiece of understatement. And what could he say in return? That she would feel like herself soon enough?

Wrong.

"You're much cuddlier since the accident." His voice rumbled against her ear. His right hand began to massage her hipbone.

"Am I?" She filed that piece of information away in the mental drawer with his name on it, and cross-referenced it with Gypsy's sexual preferences and personality quirks.

"Yeah. Used to be you'd be all over me by now."

She feigned disbelief. "I can't remember why."

He nuzzled her neck. "Can't you?"

She was beginning to think there was more than one kind of memory. There was the kind that replayed pictures and words, and there was another kind she was just discovering. When Casey touched her it felt familiar. Not because she had been touched by another man. *Casey* felt familiar. The heat of his body was familiar. His scent was familiar. Even the low growl deep in his throat when his lips touched her bare skin was familiar.

The warm ripples of desire lapping at her misery were familiar, too.

He drew up one knee and settled her more intimately against him. "You're the most uninhibited woman I know."

"Maybe that's changed, too. Maybe I'm not the same at all. Maybe you can't count on anything about me anymore."

"Let's try counting and see. One, you're still the most desirable woman I've ever known. Two, you're essentially the same woman with a little memory unaccounted for. Three—"

"What if that's not true? What if . . . whatever made me Gypsy is gone forever?"

"I don't see any signs of that."

"Don't you?"

"Look at that stunt you pulled this morning. Nothing could be more typically you. Except that you were a lot more polite than I would have expected you to be under the circumstances."

"You think going to . . . Mrs. Whitfield's room was a typical stunt?"

"I don't know why you went, but it's the kind of thing you'd do. Go right to the source, never mind who it pisses off. Find out whatever you want to know and then get the hell out before you're forced to do any cleanup. Typical Gypsy Dugan."

"You think so highly of me."

"I know you. I know exactly who and what you are."

If he thought that was true, he had a big surprise coming. She asked a question she really needed an answer to. "If I'm that obnoxious, why do you put up with me?"

"Obnoxious? You're a good reporter, that's all. You don't let sentiment stand in your way. I'm exactly the same. That's why I'm not reporting dogfights and watermelon-eating contests at some affiliate in Podunk, Iowa."

His hand rubbed her thigh, a practiced rotation of the fingertips and palm that was as provocative as it

was comforting. She could feel whatever fight was in
her draining away. She had sat this way with Owen in
the early days of their courtship, sat this way and let
him put his hands anywhere he wanted. He had been
her first lover. Her only lover. Sometimes she had
wondered if that had been a mistake. Had she let
Owen Whitfield take over her life because she had
been so grateful for the pleasure he had given her?
Perhaps if she had been sure that kind of pleasure was
possible with another man, perhaps then she would
have strived for more independence. Taken more
chances.

Reaped more rewards?

Her head had fallen back to Casey's shoulder. She
turned it a little. Just a little.

His lips touched hers, firm, warm lips. She sighed
against them. Owen's kiss was very different, more
patient, less . . .

"Gyps, are you crying?"

She was, and the moment she realized it and tried
to stop, her body began to shake with great, gulping
sobs.

"Are you trying to tell me I've lost the knack for
this?" He rubbed his stubbled cheek against hers, like
a man who wanted to give comfort and wasn't sure
how. His tone made it clear he had a sudden yen to be
somewhere, anywhere, else.

She could only think of Owen. Right now he was
probably taking or planning to take his own comfort
in the arms of Anna Jacquard. She was as dead to him
as if he had buried both her body and that indefinable
essence that was now Gypsy Dugan.

"You're exhausted. Done in. And well you should
be. I've overstayed my welcome." He wrapped his
arms around her, and she sobbed harder. "Gypsy,
don't cry. This really isn't like you. You're scaring
me."

"I'm scaring . . . myself."

"Do you want me to get Perry?"

"No. I'll be all right." There was nothing in her voice to indicate that she really would be.

"I don't know what I'm supposed to do here. I want to make you feel better . . ."

On the rare occasions that Elisabeth had cried, Owen had taken her in his arms and hummed tunelessly in her ear. And at that moment, she would have given anything, anything at all, to hear his mind-numbing rendition of "Surfin' USA."

She cried harder.

"Shhh . . ." He held her tighter. "You've been so brave. You've come so far. You've just got to give yourself time to get everything back. But we're all here to help you. Everyone wants to help. We're not going to let anything or anyone hurt you."

"Hurt me?" She sniffed loudly.

There was just the slightest hesitation. "A figure of speech. I just wanted you to know we're all on your side. And if you need anything, we'll be there to get it for you."

She wanted Owen. And she doubted that anyone could get him for her. He was no longer hers for the getting. She was no longer herself.

The world tilted crazily on its axis.

"Gyps, let's get you to bed." He pulled away from her and stood. Then he held out his arms. "Come on, brave girl. A nap will fix you up. Let's get you to bed."

Nothing was going to fix her up, but that, too, was something she couldn't tell him.

She managed to get to her feet, but her legs felt as weak as an airline martini. "Have . . . have you seen that bedroom?"

"Intimately."

"Don't expect any renditions of Salome and the Seven Veils tonight."

He smiled his sexier-than-Geraldo smile. "I can wait for that."

"I hate this apartment. I hate everything about it!"

"You can move. You can redecorate. Hell, Desmond will be so glad to have you back at work that he'll probably redecorate for you."

"All the poor animals that died for this!" One hand swept the room and fresh sobs shook her. "They were meant for better things."

"For Christ's sake, Gyps, most of it's imitation fur. Perry!" Casey bellowed the name once, then again for good measure.

Perry stuck her head into the hallway and cocked a brow.

"Help," he said succinctly.

The bed was as wide as the River Jordan. Someone, Gypsy hoped it hadn't been she, had pitched a tent over it, a tent with tassels and garish satin panels. The apartment ceilings were high, and the tent reached its peak a foot below them. There was just enough room above the peak for a small gold pennant—to match the pennants that flew from spears anchored where the tent met the floor.

The floor was another matter entirely. All the floors in the apartment were laid in a herringbone design of light oak and dark walnut that blazed across the rooms like lightning bolts. In the living room pelts— or pseudopelts—of endangered mammals littered the floor. Here the decorator had opted for subtlety. There was only one rug, a sand-colored velvety plush that stretched across most of the floor. Sitting at each corner of the rug, like mythical guardians of the four directions, were stone lions.

She had entered the lion's den. Or the lioness's.

"Oh, God." She covered her mouth with her hand. Had she really, once upon a time, wished for this life?

"Feeling better, sweet pea?" Perry pushed the door open a foot and peeked inside.

"Give me a year or two."

"Nah. You're resilient. Problem is, you're expecting miracles."

Obviously, the miracle had already occurred. She was living proof.

Gypsy swung her feet to the floor and reached for her robe. It was the closest thing to utilitarian that Perry had found in her wardrobe, a navy blue silk with tuxedo satin lapels.

"You don't have to get up," Perry said. "I could bring your dinner in here."

"No!" She gave a wan smile. "No, thanks. I keep expecting Rudolph Valentino to come popping out of the closet. I'd rather eat somewhere else."

"Old Rudolph could pop out of my closet any old day he chose."

Gypsy reached for her crutches. "Did Casey leave?"

"As fast as he could."

"Poor man."

"Water a guy like that a few times, and he might just grow."

"What do you mean?"

"It didn't hurt Casey to see you cry. Reminded him you're a real person."

"What would I be if I wasn't a real person?"

Perry lifted a brow.

"Sex symbol? Caricature?" Gypsy's voice rose.

"Let's just say that seeing the bad with the good gives a man perspective."

Gypsy thought of Owen. "Not always. Sometimes it makes them look for greener, younger pastures."

"Any man like that doesn't need to store his shoes under my bed."

"Is there a man storing his shoes under your bed?" Elisabeth would never have asked such a personal question. But Elisabeth was lying in a hospital bed with a significant portion of herself residing elsewhere. Gypsy could ask anything she wanted.

"Not storing. Renting the space on occasion." Perry gave her heart-stopping grin on the way out of the room to finish dinner preparations.

They ate canned soup and cheese sandwiches in the tiny dining area at a chrome and glass table that forced Gypsy to do the one thing she had avoided for days: stare at her own reflection. It was a table for a narcissist—or a masochist. Anyone having a bad hair day would immediately lose her appetite here.

"I look better," Gypsy said. That was relative, of course. She still looked like someone she wasn't. She *was* someone she wasn't.

"Puffiness is going away. You can cover up nearly everything with makeup now."

"What do you think of this nose?" Gypsy wiggled it and watched it dance in the glass.

"It's the one God gave you, isn't it?" Perry narrowed her eyes. "Or is it?"

It was the one God had given Gypsy Dugan. "Are you asking if I had it fixed?"

"Maybe you don't remember."

Gypsy thought of the woman who had said the rosary at her bedside. "No, I think this is mine. My mother's is the same."

"You ever hear from her again?"

Gypsy shook her head. Mrs. Dugan—she still didn't know her first name—had disappeared after their one encounter. And there had been no word from her since.

"The tape on your answering machine is about used up. Calls have been coming in all day. Maybe one of them is from her."

"I guess I ought to listen to them." Gypsy didn't look forward to that ordeal. The voices would be the voices of strangers, and once again she would be confronted by how little she knew about Gypsy Dugan's world.

"Don't have to. I can put in a new tape."

"No. I'll do it. I have to do it sometime. I'll make a list. Maybe the next time Casey comes he can help me make sense out of it."

"Before long you'll be making sense of it yourself."

Gypsy wished she could confide in Perry. She longed to tell someone what she knew, someone who might just believe her. But as delightful as Perry was, she was still a nurse, and she reported to Dr. Roney. Gypsy didn't want to end up on a psych ward searching for daisies and rocket ships on pages of inkblots.

She chewed her sandwich in silence while Perry cleared dishes from the table. Perry took Gypsy's plate when she had finished. "I'll be shopping for food tomorrow. You tell me what you like, and I'll see if I can get it."

Gypsy stared at her reflection. "It's an awful kitchen. I don't know how anybody can cook in it."

"I can manage. Or we can order out."

"I don't know what I like. You choose."

"I make a mean shrimp creole. I'll make it for you and Casey sometime."

"Are you sure you want to go to that kind of trouble? I don't think it's in your job description."

"Job, shmob." Perry shrugged. "I just want to see you get better fast, and it'll be a lot more fun if I cook something good."

Gypsy stood and reached for her crutches. "I guess I'd better tackle the messages."

"I'll be around if you need me."

In the library she settled herself in a comfortable chair by the desk. The library had no international theme. It was simple, almost cozy. Gypsy supposed she and her decorator just hadn't gotten to it yet. It took her a few minutes to figure out how the answering machine worked. She and Owen had never had one. His staff and an answering service had taken care of their messages when she hadn't been there to do it herself.

Who would take care of them now? Anna?

She jabbed the play button harder than she needed to.

Perry hadn't exaggerated about the number of messages. She took notes as complete strangers left their best wishes. Near the end of the tape another unfamiliar voice began.

"The Lord's given you another chance, Gypsy Dugan. Well, his love may be limitless, but his patience isn't. Repent or the next time you may not be so lucky." There was a click, signaling the message's end.

Gypsy pushed the pause button. "Perry?"

Perry, wiping her hands on a dish towel, came to the doorway. "You doing okay?"

"Will you listen to this?" She studied the machine a moment, then punched what she hoped was the correct button to rewind the tape. After a few seconds she punched another button.

She had gone too far back. "Wait a minute. It's the next one that's interesting."

There was a brief pause, and the voice repeated the message. It was a man speaking, a man with a vocal range hovering between tenor and baritone. The South flavored his words, but just a little, as if he had carefully exorcised all but a touch.

She paused the machine again. "What do you think?"

"I'd say that's a threat."

"My thought, too. I wonder what I'm supposed to repent for?"

"You can't remember, I'm sure not going to be the one to guess."

"I'm going to save this tape so Casey can hear it." She opened the drawer beside the answering machine and took out another tape to replace it with. "You don't think this guy had anything to do with the accident, do you?" She realized her hand had paused in midair. She lowered it and the tape to the desk.

"Do you?"

Gypsy thought about it. "No, the accident's one of the few things . . . I remember. Nobody was to blame except me and . . . Elisabeth."

"Don't eat yourself up about it, sugar."

The intercom squawked. Perry hung the dish towel over her arm. "I'll go see who that is. Want me to tell them you're asleep?"

Gypsy already had a long night ahead of her. She didn't want to make it longer. She welcomed the distraction. "No. If it's legit, I'll see them."

"Good for you to get back into things. But take it easy."

Gypsy realized she should comb her hair and do something about makeup. She hobbled into the bathroom and took her first really good look at herself.

She was young. She was passably gorgeous. And she was as pale as a ghost.

She leaned toward the mirror and examined herself more fully. This was not the glamorous anchorwoman staring back at her. The Gypsy Dugan of television fame had flawless skin, flashing green eyes, and enviable black hair. This Gypsy had bruises, enlarged pores and split ends. She needed a facial and her hairdresser, stat.

She was certainly less of a perfect specimen than poor Elisabeth had ever fantasized.

She brushed her teeth and suspected that one of the front ones was capped. The teeth were strong and white though, and she had probably never needed a root canal in her life. Her skin would glow again once she was completely recovered and the hair could be trimmed. She washed her face and smoothed moisturizer over it, combed her hair and applied some lipstick.

She looked better, felt better.

Felt better, but not like Gypsy Dugan.

There was a knock on the bathroom door. "Gypsy, Nan Simmonds is here to see you. Nan, from your show."

Gypsy stared at her reflection and wondered if she could pull this off. In the hospital she had smiled and nodded while visitors talked to her. She had asked questions. No one had expected more of her.

This was Nan Simmonds, and intuition told her that more, much more, was going to be expected.

"I'll be there in a moment." She retied the sash of her robe and unfastened the top button of her gown. Then, as gracefully as she could wielding crutches, she swung her way through her bedroom—narrowly avoiding the lion to the east—and made her way into the living room.

She recognized Nan immediately, from hours of watching "The Whole Truth." She was smaller than Gypsy had expected her to be, with abundant golden hair, a thin, pinched-off nose and Kewpie doll lips. She was dressed in a pink suit guaranteed to make Barbie trill with delight. Tears filled her eyes as Gypsy made her way into the room.

"Oh, Gypsy, you poor baby. This is just so, *so* awful. It's terrible to see you this way." Nan wrung her hands like a heroine in an old-fashioned melodrama. "Poor, poor baby," she said with feeling. "You *don't* look like yourself at all."

There were no words truer. Gypsy waved her fingertips toward the sofa. "Sit down. I don't know if there's anything in the kitchen to offer you, but I can find out."

"Do *not* trouble yourself! You take a seat. I just won't have you relapsing on account of *me*."

Gypsy had the strangest feeling that Nan would like nothing better than to provoke a little relapse—except possibly a big relapse. She lowered herself carefully to a chair that was really no more than a large drum covered in what appeared to be goat hide. "It was good of you to come, Nan," she said, knowing by now that it wasn't good at all. Her best instincts signaled trouble, even without Casey's warning.

"I brought you daisies. Your maid has them."

"Perry's my nurse, not my maid. Actually, she's more a friend than anything."

Nan seated herself on the sofa and folded her hands primly in her lap. "Well, I tried to come to the hospital, you know, but Casey would *not* let me in to see you. He's much too proprietary, Gypsy. You really *must* rein that man in."

"I'd sooner rope and brand a wild stallion."

"Well, he's been *over* the top since you left the show."

Gypsy held up her hand. "I didn't exactly leave the show. It's more like the show went on without me for a while."

"Then you really do intend to come back?" Nan batted her baby blues. "I *thought* maybe your priorities had changed."

"What priorities are those?"

"When life smacks some people in the face, they adjust to . . . a different life. They paint. They become organic farmers. They travel. I thought *maybe . . .*"

"Well, I had thought a little about joining a Himalayan monastery, but I was too tall for the robes."

"Now you're making fun of me. You *always* do that."

You always do that. For some reason the words gave Gypsy a warm glow. Maybe she was part Elisabeth Whitfield, a large part Elisabeth even, but there was still some Gypsy Dugan in the old girl yet.

"I'm planning to rejoin the show as soon as I can." Gypsy hadn't even realized that decision was made. But there it was. She had wanted to be Gypsy Dugan, and she was going to be. She had given up a lot for this. An unfaithful husband, a stultifying social whirl, newspaper articles for wealthy suburbanites. A whole hell of a lot.

"Are you *sure* that's a good idea? Have you really thought this through, Gypsy? Sure, some of the viewers have missed you, but the show *did* go on, if you know what I mean. And they've gotten used to a different look now."

Gypsy had watched "The Whole Truth" while she was in the hospital, avidly watched it, in fact. The show certainly did have a different look. Nan sat behind the anchor desk now, and apparently she liked her seat. "I've given it the gravest consideration," she said. "And I plan to do everything I can to restore order, as soon as I get back."

"Order?"

"Of course. That's what you're talking about, right? Sloppy direction. Maudlin scripts. And who's supplying your wardrobe these days? The Madison Avenue Salvation Army? I just don't know how you stood it so long without my help. But I'm back." She dimpled. "In one solid piece again and raring to go."

Nan stood. "Well, I think you may be making a mistake. It won't be easy for you to just *take* over after such a long absence."

"I've seen the ratings, Nan. Des showed them to me. He's dying for me to take over. Maybe you just didn't notice." She got to her feet.

Nan dropped all pretenses. "I'm going to be standing right in your way. Right *smack* dab in your way. I'm not going to make it easy for you. You're going to have to fight me every step. And you don't look too steady on your feet."

Without giving it a thought Gypsy swung a crutch forward and used the tip to lift the hem of Nan's linen skirt. It was a most un-Elisabeth response.

Nan pushed the crutch away. "You might be surprised what this poor, crippled baby can still do," Gypsy said.

Gypsy was standing in the same spot minutes later when Perry found her. Nan had left with a flourish.

"She told me to put those daisies in water, so I put them down the disposal. Used lots of water to do it." Perry cocked her head. "You all right?"

Gypsy wasn't sure. But she thought there was a chance, just the smallest possibility, that she might be all right someday.

❧ 9

THERE WASN'T MUCH IN THE APARTMENT TO
help Gypsy determine facts about the woman she had
become. The decor was a clue. She liked fantasy and
flash and wasn't afraid to expose that part of herself
for everyone to see. She was a sensual woman, who
liked fur and satin, long soaks in the huge whirlpool,
the feel of Egyptian cotton sheets against her naked
skin—there was a not-so-surprising lack of nightwear
in her wardrobe.

She was not a fan of subtlety. One wall of her
bedroom was nearly covered by a painting of a mighty
Arabian stallion mounting a terror-stricken mare. Her
closet was filled with designer clothes that screamed
both her flamboyant style and personal success. She
liked heavy-handed oriental scents and lingerie that
left nothing to the imagination.

There were no cookbooks to point the way to her
eating habits. There were several delivery menus. She
seemed to prefer cheap Chinese and expensive pizza.
Her appointment book was so crowded that notes ran
up and down the borders of each page. Obviously she
was an extrovert who spent as little time alone as
possible.

Her collection of videotapes was surprisingly eclec-
tic. She liked everything from *Casablanca* to *Deep
Throat*. There was a collection of Disney's greatest

cartoon hits, a dozen unfamiliar but noteworthy foreign films, and a wide selection of Hollywood's greatest blockbusters past and recent. But the bulk of her collection consisted of segments of "The Whole Truth." The tapes were carefully labeled and comprised a complete five-year history of the show and her two-year rise to anchor.

She watched the tapes of her arrival on the show, hoping to find more clues. The first one captured Gypsy, the reporter. She had investigated three mysterious deaths in a small Missouri town, as well as its sheriff, who was known to distill and distribute a powerful brand of white lightning. Some people in the town swore that the sheriff had tainted his latest batch and made sure it went to opponents of his reelection, all now conveniently dead.

Gypsy had searched out every one of the sheriff's detractors. The barber straight out of Mainstreet Mayberry, the church organist, the rival bootlegger. She'd wheedled and flirted, and by the time she was finished, the sheriff had been tried and convicted by anyone watching.

He wasn't guilty, which was briefly pointed out at the end of a show that aired weeks later. Sophisticated tests had proved that the three deaths were unrelated, victims of coincidence. The town was a victim, too. After the first show the sheriff had packed his bags and left town for good, and not a speed limit or stop sign was being heeded while the town fathers searched for someone to replace him.

But Gypsy had triumphed. Her debut was splashy enough to grab some media attention. She photographed like a dream, she was witty, sassy, and not afraid to boldly go where no reporter with an ounce of conscience had gone before.

The public loved her.

Gypsy projected none of the self-righteous belligerence that passed for style on competing shows. She was utterly female, shrewdly using every feminine wile outlawed by the women's movement. She quickly perfected her walk, her dimpled smile, her clothes and jewelry. After the first month she learned to cock her head and bat her lashes when she confronted particularly reticent subjects. She learned to lean closer, and sometimes she touched the men she interviewed with one provocative finger. She promised everything with her eyes and body language, and she delivered sensation and half-truths with such a flair that she was quickly promoted up "The Whole Truth" food chain.

Two weeks after her release from the hospital Gypsy still wasn't sure exactly who she was, but she was getting closer.

She was feeling better physically. She could put weight on her foot now and she had stopped using crutches entirely. The face that stared back at her from her bathroom mirror was Gypsy Dugan's best, unmarred by telltale bruises or swelling. Her hairdresser had arrived one morning to cut and rinse, and his partner had massaged a paste of soothing herbs over her face and neck and manicured her nails. She had been polished by professionals, prodded by therapists and personal trainers, petted by Desmond and the rest of the show's producers, and patronized by bloodthirsty colleagues who tried to convince her she was far from ready to return to work.

Her emotions pinged from despair to elation. On some mornings she awoke and thought she could cope with this strange new life. On others she closed her eyes and prayed that when she opened them again, she would be back on the North Shore, in a sun-drenched temple of a house, with Owen . . . in the room across the hall.

"You've got to get hold of yourself," Perry said on the morning of Gypsy's third week away from the hospital. "You're brooding. You keep it up, even cheesecake won't help."

Gypsy worked on her second cup of coffee. "That's a radical departure in philosophy. I thought cheesecake cured anything."

"Anything but the low down, dirt-bottom blues."

"Got 'em. Can't get rid of 'em," Gypsy admitted.

"You need to have some fun. We've been working you too hard."

Gypsy wondered what she did for fun. She couldn't see herself eating popcorn while Mel Gibson or Bruce Willis saved small cities on the big screen. She couldn't imagine roller blading or line dancing. And from the looks of things, she had no hobbies. There were no musical instruments in the apartment, no half-finished haiku, no sewing machine. The apartment was filled with flowers—more arrived each day—but there weren't even live plants to water. "Shopping." She looked up at Perry. "That's probably what I liked."

"Might do you some good to get out and spend money."

There was money to spend, although Gypsy had been surprised at how little attention had been paid to planning for the future. She lived well and had the money to do it. But precious little resided in the bank for a rainy day. Maybe she had known, somehow, that planning for retirement was futile.

Perry looked so expectant that she felt compelled to dredge up some enthusiasm. "All right. Let's do it. Let's get dressed up and hit a few stores. Then we can have lunch."

Perry was silent, but her face said it all.

"I'd like you to come," Gypsy said. "I can't think of anyone I'd rather have along."

"Sugar babe, that's because you can't think of anyone you *know*."

Gypsy smiled. "That, too. Look, I know you were hired to take care of me, but why don't you just be my friend today? You're the one person besides Casey that I've been able to count on since the moment I opened my eyes in that hospital room. I really like you."

"When you say that on TV, I know somebody's about to get screwed."

Gypsy covered Perry's hand. "I never *say* it on TV. I just pretend it's true. I'm saying it now. That's different . . . I'm different."

"How do you know you're different if you can't remember how you were?"

"Are you trying to stump me here?"

"I don't want you to get this wrong. I know I'm every bit as good as anyone else. I just don't want to be used. Understand?"

"And I'm the queen of the users?"

"That's what it looks like on TV."

"But we're not on TV." Gypsy stood. Now she was committed. She forced a brighter tone. "What'll we shop for?"

Perry stood, too. "Seems to me you need an antelope skin or two to tack up on the wall. Can't see how you missed the antelope when you decorated."

Gypsy made a face. "We could look at furniture. Or I could buy a flannel nightgown. What do you need?"

"Nothing any of the stores you shop in would carry."

"We could do your stores, then."

"First time out we'll do yours."

Sorting through Gypsy's closets had been an exercise in self-awareness. Elisabeth had dressed in classic styles and colors suitable for a pale-skinned blond. Gypsy dressed in anything she pleased. Since returning from the hospital, she had opted for the most comfortable and casual of the exotic wear available to her. But for this first foray back into the world, she knew she had to venture into new fashion territory, too.

She chose a mustard-colored jacket by Yves St. Laurent, and soft gray trousers to wear with it. The jacket, with its red piping, big brass buttons, and plunging neckline, made a statement she could almost be comfortable with. She found dangling brassy earrings and a black camisole that nicely filled in the neckline.

She was trembling by the time she finished dressing. She wasn't ready to go out in the world as Gypsy Dugan. The creature in her mirror was someone she wasn't. With every item of clothing she had assumed a new identity.

Perry gave a wolf whistle from the doorway. "Not too bad."

"I'm not sure about the fit. I haven't regained all the weight I lost."

"Why don't we stop for groceries on the way back. I'll make that shrimp creole I promised for you and Casey tonight."

Gypsy hadn't forgotten that Casey was expected for dinner. She had just pushed it to the back of her mind. "You'd do that? We could easily order something."

"Nah, I've been promising. Then I'm going out on the town while Casey baby-sits."

"You're going to leave us here alone?"

"About time."

"For you, maybe."

"For me, definitely. And for you?" Perry shrugged. "You're a big girl, honeypot. You don't want to say yes, you can always say no."

"I have a feeling that's a word I haven't used with Casey."

"The man's a sex machine."

"And I've still got a few cylinders missing."

"Just take your time. Things will happen the way they're supposed to."

They took a studio limo, which Desmond had put at her disposal. Elisabeth would have preferred one of the discreet, tasteful shops where the salesladies had known her since she was a well-behaved child. They would have found her a chair, offered simple, elegant refreshments, then, as she relaxed in comfort, they would have brought her items to examine, scarves preselected in flattering colors, shoes exactly the correct width, suits and dresses perfect for her lifestyle and taste. Shops like those were an inheritance. New customers were carefully scrutinized and usually came with a recommendation. Gypsy doubted she was known at any of them. Elisabeth's favorite salespersons at Henri Bendel or Martha would gaze at her with astonishment.

Instead she settled on Bloomingdale's, even though Perry warned her it would be crowded. But the limo driver had other ideas. He introduced himself and ushered them into the limo, but he turned in his seat to address them once they were settled. Billy was dark-haired and round-faced, an astonishingly beefy young man who looked as if he belonged in a wrestling ring, blithely yanking Hulk Hogan's blond locks. "I'm sorry, Miss Dugan," he drawled, Carolina cane syrup thick in his voice, "but I don't think Bloomingdale's would be a good idea."

"I'm sorry?" She cocked her head in classic Gypsy style.

His neck grew scarlet, and the color crept slowly up to his cheeks. "Uh, ma'am, it's just not the best place for you. You, uh, know, you've got . . . this security problem. I can't really, um . . . protect you there."

"Protect me?" She was both charmed and annoyed. "Are you supposed to protect me?"

"Well, um . . . yes, ma'am."

"Well, that's just so nice of you." Something perverse that Elisabeth would never have given in to made her wink at him. His cheeks deepened to crimson. "But Billy . . . I'm sure there's nothing to worry about. Perry and I will be just fine at Bloomies."

"Just the same, ma'am, I can't take you there."

"Can't or won't?"

"Won't, ma'am. I have to answer to Mr. Weber, and he's instructed me to keep you safe."

"Perry, do you know anything about this?" Gypsy asked.

Perry, who had dressed for the occasion in a hunter green jumper set off by a pale peach shirt and matching sneakers, shrugged. But she didn't quite meet Gypsy's eyes.

"Oh, I see." Gypsy sat back and folded her arms. "What's going on?"

"It's just that you're awfully well known, Miss Dugan. And Mr. Weber is afraid a fan or someone . . ." Billy's voice trailed off.

Gypsy silently berated herself. Elisabeth had been rich, and her husband successful, but she had been free to roam far and wide because no one—except those in the most exclusive circles—knew who she was or what she was worth.

Gypsy Dugan's life was a different story. Her face was familiar to millions of viewers, and not all of them wished her well.

She sighed. Bloomingdale's, with its cheerful bustle, suddenly seemed a long way off. "Okay, got any other ideas for us?"

He looked relieved. The high color mellowed. "Um . . . I don't shop much, ma'am. But somewhere smaller?"

"Perry?" Gypsy asked. Her world, which had already seemed as complicated as the theory of relativity, had suddenly grown even more complex. "Where do we go from here?"

They settled on Columbus Avenue, where a variety of interesting boutiques that were small enough to suit Billy lined the street. Billy dropped them off and then, to Gypsy's surprise, promised to be back at three if they hadn't called the limo service first.

She watched the limo pull away from the curb. "Does that make any sense at all? First he sounds like he's planning to throw himself in front of a speeding bullet, then he just drives away?"

"I don't think we've got anything to worry about."

"I didn't think so in the first place . . ." Gypsy stopped and took a closer look at Perry. "But what do *you* mean?"

"Just that. I'm sure you're safe."

"You mean someone else is watching out for us, don't you?"

"Can't leave anything alone, can you? Just like a snoopy old journalist to go looking for a story."

"What do you know that I don't?"

"Just that you're as safe as can be."

"Aren't they being a little overprotective? And a little secretive?"

"Everyone's scared to death of upsetting you."

"As if they could upset me any more than I am already." Gypsy turned her attention to the people moving past her. No one paid any attention to the two women standing in the middle of the sidewalk. Like typical New Yorkers, they claimed the space they moved through as their own, but everything else was up for grabs. "Where is he?"

"Somewhere." Perry waved her hand. "Nothing for you to worry about. But if you have to know, you can go stand in the middle of Columbus and see who comes to your rescue first."

"How did he know where we'd be?"

"Phone in the limo. You didn't notice?"

"I guess my instincts are pretty shot."

Perry took her arm to help steer her through the crowd. "Let's just have fun and forget everything that's worrying you for a while."

There was no chance of that, but Gypsy followed Perry through a block of boutiques, examining belts and shoes and fingering exotic costume jewelry of the sort that Elisabeth had coveted, but never owned. She wanted to have fun, deserved some, in fact. But between the natural fatigue of recuperation and a depression she couldn't shake, she couldn't summon the enthusiasm to enjoy this first excursion back into the world.

Somewhere between pith helmets and Australian stockmen coats at Banana Republic, Perry gave up. "Come on, sugarplum, let's get you out of here. We'll have some lunch, then we can go back home."

"Excuse me." A young blond dressed in olive drab and khaki stepped in front of them. "Are you Gypsy Dugan? Are you really?"

Since Gypsy had been wondering the same thing, she didn't know how to answer. She sifted through replies, and not a one of them seemed to get to the heart of the matter. "It's possible," she said, when the silence began to seem ominous.

The woman laughed with delight. "I'd love your autograph. I watch your show all the time. I'm so glad you're better. I can't wait until you're back on TV." She produced a pen as she talked, grabbed a blank sales ticket off the counter, and thrust it at Gypsy. "Please? For a big, big fan?"

Gypsy stared at the ticket. She felt like a total fraud.

"Sign it and let's get the heck out of here," Perry said in a low voice. "The natives are getting restless."

Gypsy looked up and saw that all eyes were on them. She grabbed the ticket and scrawled her name. And the signature was not Elisabeth's, but a bolder, less precise script.

"I'll treasure it." The young woman took the ticket and clasped it to her heart.

"We're out of here." Perry took Gypsy by the arm as the others began to swarm toward them. In a moment they were out on the sidewalk, moving north. "You did okay," Perry said. "Got through that nicely."

"I just signed my name." Gypsy was still mulling over the fact that her own handwriting was completely unfamiliar to her. Even the simplest things confounded her.

"Like a pro." They kept walking until they were sure no one had pursued them. Then Perry slowed the pace. "Seen enough for one day? We can skip lunch."

Gypsy almost said yes. She was exhausted, and no closer to feeling better than she had been when they set out. She was living in a stranger's body. Her handwriting was a stranger's. Nothing about this life was familiar.

Then she realized that the block they stood on was.

"Perry . . ." She put her hand on Perry's arm to stop her. "There's a shop I'd like to go in."

Perry seemed relieved. This new show of enthusiasm was obviously welcome. "Fine. Where?"

"That way." Gypsy pointed down the street. "Shu Uemura. It's a beauty boutique. I . . . buy my cosmetics there." *She* didn't. Elisabeth had. Elisabeth who certainly didn't need them now.

For a moment she almost faltered, but the lure of the familiar, the prospect of using the same cosmetics that had been a ritual in her former life, was too potent. Marguerite O'Keefe had introduced her to Shu Uemura. They had come here together, sipped wine and experimented with a dozen different lotions and powders. It was a peaceful place, uncluttered and serene. They'd had some of their best conversations on stools at the testing counter.

"Sounds like fun to me," Perry said. "Maybe I'll buy something to make me gorgeous tonight."

"You don't have to buy anything for that."

"You sure do know what to say."

They puttered for most of an hour. Gypsy knew better than to make a blanket purchase of the products that had worked so well for Elisabeth. Her skin tended to be oily; Elisabeth's had been dry. Their coloring differed, and so did the images they projected. She solicited advice, and it was courteously given. She and Perry experimented, laughed over mistakes, and crowed over successes. Even though she had to reluctantly abandon the moisturizers and foundation that Elisabeth had used, she found others that had the same familiar feel and scent. She bought liberally, and Perry, pleased enough with the prices, splurged as well.

For that hour, she almost forgot everything else. By the time they were finished making their selections, she was almost happy. Until she saw Marguerite.

She had already ceased questioning why fate had taken such a powerful hand in her life. It was far less of a twist to have Marguerite O'Keefe staring at her than it had been to wake up in another woman's body. She wondered what Marguerite would do right now if Gypsy threw herself into her arms and sobbed out the truth.

The answer was depressingly obvious. Marguerite, who had always cornered the market on eccentricity, would call for the men with the butterfly nets.

"I know you," Marguerite said.

"We'd better get out of here," Perry said in low tones.

"No, it's okay." Gypsy started toward Marguerite, stopping just in front of her. Marguerite's hair was pulled back from her narrow face in a lopsided chignon. She wore a basic black dress that had probably been passed down from a particularly stoic maiden aunt, the pearls she'd been given on the eve of her debut and a button that read: "I will not have a nice day just because you told me to."

Gypsy extended her hand. "I'm Gypsy Dugan."

Marguerite took it. "Yes, you are."

It was an odd affirmation under the circumstances.

"I believe you're owed an apology," Marguerite said.

"Am I?"

"Yes. It should come from Owen. Owen Whitfield, Elisabeth's husband. But he's in no shape to do it. So I shall take it on myself."

"I see." And she did. She doubted Owen had

apologies on his mind these days. He was probably much too busy balancing Anna, work, and the charade of grieving husband. "Well, you don't have to apologize. I understand he was upset. This must be a very . . ." A very what? Inconvenient? Frustrating? Annoying? She settled on a word that could be interpreted a dozen different ways. "A very hard time for him."

"No more than for you, I'm sure. After all, you nearly died, I'm told."

Or did, depending on perspective. Gypsy forced herself to nod. "But I'm recovering, and his wife is . . . not."

"How do you know that?"

The truth seemed the best answer. "I call the hospital and check every day."

"Do you? That seems quite conscientious."

She told the truth again. "I feel a strong link to Elisabeth."

"This all surprises me very much." Her blond head cocked, Marguerite surveyed Gypsy from head to toe. "I'm curious about one thing, Miss Dugan. Owen tells me you used my name in order to get into Elisabeth's room. How did you know I was on her visitors' list?"

Gypsy stared at her. Then she realized what any newswoman would have done if she'd wanted that piece of information. "I bribed someone to find out who was on it in case I had trouble with the nurse on duty."

"I see. And why did it matter so much to you?"

"That would be remarkably difficult to explain."

"I am remarkably capable of understanding plain English."

Gypsy faltered. She was within touching distance of her best friend. She and Marguerite had shared so many secrets over the years. They had stood together at the graveside of Elisabeth's mother and father and later, Marguerite's parents. They had crowed over the newborn Grant, cried a month later when Marguerite's own pregnancy ended in miscarriage. She wanted desperately to tell her the truth.

But how could she convince Marguerite of something she didn't understand herself?

She shrugged in her best Gypsy style. "Call it guilt. I guess that's as plain as English can get."

"You are not at all what I expected."

"You don't know the half of it," Gypsy said with feeling.

"Elisabeth was fascinated by you. That's the odd part of it, you know. I think she wanted to live your life . . ."

"I—She never told you that."

"How would you know what she told me?"

"I meant . . . From what I've discovered about her, Elisabeth Whitfield hardly seems like the kind of woman who would envy someone like . . . me."

"Oh, there were—are surprising depths to our Elisabeth. She was not—before the accident, I mean—was not happy with her life. I think . . . I *know* she wished she had done more to have a career like yours. To be perfectly honest and a bit crude, I think she envied your guts."

Gypsy swallowed tears. She had never realized how well Marguerite understood her, how much empathy had been waiting, if she'd just tapped into it. "She was . . . and is lucky to have an understanding friend."

"All the understanding in the world won't help her now. But I do not want you to believe that all of us think the accident was your fault. There is nothing to indicate that it was. Certainly not entirely. And Owen knows that, too. He is just too emotional right now to think clearly."

Gypsy stood a little straighter. "He seemed to have lots of support that day in the hospital."

"I suppose you mean Anna."

Gypsy shrugged more dramatically.

Marguerite's eyes narrowed. "I certainly hope you're not looking for a sleazy tabloid story. Because that would be the wrong place."

"I'm sure you're right." Gypsy didn't sound sure at all.

"I know Owen attacked you, but don't think you can attack back. Because we will circle our wagons around him, you know. All his friends will protect him. He is well loved."

"Well, now that you mention it, that's just the part of the story that intrigues me." No sooner had she said the words than Gypsy wished she could call them back.

But surprisingly, Marguerite smiled a little. "I think I see a bit of what attracted Elisabeth to you. You say exactly what you please. And she has always been afraid to do the same." The smile dwindled. "I have apologized, and now I'll go. Good luck, Miss Dugan. I hope you recover completely." She nodded her head in farewell.

Gypsy watched her walk away.

"Strange lady," Perry said from behind her.

"One of the best," Gypsy said.

If Perry thought her answer was odd, she didn't say so. "Shall we do lunch? Or go home?"

"There's a man standing just outside the window, lolling uselessly against the light pole like he doesn't have a care in the world."

"So?"

"He's been there since we entered the store."

"Are you worried? Should I call security?"

"No. Just go tell him to radio for the limo. I want to go home."

∽ 10

"**Y**OU COULD ASK YOUR MYSTERY MAN FOR dinner," Gypsy told Perry. "You've made enough shrimp for ten people. I'd love to meet him. Maybe the four of us could go out afterward for a drink."

"I'm going out, and you're staying in." Perry turned off the burner. "Fact is, I'm going out right about now. I'm going home to dress. And he's meeting me there."

"What can I do to change your mind?"

"Not a thing."

Gypsy followed her out of the kitchen. "I can compromise. Just come for dinner."

"No." Perry disappeared into her room and came back out with her purse over her shoulder. "Do you remember what you have to do to get everything ready?"

Gypsy made a face.

"And if I hear you called Casey and gave him some piss-poor excuse why you had to cancel dinner, I'm coming after you. Understand?"

"What if it's a stellar excuse?"

"No excuse. None. You'll have fun."

"That's what I'm afraid of."

"You'll do fine." Perry unlocked the door and stepped into the hallway. She gazed down the hall, then she nodded.

144

Gypsy stepped out after her, but there was no one else there.

"Who'd you just nod to?"

"Nobody. Now you get back inside and get ready for Casey."

"Perry . . ." Gypsy put her hands on her hips. "I mean it. Who were you nodding at?"

"You don't have a thing to worry about except getting ready."

Gypsy stepped in front of her. "Is it Billy or one of his boys?"

Perry frowned, but she didn't deny it.

"Why?" Gypsy demanded.

"Not my place to tell you, sugar bun. You want to know, ask someone from the show."

"Oh, terrific. How many secrets are you keeping from me, anyway?"

"Just the ones I'm paid to."

"Does Casey know about this?"

Perry shrugged. "Ask him."

"I have ways to make you talk."

"Not a one that will work."

"I could call my decorator and have him start on your room. How would you feel about a grass hut and a hammock?"

"Ask Casey about Billy."

Gypsy knew that was the best she was going to get. "Have fun tonight."

"You go back in and lock up so I can leave."

Inside, Gypsy started back through the apartment. Casey was due in half an hour, and she only had to change. Some of the banter with Perry had been for show, but a substantial part of her was worried about the evening ahead.

Dinner with Casey was the closest thing to a date that she'd had in twenty-five years. She was a married woman living in an unmarried woman's body, and the last time she'd gone out with a man who wasn't her husband, Gypsy Dugan had been three years old.

Casey wasn't the only man who was pursuing her, either. Since her discharge from the hospital she had used her answering machine to screen all her calls. She could only guess what some of the men wanted with her, but she didn't think it was her autograph.

Having men lined up around the block was a delicious fantasy, one Elisabeth had indulged in occasionally even when her marriage to Owen had been wildly happy. But the reality was something else. She was apprehensive, and despite herself, guilty that she was about to be alone with another man. She might be living Gypsy Dugan's life, but she hadn't yet absorbed her casual attitudes or comfort with sexual freedom.

She was ready by the time Casey was announced. She'd chosen black leggings and a sheer white organdy shirt. She had a feeling that when the shirt had been worn previously there had been nothing but skin beneath it. Tonight she wore a white satin camisole. Dressing in clothes Elisabeth would never have dared to wear was becoming the high point of each day.

Casey was dressed in a sport coat of flecked raw silk over a black T-shirt and fashionably ragged jeans. His sockless feet were jammed into dark loafers. When she opened the door he touched the tip of her chin with his index finger, then leaned forward to give her a quick kiss. "You look good, Gyps. I always liked that shirt."

"Did you?"

"I thought maybe that's why you wore it."

She stepped away from him. "Sorry. I wish I could tell you my memory's back, but you're still a stranger."

His laugh rumbled through the space between them. "We'll see about that."

"I don't think so." She watched as he conscientiously closed the door behind him, turned the dead bolt, and hooked the chain. "Can't be too careful, huh, Casey?"

"Did you forget about the crime rate in the city?"

"Did you and everyone else forget to mention why I'm under twenty-four hour surveillance?" She turned away from him and went to the dining room hutch, where she had discovered that the liquor was kept. "What'll I get for you?"

"The usual."

"And that is?"

"I'll do it." He clearly knew his way around the apartment. He found half a bottle of Jameson's and poured a generous three fingers.

He held it up to her, but she shook her head. "Do you want ice?"

"I drink it like this." He proved his point by swallowing half of it in one, smooth toss.

"What do I drink?"

"Anything you can get."

Gypsy pondered that. "Do I have a problem, would you say?"

"Are you asking if you're an alcoholic?"

"I suppose."

"Not yet. The potential's probably there. But that's true for a lot of us in the business. Too many missed meals, tight schedules. An overabundance of airport bars and meetings that last all night." He finished his drink and poured another.

The images he evoked sent a thrill up her spine. The last all-night meeting she'd attended had been with six-month-old Grant and a particularly stubborn tooth. "I don't suppose I drink Manhattans."

"I don't suppose."

"Then give me what you've got."

He did, although he added ice from the bucket Gypsy had put there for that purpose. She filed his choice in the swiftly widening Gypsy's preferences file.

She sipped, but the taste was surprisingly familiar and smoother than she remembered whiskey could be. The warm glow it left behind was the nicest feeling she'd had in a long time. "You never answered my question."

"About security?"

"You got it."

He swished the contents of his glass and stared at it as if he could find the answer in the miniwhirlpool. "You're a celebrity," he said. "Certain things come along with it. Des just wants to keep you safe."

"For the hottest reporter on a sleazeball show, you don't lie so good."

"You cut deep."

She leaned against the hutch, a starkly contemporary piece of amber-tinted glass and exotic wood that had probably been the last tree of its kind in the rain forest. "Tell me what's really going on."

"Do you remember Mark Santini?"

Gypsy searched her mind—or Elisabeth's mind. The line between the two was growing increasingly murky. "He was murdered."

"Good." He sounded genuinely enthusiastic. "You actually remember?"

Gypsy imagined Elisabeth had read about the murder in the newspaper or seen it on "The Whole Truth." For that matter, she'd seen the story on her own tapes. But mention of it seemed to resonate in every cell of her body. Her breath came quicker, and the glass in her hands grew slippery from more than condensation. "Lord." She set the glass down. Her hands were shaking.

"Are you okay?"

"I was with him, wasn't I?"

"Yes. He was murdered right in front of you."

Gypsy shut her eyes. She could almost see the scene. But was she imagining something that had really happened or one of the show's spooky recreations? "What does this have to do with my ever-present security guard?"

"After the perp killed Mark, he turned the gun on you."

"He did what?" Her eyelids flew open. "Are you telling me I almost died that time, too?"

"Nobody's sure about that. But before the accident you were perfectly certain he had intended to kill you. You were less certain why he didn't. Maybe his gun jammed, or maybe people were closing in on him too quickly and he had to get out of there."

"What do *you* think?"

"I think he had plenty of time to get you, and he didn't have anything to lose. He'd already killed a man in plain sight of a dozen people. So I don't think he meant for you to die. If he pointed the gun at you at all, it was a warning. Nothing more."

"Why Mark?"

"Looks like some of his family had Mafia ties."

"But I saw the gunman's face?"

"Four other people claimed to have seen him clearly, too. But none of your descriptions really matched. It all happened so fast, there wasn't time to make him."

"Then why the security? If I'm not really in danger, why have me under lock and key?"

"You're too valuable to the show to take any chances. And you were pretty insistent."

Gypsy picked up her glass again. She would examine this surprising memory when she had some time alone. "What did I do? Stamp my narrow little foot and raise my sexy little voice?"

He finished his drink. "Something like that."

"Am I a tyrant?"

"Sometimes."

"A coward?"

"No. You're the gutsiest lady I know. And that was part of the reason for security. If you were worried, we thought you might be right. Then, after the accident . . ."

"You don't think the accident was something else, do you?"

"Probably not."

"Well, I can reassure you about that. It was stupidity, pure and simple."

"I think you jumped in the limo and drove off because you thought somebody had just killed your driver. You probably thought you were next."

"Desmond says the poor guy was having an insulin reaction."

"Yeah, he's fine and looking for a new line of work."

"So I was paranoid then, and that's why I took off. But I'm not paranoid now. The accident was my fault and Elisabeth's and not part of some assassination plot." She looked at Casey under her lashes. "Something tells me Elisabeth and I were meant to end up this way."

"For you, that qualifies as deep thinking, Gyps."

She couldn't help herself. She dimpled despite her nervousness. "If you think that highly of my intellect, what are you doing here?"

He set down his glass and put his arms around her waist. He tugged her closer. "Do you know how sexy you look in that outfit? The camisole's a nice touch. It sets my imagination to work."

His arms were warm through the thin knit of her leggings. She could feel the imprint of his fingers against her back. She put her palms on his chest, but she didn't push him away. "We ought to set some ground rules."

"Ought?"

"I'm not ready for anything big, Casey."

"Are you referring to a relationship or something more anatomical?"

She couldn't seem to quit smiling at him. It had been such a long time since a man had so obviously wanted her. The experience was heady. "I want dinner and conversation." She couldn't end it there. "And maybe . . . dessert. A little dessert."

"Why settle for lemon ice when you can have chocolate torte?"

"Sometimes lemon ice is all you can handle."

One corner of his mouth turned up. "You can have anything you're ready for. You just have to let me know."

She was surprised at his good grace, and touched. He had been at her side since the day she woke up in a new world, and he had persevered through tears and explosions. He wasn't a patient man; he was egotistical and brash, and probably used to having his own way most of the time. But he had cared enough to put his own needs in storage. He still did.

She touched the cocky half smile with a fingertip. "Have I said thank you? For everything?"

"You've never said thank you in your life. Are you going to start now?"

"I might just." She leaned forward and brushed her lips across his. His hands slid lower and he tilted her hips against him. There was a moment when she could withdraw, and then it was gone.

He captured her lips and she didn't resist. Desire tasted like whiskey, the same heady, seductive flavor, and the warmth that had suffused her after her first sip returned. He moved his hips against hers, not a relentless grind, but a provocative sway, like some sensuous Latin dance with a name that was a conjugation of the verb "to love." His body was warmer than the air, and the heat drew her closer. She burrowed against him, and the heat simmered inside her.

She didn't know she had issued an invitation to delve deeper until he had. His hands slipped lower until they cupped her buttocks; his tongue sought refuge and refuge was granted. He was familiar and unfamiliar, a tempting and tempestuous lover who knew her body's flashpoints, but didn't know *her* at all.

"Casey . . ."

"Ah, I've missed this."

She, or a significant part of her that had once partaken, had missed it, too. Her libido had gone from zero to ninety miles an hour in record time. That significant part of her wanted to forget the other part of her completely, the part that was lost and shaken.

Sometime during their kiss her hands had clasped the back of his neck. Now they settled at his shoulders and pushed. Gently, but with conviction. He released her gradually until she was standing apart from him. "We seem to be having dessert before dinner," she said.

He didn't smile. "You're different."

Her heart nearly stopped—and she knew exactly how that felt. "Am I?"

"Something's different."

She could tell him exactly what, but knew there was no point. "How?"

"This whole experience has changed you."

"No question of that."

"You don't even kiss the same."

She supposed she was about to be rated by a pro. "Better or worse?"

He shook his head. "What do you want from me now, Gyps?"

Her body had a pretty good idea. The rest of her wasn't at all sure. "I guess I want you to come in the kitchen and help me get dinner on the table."

"You?"

She didn't understand.

"You don't cook," he said.

"Oh, it's all made. I only have to finish it off."

"No, you don't cook. You don't even open the little white cartons from Wong Chow. You've always claimed you can't figure them out."

"And you believed that?"

"Just exactly what are you going to do?"

"Finish off the rice. Toss a salad. Heat up the bread. Nothing spectacular. The entree's a surprise. Perry's specialty."

"You don't do those things."

As she had recovered, Gypsy had realized that moments like this would occur. Elisabeth knew things that Gypsy didn't. At some point along the way she had decided that she wouldn't pretend those parts of her didn't exist. She would do the things she enjoyed, and if the people around her were perplexed, that was fine. She would take a perverse pleasure in knowing that everyone else was as confused about her new identity as she was.

"I do now," she said. "Look, I'll tell you what. I stuck a tape in the answering machine that I want you to listen to. Go punch the button, then come back in and tell me what you think. Meanwhile I'll do all the things you say I can't, then we can eat."

He looked confused, with just a touch of suspicion. "You're not some sort of plant, are you? Somebody that 'Hard Copy' hired to learn all the show's secrets?"

"What do you think? I was recovering from plastic surgery all that time in the hospital?"

"I don't know. I've never heard of a bump on the head changing the way a woman kisses."

She put her hand on his arm. "Did you like it?"

"Yeah. A lot."

A warm glow spread through her again. She had liked it, too. "Go listen to that tape."

She thought about the kiss as she finished dinner preparations. Not tonight, but soon, she was going to have to decide how willing she was to really live as Gypsy Dugan. She could not assume her life as Elisabeth again, nor did she really want to. That life had ended before the accident. Even if Owen wasn't having an affair with Anna, their marriage had been on the rocks. They had become strangers, and she'd been helpless to turn it around.

Abandonment might be grounds for a divorce, but to Gypsy's knowledge, no husband had ever claimed abandonment by a spouse who had moved lock, stock, and ghostly spirit into a convenient vacant body. There was no piece of paper to declare that the marriage between Owen and Elisabeth Whitfield was over. But she had to accept the fact that it was, just as Owen would have to accept the fact that Elisabeth was never going to recover from her coma.

If she didn't.

That thought was disturbing. Her existence as Gypsy seemed precarious. There were no rules to govern it. If Elisabeth's heart stopped beating one day, what about Gypsy's? Were the two women physically linked? If Owen someday commanded hospital personnel to quit sending nourishment through Elisabeth's I.V., would Gypsy starve to death, too?

"You look way too serious. Burn the rice?"

She looked up to see Casey lounging in the kitchen doorway. And what if she began a relationship with him, or rather continued one, what then? By throwing herself into her new life, was she severing all ties with her old? Would she really become Gypsy Dugan and all that entailed? Had she already? No matter what she did?

"Need some help?" he asked.

"No. Everything's just about ready."

"You really do look like you know what you're doing. Is this what they taught you in occupational therapy?"

"No. I cut out snowflakes and made trivets from colored tiles."

"I listened to the tape."

She scraped the rice into a white pottery serving bowl and handed it to him to put on the table. When he returned she handed him the salad, and last of all, the covered tureen with Perry's shrimp creole.

She carried chilled chardonnay into the dining room and poured them each a glass to go with the shrimp. Then she seated herself, and Casey sat, too. He began scooping out the salad, and she started on the rice. "So what did you think?"

"I recognized the voice. Did you?"

"Nope. But then most of the time I hardly recognize my own."

"The Rev. George Bordmann. Ring a bell?"

The name sounded familiar. She took the salad and passed the rice to Casey. "Something to do with . . ." She shook her head, then she remembered. "I know, he's that right-wing minister who organizes all the letter-writing campaigns against the television networks."

"Bingo."

"I gather George isn't fond of me."

"'The Whole Truth' has been one of his biggest targets. And you've caught most of his public wrath."

She took the lid off the tureen and sniffed. Garlic and peppers scented the room along with the half dozen fresh herbs Perry had added to the pot. "Perry is a gourmet cook. This is spectacular."

"What is it?"

"Try it and see." She gestured for him to pass his plate, and after he did, she ladled the shrimp creole on top of his rice. After he took it, she served herself.

Casey waited patiently for her to finish. Then he raised his glass to her. "To George and all the other bigots out there who want to control the airwaves."

She reached across the plate to clink her glass against his. "Is Georgie boy dangerous?"

"Georgie boy's got the hots for you."

She nearly choked. "What?"

"Yeah. A clear case of obsession. He's after you to repent, but he's the one who needs to. You get messages like that all the time. He probably jacks off while he's leaving them."

"You're kidding!"

He started on his salad. "You don't remember any of this?"

"Not a bit of it."

"Well, it's a start that you remembered the name."

"What else should I know?"

"He propositioned you once."

"What?"

Casey nodded and dug deeper into his salad. He was obviously a one-food-at-a-time kind of guy. Grant was the same way. As a child he had refused casseroles, and to this day he hated it when one food on his plate touched another. Grant, whose mother she could never be again.

"Gypsy?"

She realized she was staring off into space. "Sorry. It's just so unbelievable that the Rev. George Bordmann would put the make on me. Do I look like I have minister's wife potential?"

He looked up and grinned. "Did Tammy Faye Bakker?"

She laughed and dug into the shrimp creole, ignoring the salad, which looked far less promising.

"Jesus, Gypsy!" Casey leapt to his feet and dived across the table. Pottery skidded across the glass top and crashed to the floor. Her fork flew out of her hand and shrimp creole splattered all over her white shirt. "Spit it out! For God's sake, spit it out!" he shouted.

She swallowed convulsively. Casey was lying across the table like a turtle on a frozen pond, his arms batting back and forth as if he were struggling for solid ground. She gasped at the absurdity of it all . . . And no air filled her lungs.

Her eyes widened.

"Christ. Jesus H. Christ!" He managed to get to his feet again and took off for the front door. He threw it open and shouted into the hallway. "Billy, get an ambulance. Get a doctor. Get somebody!"

Gypsy tried to piece it all together, but the world seemed to have switched to a slower speed. She had swallowed one bite of shrimp creole. And now, she couldn't seem to breathe.

Bit by bit the room filled with people, all moving slowly. So incredibly slowly. Her body seemed to swell. All her organs were swelling and filling every cavity inside her. She felt as though she might burst.

There was no room for air. Had she been able to breathe, she didn't know where the air would go.

She was dying. Again.

She closed her eyes and wondered if this was a habit she ought to break. Was she going to die and find herself in someone else's body once more?

She didn't want to die. And she didn't want to leave this life. It wasn't Elisabeth's life; it was the life Elisabeth had yearned for. Yet never, in all the weeks that it had been hers, had she really lived it.

"Gypsy, look at me. Don't you go out on us. Don't you dare!"

She opened her eyes and stared up at Casey. She was scaring him to death. She could see that. He didn't know that she'd been through this before, and that the worst part was knowing she hadn't done the things she should have.

She'd been given another chance, the chance she had secretly yearned for, and she'd blown it.

Again!

"Gypsy!"

Her eyelids closed on their own. And night fell like a black velvet curtain.

∽ 11

"I DON'T NEED TO BE HERE." GYPSY LOOKED around the hospital room. It was a different hospital room, and a different hospital. Roosevelt was not nearly as attractive as the University Hospital at Stony Brook, where she'd recovered before, but the paramedics hadn't been taking requests. Her room—and she'd been lucky to get one—had obviously once been part of a larger ward. There were no windows, and an empty bed sat between her and the door. She could hear noise from the rooms on each side of her, separated by makeshift partitions. "I feel perfectly fine now. I don't need to stay overnight."

Casey momentarily stopped pacing the room. "You do, and you're going to. Des is on his way over, and he says we're not going to let you out of here until the doctor says you're fit to go home."

"Great."

"You scared the sh . . . You scared me."

"I guess my allergy to shellfish was just one of those little things someone forgot to mention."

Casey still looked shaken. His hair was hopelessly rumpled and he wasn't even trying to regain his savoir faire. "It just never occurred to any of us. You were always so vigilant. You picked through everything you were served, questioned waiters and cooks . . . After

158

the accident the subject never came up, and I guess nobody thought about telling you. I know I didn't."

"It should have been in my medical file."

"I don't know if Roney ever requested records from your regular physician. But if he did, somebody slipped up or the information just wasn't there. Either way I should have thought of it. Des should have thought of it."

"Don't beat yourself up. I survived."

"You nearly didn't. Thank God for Adrenalin and paramedics who know when to use it."

Gypsy reached for his hand. It seemed the simplest thing in the world to do now. "Perry's going to have a cow when she finds out."

He linked his fingers with hers. "I called and left a message on her machine. I told her not to bother going back to your apartment until tomorrow."

"At least she gets a whole night with her honey. Silver linings and all that."

"Our night sure got shot to hell."

She brought his hand to her cheek. The contact was comforting—and something even nicer. "I bet you're starving. You can go back to my place and warm up the shrimp if you want. I sure won't be eating it."

"I lost my appetite about the time you stopped breathing."

"So did I." She didn't let go of his hand. She pulled him a little closer. She wanted him closer. "You saved my life. You and your quick thinking."

"I should have figured out what was on your fork about one bite sooner."

"I wanted the shrimp to be a surprise. Was it ever."

Casey lowered himself to the bed beside her. "I guess I'm going to call it a night. Des should be here any minute. He'll probably camp out by your bedside. I thought we were going to lose him for sure when I told him what had happened. He's been counting on getting you back on the air right away."

"Casey . . ." She tugged him closer still. She didn't know what she wanted to say. Three hours ago she'd been full of questions. Now she was full of answers, but she knew he wouldn't understand.

"It's okay." He leaned closer and kissed her lightly on the lips. "You're exhausted. It's been some night."

She put what little she could into words. "Life looks a lot different when you think you're about to leave it."

"Don't go philosophical on me, Gyps. I don't know what to make of it, coming from you." For all his macho veneer, his dark eyes were pools of confusion.

She was touched. "Sorry I keep trying to die on you."

"Yeah, would you lay off dying for a while? Give it a rest so we can all get back to work?"

"I plan to try," she said with feeling.

He nodded. He hesitated, as if he wasn't sure exactly what to do next. She solved the problem by lightly resting her hand on the back of his neck and guiding his lips back to hers. His taste was becoming familiar. Her own response was familiar, as well. She needed him. His warmth. His consolation. The assurance that her heart was still beating. His arms came around her and he pushed her harder against the pillow. Her heart beat even faster. They were engrossed in a passionate kiss when the door wheezed open.

A familiar voice bellowed from the doorway. "Jeez, Gypsy. What in the hell are you trying to do to me?"

"Des is here," Casey said, without turning. He smiled a little, kissed her again, then straightened. "I'm gone."

"I'll see you soon?"

"Yeah. In a couple of days. When I get back from assignment."

"I'll look forward to it."

Casey passed Des on his way out of the room. "She

didn't see Elvis or Hoffa before the paramedics got to her. I checked."

Des didn't rise to the bait. He bustled across the room and folded his arms to stare down at her. "I can't take much more of this, Gypsy. My heart won't stand it."

"If you're worried about your heart, you'd better pull up a chair."

He did, but he leaned forward as if he planned to leap to his feet again if necessary. "Why in the hell were you eating shrimp?"

She took a moment to compose herself, although it was going to take a lot longer than that. "I didn't know that I couldn't."

"Why the hell didn't somebody tell you?"

"Des, you're not making sense."

He ran his fingers through the wiry strands of his hair until it was as rumpled as Casey's. "I never thought about it. None of us did."

"It's over now. Unless there's something else I should know? Something else that's threatening my life?" She waited expectantly.

He looked down at the floor and didn't answer for a moment. "Casey's been talking to you, right?"

"Yes."

"So you know about Mark. Well, that'll make it easier to keep you safe. We won't have to scurry around behind your back."

"Why didn't you tell me?"

"Roney said not to. He thought it would be one more thing to worry you, and you had enough on your plate."

"Well, that part's true, at least. But it's time to tell me all my many secrets. I'm not going to remember things on my own, Des. I think that's pretty clear by now. And I don't want to take any more chances with my life. It may very well be the only one I've got left."

He looked up and glared, as if she were making a

lousy joke. "How in the hell are you going to get along? I've got a show to produce, and you're the star. How are you going to work if you don't remember anything? How are you going to sit there and read copy if none of it makes any sense to you?"

"I've seen every episode of the show from the moment I went on as reporter. None of the copy makes any sense anyway, so what's the problem?"

"Are you kidding?"

In the last hours Gypsy had thought this over carefully. For better for worse, she had been given this life. She didn't know why, and she didn't understand how. But there it was. At the moment when she thought she'd lost it forever, she had realized just how precious a chance it had been. She had been given her heart's desire. And she had nearly thrown it away.

"*You* know I can't remember anything, and *I* know it. But I'm nothing if not an actress. Everyone knows my brain got badly shaken. That's all they have to know. Nobody has to know it's not going to get any better."

"Maybe it will. Maybe you'll—"

"No." She shook her head. "We've got to assume this is what we've got to work with. And we can't assume I'm going to regain any memories. Knowing that, with your help and Casey's, I think I can pull this off."

He was silent, probably searching every which way for angles on what she'd said. "You think you can do it?"

"I know I can. But I'm going to need your help. No more episodes like tonight. I've got to know everything about myself, about the show and my job. Everything. There's no point in keeping silent, hoping I'll remember on my own. If I couldn't remember not to eat shrimp, I'm not likely to remember colleagues or components of my job or any of the other ten thousand things I'll need to know."

"It's going to be a whole hell of a lot of work."

"For both of us. Are you willing?"

"Willing?" He stood up and started to pace. "My frigging job's on the line! If our ratings don't go up soon, Callahan's going to be looking for a new producer. And I'm not the only one. He'll make a clean sweep. There won't be anybody left except the janitors."

"So even if I did recover in a couple of months, there wouldn't be a show to go back to?"

"Not the show you're used to . . . or were."

"Then neither of us has anything to lose and everything to gain. Are you with me on this?"

"When are you coming back?"

She took a deep breath. She had expected Desmond to agree. She just hadn't expected this to be so easy. She was making more than a commitment to her job. She was making a commitment to this life, Gypsy's life. She was going to seize this opportunity, no matter how long or short her sojourn in this body was destined to be. She didn't understand anything that had happened or why, but now she understood something more important. It could happen again. She could be faced with death at any moment, and somewhere along the way she was going to run out of chances.

If she wanted to be Gypsy Dugan, the time was now.

"Monday," she said decisively.

"That's only three days away. Roney's gonna piss in his pants! Especially after this latest scare."

"I don't care what Roney does. He's my doctor, not my keeper. I'm coming back, and I want to get back on the air as soon as I can."

"*Nan's* gonna piss in her pants."

"Now that I'd like to see." She dimpled seductively, and she knew that if she were looking in a mirror that the face dimpling back at her would be classic Gypsy Dugan.

* * *

It wasn't even light the next morning when Gypsy got out of bed. Sometime during the night a nurse had removed her I.V. and allowed her to get up on her own to use the bathroom. She was steady enough on her feet, considering what she had been through, and even steadier in her mind. She knew exactly what she had to do next.

She was going to live Gypsy's life. She was already, in very real ways, Gypsy Dugan. But she was also part Elisabeth Whitfield. And the part of her that was still Elisabeth couldn't completely abandon the life that had been hers.

She had stared at the ceiling through the long night, scheming like Gypsy and worrying like Elisabeth. But as the city below her had begun to come awake again, she had realized exactly what she had to do and how she had to do it.

She needed a connection to her old life. She couldn't forget forty-eight years and all they had brought with them. She might eventually be able to banish Owen from her heart, but Grant was another matter.

And so was Marguerite.

She dressed quickly in clothes Casey had brought for her. Her purse was locked up, and there was no hope of getting it until she was officially checked out later that morning. But she had already learned that Gypsy had a habit of keeping change in her pockets, and a quick perusal of the clothing Casey had provided had revealed about four dollars in quarters and dimes.

Enough for the subway.

If she was lucky, Marguerite would be at home on Central Park West and not at Birch Haven in Connecticut.

She dialed the familiar number and waited while it rang. Marguerite was an early riser, but this early was unheard of for her or her household staff.

"This had better be good," said the voice that

answered, carefully enunciating in flamboyantly frigid tones.

"Marguerite . . . This is Gypsy Dugan."

There was no answer, but Marguerite didn't hang up.

"I know this is early," Gypsy said. "It was the only way I could be sure that this would be private."

"I would not have taken you for a morning person."

"I have something to tell you, something that's going to come as a terrific shock."

"Just the fact that you have my phone number comes as a shock, Miss Dugan."

"I'm afraid that's only the beginning."

"Exactly what do you mean by that?"

"I can't tell you this over the telephone. I have to meet you. I know where you live. Could you meet me right across the street in the park? For a quick walk?"

"No."

Gypsy had expected exactly that. "It's about Elisabeth. Something only I know. Something she would want you to know, too."

"You know exactly what buttons to push, don't you? But I suppose that's why you do what you do."

"Please meet me."

"And will there be a film crew? Microphones and crude reporters?"

"No. Just us. You can search me, if you want."

Marguerite was silent. Gypsy hoped she was considering. "When?" she asked at last.

"Thirty minutes?"

"If I have to wait, I will not."

"I'll be there."

"Very well." The line went dead.

Gypsy wondered if she could make it on time. First she had to escape. She had discovered last evening that the door between her room and the one beside it was locked from her side. Des had checked it last night to guarantee her security. But when she'd unlocked her side and tried it in the middle of the night, she'd discovered it wasn't locked from the other. She hoped the doors were unlocked for at least several more rooms. If she could exit farther down the corridor, her chances of being caught by whoever was guarding her room were substantially lessened.

Luck was with her. She stole quietly through the first room where an elderly lady wheezed pitifully in her sleep. The next room had no inhabitants, but the next had two, and one of them, a middle-aged man with a handlebar mustache, was awake.

"Housekeeping," Gypsy said with a smile. "Just making an inspection. Have you been satisfied with the condition of your room?"

"Room's better than the goddamned nursing care. What do you mean waking me up before it's even light outside?"

"Just not enough hours in the day to do everything." She smiled again. "Go back to sleep now. Pleasant dreams."

She stepped into the hallway and closed the door behind her. If she was really lucky no one would even know she was gone until she returned. With summer camp flair she had piled her pillow and the one from the other bed in the semblance of a human shape and covered them with her spread. The resulting lump would pass inspection if no one turned on the overhead light. And if this was like most hospitals, what passed for breakfast didn't start for another hour and a half.

The escape was melodramatic to the extreme, much more Gypsy than Elisabeth. But she knew that once she was back in her own little world, every move she made would be carefully noted. At home there was Perry and the ever-present Billy Boys. At the studio her colleagues would be watching her for suspect behavior. It would probably be weeks before she had the opportunity to steal away to see Marguerite. And she couldn't wait weeks.

Her exit from the hospital was trouble free. New

York stretched and yawned as she made her way to the nearest subway station. The ride was blessedly peaceful, and the short walk to the section of the park closest to Marguerite's Gothic Revival apartment building was, too. With everything else that had happened to her in the past months, she had expected terrorists, or at least rapists and muggers, but the human scenery consisted of dog walkers and professionals heading to jobs where an early start was the first rung on the climb up the corporate ladder.

Two joggers crossed her path, brightly decked out in iridescent spandex, and so did a young woman with a baby in an expensive perambulator. The baby looked content, but the woman looked as if they'd been up all night. An old man dressed in several layers of ragged clothing dozed upright on a bench, as if now that the sun was about to rise, sleeping was a safer activity.

Marguerite was nowhere in sight.

Without the sun, the morning was cool, and Gypsy rubbed her hands up and down her arms as she waited. She wondered if Marguerite had changed her mind. Had she thought better of this visit? Worse, had she called Owen and told him that Gypsy Dugan claimed to have important information about his wife? She hadn't cautioned Marguerite against calling Owen because she had been afraid it would plant the idea in her head. But now she wondered if she should have taken that chance.

A woman's figure emerged from a small clump of trees that hid a bend in the sidewalk. She wasn't jogging. She was walking slowly and regally, Queen Victoria out for her morning stroll in Hyde Park.

Gypsy waited for Marguerite to join her. Marguerite's blond hair was pulled back in a dime store barrette and she wore an army surplus parka over a pale blue designer sweat suit. "Shall we walk while we talk?" Gypsy asked.

"I do not intend to have more than a brief conversation."

"Wait and see. You might change your mind."

"If you knew me, Miss Dugan, you would find I rarely change my mind."

Gypsy began to walk. "You did at least once. You and Elisabeth were six. You had invited her to your birthday party. A magician was scheduled, and Elisabeth, in a rare, undiplomatic moment, said that she was tired of magicians. So you told her you had changed your mind, and she was no longer invited. Your mother wouldn't allow that, of course, but you refused to speak to her the entire afternoon of the party. The next year you had ponies, and even though Elisabeth was tired of ponies, too, by then she knew better than to say anything. You were quite a tyrant."

Marguerite betrayed no emotion. "It does not warm my heart to hear that you've been doing research about people who have absolutely no connection to your life. Except, of course, that you were at exactly the same place and time as one of them and she is now in a coma from which she will probably never recover."

"I haven't been doing research, Marguerite. I've been recuperating. I've hardly left my apartment."

"Then how do you know that ghastly piece of childhood whimsy? Did it just happen to come up in a conversation with someone who knows me? I find that doubtful unless you were probing for information for that show of yours."

"I don't need to probe. I know more than I could possibly tell you. I know that on the eve of your wedding to Seamus you had one too many glasses of Dom Perignon, took Elisabeth aside, and asked her if she would help you escape to Bora Bora."

"Zimbabwe."

"No. Bora Bora. You said that you'd always had a yen to wear flowers in your hair and dance naked in the sunshine. Zimbabwe was Rhodesia back then, and far too colonial for your purposes."

"I can not believe Elisabeth ever told anyone that story. She was the soul of discretion."

"She didn't, and she was. And I know because I *am* Elisabeth. At least the part of me that's not visible to the naked eye."

Marguerite stopped walking. "I suppose about now some sordid chain-smoking little man will come leaping out of the shrubbery with a state-of-the-art video camera."

Gypsy faced her. "This isn't about 'The Whole Truth.' It's about you and me and the incredible reality of my waking up in another woman's body."

"I am not the pushover I seem, Miss Dugan. I have far-flung interests, it's true, not all of them terribly mainstream. I had a great-aunt who was a Spiritualist medium, and for a time I attended services with her. But never did I see the tiniest shred of proof that anything she believed was true."

"I remember going to one of those services with you. We were what, fifteen? Sixteen? Everyone brought a flower and laid it in a basket. The woman leading the service held each flower in the air and talked about the person who had brought it. She said that you would experience an extraordinary event in your life that would make you question everything traditional religion had ever taught you."

"How *do* you know that?"

"I took a white rose to the service. She held it up and said that I would lead two very different lives. I always thought she meant my life before my marriage and my life afterward. Now I know that's not what she meant at all."

"This is outrageous. Ridiculous!"

Gypsy touched Marguerite's arm to keep her from turning away. "Marg, no one is more aware of how outrageous it is then I am. Do I have to keep proving my point? I can tell you the name of the first boy who touched your breasts and the first man you slept with.

I know that if the baby you lost had been a girl, you were going to name her Anne after your favorite nanny. I know you didn't really want to go to Bora Bora at all, but you were afraid Seamus didn't love you enough to put up with all your little quirks. I also know that he did and does and that you've made a wonderful life for yourself with him."

Marguerite took a moment to examine her from head to toe. Then she shrugged. "Do you remember the time we stole butternuts from a neighbor's grove in Newport?"

"It was apples at your grandmother Warrington's summer house in Bar Harbor."

"What was my grandmother's maiden name?" Marguerite held up her hand. "No, that is too easy. What was the name of the Birch Haven butler who was fired for peeking at us when we were changing for bed the year we were twelve?"

"*That's* too easy. Wyman, and we were thirteen. I'd just had my birthday. I don't know if Wyman was his first or last name. Poor man, I never was sure he really peeked or just happened into the wrong room and was trying to leave without embarrassing us."

"He was a convicted child molester."

"You never told me that! When did you find out?"

"What was the name of the first man *you* slept with?"

Gypsy was silent. Marguerite raised an eyebrow.

"There was the first man I really slept with and then there was the one I told you about," Gypsy said at last. "They weren't one and the same."

For the first time that morning, Marguerite's surprise was discernible. "What?"

"I'm sorry I lied. I never slept with Lyle Bennett. I know I told you I did. I almost did, but I just couldn't go through with it. I couldn't tell you the truth. You were so smug back in those days. You were into free love and women's lib, and I was just repressed. Owen was my first lover. My one and only."

"I knew that."

"How did you know?"

"You could never lie. Your face . . ." Marguerite shook her head. Then she started walking.

"Marg, do you believe me?"

"No!"

"Yes, you do!"

"No! I don't know why you're doing this, Miss Dugan, but it's unconscionable."

Gypsy caught up with her. "You're afraid of spiders, but you love lizards. You wouldn't wear lavender if it was the only color in the world and you've always wanted to be a jockey but you were already too big by the time you were ten. Your mother sent you to bed without your supper when you were eight for telling a houseguest that her feet smelled, and your father brought you a tray that night when she pretended she wasn't looking. You adored them both, but you weren't allowed to tell them so. They adored you silently, too, and spoiled you rotten."

"They did not."

"They certainly did, but they were good parents. They taught you to look for the truth in unlikely places. And they would be disappointed in you now for ignoring what your heart tells you to believe."

"Stop it!" Marguerite stopped walking again. They had attracted attention this time. Fifteen yards away two men in business suits were staring at them as if they might need to leap to the rescue.

Gypsy took Marguerite's arm to allay their fears. "Look," she said softly. "It's me. Elisabeth. I don't know why or how. I remember seeing Gypsy Dugan's face staring back at me from that limo. The next time I saw that face, I was staring in a mirror."

"There's something only Elisabeth knows. Something about me, my life, that nobody else suspects . . ." Marguerite looked off into the distance.

"I would never have used that as evidence."

"Say it."

"Marguerite . . ."

"Say it."

Gypsy lowered her voice. "You have a child living somewhere in Europe. You got pregnant your first year of college, and you went to Paris to have the baby that summer. Everyone thought you had gone to perfect your already-perfect French. I was the only one you told. I went to stay with you on the Left Bank for those last weeks of your pregnancy. And I was with you when you gave your son to his new parents. You came home in the fall, thinner and quieter, and picked up your life as if nothing had happened."

"He is nearly thirty now. I have never contacted him."

"And we haven't talked about this since the day you put him in his new mother's arms."

"Do you know how I have regretted giving him away?"

"I've guessed."

Marguerite looked at her. "Either you are Elisabeth, or you are the most despicable, devious snoop and liar on the face of the earth."

"I'm neither and somewhere in between. I'm part Elisabeth Whitfield and part Gypsy Dugan. I have Gypsy's impulses and Elisabeth's memories. You were right the other day when you said that Elisabeth envied Gypsy. My life was a mess, Marg. I was sinking fast. I'd watch Gypsy's show and I'd think: 'Why didn't I try harder to be all the things I wanted? Why did I settle for so little . . .'"

"I cannot absorb this. It's simply impossible."

"I know."

"Why . . . Why did you tell me?"

"Because I need your help."

"What could I possibly do for you?"

"I'm going to be Gypsy Dugan. I . . . realized last night that I've been given a miraculous chance, a chance most people can't even imagine. But there's a part of me that can't let go of Elisabeth and her life. Not completely. I have to know what's happening. I have to know about Grant and my friends—"

"And Owen?"

Gypsy was silent.

"He is devastated, Elisabeth."

"Gypsy. You have to call me Gypsy, because that's who I am now. And Owen didn't look too devastated that last day in the hospital. He looked as if he were getting all the comfort one man could handle."

Marguerite sighed. "Anna."

"I don't want to know about Anna. Nothing about her. And I don't want to know about Owen, either. Or I won't be able to do this, Marg. I can't live this life if I'm always thinking about him."

"All right."

"Will you do it? Will you help me? Will you be my eyes and ears?"

"I think I am in the midst of a very bad dream."

"I felt that way. But it's not a dream. It's an opportunity."

"Pardon me, but you sound like an advertisement for the afterlife."

"I don't think this *is* the afterlife. I think it's . . . something else, something that's not supposed to happen and did. I think Gypsy Dugan . . . the other Gypsy Dugan, could sell heaven with a lot more assurance than I can."

"Then you don't think she . . . that part of her . . . is in Elisabeth's body?"

"No. I think she died. Period. Whatever that means."

"Why is Elisabeth still alive?"

"You're asking me? I'm not the expert. I've just been caught up in the whirlwind."

"I'm going home, and when I wake up, it will still be early morning, and none of this will have happened."

"Good luck." Gypsy took Margucrite's hand and squeezed it. "Be with me on this, Marg. Please. Help me. You're the only person I could tell."

Marguerite didn't respond.

"Will you answer my calls?" Gypsy asked.

"I suppose I should be grateful you only want a little information. You came back from the dead. You could have asked me to help you found a new religion."

"Then you'll help?"

Marguerite withdrew her hand. "Let me go now. Let me think." She walked away, her back straight, her head high. But the woman who stood and watched, the woman who knew her better than anyone in the world, could tell from the way Marguerite held her shoulders that she wanted to cry.

∽ 12

"**T**HE WHOLE TRUTH'S" STUDIOS WERE located in a red brick building on the Upper East Side, in a neighborhood with enough bars to keep the hard-drinking reporters happy and enough churches to give them a fair chance at repentance. Rockefeller Center, with its tourist charm and broadcasting elite, had little in common with the rough-hewn city block where "nothing but the truth" was supposed to flourish.

Gypsy, with one of the Billy Boys keeping careful watch over her, stood in front of the studio and indulged in her own moment of truth. "Well, it looks . . ." She was speaking to Perry, so there was no need to pretend. "Like a building," she finished.

"Try, 'nothing much has changed, has it?' That ought to be as good as anything else once you get inside."

"I'm going to be the mistress of vague by the time today is over."

"You're going to do fine, sugar lump. No reason to think any different. You're going to walk on in there and they're all going to throw themselves at your feet."

Gypsy practiced her smile, but it was a strained version at best. "Thanks for agreeing to come with me."

"They're going to figure out right off that you don't need a nurse," Perry warned. "They're going to wonder why I'm there."

Perry was there to help Gypsy pick up clues. The two women had discussed her role at length. Perry, who seemed in no hurry to get to her next nursing assignment, had promised that she would stay on for a few more days. Then she was moving out and on.

"Just take my pulse every once in a while, or warn me I ought to sit down and rest a little if someone starts grilling me too closely."

"Kind of business you're in, there's always someone grilling you. High pressure all the way. By the end of the day your pulse'll be beating time faster than Green Day's drummer."

Gypsy was already later than she'd planned. She hadn't realized how much time it would take the Billy Boy in attendance—a young man named Dan who was interchangeable with all the other young men who guarded her—to take one of a thousand long routes to the studio. He had informed her that the direct route was too predictable.

She took a deep breath and six steps to the front door. The chaos began the instant she stepped into the lobby.

Security waved her through with a smile.

"Miss Dugan." The receptionist at a desk by the elevators rose to her feet. "No one told me you were coming back today." She gave a wary smile, as if she wasn't sure to cheer or stick out her tongue. "You look wonderful."

Gypsy guessed that this plain-featured woman in the no-nonsense blue suit had hoped that she wouldn't look wonderful at all. She wondered how many of the other people she was about to encounter would be filled with the same kind of ambivalence. "Thank you . . ." Her eyes flicked to the woman's badge. "Carol."

Carol had seen the slight movement of her eyes. She smiled almost smugly. "It's so brave of you to come back after such a serious injury."

"Not serious enough for some people, I suspect." Gypsy dimpled, to take the sting out of her words. "How's your husband?" She had noted the wedding ring on Carol's finger. "And the kids?"

Carol's eyes widened. "Great. Thanks for asking. I brought my oldest daughter in to spend the day here a couple of weeks ago. You know. To see what I do."

"I'm sorry I missed her. Next year bring her in and she can spend the day in the studio with me."

If Carol's eyes had widened any farther, they would have taken up most of her face. "That's so kind."

Gypsy smiled her good-bye and started toward the elevators. "How'd you remember she has kids?" Perry asked.

"I didn't. But she has a crayon smudge on her blouse."

"Good detective work. Keep it up."

The elevator doors opened and a small army stepped off. Gypsy was immediately enveloped in hugs and coos. By the time she and Perry got on and the doors closed again, she had learned a few important points. The men who knew Gypsy Dugan were genuinely happy to see her back at work. The women weren't quite so sure.

"I don't think I'd be at the top of an in-house popularity poll," Gypsy said as the elevator squawked its way from floor to floor.

"Oh, I don't know. The older guy was trying to look down your blouse, and the younger one was resting his hand on your butt like he owned it."

"He did not."

"Maybe you didn't feel it, baby doll, but it was there."

"I think the women were hoping I'd turned into a slobbering idiot."

"Any of them familiar?"

"Two." Gypsy had recognized the oldest man, Kevin O'Flynn from her hours of viewing. He was a regular reporter, usually off on location in some Kansas cornfield looking for U.F.O. landing sites or haunted Indian burial grounds. Kevin was the leader of a rat pack of roguish Irishmen, one of Tito Callahan's homeboys who was reputedly quick with his fists and razor-sharp comebacks.

One of the women, Loretta Somebody-Or-Other, had been familiar, too. Along with some other staff, she had made a brief visit to the hospital.

All hell enveloped Gypsy when she stepped off the elevator. She hadn't really known what to expect, but she hadn't expected chaos. The newsroom was a free-for-all. What passed for desks looked as if they had been strewn around the huge room at random. A table in the far corner was being used as a cot. A black man of Sumo wrestler proportions lay sprawled across its surface, arms and legs dangling. His snores were audible over the hubbub. The desks were as likely to be used for chairs as surfaces to write or store papers. People, most in casual dress, wandered from desk to desk, using the closest telephone or pencil sharpener as if the concept of ownership was a bourgeois dialectic they had rejected.

She was immediately scooped up, pummeled, and crowed over. She looked over her shoulder to see how Perry was faring. She had been swamped by the newsroom horde, but she was holding her own, introducing herself and making her way to Gypsy's side with single-minded tenacity.

"Hello, everybody," Gypsy managed. Some of the horde looked familiar, either from telecasts or as hospital well-wishers—although in the confusion she wouldn't have been able to say exactly which was which. "Look, I'm thrilled to be back, but you're going to have to give me a little air here, or I'm going right straight back to the hospital."

The seas parted. She was surprised by the fervor of the greeting. The people who had surrounded her seemed genuinely pleased to see her. Male and female alike.

A vaguely familiar-looking brunette with tortoise-shell glasses and a Dutch boy bob took her arm. "Do you need to sit down? Can we get anything for you?" She popped a wad of gum in emphasis.

Gypsy measured the question. She couldn't detect a trace of malice in the woman's voice. "Nope. Listen everyone. Thanks a lot for the welcome. Really. But I just want to get back to work. That's all. I'll need your help, because frankly, I'm not a hundred percent yet. But I know I can count on everyone here." And strangely enough that seemed to be true.

The brunette squeezed her arm, then dropped it. "Let's get you to your desk." And as naturally as if she had always escorted Gypsy there, she steered her to the wall lined with large cubicles separated by dark paneling and giant panes of glass. Gypsy's, it seemed, was in the corner.

The woman stepped back at the doorway, then followed her in, with Perry trailing behind. "I visited you in the hospital for a few minutes just before you were discharged. I'm Kendra Scott," she said. "And Desmond told me you're still having problems with your memory. We're not going to tell everyone exactly how much trouble unless it seems absolutely essential. I'll hover for a while, if that's all right with you, and help you get reacquainted."

"I can't thank you enough." Gypsy wandered the small office, lifting a blown glass vase off the desk. "What's your job here, Kendra?"

"Research. Token head of the snoop department. That means I get to give the newbies the jobs I'm not interested in. But everyone on staff does whatever they have to. They need someone to hop a plane and set up a shoot in Rangoon and I'm the only one that's not already off in Timbuktu, then I do that, too."

"I don't remember everything being so . . . uncontrolled."

"Hey, this is controlled. It's still early. Wait until it's time to ride the bird and Des finds out that his lead story's a minute short because the legal suits say we have to cut the best part."

"That happens often?"

"That or something worse. We're glad you're back, Gypsy. There are people in this room who would cheerfully have taken your place in that wreck."

Gypsy looked up. Someone *had* taken her place, but she knew better than to go into that. "Why?"

"You can be a real bitch," Kendra said cheerfully, popping gum with every other word. "But everyone knows where they stand with you. And you've gone to bat for us more times than I can say."

"I have?"

"Oh, the self-serving lies I could get away with today. My integrity's in for a big test, isn't it?" Kendra grinned. "But that was the truth. See, the way you play it is this. You have a hierarchy . . ." She paused. "Do you remember this?"

"Go on. You're doing fine."

"Well, you have people on lists. The people you compete with directly, you know, Nan, in particular, hate your guts and you hate theirs. That's list number one. There there are the people you tolerate, but you watch your back with them. People like Kevin and Loretta—"

"Why them?"

"She's got anchor potential if she ever loses the lisp and the nervous blink. He's so close to Tito, you know you have to watch everything you say in front of him."

"Okay. Go on."

"Then there's the hoi polloi. Us." She waved toward the newsroom. "We cover your ass. We make you look good. You're smart enough to know which side your bread is buttered on, and besides, you have a soft spot for us, because this is where you started. And someday, when you lose your looks, you might just end up back here."

"You wouldn't want to commit those lists to paper, would you?"

"Not on your life. I don't trust you that much." Kendra grinned and popped simultaneously. "Desmond wants you in his office right away. Next floor, third door. Use the stairs whenever you can. Casey sends his love, but he's in Baltimore covering a private eye convention and won't be back until tomorrow. Nan's going on today and tomorrow and Des wants you back on the air by Wednesday. There's a story conference in Abram's office in an hour. Des hired a new assistant for you, but I think she's about as smart as grass and just as green. Don't think she'll make it past the end of this week." Kendra paused. "Oh yeah, there's an armful of new clothes for you to try on in your dressing room—"

"Dressing room?"

"One of your many perks. You hang out up there when you need quiet or when you and Casey have time for a little hanky-panky."

"Do I put up a sign so you people will know which it is?"

"Nope. We make bets." Kendra started for the door. "I'll take you up to the dressing room when you're ready. I'd draw you a diagram of the desks, but nobody respects anybody else's space, so it wouldn't help. I'll make a list of names and try to attach comments. But your best bet is to read badges for a while."

"Kendra . . ."

She didn't pause. "Yeah?"

"Do I like what I do?"

"You were born for this."

"Good."

"Break a leg. Never mind, you already did that. We can't afford another hospital stay, or we're all toast." Kendra slammed the door behind her.

Gypsy stared at the spot where Kendra had been. Words failed her, but not Perry.

"Whew!" Perry's eyes were dancing. "Sugar cakes, I think we've landed on Mars."

"The green's good," Perry said about four hours later. "Trash the polka dots and the suit with the Joan Crawford shoulder pads. Try on the yellow next."

"Are you sure about the polka dots?" Julie of the blond pageboy asked. She was the assistant Kendra had mentioned, a straight-out-of-Vassar debutante whose father had gone to Yale with Des. Gypsy had already learned that she was arrogant, lazy, and unhappy to be connected with such a lowbrow show. She was just marking time at "The Whole Truth" until her med student fiancé became a resident.

"Perry's right." Gypsy stripped off the dress in question. "It looks like a bad case of the measles."

Julie arched one perfectly plucked brow. "I think it lends some badly needed class."

"This isn't a Barbara Walters special." After a morning when she'd expected everything to go wrong, Gypsy was finally having fun. Even the worst moments had flown by. Half an hour into the morning her nerves had settled into neutral. She had survived her first story conference and meetings with Des and three more of the show's producers. With Kendra and Perry's help she'd navigated her way around the building and the business at hand. She had missed Casey, but not Nan, who had been busy taping the lead-ins for tonight's story, a job Gypsy would take over at the end of the week. They were already running promos about her return, vintage clips of a pre-accident Gypsy.

Trying on the new wardrobe was Halloween and Christmas rolled into one, a chance to be someone else entirely, with surprises to be unwrapped, one right after the other. Her dressing room had been a particularly nice surprise. She had expected it to be as austere as the rest of the studio, but instead it was an oasis. Unlike her apartment, it was in moderately good taste.

"Maybe this isn't 'Barbara Walters' or 'Sixty Minutes,'" Julie said, "but a little discretion and taste wouldn't hurt."

Gypsy paused in the act of smoothing the yellow skirt over her hips. Julie had already progressed beyond irritating. Someday she would be a clone of the worst women Elisabeth had been forced to make conversation with at important dinner parties, an empty-headed socialite whose days revolved around invitations to the best parties in the Hamptons and the search for the perfect fat-free salad dressing.

Elisabeth would have said something tactful and defused Julie's irritation. But Elisabeth wasn't in this room. Gypsy Dugan was, a Gypsy who didn't have time or inclination to placate the rude and ignorant of the world.

"You know, Julie," she said with deceptive calm, "I sense a certain unbecoming hostility toward the show. Or is it just toward me?"

"I don't know what you mean."

"What have you been doing while I've been on leave? You were hired as my assistant, but I wasn't here to assist."

"I've been working with Nan."

"I see." Gypsy turned her back to Perry, who slid the zipper into place, then she turned to the full-length mirror again for an objective critique. She decided to see how the color looked on camera before making a final judgment. "And what did you do for Nan?"

"Whatever needed to be done."

"Okay. Then I think that's what you'll need to do again."

Julie pouted. "I don't see how I can be any help to you when you don't want my advice."

"I think you've misunderstood me. I think you'll need to assist Nan from now on, not me."

"Nan already has an assistant."

"That's too bad. I can see that the two of you would get on well. And the two of us will not." She presented her back to Perry to be unzipped. "I think you should go find Nan right now and plead your case, because it's the only case you have."

"You're firing me?"

"Let's just say I'm rearranging your schedule. You don't work for me anymore. The rest is up to you."

"I'm not going to talk to Nan. I'm going to talk to Desmond!"

"Make a few more suggestions about the quality of the show, while you're at it. I'm sure he'll be delighted to get your seasoned input."

Julie's debutante training had not yet progressed to the proper way to close a door.

"You can be one righteous bitch goddess, you know that?" Perry said.

Gypsy was marveling over her newfound assertiveness. "I thought I was fairly tasteful. I didn't scream or pull hair."

"A little discretion and taste wouldn't hurt," Perry said in a precise imitation of Julie.

"Oh, you're good. Who else can you do?"

"Let's just say I'm rearranging your schedule. You don't work for me anymore. The rest is up to you." Perry dimpled in a familiar way. No one could have told the dimples or voice from Gypsy's own.

"Very, very good. Where'd you learn to do that?"

"I was a theater major in college."

"How'd you end up as a nurse?"

"I got tired of waiting tables to pay the bills. Not a lot of call for funky-looking black women with dreadlocks. Whoopie's got the market sewed up. I still go out on an audition every once in a while. Just to stay in shape. That's why I'm doing private duty instead of a regular job."

There were three sharp taps on the door, then three more. Gypsy had heard metronomes with a less precise cadence. The door opened before she could respond. Nan, in palest lavender, stepped over the threshold. "Oh, you *are* here . . . When you didn't answer, I thought maybe you hadn't made it through the day . . ."

"Come in, Nan." Gypsy widened her eyes. "I'm sorry, you already have, haven't you?"

"What a *brave* soldier you are, Gypsy. Most of us would have stayed away until we were fully recovered." Nan stepped all the way inside and closed the door behind her. "I don't know a *single* person in this world who would have tried to come back under the circumstances."

"Which are?"

Nan touched her forehead with her index finger.

"Are we playing charades?"

"Gypsy, you *don't* have to try to hide the truth from me. I *know* what you're going through."

"Enlighten me."

"Your memory. Gone. Shot. Destroyed."

With great effort Gypsy didn't flinch. "You forgot kaput."

"Everyone's talking about it, you know. You haven't *fooled* a single person. How *can* you survive? I mean, how *are* you going to do your job here? There are so many things you probably don't know anymore. It must be *too* devastating."

"Nan, are you speaking in code? I mean, if the words you're stressing are the directions to buried treasure, I don't want to miss my chance."

"Don't make jokes to hide your pain. It's *just* not necessary. I can't believe how courageous you are."

For a moment Gypsy's confidence faltered, and she wondered if Nan had won this round. She had managed to get through the first part of the day with help from Kendra and Perry and lots of fudging, but how could she possibly continue to pull this off? Already her colleagues were suspicious, although she doubted they understood the extent of her memory lapses. She had to give Nan credit for finding and targeting her Achilles heel so expertly.

She was grasping for something to say when Perry spoke.

"I'm afraid she's more courageous than anyone else could guess." She aimed her comment to Nan but inclined her head toward Gypsy.

"Excuse me?" Nan's ice blue eyes stared straight through Perry.

Suddenly Perry looked confused. She turned to Gypsy. "Oh, I'm sorry, Miss Dugan. I thought she knew . . ."

The "Miss Dugan" was a tip-off. In all their weeks together Perry had called Gypsy every pet name imaginable, but never Miss Dugan. Gypsy played along. "That's all right, Perry. You were trying to help."

"Help? What do you mean? What's going on?" Nan said.

"It's just that . . ." Perry hesitated. "I mean . . ."

"Go ahead, Perry. She should know." Gypsy wanted to know, too.

"Well, it's only . . . You see, there were problems after the accident, of course. I'm sure you know about Mediacranial Syndrome, Miss Simmonds. As well informed as you are, you've probably done stories about it. We expected it, of course, but we hoped . . ."

"Hoped?" Nan tilted her golden head.

"Yes. After injuries as serious as Miss Dugan's, we were afraid she might be prone, and we did everything we could . . ."

"But?"

"Well, we just couldn't do enough, unfortunately. And poor Miss Dugan . . ." Perry shook her head.

Tears filled her eyes. "And you're right, of course. She's so brave about it all. She had the full-blown syndrome, of course. Every last symptom, but she insisted on coming in today. Despite everything. Even though she may still be . . ." Her voice cracked. ". . . Contagious."

Nan's eyes doubled in size. "Contagious?"

Gypsy waved her hand in dismissal. "Oh for Pete's sake, Perry. You know that's very unlikely. What were the odds? Three in seven?"

"Five. Three in five. But that's just on paper, of course. We have every hope that the infection is completely out of your system."

Nan's voice rose an octave. "And if it isn't?"

"There's nothing to worry about," Gypsy assured her. "Do you think I'd put any of you at risk? If you're relatively healthy to start with, there's a series of injections you can take, starting the moment you notice the first symptoms."

"Very similar to rabies vaccine," Perry said. She managed a watery smile. "And just as effective. I've had them, myself. I only missed a week of work . . ."

"I can't believe you came back so soon and exposed the rest of us!"

"But I had to," Gypsy said. "The show was going to hell. You know that. You needed me. How could I let you down? Sure, my memory's not as good as it once was. But the moment the infection's all cleared out of my . . ." She frowned. "I'm sorry. What was I saying?"

"Holy shit!" Nan threw the door open and stomped through it.

Like Julie, no one had taught Nan the proper way to close a door.

There was a long silence.

"*Media*cranial syndrome?" Gypsy asked Perry.

"Seemed appropriate."

"You ever consider working in television?"

"Television just never considered me."

"I suppose you love nursing so much now that you wouldn't consider a change."

"Never did love it. No! Hold on there! Wait just a minute . . ."

Gypsy was already heading for the telephone. She didn't know any extensions by memory, but she found the one she needed in the index beside the phone. "Hi. This is Gypsy. Des busy?"

He was, but not too busy to speak to her apparently. She waited until he was on the line, then explained what had happened with Julie. "No, I couldn't wait another day or two to see if I warmed up to her," she said as soon as she had the chance. "Besides, I've found someone better. Do I have your permission to hire her?"

She hung up a few moments later. Perry was still shaking her head. "I never had the foggiest notion to do news," Perry said. "Never did, and don't think I've changed my mind."

"Does this look like the news to you?"

Perry searched for an answer. Finally, she shrugged in defeat.

"Welcome to 'The Whole Truth.' " Gypsy slung her arm around Perry's shoulders. "Baby doll sugar, I think we're going to make you a star."

13

"**A**RE YOU SURE THIS IS THE PLACE, ma'am?" Billy himself was driving Gypsy home after her first day at work, and she had demanded a detour to the Bronx. They were alone. Perry had taken a cab back to her own apartment.

Sometime during the afternoon the limo had been replaced by a dark blue straight-from-Detroit sedan. Tito gave, and Tito snatched away. Now that Gypsy was back at work, Tito clearly didn't want her to have an overblown estimate of her own worth. And besides, for security purposes the sedan was far less conspicuous.

"This is the place." Gypsy stared at the building where Grant taught English. Norman Carroll High School had been built near the turn of the century by immigrants and second generation Americans who had dreamed of the things their children would accomplish after graduation. Stone turrets framed the doorway and wide windows looked over the busy street. Once there had been trees and a signboard proudly announcing the accomplishments of each senior class. Now there was only concrete and an eight-foot chain-link fence. For the past decade senior accomplishments had vied with spray-painted graffiti, and last year, the graffiti had won. The sign was no more.

189

Elisabeth had been dismayed that Grant would choose an environment like this to display his teaching talents. She was a liberal in the best sense of the word, but she was also a parent. There had been shootings in these halls, and one teacher who had tried to interfere in a fight between two rival gangs was buried not far away. She had wanted her son to stay safe. Owen had accused her of wanting him to stay a little boy forever. It had been one of the rare times that Owen had ever criticized her parenting.

Grant lived on the next block in a building forty years older than the school and forty years more dilapidated. Many of his students lived nearby, and Grant wanted to be accessible to them after school hours. His door was always open, so open, in fact, that he'd been robbed twice, once while he was in his bedroom changing clothes.

It wasn't unusual to visit Grant and find a teenage boy sleeping on his couch. He farmed out the girls who came looking for a place to stay, but it was Grant who went back home with all of them when the worst had blown over, to help them work things out with their parents or foster parents or grandparents. It had dismayed Elisabeth to discover how many of Grant's students lived one step from the streets, and how many of them saw Grant and the other teachers at the school as the only caring adults in their short, sad lives.

School, which had just started again after the summer break, had been out for an hour, but Gypsy knew that Grant would still be in the building. He worked with the literary magazine staff and coached the wrestling team. Often he wasn't finished until the janitor threatened to lock him in the building or the security guards threatened to escort him personally to the front door.

"You're sure you want to go in?" Billy asked.

"I'm sure."

"You know I'll have to come with you."

"Just don't hover."

"Please don't try to escape again. Okay?"

"Nobody knows about that but you and me and the guy on duty at the hospital." She dimpled. "And that's the way we'll keep it if you promise not to get too conscientious."

"Try to see this my way, ma'am. I'm being paid to keep you safe."

"Try to see this my way. There's no good evidence anyone's trying to get me. And I have to have some space to do my job." She opened her door and stepped on to the sidewalk. "Follow if you have to, but just stay at a distance. Okay?"

He shook his head, but he got out and leaned against his door until she was halfway up the wide stone steps.

She knew exactly where to go and what to do, but since Gypsy Dugan was a stranger here, she wandered a little. She was wearing sunglasses, but she wasn't counting on them for anonymity. She was hoping that no one would notice her simply because no one expected her to be there.

She had rehearsed exactly what she would say if she actually confronted Grant, but her real purpose in coming to the school was to watch him from afar. Motherhood was a steel bond. Her maternal instincts had been transplanted in her new body right along with everything else.

She had hoped a wrestling match might be in progress, that she could stand on the sidelines and watch Grant with his team. He was average height and weight, but he had wrestled all through high school and college, the quintessential team player who was never star material but who kept spirits high through good times and bad. His fondest wish was to pass on his love of sportsmanship to his students.

It was obviously too early in the school year for activities. The gym was empty, locked securely against after-hours basketball games. She wandered down the wing where she knew the literary magazine staff gathered, but there, too, she drew a blank. A security guard stopped her, and as she flashed her press badge she told him she was a reporter preparing a piece on secondary education. Several teachers and students passed her in the hallway and didn't even look at her.

Then she saw Grant.

He was standing outside the office, talking to another teacher, a bleary-eyed young woman who looked as if the demands of the day had nearly finished her. Grant wore a blue oxford cloth shirt and a three-dimensional geometric print tie that his father would covet. His khaki trousers needed ironing and his hair needed cutting, but he was Grant, in the flesh, and he looked wonderful.

It was time to turn and walk away. She had prepared what to say if she was caught and had to explain herself, but her story was far from believable. She made herself turn and start back the way she had come. She heard footsteps following her, and she slowed, so that if someone was trying to overtake her, she wouldn't look as if she was running away.

"Excuse me."

There was no doubt who was speaking. She stopped, turned, and she was face-to-face with her son.

"You're Gypsy Dugan, aren't you?"

"Yes."

"I thought so." He gave the same smile that had captivated her the first time she met his father. Her heart turned over, and she wanted to cry. For a moment she missed Owen so much that his absence was a black hole in her life, sucking up everything else in its orbit.

"I suppose you've seen me on television," she said. She couldn't dimple on cue, no matter how much she knew it was called for.

"Once or twice. I . . ." He shrugged. "You don't know who I am, do you?"

"Should I?"

"My name's Grant Whitfield."

She acted as if the name meant nothing. "Are you a teacher here, Grant?"

"Yes."

She had always been able to read his expression. Now she watched him struggle to decide whether he should reveal their peculiar connection. She saved him the decision. "Whitfield? Not . . . Are you related to . . . ?"

He nodded. "She's my mother."

"I see." She did, of course, and he didn't and never would. She put her hand on his arm and lied. "I'm so sorry. I had no idea that Mrs. Whitfield had a son who worked here. . . ."

"What are you doing here, anyway?"

She gave the explanation she had rehearsed. "I'm interested in doing a piece on schools in the city. I've chosen half a dozen at random to investigate. I thought we might come in and follow students around for a day, or maybe even longer. See what they have to put up with. I'm just doing a little advance scouting before I approach anyone."

The explanation sounded even lamer than she had expected it to. "The Whole Truth" didn't concern itself with anything as socially responsible as what she pretended to propose. Had there been an ax murderer custodian or a principal who exposed himself during school assemblies, then her colleagues might have been first in line at the door. But reporting on kids imperiled by the rigors of urban America was too close to real life. It was neither horror nor fairy tale, and most of the stories the show took on were one or both.

"It seems like a good idea," Grant said. "But not particularly your style."

"I guess we can say my style's changed considerably since the accident." That was certainly true.

"What have you seen so far?"

"Just the basics. I've wandered the halls. That's all."

"Would you like a tour?"

She'd had one as Grant's mother, of course. A reticent Grant had walked her through every classroom. She had tried to manufacture enthusiasm as she counted smoke alarms and metal detectors. Now she regretted she hadn't let him know how desperately proud she was of him for never taking the easy way out, for championing kids with no champions, and for caring so much.

"I'd like that." She wanted to spend the next minutes beside him. She didn't know how long it would be before she could see him again.

They talked about his job as he led her into classrooms. He showed her the former band room that was used as an in-school suspension center because so few of the students could afford to rent or buy musical instruments, the metal and woodworking shop that no longer was in use because liability insurance was too costly, the art studio where a large metal bucket sat under a broken skylight to catch leaks.

"You know, everyone tries," Grant said. He pointed to the new paint on the studio walls. "We painted this room ourselves. The kids did most of the work. It took half a day, and they did a great job. Some of the teachers and the parents came in and made lunch for them. It was a real community affair. Then someone got up on the roof a couple of weeks later. We don't know how or why. They threw a brick through the skylight. The school's trying to find the money to replace it. But I don't think they'll find it this year."

"One step forward, two steps backwards."

"No, we're keeping pace. But barely. Drugs hit this neighborhood hard. The parents who work are working more than one job just to put food on the table. The parents who don't work are too strung out to remember they have kids. Either way there's nobody home to listen to them or set limits." He paused. "What were your parents like, Gypsy?"

It was a question she couldn't answer. She guessed, based on the little she knew. "Rigid. Disapproving."

"Mine were perfect. *Are* perfect." He looked away a moment as if he needed to get hold of himself. "They were always there for me. I guess you know what a difference that can make in your life."

"Perfect, Grant?"

"In the ways that really matter. Sure, they screwed up sometimes. My father has a hard time expressing his emotions, but I always knew he loved me. And he was crazy about my mother."

Her skin prickled all over, almost the way it had after her one fateful bite of Perry's shrimp creole. Owen had fooled almost everyone, even this remarkably perceptive young man. "That sounds almost ideal."

He looked away, as if to compose himself. "It's not ideal now."

"I'm sorry. I can only imagine what you're going through."

"It wasn't your fault. Everyone knows that."

Not everyone, of course. Owen had made it clear that he blamed Gypsy for his dilemma. He had half a wife now, and that was certainly harder to get rid of than none. "I check on your mother every day," she said.

"Do you?" His eyes flicked back to hers. He seemed genuinely surprised. "Then you know she's been moved to a nursing home in Great Neck."

Gypsy nodded. She'd had the home checked out. It was the best that money could buy. "I may not be responsible, but I feel responsible."

"She wouldn't want you to. She never blamed anyone else for anything."

Gypsy was struck by how little he had known Elisabeth. For months before the accident she had blamed everyone but herself for her unhappiness. She had blamed everyone but the one person who could have made real changes in her life.

Grant put his hand on her arm. "Are you all right?"

"Yes. I'm fine. Thanks."

"Are you sure you don't want to sit down? You look pale. You're still recovering from the accident, aren't you?"

"I'm fine. I appreciate the tour. I can't promise anything about the show. I'll admit this is out of line with our usual. But it's intriguing." As she said the words, she realized they were true. Could she find an angle here that would interest Des? If so, it was the answer to a prayer. She could stay in touch with Grant and live Gypsy's life at the same time. She could have the best of both worlds.

Almost.

"Can I call you if I need more information?" she asked.

"Sure." He grinned, and for a moment she had a glimpse of the young boy who had been the greatest joy of her heart. The child she had *willingly* given up her career to raise. "Has any man ever turned down a phone call from Gypsy Dugan?"

By Wednesday she had ping-ponged between hope and despair so many times that she was keeping score. So far despair was in the lead.

Elisabeth had worked in a television newsroom in the early seventies. How could she ever have believed that her limited training would prepare her to anchor "The Whole Truth?" She was a Stone Age hunter trying to figure out how to launch a nuclear missile. Even the language was unfamiliar.

"Now we're gonna run through it one more time, Gypsy." The floor manager, a potbellied man named

Hal, whose headset took the place of hair, looked toward the control room where no one was sitting at the moment. He started to count down, and more sweat ran from his pores with every number.

He pointed to her and she dimpled on cue as if the TelePrompTer was an incredibly sexy man. "Good evening. Welcome to 'The Whole Truth.' And before we begin tonight's top story, may I say that it's good to be back? Your cards and letters made my recovery speedier, and I'm grateful to all of you for your support." She smiled again, then followed the prompter with her eyes as the camera changed position.

"We're starting tonight with a story that will touch the hearts of anyone who knows a teenage girl who is worried about her weight. You'll want to pay close attention, America, because even though our subject is anorexia in the royal family, *your* family could be next."

She stared at the camera until the floor manager cued her again. Then she slumped in her chair. "Better?"

"You're not putting yourself into it, Gypsy. I'm no director, but even I know you're not punching the right words. It's lacking."

"At least I didn't drop my eyes at the end."

"Yeah, you're learning. At this rate you'll have it down by next month." Hal ground the sole of one shoe against the studio floor as if he wished she were under it. "Put some sex into, huh? Jeezum. You sound as soppy as Nan. I want to cry every time you say that bit about your recovery."

Her temper flared. She was learning that Gypsy's boiling point was a lot lower than Elisabeth's. "Then tell them to give me something sexy to say, for Pete's sake! Anorexia's not sexy. Cards and flowers aren't sexy! What do you want me to do? Strip on cue?"

"That's more like it. A little spirit. Try it again."

"In your dreams." She stood up. She and Hal had been practicing for most of an hour. In two hours they would "ride the bird." The entire show had to be in the can by then, ready to be sent by satellite to the 170 affiliates who broadcast it. Before that moment the anchor lead-ins had to be seamlessly spliced to the segments that were already recorded.

Before Gypsy's accident there had been 174 affiliates.

"Maybe I should be standing beside the prompter." Casey materialized out of the shadows.

"Well hi, stranger." She came out from behind the desk and held out her hands.

He ignored the hands and put his arms around her. "Hi yourself." He kissed her, and his hands slid lower to cup her bottom and bring her closer.

"Hey." She placed her hands against his chest and pushed. "When did you get back?"

"About an hour ago."

She hadn't seen him since the night she'd landed back in the hospital, but he'd kept in touch. He'd been to San Francisco, Baltimore, a private island in the Caribbean, and back to San Francisco again. Obviously the travel agreed with him, because he didn't look exhausted.

He looked ravenous, and she was on his menu.

"How long are you going to be around?" she asked. It seemed imperative to keep him talking.

"About three hours. I'm flying back out after the taping."

"I'm not sure if I'm glad you'll be here watching today."

"You're going to do fine. It'll all come back to you when the camera starts rolling for real."

"Will it?"

"You can't miss. You're Gypsy Dugan."

"That's what they tell me."

"Memory getting better?"

"I'm picking up the things I need to."

He relinquished her with obvious reluctance and stepped back. "I've got to retape some commentary on the P.I. story, but I'll be back to give you support if you need it."

She suspected he was going to be nothing more than a distraction, but she smiled. "Great."

"Better go finish getting ready," Hal said. "You'll need to be back on the set in thirty-five minutes."

She picked her way over cables snaking across the floor, brushing shoulders with more technicians who were arriving to set up. She found her way to her dressing room by pure instinct. From the moment she had awakened that morning with her postaccident debut just hours away, she had considered finding a new body to inhabit, preferably one without such a terrifying occupation. All week she had tried to convince herself that she could do this. All week she had known, deep down inside, that she wasn't going to make it. She had Gypsy's body, her instincts, sensory memory, and come-hither smile. She had Elisabeth's intellect, memories, and scruples. The combination did not an anchorwoman make.

Perry had taken to her new job like the proverbial duck to water. She was waiting when Gypsy walked in, the lemon yellow dress hanging from her arm. "Found a navy blazer that looks great with this. Want to try it on?"

Gypsy had settled on a more conservative teal green suit for today's taping, but now she was tempted to wear something brighter. "Maybe that dress will cheer me up."

"You're going to be fine. Terrific."

"I don't think so."

Perry looked sympathetic. Too sympathetic. "Don't worry, sugar lump. Nan's been in twice to tell you that she's ready to go on if you need her."

"I'll just bet. When's makeup getting here? The

hairdresser's scheduled to come in fifteen minutes and I don't want them working on me at the same time."

Perry hesitated just a moment too long. Gypsy's head shot up. "Perry, didn't you get my note?"

"What note?"

"I left you a note and asked you to make the arrangements."

"Didn't get it. And I cleared my desk just fifteen minutes ago."

Gypsy believed her. Perry was as organized as an air traffic controller. "That's odd. Call, will you, and see if you can get someone? I really don't trust my own hands today."

"I'll run out and see what I can do. It'll save time."

Gypsy tried on the yellow dress again while she waited. It was brash and eye-catching. While she was still wearing it she took the teal suit jacket off a hanger and held it up for contrast.

A brass button fell off in her hand. Frowning, she held the jacket at eye level. There was a conspicuous stain across the breast pocket.

"No one." Perry came back into the room at a trot. "Anyone who could help has disappeared. Somebody out there said you always do your own preliminaries."

"Look at this." Gypsy held out the jacket.

"Wait just a minute. I checked it myself about two hours ago. There wasn't anything wrong with it then."

"This is beginning to seem like more than a coincidence."

"Take off the dress and sit over there. I'll do your makeup."

"Perry, do you know what you're doing?"

"No one better. You major in theater, you learn to do everything. You want to look like Romeo's Juliet or Blanche in *Streetcar*?"

Gypsy flopped into a swivel chair in front of a bank of mirrors. "Get ready to help with my hair, too.

Something tells me the hairdresser may not show, either."

Fifteen minutes later she stared at herself. Between her efforts and Perry's they had transformed her into a creature of the camera. She knew enough to realize that she needed the more vivid makeup to photograph well, but she felt like a painted lady. "Yellow dress?"

"Got no choice that I can see. Put it back on and I'll get that blazer."

The navy blazer sobered the dress just enough. Perry held up a circle of heavy gold links. "Try this."

"Looks like something Casey would use to chain me to the bedpost."

"If that's what it makes you think of, it's perfect."

Gypsy added round gold earrings with a matte finish that wouldn't distract on camera. "That's it. What do you think?"

"I think I'm glad someone was playing at sabotage. We did all right, didn't we?"

"Why don't you go on for me?" Gypsy put her head on her arms. In the rush she hadn't had time to be nervous. But staring at herself in the mirrors now that she was ready brought it all back. She looked like Gypsy Dugan. She looked like her.

But she was someone else.

A knock rattled the door. Des didn't wait for an invitation. He strode in before the sound had died away. "They need you on the set."

She sat up. He was wearing a maroon sport coat and plaid pants that belonged on a golf course. She couldn't think of a thing to say.

"Come on, Gyps. Don't screw this up now. We've got everyone waiting. You had a chance to practice with Hal. You know what to do. Now you've just got to do it."

She knew what the last mile felt like. She got to her feet, standing on legs that were already wobbly in three-inch heels. "Do you really think I'm ready?"

"Hell, I don't know. But if you're not, you have to

be anyway. We've got to get that show in the can and
send it off. And if we don't, we're through. Tito's
going to be watching what we do."

"You didn't get where you are today because of
your counseling skills, did you Des?"

"Don't frigging let me down, Gypsy."

He waddled out of her dressing room on his incongruously short legs. She teetered in her ridiculous
pumps behind him and wished she was wearing Air
Nikes for a quick getaway.

The studio was crowded. She had watched a taping
yesterday and rehearsed with Hal today, but she
hadn't really noticed how many people it took to put
together the show. The control room, glassed-in and
high-tech, was bursting at the seams. She recognized
the director, an associate director, the technical director, and the associate producer who would oversee the
taping. A row of monitors in front of the control panel
was blank except for one that was rolling a segment
with a young woman walking along an ocean board-
walk, footage from their feature story.

The anchor desk was teak, a simple curving Scandi-
navian design that called no attention to itself. Behind the desk to the left was a large globe like the one
used at the show's opening. When she finished her
lead-in a camera would focus on the globe and zoom
in for a close-up. The opening of each report would
appear to be projected directly on the globe's facets,
although that was really just a technician's trick,
performed in the control booth.

Des waved her to her seat as the crew worked out
the final details of the taping. A young woman in
ragged jeans spoke into a headset, changing the position of one of what must have been a hundred lights
as she chattered away. A man in a T-shirt and a tie
adjusted one of the cameras. Casey stood in the
corner conferring with an unfamiliar man in an
expensive suit.

A woman wearing an institutional green smock

hurried toward the desk where Gypsy was attempting to clip on her mike. "Who did your makeup?"

"Perry. My assistant."

"Not bad. But you should have let me get it today. You look too good, like you haven't been sick at all."

"Isn't that what we're after?"

"Uh-uh. Des wants people to feel sorry for you, so they can forgive you if you screw up."

"Thank him for the vote of confidence, would you?"

The woman pulled a soft brush and a container of pale powder from one of the voluminous pockets of her smock. "This'll help."

"No." Gypsy turned her head. "Unless my nose is shining or I've smeared my lipstick, I don't need you."

"But Des—"

"I don't give a flying—" She stopped herself, appalled at what she had almost said. "I mean it. Thanks, but I'm fine the way I am."

The woman shrugged. "Your call."

The studio was cool, but under the lights the temperature quickly climbed.

"Let me get that."

Gypsy looked up and gave Casey a nervous smile. He took the microphone from her trembling hands and clipped it under her jacket lapel. "Gyps, listen. All you have to do today is read your lines. That's it. The viewers will be so thrilled you're back, they're not going to notice anything else. There's not a viewer in television land who won't cut you some slack when this airs tonight."

"You don't think I can do it, do you?"

He straightened. "I didn't say that."

"None of you thinks so. Everyone expects me to fall flat on my face!" As if to prove Gypsy's point, Nan stepped out of the shadows and up to the closest cameraman. They put their heads together in conversation. Nan was dressed in a Kool-Aid purple suit and a peppermint-striped blouse, and she looked ready for anything. Nan, who was ready to go on if Gypsy failed.

"What's she doing here?" Gypsy said.

Casey tightened his lips. "She's just watching."

"Bullshit." She didn't have time anymore to be appalled at her own language. "Who asked her to come? Des? Tito?"

"She's here because you probably won't make it through the taping. Is that what you want to hear?" He leaned toward her again, but this time he stared straight into her eyes. "You don't have what it takes anymore, Gyps. Everyone knows it. You're too nice, too vulnerable. Hell, anybody on the show could do better than you did with Hal today. Any kid right out of high school could do it better!"

"You bastard!"

"And Nan's in her element knowing you're going to make a fool of yourself. You think Hal went to her after he worked with you today? Goddamned right he did. You can count on it. And he told her that you were washed up, that nobody will want you behind this desk ever again. So she's ready. And she's a professional. Nan can step in the second you fail, and she can be the one to save the show."

Her hands clenched in her lap. "Drop dead, Casey. And do if off the set. I've got a show to tape right now."

"If you can." He raised one skeptical brow. Before she could respond he started toward Nan. She left the cameraman and followed Casey back into the shadows. Gypsy could just see them, heads together. Watching her.

Des sped toward the desk. He leaned over, as Casey had done. "We're about ready. You okay?"

"I'm fine. Just stand back and let me do my job."

"Just remember, the camera with the red light is the one that's taping. And——"

"Get the hell out of here! Now!"

"Fine. Great. See you."

He shook his head as he walked away.

Hal appeared, sweating more than ever. "Count-down's on. Get ready for your cue."

She sat up a little straighter. She could just see Casey and Nan, heads still together. She wanted to strangle him. She wanted to strip off the mike and go right for his throat. And she wanted to mop up the carnage with Nan's pretty grape-flavored suit.

There was only one thing better than murder. Revenge.

The TelePrompTer operator moved into position. She adjusted accordingly and waited for Hal to point his finger.

The studio suddenly seemed truly familiar, not a place she had recently visited, but a place where she had lived. The cool, dark cavern beyond the cameras, the overly warm, brightly lit anchor desk. The soft padding of her chair. The globe turning slowly behind her with a sound like the muted whir of an electric fan. Even the smells were familiar, although she couldn't identify any one of them.

Hal's hand came down. She looked straight into the camera and gave her most outrageous smile.

"Good evening. Welcome to 'The Whole Truth.' And before we begin tonight's top story, may I say that it's good to be back? Your cards and letters made my recovery speedier, and I'm grateful to all of you for your support."

She flirted with the camera the way she had flirted with Owen on their first date. She made love to each word, lingered over vowels and punched consonants. When the camera shifted, she shifted, too.

"We're starting tonight with a story that will touch the hearts of anyone who knows a teenage girl who is worried about her weight. You'll want to pay close attention, America, because even though our subject is anorexia in the royal family, *your* family could be next."

And by the look on Des's face as the tape of that first segment began to roll and she was no longer on camera, she knew not one viewer who was the parent of a teenage girl would sleep easily tonight. Gypsy Dugan had sold them anorexia in her most persuasive tones.

Des sprang out of the shadows. "Goddamn it, Gypsy. That was terrific. Why in the hell have you been playing with us like that? I've cornered the frigging market on Rolaids!"

The man in the suit who had been talking to Casey before the taping stepped forward.

No one had to introduce her. There was a sudden electric silence on the set, and now that he was closer Gypsy knew that she was facing the great Tito Callahan himself. His face was tan—and familiar from the news. His hair was gray and closely cropped, his build that of a man who regularly worked out at the gym— probably with a telephone in both hands.

She dimpled. She was not going to be easily cowed again. Not ever again. "Tito. Like what you saw?"

"Not bad." Tito didn't smile—she suspected he was too busy thinking about his next billion-dollar deal. There was a slight Irish lilt to his voice, but this was no leprechaun, no charming barroom tenor. This was a man bent on controlling the world's communications, one medium at a time. "You've still got it. Just be sure you keep it."

She tossed her head. "I wouldn't know how to get rid of it if I tried."

He strode off, and technicians parted for his exit like knights before their king. She turned to the spot where Casey had been standing with Nan. Nan was gone. Casey stood alone.

As she narrowed her eyes and glared at him, he lifted his hands and began to applaud.

Everyone, down to the lowliest technician, joined in.

∽ 14

IF THERE WAS A BLOOD RED ROSE WAITING ON Gypsy's desk when she arrived for work, then the day was clearly a Tuesday. Tuesday's rose was always accompanied by a note that graphically described some portion of her anatomy. The notes had arrived every Tuesday for three years, and the show's technical crew started a pool every Wednesday to see who could guess what body part Gypsy's fan would describe next. So far the records showed that her admirer was particularly fond of kneecaps and elbows.

There were other eccentric viewers who wrote long rambling letters of commentary, who asked to talk about their grisliest delusions on camera or made obscene suggestions. There were phone calls from the subjects of previous shows whose lives had changed after their stories aired—not necessarily for the better. And much too often there were calls from the Rev. George Bordmann.

"Rev's on the phone again," Perry said on Tuesday morning three weeks after Gypsy had resumed her job as anchor. "Want to have a little talk with him?"

"About as much as I want to have a little case of the bubonic plague." Gypsy was systematically tearing the petals off the weekly rose and dropping them into her trash basket. In the first year of their marriage, despite sitting squarely on the poverty line, Owen had sent her a rose every week, too.

"Rev says you're going to hell."

Gypsy tried to summon the Bible training Elisabeth had absorbed in Sunday school. "Judge not that ye be not judged. Or something like that. Tell him I said so."

"He's breathing kind of heavy. Don't know if I can make myself heard." Perry put the receiver back up to her ear. "Nope." She set it back in the cradle.

"The world is full of crazy people. You know that?" Gypsy stared at the last rose petal clinging to the leafless stem. "Very, very crazy. . . ."

"Yep. And sometime, some way, in their kinky little lives they get involved with this show."

Gypsy plucked the last petal. "Perry, what if we did something that was more serious?"

"What? You don't think that piece Kevin did about the love slaves of Martian men was serious?"

"*I'm* serious."

"You said *we.* You mean like you and me? Or this whole nutso show?"

"I want to spend a day at a high school in the Bronx. Shoot the day or maybe even a week, just the way one of the students there sees it. You know? Show the drugs, the violence, the overcrowding."

"You think this is PBS, honeysuckle?"

"I'm going to suggest it at today's story conference."

"They're gonna wonder if you banged your head again."

Gypsy suspected Perry was right. No one expected her to be a pretty face and nothing more. By the same token, no one seemed to think she wanted hands-on involvement with a story either. She conducted occasional interviews and taped lead-ins. Now that she was back at work full-time she wrote her own copy and worked with the producers to put together a seamless, visually attractive show. But she didn't suggest story ideas and particularly not ones that the production staff might find socially redeeming.

"There's this high school in the Bronx. I visited there a couple of weeks ago. I think they'd let me do it." Gypsy glanced at her watch. "Show some enthusiasm when I make the suggestion, would you?"

"Me? I don't go to story conferences."

Gypsy stood. "You do now. Because if they let me do this, you're going to be doing a big chunk of the work."

The conference was in Des's office, a small, fussily decorated space with one narrow window. By the time Gypsy and Perry arrived all the seats had been taken and there was minimal room on the floor. No one gave up a seat for Gypsy. She had proved she was fully recovered—at least physically. She and Perry leaned against bookcases, gossiping with the others and sipping muddy coffee from battered foam cups while they waited for the remaining reporters to arrive.

Gypsy had learned to look forward to these meetings. Her colleagues were sharp and creative, and with the exception of Nan, every one of them had a wicked sense of humor. There was an irrepressible enthusiasm that accompanied even the most outrageous suggestion. In this room the sacred cows of journalism were only calves.

She let the meeting crank into full gear before she made her pitch. There was a brief lull while notes were made between ideas. Nan, wide-eyed and springtime fresh in mint green, was batting her navy blue eyelashes at Kevin, whose mouth was said to be close to Tito's ear. Gypsy knew her time had come.

"I have an idea."

"Somebody ring a bell," a bored voice proclaimed from the corner.

"Idea number one. Fire whoever said that," she shot back. "Idea number two. I visited a high school in the Bronx a couple of weeks ago. It's a typical example of what goes on in the inner city schools in this country. I think we should spend a day there taping, maybe even longer. I thought we could follow a student, maybe even plant someone there. Give the viewers a taste of what urban education is really like."

The lull, which had been little more than an indrawn breath, was now a roaring silence.

"You lost your mind?" Kevin asked at last.

There was another silence as everyone remembered that she *had* lost her mind, or at least a large chunk of her memory.

She dimpled to show there were no hard feelings. "Look, Kevin, I know how it sounds at first. I felt the same way. But this story's got everything. Sex. Violence. Sentiment. We'll get down with the kids and look at stuff from their viewpoint. We won't pretty it up like some of the network news magazines might. We'll let our footage speak for itself. No self-righteous commentary. Just a quirked eyebrow or two."

"What's the point?" Des reached for a jar of Rolaids on his desk.

"Education. Letting the viewers know what's happening. Isn't that always our point?"

"Not if it's not entertaining. And I don't think footage of kids learning Shakespeare and calculus is high drama."

"Des is right," Nan said sanctimoniously. "There's no heart. No pathos."

"There's as much heart and pathos as we're willing to find. It'll just take the right person to find it. And that person's me."

"You?" Kevin narrowed his eyes. "Since when did pathos interest you, darlin'?"

"Yeah. This ain't like you, Gypsy baby," one of the field producers said.

"There's more to me than you know," she said— and certainly meant it. "Look, no one or hardly anyone's learning Shakespeare and calculus in that school, Des. Sure, some of these kids have normal

lives, normal enough that they can pursue their stud-
ies and think about college for the future. But there
are a whole lot more that are just worried about
whether they're going to survive another week and
how they're going to do it."

"Frigging bleeding heart," Des said. He put his
head in his hands. "Jeez Marie, Gypsy's turned into a
frigging bleeding heart."

Her bleeding heart sank. She hadn't prepared well
enough. She hadn't presented her idea with the right
kind of enthusiasm or skill. Not only had she destroyed her chances of doing the school segment and
working with Grant, but she had lowered her standing
in the eyes of her colleagues.

Des straightened. "We'll do it. And the more you
bleed on camera, Gyps, the better it'll be. Just don't
get sappy. We've got Nan for that. But let 'em see that
this really matters to you. It'll give your work a whole
new dimension. The rest of you get out of here and go
find some ideas this good. Only let's dole 'em out. We
don't want all our viewers rushing out at the same
moment to join the NEA or the ACLU or any other
frigging group with initials. We'll educate 'em a little
at a time. Gypsy pick your crew for this and get on it.
Who's next?"

Grant returned Gypsy's phone call late in the
afternoon after the day's show had already gone out to
the affiliates. She told him about the story conference
and invited him out for a drink. An hour later they
were sitting in a smoky bar across from the studio
with an AM radio station blaring commercials in the
background and straight-backed chairs that would
have been suitable for the Spanish Inquisition.

Grant looked tired but wonderful, her son of the
preppy shirts and the inherited taste in ties. He'd
gotten a haircut since she'd seen him last. She longed
to tell him to get another barber.

"So they went for the idea?" He was sipping

Foster's. He had spent his high school junior year in Australia as an exchange student and a taste for Foster's was the main thing he'd brought back from down under.

"With enthusiasm." She was working on a Jameson's. Straight. Along with her body and diplomacy she had lost her taste for Manhattans. "Now I'll have to get permission from school authorities. I thought you might be able to tell me the best way to go about doing that."

"The school administration's okay. They'll be able to guide you through the bureaucracy." He gave her some names and she wrote them down.

"I want your help, Grant. I was impressed with your commitment. I think our viewers would be, too."

"Don't make me out to be a saint."

"You don't have to be up for canonization. Just a good, committed guy."

"You know, the funny thing is that I took this job as a rebellion against my parents."

She didn't know what to say. She couldn't believe he had admitted that to her. Then she realized who she was. Not his mother, but a woman just a few years older than he was. "It's an odd kind of rebellion," she said cautiously. "Didn't they want you to teach?"

"They never said so. But I think I was always a disappointment. I was that square peg in a round hole. Never brilliant at any one thing. My father's such a brilliant architect that people from all over the world come to study with him. They'll empty wastebaskets and sort mail, just to be in his presence for a little while."

She refused to think about Elisabeth's brilliant husband. "And your mother?"

He looked up, because her voice had caught. His eyes gleamed compassion. Gypsy knew that he believed she was wallowing in guilt about the accident. "My mother was . . . is a brilliant hostess. She makes

Martha Stewart look like Tugboat Annie. She's one of these people who does everything well."

"Including being your mother?"

"She was—is absolutely the best. And that's probably why I had to rebel. I had to get away from my father's brilliance and my mother's perfect love. I had to get away from them and function in my own sphere. And the Bronx is a million miles away from the Gold Coast."

"What about now?" She sat back and toyed with her glass as she watched him. She wasn't sure what to think about Grant's feelings for Elisabeth.

"I thought I might like teaching. I had no idea how much. I can't tell you what it's like, knowing that something you've said or done, even something that seems insignificant, can change a life."

"From what I hear you do more than your share. Is it true you moved into the neighborhood so you could be available to kids who needed you?"

"Where did you hear that?"

"Can't reveal my sources." She smiled.

"Partly true. Part of it was a need to get away from everything I was familiar with. I was an exchange student in high school. I lived in Sydney, with another wealthy family. Learned the accent and how to eat a meat pie, but I didn't learn anything like the things I'm learning now."

"Don't you feel helpless sometimes? Overwhelmed?"

"Sure. Nine hours out of ten. Then something happens, usually something so small it's nearly hidden, and I realize that I'm doing what I'm supposed to. And that's really what I was looking for, because that's what I learned at home. Both my parents were always sure they were doing what they were supposed to. They never had any questions at all." He favored her with his charismatic "Owen" smile again. "You're easy to talk to. But I suppose that comes with the territory."

She couldn't believe Elisabeth had allowed her own son to believe she was so perfect, so satisfied. "I suppose."

"Did you always know what you wanted to do?"

"I guess I always wanted to be rich and famous." She hadn't discovered much more about Gypsy Dugan's motivations than that. She had dug and dug and found a hopelessly shallow life.

"So what do you do next? Get richer? More famous?"

"Right now I just plan to enjoy what I have and what I do."

"Are you enjoying it *with* someone, Gypsy?"

"A man?"

The grin didn't diminish. "That's what I had in mind."

She was stunned at her own son's charm. She had never seen him this way. As a mother she'd known he was good-looking, intelligent, sensitive. But as a woman nearly his age, the effect was completely different. He had his father's way of gazing at a woman, his brown eyes laughing and searching at the same time. He conveyed more with that devil-may-care grin than most men probably conveyed in a full night in the bedroom.

"There were dozens," she said. "And when I came to in the hospital after the accident, I couldn't imagine why. Some of them were real losers."

"There must have been something that attracted you."

The conversation seemed headed for dangerous waters. "I believe it must have been their astonishing intellects." She chugged back the rest of her whiskey and stood, holding out her hand to him. "I'm going to be seeing a lot of you in the next weeks. I'm glad. I need high-minded friends."

"My mind can sink just as low as anyone's." He took her hand and held it. "Let me know if you need me. I'll be happy to do whatever I can for you. Anything at all."

She was too keyed up to go home. Now that Perry had moved out, the apartment seemed empty and sterile. She had an appointment with an interior decorator for the following week, but until then she had little desire to relax among a herd of dead animals.

She grabbed a corned beef sandwich and a Diet Coke at the closest deli and went back to the studio. There were no quiet moments here, no chances to dissect what she had gained and lost. There was always some detail that needed to be taken care of, some late-breaking news story that needed attention. She could spend the entire evening returning telephone calls and only make a dent in her message pile.

She said hello to the people who were still hanging around. Kendra was there, already beginning to pull together threads for the story on Grant's school. Kendra waved with her free hand as she shuffled papers with the other. The telephone receiver was tightly tucked in the crook of her neck.

Gypsy chatted with one of the assistants and asked him to locate some files for her. One of the field producers wandered by and she asked for his suggestions on a crew for the shoot at the school. By the time she arrived at her desk, she had made considerable progress on her story.

She sank into her chair, rested her head against the back and closed her eyes. Being with Grant was heaven and hell. She had wanted more children, and she had been devastated when no more were conceived. Now she was glad she hadn't had more. Losing Owen and Grant was bad enough.

Being with Grant had another effect, too. He was a painful reminder of Owen. But she didn't really need a reminder. She couldn't make herself stop thinking about the man who was Elisabeth's husband. She was still angry with him, still desperately hurt that he had turned to another woman, still confused about how their life together had all fallen apart at the end. And there was another part of her that she couldn't exorcise, the part that clung to the good times when Owen was nearly as young as Grant and she had fallen so completely in love with him that none of her other dreams had mattered.

"Gypsy?"

She opened her eyes. Kendra was staring at her strangely. She pulled herself back into the present, back into this new, odd life. "Got a problem?" she asked.

"No, but I thought you might."

Gypsy sat up straight. "What?"

Kendra looked down at Gypsy's desktop. Gypsy's gaze followed hers. She hadn't paid any attention to the clutter there when she'd sat down. Now she wondered how she had missed the object of Kendra's fascination.

She leaned over and stared at the magazine, opened wide to a two-page spread about the Whitfield family tragedy. Owen stared back at her, an Owen in formal wear and a brooding expression. His wide Slavic cheekbones and hooded eyes were strikingly photogenic. On the glossy page he was a tragic figure, a sensually powerful man to whom any woman reading the article would want to offer comfort—and anything else she was free to give.

The photo beside him showed Elisabeth in better days, so poised and patrician she would have been an advantageous match for Prince Charles. There were photos of the two of them together at social functions, a photo of Grant, and last, but certainly not least impressive, a photo taken at the accident scene. Someone had adorned that photo with what looked like blood. Beneath it was scrawled in red ink: *See what you've done?*

"Where in the hell did this come from?" Kendra asked.

"I don't know." Gypsy closed her eyes, blinking back tears.

She felt an arm around her shoulders. She choked back sobs.

"Whoever did this is a real slimeball!" Kendra said. "Talk about hitting below the belt. The accident wasn't your fault. Everyone knows that."

Gypsy couldn't tell her the truth, that the sobs were for Owen and Grant and everything she'd lost. "I'm okay."

"No, you're not. Here, open your eyes." Kendra held out a tissue. Gypsy took it. The magazine was closed now and off to one side, courtesy of Kendra's fast maneuvers. "You didn't notice it when you came in?"

"No. But I didn't even look at my desk."

"How about right before you left?"

Gypsy tried to recall if she'd paid enough attention to her desk to notice the magazine at that point. "No, I'm pretty sure it wasn't there. I went through that pile last thing before I left the building." She gestured to the center of the desk where the magazine had been.

"Well, I've been here since noon. I don't think I've even left the newsroom to hit the john."

"Did you notice anybody coming in my office?"

Kendra shook her head. "I was superbusy. I'm sorry." She perched on the edge of the desk. Gypsy had noticed that in the last week people had begun to make themselves at home in her office. And even the most reticent were more inclined to be chatty.

"Get some paper. We'll make a list," Kendra said.

"Of what?"

"People who were around here in the last hour."

"Okay." Gypsy opened her drawer and got out paper and a souvenir pen with "The Whole Truth" crystal globe at the end.

"Kevin. Me. Harry. Tracy." Kendra ticked off about six other names.

"That's it?"

"No." Kendra shut her eyes, as if she were concentrating. "Des streaked through. But he's the last person to want you upset. I think Nan was here. I remember getting a whiff of concentrated rose essence. Casey."

"Casey?"

Kendra opened her eyes. "Yeah. He got back from Seattle about an hour ago. Come to think of it, he asked where you were. I told him off with another man. Keep him on his toes."

"Thanks," Gypsy said wryly.

"I can't think of anyone else."

"Where did Casey go?"

"I wasn't paying attention. Sorry."

"And you didn't notice any of them going into my office?"

"No, but I can ask around."

"Would you?" Gypsy stood. "I'm going to see if I can find Casey. I'd rather we kept this between us for right now. Okay?"

"Sure. No problem." Kendra slid off the desk.

"Thanks for your help."

Kendra was almost to the door. She turned and made a funny face. "You know, you really ought to stop doing that."

"What?"

"Thanking people."

"Really? Why?"

"Before the accident you'd probably never said thank you to anybody in your whole life. There's a rumor going around that they transplanted some nicer person into that gorgeous bod of yours while you were in the hospital. You keep thanking people, you're just adding fuel to the flames."

∾ 15

G YPSY SEARCHED ALL OF CASEY'S USUAL haunts in the building, but he wasn't anywhere she looked. She was still shaken by the photo spread, and she didn't want to go back to her office right away, where she'd probably be forced to make conversation. Instead she started toward her dressing room, where she could be alone to consider who, among the sizable list of Gypsy Dugan's enemies, might have left the bloodstained magazine on her desk.

When she unlocked the door she was surprised to find that she'd left a lamp burning. Maybe once upon a time an unenlightened Gypsy Dugan had left lights on without a thought—she didn't know. But she certainly tried not to leave them on now. Elisabeth had been a rabid environmentalist, a relentless recycler. Comments had been made since Gypsy's return to the studio about the tactful way she lectured newsroom staff who turned the thermostat too low or tossed their soft drink cans in with the paper trash.

Nothing in the room looked as if it had been disturbed, and she relaxed. She sank to the sofa and closed her eyes. In the darkness of her own mind the photograph of Owen stared accusingly at her.

Resigned, she opened her eyes and searched for a scrap of paper to make another list of the names Kendra had given her. Most of them were people she'd had little interaction with since her return. They were assistants, research staff, gofers. She tried to be pleasant to all of them, and she'd sensed no hostility. Casey and Des had no reason to rub her face in the accident. The only person on the list who might want to upset her was Nan.

It was possible that she had made enemies she didn't know about. Any one of the people on the list might dislike her for some past encounter. She might have stolen a boyfriend, fired a colleague's mother, broadcast evidence that someone's beloved uncle was a transvestite. But wouldn't she have felt their animosity? Elisabeth had always been sensitive to those around her, too sensitive most of the time. And since the accident Gypsy had been forced to rely on subtle clues in order to make it through each day. She had struggled to read and interpret people the way the young Elisabeth had read and interpreted *The Scarlet Letter* and *Moby Dick*.

Nan continued to stand out as the most likely saboteur. But would she be so obvious? She was not a subtle woman or even a bright one, but would she risk a stunt like this? The chances were good that she might have been seen near or in Gypsy's office. On the other hand, perhaps she'd had an alibi all prepared, just in case.

Gypsy was considering how to confront Nan when her dressing room door swung open. "I wondered if I'd find you here."

"Casey." She got to her feet. "You look like hell." He was wearing jeans that looked like they had permanently molded themselves to his body and a shapeless gray T-shirt with a darker outline where the pocket had been ripped away.

"I caught a ride from Delhi on a cargo plane. We went by way of Singapore. At one point they threatened to put me off in some remote island near Fiji to make room for a tank of tropical fish."

"Kendra said you'd flown in from Seattle."

"That's where I switched to a commercial airliner. The only way I got that seat was to hold some kid with an ear infection in my lap the entire trip to Chicago. He got off, but not before he threw up on my shirt. I thought my luck was changing when one of the flight crew found this one for me." He pulled the shirt away from his chest. "Then a deaf nun took the seat next to me and shouted the Lord's Prayer all the way to Kennedy."

"You poor baby."

He didn't look like anyone's baby. He looked dark and dangerous, a man with all barriers lowered. A hungry man.

"Got anything to drink?"

"Come here and sit down. I'll fix you something."

They should have passed, he on the way to the sofa, she on the way to the refrigerator in the corner. They didn't pass. They stood and eyed each other. Calculating changes, multiplying all the things that were still unsettled between them.

"Ah hell, Gyps." He tugged her against him and brought his lips down hard on hers.

She was a woman confused about everything, particularly about the men in her life. She still mourned for the husband she'd lost, yet in Casey's arms it was almost possible to forget Owen. Even the good times.

Something surged inside her, something hot and liquid, forbidden to a woman who was married to someone else. But Gypsy Dugan wasn't married to anyone and never had been. And this man wanted her.

"I missed you." The words were the briefest of interludes. His lips opened against hers and his tongue sought the inner recesses of her mouth. Her arms circled his waist and she pressed herself against him. Her breasts tingled against his chest. Her hips slid into place against his like they had been tailored to fit.

He broke away just long enough to jerk her unceremoniously toward the sofa. He tumbled down and took her with him. She landed across him and he tunneled his fingers into her hair to bring her head down and her lips back to his.

He wrapped his arms tighter around her and turned her so that they were lying on their sides, face-to-face. "You're like a sickness in my blood."

"You say the sweetest things."

"I can't get enough of you. You're an addiction. It doesn't matter how long I'm away. I still need you."

His desire for her was the most seductive thing imaginable. To be wanted this way, to be longed for with this visceral intensity was dizzying. She had never felt as alone as she had since waking up in this body. Now she wasn't alone anymore. She was desired. She was needed. She responded as women had responded to flattery from the beginning of time. She opened herself to him in every way, sighing as his hand found her breast, pressing closer as the heat of his body melted into her own.

"Gyps, you're not teasing me, are you?"

Her head arched back as his lips found the pulse at her throat. It was racing, roaring like a freight train one mile out of the station. She wasn't teasing. She couldn't think that clearly. Her body was enveloped in a sensual cloud that threatened to steal the breath from her lungs and whatever good sense the accident had left her.

He didn't wait for an answer. He pulled open her blouse with one smooth motion, and buttons willingly abandoned buttonholes. His obviously practiced fingers made quick work of her bra. The weight of his palm against her breast caused an ache that needed soothing. His fingers moved, weaving magic everywhere they touched.

"What do you want me to do?" he said, and the words were a growl against her earlobe.

She wanted him to make her forget everything. She

wanted to feel again and find no guilt in it. She guided his lips back to hers, and he took it as a sign that all signals were go. He slid his hand to her waist and freed that button, too. Then his hand slid over her hip and under her skirt. He paused momentarily. "You're wearing panty hose . . ."

She was sorry, but he seemed stunned. "They aren't plastered to my skin. They come off."

"You never wear them." He didn't give her a chance to answer. He dug his fingers inside the waist and tugged.

She understood why she had never worn them before the accident. "Goddamned chastity belt," he muttered, tugging again.

She had the absurd impulse to giggle. She didn't want to laugh. She wanted to lose herself in this, lose the sadness she'd felt at seeing Owen's photograph and the guilt that another man was making love to her.

She tried to help him, and their hands tangled. "Casey—" She struggled with the hose, and so did he. Slowly, together, they inched them down. She could feel his belt buckle against her bare midriff and the rasp of denim. She could also feel the tight elastic of the waistband of her hose cinching her legs together. "Casey, slow down!"

He went rigid, as if he realized for the first time how fast he had been rushing her. "I'm sorry. I—"

Something crashed to the floor.

Both of them went rigid.

"What was that?" she whispered. She tried to sit up, but he held her down.

"Don't move." There was no sound attached to the words. He mouthed them, but there was no mistaking what he'd said.

She nodded just a fraction to show him that she'd understood.

"Gypsy, Gypsy, you're such a turn on." He didn't even look at her as he said it. He was removing himself from her, an inch at a time. Quietly. Carefully. He slid to the floor beside her, and motioned for her to stay where she was. "The things you do to me." He sounded like a man at the border of nirvana.

The sofa was placed at an angle near the center of the room. She tried to picture the room behind it. At the far end there was a walk-in closet large enough for a sizable wardrobe. She tried to remember if the louvered doors leading into it had been opened or closed when she'd entered the room.

The lamp had been on.

She wanted to tell Casey, but he was already rounding the sofa on his hands and knees. She could see his feet, then nothing at all. She heard a scuffle, then another crash. Finally, she heard a scream.

A woman's scream.

She pulled her hose up and her skirt down and sat up, in spite of what Casey had said. She peered over the sofa to see Casey locked in a furious embrace with Nan.

"Gotcha," he said, wrestling her arms behind her.

"Nan," Gypsy said. "Doing some research?"

"Let go of me, you big ape." Nan struggled, but it was futile.

Casey shook his head. "Gypsy, did you invite Miss Nanny in to watch?"

"I just didn't think of it." Gypsy pantomimed regret. "Sometimes my manners just aren't what they should be."

"See, Nanny, if you'd only asked, Gypsy would have let you watch. You wouldn't have had to pick her lock or peek through her closet doors."

"You're insane, Charles. Let me go!"

"Should I?" he asked Gypsy.

"I don't think so. You look so strong and sexy holding her that way, I could watch all day long."

"You're both insane!"

"How did you get in, Nan?" Gypsy asked. She

moved around the sofa and stood in front of her. "Do you really know how to pick a lock? It might be a good feature story. I could suggest it."

Nan stared daggers at her, but she didn't respond.

"Let's see if we can figure it out," Gypsy said. She rested her index finger against her cheek. "I know! I'll search her. Won't that be fun?"

"Don't you dare! I'll sue. I'll have you fired."

Gypsy moved forward and began to pat Nan down like a television cop. "Have me fired. Now that might be interesting. Your side of the story would go something like this? I broke into Gypsy's dressing room and she had the nerve to try and find out how I did it? Fire that woman!" Her hands stopped at the hip pocket of Nan's skirt. She delved inside and produced a key.

She held it up in front of Nan's face. "Shall I try it in my lock?"

Nan pursed her lips.

"Where did you get that?" Casey demanded. "Who gave you a key to Gypsy's dressing room?"

"Don't bother. I know who must have done it," Gypsy said. "Julie. My four-hour assistant. She worked with Nan first, but officially she was my assistant. I'm sure someone must have given her a key to transfer my new wardrobe. When I fired her, she must have given the key to Nan, just to spite me."

Nan didn't deny it. "I forgot to return it for her. That's all."

"And I'm sure that's why you were in here. You just wanted to leave it for me?"

Nan tossed her head, Southern style. "That was my intention."

"Were you planning to leave it in her closet?" Casey asked.

"No! But when I heard her unlocking the door, I panicked and hid. That's all. You're making a mountain out of a molehill."

"It's too bad you got so interested in seeing the show on the couch. We probably wouldn't even have known you were there," Casey said.

"I was just trying to get out. That's all. And give you some privacy."

"Nan. Nan." Gypsy shook her head. "A better friend no woman's ever had."

"Would you please let me go now so I can retain a little dignity?" Nan said.

Gypsy appeared to consider. "Sure." Before Casey could move an eyelash she held up her hand. "No. Wait. We can't let you leave without being sure you haven't left anything important behind. We wouldn't want you to run off and forget something. Just let me check the closet before you go."

Nan struggled and Casey held her tighter. "Maybe you'd better let me check," he said.

"You've got your hands full." Gypsy brushed past them. The closet door was open, but the light was off. She flicked it on. Her eyes adjusted immediately. It took the rest of her a moment to adjust to the sight of her entire wardrobe in heaps on the floor. The same bloodlike substance that had adorned the magazine on her desk was splattered over everything.

She backed out. Horror had filled her in her office. Now it was eclipsed by rage. She took a moment to master herself. Katherine Brookshire Vanderhoff would have been proud.

"Casey, can you hold Nan just a little longer?"

"All night and then some."

"Long enough so that I can call security?"

"I'll manage somehow."

"Then I think Nan will need some help packing her things."

He grinned diabolically. "No problem. The way Tito lops heads, security's had plenty of practice."

"How about that drink?"

Almost two hours later Gypsy stood at her apartment door and considered Casey's request. "A short one."

He nodded. "No problem. I'll be in and out in a flash."

She dimpled. "That's the problem with most men."

He laughed, and the rumble seemed to fill the short hallway with electricity. "I could stay as long as you want me to."

"A quick drink and out the door."

He held up his hands. "I understand the ground rules."

She unlocked her door and waved to Billy, who disappeared to wherever bodyguards went when they were off duty.

She stepped into the entranceway. "I don't need Billy anymore. I'm going to talk to Des tomorrow and see if we can get rid of him. For a moment when I saw that bloodstained magazine, I thought maybe someone really was trying to get me. But now I'm back to thinking it's all an overreaction."

"It would be hard to blame Mark's death on Nan. She doesn't have the brains to hire a hit man."

"I gather I've made more than my share of enemies along the way. But I don't really believe any of them are trying to kill me."

"I've never thought so."

"That settles it. I will talk to Des."

She turned on the lights. He whistled softly. "What have you done to the place?"

"Not nearly enough. Just got rid of some of the trappings until the decorator comes next week. Does it look better?"

Casey examined the room, and she could tell he liked what he saw. She hadn't had time to do much. She'd stuffed closets with everything she could fit into them and bought a ficus and a dracaena that nearly grazed the ceiling. She'd missed having a garden to tend.

"I took down the tent in the bedroom." She

stopped. She wished she hadn't brought up that particular subject.

"Good. I was tired of playing the sheik."

"I'm negotiating with the old lady down the hall. She has a garden on the roof and she wants the lions."

"I'll carry them up there for you."

"You'd get a hernia." She crossed to the bar and fixed him the drink he'd asked for hours ago. She held it out to him. "Casey, we ought to talk."

"No need." He swallowed half of his Scotch like a man at a desert oasis. "You're beat, and so am I. You were great with Nan. I expected you to pull out every hair on her head, but you were every inch a lady."

Obviously Casey saw it differently than she did. In her opinion she had acted in a very different way than Elisabeth would have. Elisabeth would have tried to work things out with Nan, perhaps tried to understand her motivations and address them. Gypsy had booted Nan out the door. Gypsy could assert herself when the time was right. Elisabeth had never quite managed assertiveness—at least not until the moment of her death.

"Whatever possessed Nan to do something so stupid?" she asked.

"She was desperate. She always thought she had a chance to eclipse you. But since the accident . . ." He shrugged.

"What do you mean?"

"Gyps, you're different. There's no denying it. It's like that movie that came out a few years ago, about the lawyer who gets shot in the head and turns into a nice guy."

"A nice, stupid guy. I saw it. Harrison Ford. Are you saying I've turned into a nice, stupid anchorwoman?"

"No." He finished his Scotch and held it out for a refill. "Please?"

She grimaced, but she fixed him another.

"You're the talk of the show. You're not the same person."

"Well, that's true." She decided she needed a drink, too.

"You're kinder. You're more insightful. Never mind that you can't remember half of what you're supposed to. You've got people on your side. They're willing to go the extra mile to get you out of jams. Nan saw that and realized her shot at the big time was just going to go downhill from here."

"So she started a sabotage campaign to shake me up. What? Was she hoping I'd fall apart, turn back into the vixen she knew and loved? I'd lose my following because she poured blood on my clothes?"

"She was desperate. And dumb."

"And now she's gone." It hadn't taken much to get Nan fired. A call to Des, a visit to her dressing room by the senior executive still in the studio, a brief explanation. And Nan was gone. *Poof!*

"The show's better for it," he said. "She was a weight around our necks. We don't need a sob sister to make our point."

"What do we need then?"

"The combination you're bringing to the anchor slot. Intelligence, irony, sizzle, and just the faintest touch of emotion. It's a winner."

She hardly knew what to say. She'd been struggling to find her way, moving in what she thought was the right direction, and now Casey was affirming her attempts. "Thanks." She sipped her drink, watching him over her glass.

"You're more polite, too."

"That's right. Kendra told me that today. She says it's throwing everyone for a loop."

"Let them scurry a little. It never hurts."

"So where do I go from here?"

"Out on location."

"Oh. . . ." She'd wondered when that suggestion was going to come up. "Do you think I'm ready?"

"No question. And there's an opportunity."

"Where?"

"Cleveland."

She'd been hoping for somewhere more exotic. "That's one place I've never . . ." She stopped. She'd nearly said "been." But, of course, she'd been there. She'd grown up there. And according to everything she knew about herself, she had a large family that lived there still, including a mother whose dexterity with a rosary was undoubtedly legendary.

". . . wanted to go back to," she finished lamely.

"Maybe it's time to mend some fences."

"Think that's a good idea?"

"That's up to you."

"What's the story?"

"The Tracy Hart trial."

Tracy Hart was a Hollywood almost-made-it, an aging actress with a face that was instantly recognizable and a name that made most people scratch their heads. Her career had fallen short of stellar. She'd worked on good films, but she'd never gotten the starring roles. She was nominated for Oscars but never won them.

Three years ago Tracy had married a Shaker Heights businessman and settled down to the good Midwestern life. One year ago she had shot him in the head. Her trial was set to begin in two weeks. Rumors were circulating that in her marriage, as in her career, she had been eclipsed by another leading lady.

Now that she thought about it Gypsy felt a real affinity for Tracy Hart. She hoped the poor woman was acquitted. She finished her drink and set down her glass. "You think that's important enough to go on the road for?" she asked.

"It's not O.J., but it'll play big in the Heartland."

She couldn't think of a better way to try her wings. She was a hometown girl. The Cleveland press would be thrilled and the publicity would be excellent. Her ability to fudge her memories would be severely tested, but she was probably up to the challenge.

Mending fences. Since the moment she had realized that she had indeed assumed another woman's life, she had been suffering guilt. She possessed everything Gypsy Dugan had worked so hard for. She had longed to make amends somehow. She had not been able to shake the feeling that she owed Gypsy something for what she had taken from her.

Gypsy had been estranged from her family. As a memorial, could a reconciliation be engineered?

"I'll do it." She hoped she wasn't making a mistake.

Casey put down his glass. "You're a trouper."

"Am I?"

"Among other things." He reached for her, and she let him pull her closer. He wrapped his long arms around her waist, but he didn't kiss her. He just stood there, looking into her eyes. "I got carried away tonight, didn't I?"

"We both did."

"I guess you're not ready to play harem again?"

She answered truthfully. "You have no idea how confused I am about everything."

"What's there to be confused about, Gyps? You wanted me in your dressing room. The signs were unmistakable. We've always had fun together. The sex was outstanding. I've never pushed you for anything else. I'm not pushing now."

"There's no way you could understand."

"Is there somebody else?"

There was. Another woman's husband. A man who probably loved his protégé. A man who ironically thought that Gypsy Dugan was a hopeless slut.

"I can't explain any of this. You're just going to have to give me some time."

"The spirit's willing." His grin was lopsided and forced.

"I'm sorry."

He released her. "Don't be. It's not like you."

"You're going to have to get used to a whole new me."

"I'd like nothing better. The whole new you. Every bit of it."

"I don't think I'm as much fun as I used to be."

"Maybe you just need time."

Or a values transplant. She didn't know. She wished with all her heart that in this, she could be a little more Gypsy and a little less Elisabeth. She needed Casey as much as he purported to need her. "I'll talk to Des about Cleveland tomorrow."

"Yeah. Do that."

She kissed him, then she stepped away.

At the door he turned. "It's the strangest thing. I like you better this way. But at the same time I miss who you were, and not just the sex. Can you beat that for confusing?"

"Probably."

He smiled the same tense smile before he closed the door behind him.

∽ 16

THE DUGAN HOUSE WAS ON A SIDE STREET, one of a dozen two-story homes that looked almost exactly like it. This section of the west side had sprung up to provide housing for Eastern European immigrants who had come to the city at the beginning of the century to provide labor for the steel mills. Cleveland had changed over the decades, but the view in this neighborhood was still the same. Smokestacks rose high and belched pollutants into the tired, gray air. The lakefront with its colorful sails and sandy beaches, the picturesque Tudor and Colonial houses of Shaker and Cleveland Heights, the endless green of the city's extensive park system seemed a continent removed instead of a matter of miles.

"This is it?" Gypsy stared up at the house. The damp gray air had a familiar chemical smell, and it felt familiar against her bare forearms. But she didn't recognize anything she saw.

"This is it." Casey stood beside her, thumbs hooked over his leather belt. "No place like home. Remember?"

"I still think I should have called."

"Trust me. From the little you've told me about your family, it was best not to warn them you were coming."

"You don't think they know? You don't think they watch the show?"

"No."

The house was covered with gray asphalt shingles. There were no shutters adorning the small windows, and the stoop was a square of concrete with no overhang to shelter the visitors who dared to knock on the battered metal storm door.

"The petunias are a nice touch," she said. There was a narrow bed in front of the stoop planted with pink petunias that were gasping their last as Gypsy watched.

"Soil's probably poison."

"I understand why I left."

"I wonder why they never moved? The city's filled with interesting neighborhoods that have better views and cleaner air, and some of them aren't far away. Real estate's a bargain here compared to New York."

"Maybe my father likes to walk to work." With the help of Kendra Gypsy had learned everything she could about the Dugans before the trip to Cleveland. Her father, John, was a foreman at the nearest steel-processing plant several blocks away. Her mother, Rose, stayed at home to finish raising the children who hadn't yet left the nest. There was a brother, Peter, who was nineteen and a sister, Joan, who was sixteen. There were three more brothers, none of whom lived in the area, and a sister, Theresa, who was married to a man who worked with their father. Theresa, the mother of two little boys, lived just several miles away.

"Maybe he just couldn't find anybody to buy this house," Casey said.

"They could rent it out. I wonder if I ever offered to help them buy another?"

"I doubt it. And I wouldn't rush right in and offer. Feel your way."

"If they give me a chance." She faced him. "Are you sure you don't want to come with me?"

"Completely."

"But you'll be within hailing distance?"

He patted his pants pocket where a beeper resided. "Just buzz me."

She kissed his cheek. "Thanks, Casey."

"Don't thank me, thank Tracy Hart. If she hadn't shot old Rodney, we wouldn't even be in town."

She started up the walk and he started for his car. He opened the door and slid behind the wheel, but he didn't leave. Gypsy suspected he was waiting to see if her parents let her in. As far as she knew, all bets were covered.

She rapped on the door because the buzzer didn't look trustworthy. For a moment she thought she'd struck out. Then, from somewhere toward the back of the house she heard a baby crying. The crying got louder and louder and culminated in the door being thrown wide so that the baby, a healthy-looking child with a full mop of dark hair, was screaming in her face.

"Well, your timing's as great as it always was. I'm trying to change a poopy diaper. Do you mind?"

"Actually, I think I'd mind if you didn't." Gypsy waved her hand in front of her face to disperse the smell, but she didn't take her eyes off the young woman who'd spoken. She was in her early twenties, with shoulder-length brown hair and Gypsy's own pert nose. Gypsy made an educated guess. "You're looking good, Theresa."

"I got married and had two kids, in case you never heard."

"But you're still as pretty as you were when we were kids."

Theresa narrowed her eyes. "Yeah? Considering that you called me Dump Truck for most of my life, I guess that's not much of a compliment."

"Dump Truck? I don't remember that."

"No? You got the good nickname. Dump Truck Dugan would never have made it on television."

Gypsy tried not to laugh. Theresa looked absolutely serious, but when she saw Gypsy fighting a smile, she smiled a little herself. "It's good to see you, Maggie. I guess."

Gypsy remembered her research and the little she could recall of Mrs. Dugan's hospital monologue. "Is this Timmy?"

"Jason. Timmy's two."

"Stair steps."

"A real short flight. I got fixed. No more for me."

"What'd . . . Mama say?"

"I didn't tell her, and you'd better not, either. Damn, I wish I hadn't said anything. You're going to blab it, aren't you?"

"Of course not." Gypsy put one foot on the threshold. "Why would I? It's your body and your decision."

"You're not above using either to get your way."

"Look, Theresa, have you changed at all since we saw each other the last time?" Whenever that was.

Theresa tossed her hair over her shoulder so that Jason would stop trying to yank it. "Of course I have. I'm married. I've got kids, a mortgage, and a part-time job. What do you think? That the world stayed the same while you were sleeping your way around New York?"

Gypsy ignored the last part. "Well, if you've changed, don't you think I might have changed, too?"

"Not real likely."

"I have."

Theresa stepped back, as if that was as much of an affirmation as she could manage. "Mama's upstairs cleaning. You might as well go on up while I finish changing the baby. I don't want to be there when she sees you."

Gypsy stepped inside and closed the door behind her before Theresa could change her mind about letting her in. "Do you think she's going to be upset?"

"Yeah. You're not her greatest success story."

"Who is?"

"Well, she's hoping Joanie will be a nun."

"Boy, if that's what she wanted for me, I was a *real* disappointment."

Theresa smiled again. Wider this time. "So was I, seeing that I had to get married."

Gypsy touched Jason's plump downy cheek. "Change this baby, and I'll bounce him on my knee."

"It's a deal. I'll do whatever I can to get someone else to hold him."

Theresa disappeared through the kitchen and Gypsy was left standing in the stairwell. The entrance hall opened into a small living room on the right. Glimpsed through the doorway, it was neat and utilitarian, with sculpted avocado green carpeting that hadn't been available in stores for decades and a pale glass-topped coffee table. The sofas were covered with orange flowered spreads, and the Naugahyde slingback chairs looked as uncomfortable as the ones in her apartment.

Give Rose Dugan a sizable income, a healthier libido, and several years in the Big Apple, and she would probably decorate in leopard skin, too.

Gypsy started up the stairs. At the top she paused in the narrow hallway and listened for serious scrubbing. She knew from the little she'd seen that her mother was a fanatic housekeeper. There wasn't a fingerprint or a smudge anywhere. Even the living room carpet looked brand-new, as if the room had been roped off as a museum exhibit of the sixties. Where had the Dugan children played? In the backyard inhaling factory fumes?

"Mama?" She listened for a response, then tried again. "Mama? It's . . . Maggie."

For a moment Gypsy thought Rose wasn't going to respond. Then a weary voice sounded from the room at the end of the hall. "What are you doing here?"

"Right now I'm looking for you."

The door opened. Rose was sitting on the edge of a

tub in a closet-sized bathroom surfaced in tiny white octagonal tiles. "What do you want?"

Rose was wearing a dress much like the one she'd worn to the hospital. This version was navy-issue green with only a crisp white collar for interest. Her hands were folded, as if she'd been sitting on the edge of the tub for hours contemplating the mysteries of the universe.

"I'm in town covering a story," Gypsy said. "And I wanted to see you."

"Why?"

"Because you're my family."

"What happened, Maggie? Did you see the face of God when you almost died? Did you decide it was time to repent?"

"I decided it was time to come home and see my family."

"You were told not to set foot across this threshhold again."

"I suppose I'd conveniently forgotten that."

"You broke your father's heart."

"Did I?" Gypsy tried to keep her voice neutral. Faced with this wall of hostility, she didn't know what to do. She only knew that she needed this reconciliation. She felt compelled to pull it off somehow for the Gypsy who'd lived here as a child.

"He was the one who told me to lay off of you. He was the one who spoiled and petted you and made you what you are. Then you turned on him."

Gypsy had learned *when* she'd left home, but not what she'd done. She made a safe guess. "I was a teenager, Mama. Teenagers make mistakes."

"Is that all it was to you? A mistake?"

"What do you think it was?"

"A sin. A terrible, black sin. And you are a sinner."

"Let her be, Rose."

Gypsy turned and saw a man standing behind her. She had been so riveted by Rose's accusations that she hadn't heard him coming up the stairs. He was a pale man, thin and bent. What hair he had was nearly all white, but his eyes were still young. "Hello, Maggie."

"Daddy." She nodded in greeting, and knew she'd guessed correctly.

John Dugan looked past her to his wife. "I'll have no more of these accusations in my home, Rose. Maggie's come back. We'll forget the past."

Rose's lips tightened, but her eyes blazed.

"Mama, I don't expect the fatted calf," Gypsy said softly. "I just wanted to come home and be with all of you for a little while. I've changed. Maybe we can start again."

Rose didn't respond, but John did. "Will you stay for supper?"

"I'd like that."

"We're having a chipped beef casserole. You won't like it," Rose said.

Gypsy suspected Rose was right about that much, at least. "I'll eat every bite. I'll even help you get it on the table."

"You?" Rose exhaled a whoosh of disbelief. "You couldn't find the door to the oven."

Gypsy was completely in the dark about what lay behind her mother's anger, but she felt no need to react defensively. She had no real emotional ties to the Dugans, although she had compassion for their pain. She was becoming more and more certain she could navigate her way through these troubled waters and pour soothing oil on them to boot. For the first time since waking up in Gypsy's body, her lack of memory—and feelings—about Gypsy's past were a bonus.

She dimpled. "Just try me. I can open an oven door with the best of them."

"We've missed that smile at our dinner table," her father said.

"And I've missed both of you." She looked at her father and saw the quick flush of color to his cheeks. His dark eyes sparkled suspiciously with tears. Surprisingly something clutched at her throat, and she cleared it solemnly. She was glad that she'd come here to make amends.

She was very glad she'd come.

"When I was seventeen I got pregnant. I was too young to want the baby, of course, and marrying the boy was out of the question. So I had an abortion. I didn't tell my parents, but they found out later from someone who'd seen me going into the clinic. I was supposed to go to college. They have a college fund for all their kids. That's why they live in that awful house. So they can save every extra penny."

Gypsy turned her back to the Ritz-Carlton windows and faced Casey. "When they found out about the abortion, they wouldn't let me go away to Ohio State, like I'd planned. They told me I had to stay at home and go to the local community college so they could keep an eye on me. Instead, I apparently sold everything I could get my hands on, including their only television set, and took off for New York. I pieced together the whole sordid story from things my sister Theresa said tonight."

"I knew an abridged version." Casey leaned against the door and crossed his arms.

"Why didn't you tell me?"

"I didn't know enough. And I didn't know how much of it was true."

"I suppose I lie with facility."

"I suppose you used to."

She turned back to the windows. The view here was stupendous. Her room looked over the Cuyahoga River and the Flats, Cleveland's answer to Greenwich Village. The river was famous for having once caught on fire, but there were no signs of pollution now. The Flats was home to nightclubs and restaurants, and pleasure boats crowded the river. Under creative political leadership the city was undergoing a tremendous renaissance.

"My father's a sweetheart. A martyr to my mother's fanaticism. But she has her warmer moments, too. She softened up as the night wore on. I told her that I'd been wrong about a great many things, and I hoped she'd give me another chance. But I made my best impression when I changed Jason's diapers."

"It sounds like you survived hell tonight."

"Joanie's a sweet kid. She looks like a nun, but I'm afraid she's got more of Theresa and me inside her than Mama gives her credit for. She has a boyfriend. She asked me about the abortion."

"Did she?"

"I told her it was probably the right thing to do under the circumstances, but I regretted the necessity. I'd have a ten-year-old son or daughter now. It makes you think, doesn't it?"

"Gyps, you hate kids."

"Do I?" Elisabeth certainly hadn't hated them. She had wanted more. For years after Grant became a toddler she had yearned for the feel of a baby's soft flesh cuddled against her own.

"You're as religious about birth control as your mother is about attending Mass."

"I'm not the same person I was before the accident."

"What are you trying to tell me? That you suddenly want a tract house in Connecticut and 2.3 kids? You want to bake apple pies and teach flag folding every Wednesday afternoon to a denload of hyperactive Cub Scouts? Come on. You haven't changed that much."

"There are compromises. The choice doesn't have to come down to den leader or anchorwoman, with nothing in between." She wished that Elisabeth had seen that more clearly. But at least Gypsy could see it now.

"What does it come down to?"

"Maybe it comes down to not being perfect at anything. Doing some of this and some of that.

Having fewer children than my mother did and working fewer hours than I do."

"Are you complaining about the job? Is that what this is about?"

"No." And it wasn't. Because her situation was thoroughly unique. She'd been a den leader. And now she was an anchorwoman. She knew the joys and disappointments of both. "It's about me. About what I want and what I'm willing to do to get it."

He pushed away from the door. "What do you want?"

She was still as unclear about that as she had always been. She just knew that Gypsy's life, as exhilarating as it was, wasn't turning out to be enough for her.

She shook her head. "I don't know, Casey. Right now I just feel drained."

"Come here."

She was reluctant to comply. In the weeks since Nan's departure from the show, she and Casey had been too busy to explore their relationship. They had met for dinner between his forays out of town, but he hadn't pushed, and she hadn't suggested a deeper commitment. The other men who had scurried around the borders of Gypsy's life had begun to drop away from a lack of encouragement. She was frequently lonely, despite the warm camaraderie at the studio and her strong friendships with Perry and Kendra.

She needed love. She needed what she knew Casey could offer her. And still, she was afraid.

"Come here, Gypsy."

She came. There was no point in pretending she didn't want him. Despite the bizarre twist that had landed her in this body, it was a normal body, with normal urges. She more than liked Casey. He was intelligent and perceptive, sometimes egotistical but always fair. His touch was as exciting as anything she'd ever experienced.

"Sit there." He pointed to a wing chair upholstered in soft floral hues.

She sat. "Why? Am I about to get the third degree?"

"No. A massage. Stay there." He went into the bathroom and returned with a bottle in his hands. "Take off your shirt."

She hesitated.

"You can leave the bra on. If you're wearing one."

It seemed a challenge. She stripped off the man-tailored linen shirt and tossed it on the bed. She *was* wearing a bra, a sturdier affair than anything she'd found in her lingerie drawer after her release from the hospital. But it was provocative enough. Peach colored lace and a cleverly engineered design that Howard Hughes would have approved of.

"Good," he said noncommittally. "Now lean forward a little."

She did as she was told, but she was edgy. She could feel her muscles screaming as she forced them into stern resistance. The afternoon had taken more out of her than she'd realized.

She jumped when he rested his hands on her shoulders.

He stroked his thumbs along her neck. "I didn't even know you could be so tense. You create stress for other people, you don't experience it."

"It was a tough afternoon."

"Is that it? Or are you all wired up because I'm touching you?"

"Why should that make me tense?"

"Excellent question." He lifted his hands. "Stay right there."

"Casey, I don't know if this is such a great idea."

"Why not? You've got a problem, and I've got a cure."

She knew what kind of cure he meant. And she suspected he was right, at least partially. She was tired of celibacy. She ached for the comfort of Casey's body, the delirium of passionate, skillful sex. She yearned for boneless, drifting reverie.

This time when he touched her his hands were warm and slippery. She smelled heliotrope and hyacinths and felt the lotion on his hands seeping luxuriantly into her skin. "Ahhh . . ." She closed her eyes. His thumbs settled at the back of her neck and began slow, delicious circles.

"I always wanted to do this for you, but you never let me. You were always in too much of a hurry."

"Was I?" She could already feel the warmth of his hands moving inside her to places he couldn't touch.

"So you said. I always wondered if that was the real reason."

"What other reason could there be?"

"I always wondered if you felt safe with me. Safe enough to give me this much control."

Her head fell farther forward. "Why wouldn't I feel . . . safe?"

"Maybe when you're heading for the top, you can't trust anybody. You can't be even a little bit vulnerable."

"Are *you* vulnerable?"

He was silent, but his thumbs pressed harder.

"Are you?" she asked again.

"Just occasionally." His hands slid to her shoulders. He pressed with his palm as his fingers gripped and kneaded.

She could feel her muscles giving up the fight, one by one. She could understand why she had once been reluctant to let Casey work this kind of magic. "What makes you vulnerable?"

He didn't answer. He trailed his fingertips along her collar bone, back and forth, as his palm pressed harder.

"Do I make you vulnerable?" she asked.

"You'd love that kind of power, wouldn't you?"

"No."

"Come on, Gyps. You'd like nothing better than to have me at your beck and call."

"Slavery has no appeal to me. I come from a long line of abolitionists."

He stopped working on her shoulders. "Lean forward."

She complied.

He put his hands on her back, then lifted them again. "This isn't working. I can't reach you. Lie down on the bed."

Warning bells sounded inside her head. "Casey . . ."

"Afraid of giving up control?"

She sighed. "You have no idea how little control I have."

"Lie down on the bed."

She got to her feet. Her body felt as heavy as a sultry summer breeze. Without looking at him she stretched out, facedown across the comforter. He joined her, straddling her with his knees. She could feel his hands against her back. Then she felt the clasp on her bra giving way.

"You have such beautiful skin." He stroked his hands the length of her back. Once, then again. "Does that feel good?"

She made a noise low in her throat. It was all she could do. She was melting. Dissolving.

"Good." He rested his thumbs along her spine and began to press lightly, sliding them slowly downward. "I love touching you. I tell myself I'm going to purge you from my blood, and then I remember what it feels like to touch you."

"Purge?"

His hands grazed her sides, feather-light and provocative. His fingertips inched toward her breasts, then withdrew. Inched, withdrew. He had long fingers and wide, square hands. He knew exactly what to do with them.

"You're selfish and thoughtless and perfectly capable of sleeping with a man to get something you want." He hesitated and his hands stilled. "Or at least, you were before the accident."

She could hardly think about what he was saying. Heat pooled inside her, an unpredictable, unstable geyser. "You've stayed just because . . ."

"Because of the sex?" His hands began to move again. With assurance and skill. "What do you think?"

"I . . . don't know." If what he said was true, her life would certainly be easier to compartmentalize.

"I guess I don't know, either. I've told myself that's all it was for so long, it's hard to get past it."

"But when you try?"

He slid his fingers under her rib cage, just inches from her breasts. His thumbs rotated in lazy circles along her back, dissolving tension everywhere they touched and creating a different kind of tension entirely.

"What are you looking for, Gyps?"

She was looking for oblivion. Her body was yearning for it; her mind was succumbing to it. She was having trouble thinking of anything else. The only sound she could make was no answer at all.

It seemed to be enough for him. "You want me to tell you that I love you? That I see things in you no one else ever did? That right from the beginning I saw the hurt little girl who could never be good enough, no matter how hard she tried? So she set out to prove she really wasn't any good at all?"

It took her a moment to realize what he'd said. The sensual haze began to change to something less defined. "Casey . . ." Tears unaccountably filled her eyes.

"I'm not going to tell you any of that. Because I don't know who in the hell you are anymore. You feel the same. You taste the same. But you don't seem to be fighting the same battles. Or using the same weapons.''

He shifted and pressed his hands against her shoulders. Then she could feel the warmth of his breath against the back of her neck and finally, his lips in the same place.

She shivered. Her body had never been more alive. He moved to her side and stretched out beside her, bringing her with him so that she was lying with her bare back against his chest. His arms circled her, and her bra slid down over her arms.

He cupped her breasts and his lips traveled along her nape to her shoulder. ''There was a time when you wore me out with demands, like you wanted to keep me as far away as possible, even when we were as close as two people could get. But when we were right in the middle of making love I'd look in your eyes and you'd really be looking at me. Like you couldn't help yourself, even though you were fighting against it.''

She wanted to turn to him. She knew that's all it would take. She could turn, press her breasts against his chest, and, in deliciously sweet moments, he would be inside her. There would be no turning back. She would be taking over Gypsy's life in every conceivable way.

Except that it wasn't this Gypsy that Casey wanted. She hadn't understood that until now. He was not in love with soft, smooth skin, with chorus girl legs and a come-hither smile. He was in love with a woman who no longer existed. He loved a woman he would never see again.

She might have been able to conquer her own doubts. She might have been able to tell herself that Owen loved someone else, and his comatose wife was as good as dead to him. She might even have been able to tell herself that she could start a new relationship with Casey and forget the past.

But she couldn't tell herself any of those things

now. Because neither she nor Casey could forget what had passed before. And when they were finished here tonight, it would still haunt them.

"I'm not that woman anymore," she said. She took his hands in hers and held them still until they curled into fists. "I want to be, Casey. For your sake and mine. But I can't be."

He was silent. She had expected an argument or sweet persuasion. He was silent, instead.

"You understand, don't you." It wasn't even a question. She knew that Casey didn't understand the same things that she did. Not exactly. But he understood the truth on some level where words no longer mattered.

He understood.

Little by little he withdrew. She missed the heat of his hands immediately, then the erotic brush of his body against hers, his erection grazing her back, his legs capturing hers.

"I'm going now," he said when he was no longer touching her.

"Did she ever know how lucky she was?"

He didn't ask what she meant. He didn't even seem to find the question or the pronoun strange. "I don't know."

"She was very, very lucky. If she didn't know it, she's not worth mourning."

"Go to sleep, Gypsy."

She was crying before the door closed, but he didn't come back to comfort her. He needed comfort himself. And she knew that neither of them could ever provide it for the other again.

⌒ 17

"**T**HERE'S A WOMAN ON THE PHONE SAYS she has to talk to you." Perry slumped comfortably in an armchair in Gypsy's dressing room and held the telephone receiver to her chest. "Says it has to be now."

"It always has to be now." Gypsy looked up from a script she had been reading. "It's not Sal, is it?" Sal, Gypsy's agent, was a chain-smoking dynamo who called at least once a day to warn her that she was the talent and she'd better stop reinventing her job without a new contract in hand. Lately he had begun to disguise his voice as a woman's so that she would be fooled into taking his calls.

"Nah. Very upper crust, dahling."

"Does she have a name?"

"Won't give it. Says she's a friend of Elisabeth's, if that helps."

"Look, will you go out and see if they're going to need me for that voice over after all?"

"Sure. How long should I stay away?"

"Depends on how long the phone call lasts."

Perry grinned. "Gotcha."

Gypsy waited until Perry was gone. Then she crossed the room and punched the blinking light. "This is Gypsy Dugan."

There was a pause. For a moment she wondered if

the caller had hung up. Then a familiar voice spoke. "Are you really Elisabeth?"

"Marguerite." Gypsy sank to the chair. "I hoped it was you."

"I've been watching the show."

"Have you?"

"Sometimes . . . I catch a glimpse of someone I used to know."

Gypsy closed her eyes. "Do you?"

"I don't want to believe anything you told me."

"Neither do I."

"I think, perhaps, we should have lunch."

"When and where?"

Gypsy was still staring at the phone long after the call had ended. Perry came back into the room. "They needed two sentences. I did them for you."

Gypsy knew Perry could do a perfect Gypsy Dugan. "Great. Thanks."

"Gypsy?" Des followed in Perry's footsteps. "Got a minute?"

"Sure."

"Perry?" Des jerked his head toward the open door.

"I'm getting real practice on my entrances and exits today." Perry rolled her eyes and closed the door behind her.

"She's something," Des said.

Gypsy was still thinking about Marguerite's call. "You're telling me."

"No, I mean she really is. I heard her do your voice over. She's incredible. So I asked her to read a few lines of copy. Then I asked her to read it a couple of different ways. She can do anything. And with those cheekbones and that smile, she'd photograph like a dream."

"All that and CPR, too." Gypsy dimpled. Desmond had her attention now. "What are you getting at?"

"I want to move her up to reporting. We need somebody to take Nan's place."

"That's a super idea. I hoped she'd move up, but even I wasn't going to push this fast."

"You wanted me to promote her?"

"Sure. Why not? She's just what the show needs. And she's not just a good actress. She's perceptive and funny and she works hard."

"Wait a minute. She could be your competition one of these days."

"So? There's room for both of us. It's a big business."

Des flopped down on the nearest chair and stretched out his stubby legs. "Everything they're saying about you is true. I thought maybe you were just putting us on, trying to throw us off-balance. But it's more than that, isn't it? That bump on the head changed you but good."

Gypsy turned her hands palms up in surrender. "I could try to be a bitch. I could work at it."

"That's the thing. It doesn't come naturally anymore."

"Was that a prerequisite for the job?"

"It's not just the attitude adjustment. You're doing some good work on this piece at the high school. You're sinking your teeth into other stuff, too."

"I hope you see that as a positive thing." She couldn't tell from his voice if he did or not. It was possible she was pushing for change too hard and too fast.

"Sure I do. It's just hard to figure. That's all."

"Well, what you see is what you get."

He stood and started for the door. "Just don't forget what you were hired for. All the other stuff's fine. Great. But we got you to sell stories, not to create 'em."

"In other words back off a little?"

"Just don't delve so far below the surface that you forget to come back up for air."

* * *

Marguerite hadn't wanted to meet in any of the fashionable restaurants where they had lunched in years past. Gypsy was just as glad since she would have had to pretend that the friends who came up to the table to visit with Marguerite—and examine Gypsy under their lashes—were strangers to her.

They met at a Thai restaurant on the lower east side where the air was scented with lemongrass and coconut. A high soprano wailed convulsive lyrics over a faulty sound system and the tables were covered in gold vinyl.

"Not your style," Gypsy said, when Marguerite arrived. She had worked on her opening line while she'd waited, abandoning sentiment and gratitude and settling for casual intimacy. She was determined that this lunch would go well, that she would not lose this fragile link to her former life.

Marguerite, in a man's tweed smoking jacket that was fraying at the wrists, took a seat across the table. "Seamus dragged me here last month. It's the best Thai food in the city."

"Seamus knows the best places. I always thought he should be a food critic."

"The man eats, the man does not write."

They kept up the patter while they examined the menu. Gypsy knew better than to push Marguerite for information. When she was ready, and only then, would she talk.

The server, a young man with tattooed forearms and a patch over one eye, took their order and their menus, and they were left to contemplate each other.

"I've thought a lot about our last conversation," Marguerite said at last.

"I'm sure you have."

"You were there for me when I needed you in Paris. The least I can do is be here for you now."

Gypsy didn't know how tense she'd been until she felt herself relax. "I don't know what to say."

"Nothing gushy I hope. This certainly isn't a Kodak moment." Marguerite looked away.

"Do you remember the time I burst into tears at the yacht club ball? I don't even remember why, but I embarrassed you so much you wouldn't speak to me for weeks."

"You were crying because your date sneaked outside with that awful redhead from Palm Beach. What was her name?"

"Cherry Stone."

"She should have been a stripper," they said in unison. They followed with shy laughter.

"This will take some getting used to," Marguerite said. "I find it disconcerting to be best friends with someone so young and luscious."

"I find it disconcerting to *be* someone young and luscious." Gypsy leaned forward. "Marg, tell me what's going on in your life. I want to hear it all. I've missed this so much."

By the time they were sipping their final cups of jasmine tea, Marguerite had detailed the lives and loves of everyone in the mutual social circle of the Whitfields and O'Keefe's. Everyone except Owen.

Gypsy sat back, satiated by gossip and *pad see eow*. She toyed with her cup. "I've made contact with Grant."

"Have you?"

"I'm producing a segment on Norman Carroll High." She explained the story and her angle. "It was a way to be close to him."

"I'm sure Owen doesn't know, or he would have mentioned it to me."

The name stopped Gypsy like a kick to the abdomen. She took a moment to recover and knew that Marguerite had noticed. "I suppose Grant felt it would be better not to mention it. Owen's feelings about Gypsy Dugan are crystal clear."

"Owen still goes to the nursing home every day."

"With or without his protégé?"

"Without, most of the time." Marguerite sat back, too. "Anna goes by herself quite frequently."

Gypsy tried to imagine that scenario. "I hope they check the life support after she visits."

"I don't think she wishes you . . . Elisabeth any harm."

"Really? You're sure she doesn't sit there sticking pins in little blond matron dolls?"

"Oh, you've gotten so deliciously nasty." Marguerite smiled.

"What could be better for Anna than my . . . Elisabeth's demise?"

"Her recovery, I think."

"What do you mean?"

"I think Anna's praying for a complete recovery."

"Why? She prefers her competition alive and well?"

"There is no competition." Marguerite fidgeted with a spoon. Picking it up. Putting it down. It was completely unlike her.

"Get to the point, please. I know you're working up to something."

"I'm sure you were right about Anna's feelings for Owen. I think she has or had what we called a crush when we were girls. She worships at Owen's feet. Don't you suppose that in that state, she wished, quite frequently perhaps, that Elisabeth would be hit by a car or at least jump off a bridge? Anna's only human, after all. And can you imagine the guilt she might feel when her fantasy suddenly comes true?"

"Isn't that rather farfetched? Maybe the guilt's a little more basic than that. Maybe she feels guilty because she's been screwing Elisabeth's husband."

"Maybe. But even if that *was* true, I doubt that it's true now. Owen does not look like a man who is having any fun."

Gypsy wanted to shout "good." What emerged was only slightly more polite. "I'm having trouble drumming up sympathy."

"Perhaps, under the circumstances, it's easier to be angry at Owen. What good could come of feeling anything else?"

"What on earth do you mean?"

"Well, let's suppose you discovered that Owen is not unfaithful to Elisabeth anymore. Suppose you realized that he loves her, has loved her all along even if he strayed just a bit. What could you do about it? You're the woman in the other car. The woman who put his wife in a coma."

The cup slid from Gypsy's hand and clattered against the saucer. "But it's not that way."

"All right." Marguerite folded her hands to stop them from fidgeting. "Then it's not."

"I don't even want to think about Owen. There's another man in my life." Gypsy stopped, then she shook her head. "There was."

"I see."

"No, you don't. I wanted him. He's the sexiest man I've ever met." She looked up. "One of two."

"And?"

She shook her head again.

"You were never any good at sex without love," Marguerite said. "No matter how badly you wanted to be."

"Maybe I'd better learn to be good at it. Or I'm going to live the life of a nun."

Marguerite covered her hand. "I'm afraid you can take the woman out of the body, but you can't take the heart out of the woman."

For weeks Gypsy had contemplated going to see Elisabeth. There was no reason that she should. What could she say or do that would change anything? Elisabeth was in a coma, and Gypsy was alive and well. Going to see Elisabeth was too much like the afternoon years ago when she had driven past the first house she and Owen had lived in together. It had been disheartening to see what the new owners had done.

She had been powerless to replant the lilacs and bridal wreath they had removed or restore the original shingles and shutters. The house was forever changed; it no longer belonged to her.

Despite that, *knowing* that, she still felt compelled to make the trip. And her lunch with Marguerite only reinforced the impulse. That afternoon she sat at her desk and considered all the consequences. She longed to talk to Casey about it, but she had hardly seen him since the trip to Cleveland. They had scrupulously avoided each other, and when they had been forced to work together, they had been polite and distant. Rumors were flying at the studio that their romance had ended.

"You're sure about Billy and his boys, now?"

Gypsy looked up from the jumble of papers that she hadn't touched in ten minutes. Desmond was planted in her doorway. "Absolutely."

"You feel safe?"

"I feel perfectly safe. No one's batted an evil eyelash at me since Nan left. Hey, it's Tuesday, and I didn't even get a rose. All bets are off this week and the grips are fighting mad."

"Maybe the guy's florist went belly-up."

"Maybe he's just found someone else to pester." Gypsy stacked the papers and stood. "I'm tired of being tailed, Des. If someone wants me out of the way badly enough, they'll get to me whether Billy's there or not. It just doesn't make sense to spend more money on this."

"Okay. Then we'll pay him off."

"As of when?"

"Now?"

She nodded. "I'll be careful. If anything looks odd to me, I'll let you know."

"Do it. And we'll take all the normal precautions here."

"There haven't been any new leads about Mark's murder, have there?"

"Don't you watch your own show? We get a lead, you'll be the one telling Mr. and Mrs. America."

"I've wondered . . . Exactly how long was he working here, Des?"

"Not even three full months."

"Did he have time to get involved in a story that someone didn't want him to tell? Could his death have had something to do with the show?"

"We looked into all that. We read his notes, checked his mail and messages, went through everything in his office. Zip. *Nada.*"

"I guess that wasn't exactly a world-class hunch."

"Not a bad hunch, but you're underestimating your colleagues. We didn't leave any stones unturned."

Gypsy knew the prevailing theory about why Mark had been murdered. "If it was an organized crime hit, then we'll probably never know."

"Probably." He grimaced. "You just stay out of harm's way now. We can't afford to lose anyone else."

She stared at the empty doorway after Desmond left. The Billy Boys were off her case, and she was free to come and go without explanation. She was never going to be certain that seeing Elisabeth again was the right thing to do, but if she waited, she might lose her nerve entirely.

She gathered work to take home for the night and grabbed her purse. If she was going to see Elisabeth, now was the time.

It was early evening and quickly growing cooler by the time she stood outside the home in Great Neck where Elisabeth had been moved. The unimaginative tan brick had been softened by Virginia creeper and wide beds of snapdragons and asters, but she'd bet her bottom dollar that Owen winced every time he had to walk through the front door.

Inside, the halls smelled of antiseptic and floral air freshener without even a subtle bottom note of stale urine. The walls were painted a soft cream color and cheerful blue plaid curtains hung at every window.

Plants flourished in corners and beside conversational groupings of chairs and sofas. Not far away an old man in a maroon robe was carrying on a sparkling—and one-sided—conversation with the closest schefflera.

An attendant approached and offered his help. She explained her purpose for being there, and he pointed her in the right direction. She started down the hallway to the mellow piped-in refrains of Frank Sinatra's "My Way" and arrived to Barry Manilow's "Mandy." Along the way she was greeted by three different employees and a resident but stopped by no one.

At Elisabeth's door she removed her trench coat and stood silently, gathering courage. She remembered the day in the hospital when she had stolen into Elisabeth's room to prove to herself that the Whitfields were really strangers. There was nothing to prove today. She was here because she wanted a peek at her past and because she felt she owed something to the woman lying in the bed beyond this door. She didn't know *what* she owed Elisabeth exactly. Regrets. Apologies. Explanations. There was no protocol for this situation. Elisabeth's mother had prepared her for every conceivable social occasion, but no one had prepared Gypsy to face the woman she had been.

The room was silent, and the only light oozed in from a window to the right of the bed. The spring green curtains and framed New England landscapes couldn't make up for the fact that this was an institution, and the woman lying as still as death in the narrow bed with the iron rails didn't care what color the walls were painted or whether there were roses on the laminated nightstand.

There was no one else in the room. Obviously there was no need for round-the-clock nursing care. Gypsy imagined that Elisabeth was checked and fussed over frequently, with little expectation that anything important would change. She looked much as she had in the hospital. Her hair fanned over the crisp white pillowcase. An I.V. dripped patiently into a vein. Her hands lay one on top of the other. Her eyes were closed, and a casual observer would probably say she looked at peace.

Gypsy was anything but a casual observer. To her eyes Elisabeth looked like she wasn't all there, a chipped and faded conch shell deserted by the ungrateful conch who had gone looking for jazzier quarters. Elisabeth looked as if no one was at home. And, of course, no one was.

Gypsy put her coat on a chair and crossed to Elisabeth's side. "Elisabeth?"

Gypsy would have been shocked if Elisabeth had answered. The puzzle was complex enough as it was. But the fact that she didn't answer, didn't moan or even flick her eyelashes was disconcerting, too. It was impossible to know what to expect, or even what to hope for.

"Elisabeth, it's Gypsy Dugan," she said. "Or a facsimile thereof."

She wanted to hold Elisabeth's hand, but she couldn't make herself touch the other woman. It seemed taboo, a twisted corollary to childhood rules against touching intimate parts of the body.

"I'm what you dreamed of being," she said softly. She leaned over the bed. "I'm your dreams come true, Elisabeth, but I don't know if that's any consolation. I don't even know if consolations are in the realm of possibility, here. I mean, is anything going on inside that body to be consoled?"

She was babbling. She knew it. But there was nothing she could say that would make any sense, and she knew that, too.

She looked around for a chair and found one not far away. She pulled it closer and perched on the edge, leaning forward so that she didn't have to shout. "I'm back at work. I like the job. No, that's not true. I love it. It's a little sleazy, even by Gypsy's standards, but the fact that no one's uptight about dotting every 'i' or crossing every 't' makes it possible to be creative. And they're letting me expand my job description a little. I'm doing some serious stuff, stuff you'd approve of. Of course you had your raunchy side, didn't you? No one knew it, but you did."

Elisabeth didn't even twitch.

Gypsy switched topics. "I saw Grant. He looks well. He looks different from this perspective, too. You never realized what a hunk he was, did you? Well, he's not your brown-eyed baby boy anymore. He's gorgeous. You ought to see what he can do with those brown eyes when the spirit moves him."

Elisabeth looked as cool and impervious as a white marble sculpture.

Tears rose in Gypsy's eyes. She realized she was twisting the covers that were hanging over the edge of the bed. She cleared her throat. "Look, let me give you some advice. If you're lying there thinking, if there's something left to think with, just remember. Wishing is a dangerous thing, Bess old friend. Don't make any foolish wishes while you're lying there, because God knows where you might just end up."

Elisabeth looked as if wishing were a thing of the past.

There was nothing left to say, but Gypsy wasn't ready to leave. She leaned back in her chair. The room was peaceful, and she had come a long way for this. She probably wouldn't return; this would probably be her last time at Elisabeth's side. Since there was nothing else to say, she said nothing. She closed her eyes, and thought about the woman lying in the bed. Much later, when she opened her eyes, Owen was standing beside her.

ᴄᴏ 18

OBVIOUSLY OWEN HADN'T COME TO THE nursing home from work. He never stepped foot into midtown Manhattan in slacks and a sweater. And only on the rarest occasions did he return from the city this early in the evening. Gypsy had assumed that if he visited Elisabeth at all today it would be sometime after dinner. She had been certain she wouldn't run into him.

Or perhaps she had only told herself as much.

He towered over her, stiffly erect and seething. "What are you doing here?"

She took a moment to examine all the subtle changes. He was still thinner than he'd been when the woman lying in the nursing home bed had been taking his suits to the tailor for alterations. There were lines in his forehead that were new but not unattractive. He was wearing the wire-rimmed glasses he had once saved only for reading, but if anything, they gave an arresting face even more character. She had always known he would age with style while Elisabeth sagged and faded.

"I'll leave." She got to her feet.

"Why did you come in the first place? Are you looking for another installment of your tragic tabloid story?"

Anger flamed inside her, anger that had little relation to his questions. "Look, I'm not going to bother trying to explain myself to you. You're obviously one of those men who's so sure the world revolves around him, you can't recognize anyone else's place in it, anyway."

"You don't know anything about me, Miss Dugan!"

"No?" She faced him, hands on hips. "I know what I see. You're arrogant and insensitive. I almost died in the same accident that put Elisabeth into the twilight world, but you conveniently forget that every time you meet me. You're incapable of giving anyone else's pain a moment's pause. I'm curious. When you come here and sit by this bed, who is it you're sorriest for? Her or yourself?"

"What in the hell are you here for?"

"I came to be with her. To talk to her. That's all." There were two routes to the door. She chose the one that put the chair between them, but he grabbed her arm to stop her.

"What do you have to say to my wife?"

"Nothing I plan to repeat."

"How does she look to you, Miss Dugan? Are you going to describe her on the air? Have you taken in enough details?"

"Let go of my arm."

He didn't even seem aware that he was holding it. He looked down. One by one his fingers unclenched.

She moved toward the door, grabbing her coat and tucking it under her arm. He reached the door before she did. "She's not any better," he said. "She's probably never going to get any better."

"No. She probably isn't." Staring just past his head Gypsy waited for him to move. But he didn't.

"Are you going to tell the world?"

"You really don't listen, do you? Did you listen to your wife when she was awake and able to communicate with you?"

"My relationship with Elisabeth is none of your business!"

"No? You know what? I've got your number, pal. I bet you've probably spent more time at her bed since she's been in the coma than you did when she was alive and well!"

He looked stunned. And in that moment, when all his defenses slipped, she saw what she'd refused to see before. He was standing at a precipice where he'd never had to stand. And it wouldn't take much more to push him over the edge.

"I'm sorry." She looked away. "I have no right. I'm sorry."

He stepped away from the door. She rested her hand on the knob. "I won't come back," she said. "And I have no plans to do a follow-up story on the accident."

The door was heavy enough to protect Elisabeth from tornados, fires, and floods. Gypsy hauled it open and stepped through the doorway. The door was closing slowly behind her when Owen spoke. "Forgive me."

The door hissed its final six inches and clicked into place. She was standing in the hall listening to Johnny Mathis sing "Chances Are." Owen was standing in the deathly silence of Elisabeth's room.

The biggest part of her wanted to turn and leave. That was the part that was now Gypsy Dugan, a woman who went after what she wanted. She wanted to leave. She wanted to let Owen suffer in his own private hell, whatever its origins.

There was another part of her. A part that was still Elisabeth and still loved this man. No matter what he had done to her. No matter with whom he had done it.

She was weighing the parts, dissecting them, analyzing them, sorrowing over them, when he opened the door.

"For what?" She folded her arms over her chest in primitive protection. "For reacting like a human being under stress? Don't worry, I understand."

"None of this is your fault. But I want to blame somebody." He ran his hand through his hair in a gesture that was so familiar she could almost feel him do it. Had she still been his wife, she would have reached over and smoothed his hair back into place. But she wasn't his wife.

Not anymore.

She looked away to compose herself. "That's natural."

"I keep thinking it's going to get better. That I'll wake up one morning and accept what's happened. That the anger will disappear. But it doesn't."

She swallowed. "Are you angry at her?"

"Goddamn it, yes! I'm furious. And I'm furious at you and at the man in the car that you swerved to avoid and at God and the world in general. I want things the way they were, so I guess I'm furious at time, too. And most of all, I'm furious at myself."

Her gaze stole back to his. "Why?"

This time *he* looked away. "Because there were things I never said. Things I kept waiting for the right moment to say. And now it's too late. I say them every day, of course. I sit by that goddamned bed and say them, but she's not there to hear. They say people in comas can hear you. The doctors say they can still hear. But I know she doesn't. She's not there anymore. She was my wife for twenty-five years! I know she's not there."

She wanted to beg him to tell her what he said in those dark hours. She wanted to tell him that she was here now, and he could say whatever he had to. It would be best for them both if he did. They could get on with their lives. Perhaps she could finally let go of this sham of a marriage. Perhaps she could go to Casey and ask for another chance.

But as far as Owen knew, she was Gypsy Dugan born and bred.

"I don't know what to say." It was only a little bit better than nothing.

"Of course you don't. I'm making a fool of myself."

She put her hand on his. She wanted to cry. She wanted to slap him. "No."

"I haven't said any of this to anyone, and now I'm standing in the hallway pouring out my heart to a stranger."

"I'm not exactly a stranger."

"Fate thrust you right in the middle, didn't she?"

"That's a good way of putting it."

Her brain insisted she drop his hand, but her fingertips resisted. Touching Owen was so familiar, even if this wasn't exactly the hand that she had touched him with so many times before. Her flesh warmed, and she felt an instant connection.

"You're not who you appear to be, are you?"

Her eyes widened. Her hand fell to her side. "What?"

"You're not who you pretend to be."

For a moment, one stunned moment, she thought he knew the truth. Then she realized he was talking about her celebrity persona. "You mean the person I pretend to be on television?"

"I've watched the show. You're very different in person."

"Most people have a public and a private side."

"Why did you really come here tonight?"

"I told you, I have things to say to her, too."

"We're quite a pair, aren't we?"

She tried to smile, but tears filled her eyes. Once they *had* been quite a pair. "I suppose."

"Look, it's dinnertime and there's a decent café a couple of blocks away. I think we both need a drink and something in our stomachs."

"You haven't had any time with her by yourself."

"Oh, I'll come back. I usually spend at least an hour here in the evenings. I read poetry out loud. Her favorites."

She remembered evenings at the beginning of their marriage, evenings in front of a roaring fire when she could feel their baby moving inside her. Owen had held her in his arms, one hand across her abdomen, and read poetry in his musical baritone. He had alternated between her favorites and his. His were in Polish, but it hadn't mattered that he'd had to translate. It had only made perfect evenings longer and more perfect.

"Please?" He wasn't a man who let his emotions show. They were showing now. He was as close to losing control as she had ever seen him.

There were things they needed to say to each other. She wondered if they could say them anyway, even if Owen didn't know exactly who she was . . . or wasn't.

She looked at her watch, although it was just an excuse to look away. "All right. Then I've got to get back to the city."

"I don't want to keep you if—"

"No, it's fine. It will be good for both of us."

"Let me tell someone I'm coming back later."

She waited for him in the reception area. The old man in the maroon robe was now conversing enthusiastically with a visitor. Gypsy wondered if he could tell the difference between the sad-eyed young woman holding his hand and the schefflera.

Owen joined her. "I'm surprised they let you in to see Elisabeth without authorization."

"I'm rarely stopped no matter where I go. I suppose if you look like you know what you're doing, people just assume that you really do."

He opened the door for her, and she passed in front of him, holding herself carefully so that she didn't brush against him. His voice rumbled in her ear. "Well, you obviously don't need my help, but I just asked that you be put on her visitor list anyway."

"Thank you."

"I can't imagine Elisabeth doing that."

"Doing what?"

"Just walking in that way and expecting to get what she was after. A long time ago she was a television reporter, too, but she was scrupulous about going through the correct channels."

Gypsy had often wondered what Owen thought about Elisabeth's ability to do her job. "How good a reporter was she, then? Because sometimes you have to brazen your way into a situation to get the information you need."

"She was wonderful. There's nothing brazen about Elisabeth. But she charmed her way into people's hearts and lives. And she was absolutely genuine. People fascinated her. She wanted to know about them, to feel what they were feeling. They knew that, and they talked to her as if she was a close friend."

His words gave her a warm glow. She probed a little more. "Was she working . . . at the time of the accident?"

"Not in television. She wrote articles for our local weekly. She was going to interview you for the paper on the day of the accident."

"I'm sorry. My memory of that day is still cloudy. Did she miss television?"

"I don't know."

"No?"

"You'd have to know her to understand. She never complained. Never. Not about anything. I had to read between the lines, and I'm not very good at that. Maybe it was just one of the ways I failed her as a husband."

Gypsy was surprised she was instinctively reacting with sympathy. Owen had failed Elisabeth in many more important ways, and apparently, he realized it. "Was she one of those women who gave up everything for her family?"

"We're talking about her in the past tense."

"I'm sorry."

"Don't be. It's impossible to know what tense to use. Even if a miracle occurs and she regains consciousness, the woman I was married to probably won't ever exist again." He pointed to his car, a dove gray BMW still sporting a dent on the fender from the night of Grant's college graduation party.

He helped her into the passenger seat and went around to his own door. She fastened her seat belt while she waited. The car was nearly as familiar to her as the one she had totaled in the accident, but the seat didn't fit her body in the same snug way. The seat was the same, but she was not.

"This place isn't fancy, a dive by Great Neck standards." He pulled out of the parking lot. "I hope you don't mind, but it's easy to get to and quick."

"And you want to get back to your wife."

"I doubt that it matters to her. But, yes."

"Anyplace will be fine."

The café was small and dimly lit, as if the owners wanted to save money on electricity or health department law suits. Plate glass windows looked over a blacktop parking lot. There were crumbs on the dark green tablecloth and the menu had coffee stains.

She closed her eyes and remembered another dimly lit cafe, the first they had ever eaten in together. The two were almost interchangeable.

Owen put his hand on her arm. "Are you all right?"

What could she say? That she was having flashbacks? "I'm fine, but maybe I do need something to eat."

"Would you like a drink first?"

"Jameson's. Straight."

He ordered two.

She wanted to tell him he never drank whiskey, much less straight. She looked away and bit back the words.

"The veal's good here," he said.

"I don't eat it."

"Elisabeth wouldn't, either. I always felt guilty if I ordered it when she was at the table."

"Feeling any guilt now?"

He smiled, and the smile launched itself, arrow-straight to her heart. "The chicken's good, too. And the pork and sauerkraut is almost as good as my mother's."

"That's what I'll have."

"I pictured you as more trendy than that. Tapas. Sushi. A nibbler."

"Looks can be deceiving." He couldn't imagine how profound the old saying was in this case.

His smile faded, as if he just didn't have the strength to maintain it. "I keep trying to put you in a box, and you just won't let me, will you?"

"Which box? Vicious bitch? Bloodthirsty reporter? Airhead anchorwoman?"

"Some combination. Does projecting that image on the air protect you?"

"Protect me from what?"

"Men who are trying to get too close."

She smiled her best vicious bombshell smile. "Can men get too close?"

"You're amazing. You can turn that on and off on cue."

"You'd be surprised how much pretending I'm called on to do." He would be particularly surprised if he knew why.

They ordered dinner and started on their drinks. Owen asked her about herself and her job. Small talk with tidy, easy answers. "I suppose I should tell you that I've met your son," she said when the subject turned to stories she was involved in. "We've decided to do a piece on a day in an inner city high school, and we chose Norman Carroll. Your son recognized me while I was investigating the school as a possible story site, and he introduced himself."

"That seems like quite a coincidence."

"Doesn't it?" She took a particularly large swallow of her whiskey.

"What did you think of Grant?"

"I like him a lot. You should be proud."

"I like him, too. It's funny. He and his mother are especially close. I always felt a little left out. Now that she's . . ."

She picked up the conversational ball. "You've gotten closer?"

"I don't know. I want to be there to help him, but I'm not always sure how. Sometimes I think he'd rather just help me instead. He's like Elisabeth in that way. When something went wrong in her life, I'd try to step in and help her, and she'd turn the tables and make it my problem so that she could help me."

She stared at him. Had she really done that? Had she cut off his attempts to offer solace? "I'm not sure what you mean. How could she do that?"

"Well, I remember after her mother died, I tried to comfort her. She talked about how sad I must be because her mother and I had become good friends. The next thing I knew, she was consoling me. Sometimes when I go into the nursing home to see her, I almost expect her to start talking about my feelings. What the accident has done to me. How it's affected my work or my schedule." He shrugged. "If she could, she probably would."

Her hands were trembling. She clenched them in her lap. "You don't sound as if you admire that about her."

"I admire it immensely. Who doesn't want to be the center of someone else's world? I just don't admire the way I took advantage of it. I let that happen. Eventually I began to expect it. At the end I even made a fuss when she tried to assert herself."

"Did you?" Her voice was huskier than it had ever been.

"The night before the accident I asked her to give up going to Stony Brook to hear your speech. I needed her to entertain the wife of one of my clients. She told me how important it was to do the interview with you, but the only thing I could see was that she wasn't putting my needs first. So she compromised. And that's why she's lying in that bed right now."

"What on earth do you mean?"

"She was driving too fast because she'd spent the morning helping me, and she was running late. She was probably afraid she was going to miss seeing you entirely. She never drove over the speed limit. Elisabeth followed all the rules. Always. Just that once she didn't, and it was my fault."

"Owen . . ." She stopped herself.

"Please, go ahead and call me Owen."

"Your wife was a grown woman. She made her own choices."

"I shouldn't be telling you this. You didn't bargain on instant intimacy when you came here today."

She wondered if that was true. Had she really come to see him as much as Elisabeth? "I'm glad I'm here."

They switched to safer topics, the weather, baseball scores, books they'd read. The meal arrived in stages, and it might have been as good as Owen promised, but Gypsy hardly paid attention to it.

They were alone in a restaurant, discussing their lives and their days as comfortably as old lovers. Once upon a time they had done this often. They had made time in their busy schedules for each other, crossed off parties or business appointments on their calendars just to be together. Nothing had kept them from enjoying each other's company in every way.

When had it all gone wrong?

"It's funny. . . ." Owen sipped his after-dinner coffee—black with three lumps of sugar, just the way he always drank it.

"What's funny?"

"I think you and Elisabeth might have been friends if you'd had the chance. You're much more like her than I ever would have believed."

She had been stirring cream into her coffee. Her spoon clattered to the table. "Is that so?"

"Not in looks, of course. But you listen with the same enthusiasm that she did. You share your opinions the same way, too. I know exactly where you stand, but you make me feel like my opinions are every bit as important."

"Maybe that's something all women learn at their mothers' knees."

"Not all women. My mother could shut down a conversation so quickly that no traces of it lingered in the air."

"Actually, mine's that way, too," Gypsy said, thinking of Rose Dugan.

"My mother was born in a different time and a different country. She and my father were sturdy Polish peasant stock, and there wasn't a question in their minds that children were sent by God to work, say their prayers, and keep their thoughts to themselves."

Gypsy wondered how much of his life story he'd admit to a stranger. He had grown far beyond his roots, and he rarely discussed them. "There's just the faintest trace of an accent when you speak. Something not quite New York."

"The family name is Witovicz, changed to Whitfield by my grandfather the moment he stepped off the boat. But the next generations were never allowed to forget who we really were. My father knew he'd better marry a Polish girl or face complete rejection by his family, so he found and married my mother, whose background was every bit as pure. We spoke Polish and nothing but at home, even though both my parents did most of their growing up in this country. I still dream in Polish."

"And Elisabeth?"

He smiled, as if his thoughts were pleasant. "As much of a WASP as they come. Her blood is so royal blue it could be matched by color instead of type. She's never done an improper thing in her life, except marry me."

"Marry you? But look at you. You're known internationally for your work. You're wealthy, handsome."

He didn't blink or blush. Owen knew who and what he was, and he was comfortable with all of it. "At first I was so in awe of her, I could hardly stammer out a sentence. She was every dream I'd ever had. Beautiful, sophisticated, intelligent. She was absolutely sure what to do in any situation. And I was a long-haired, tongue-tied Polack who was so poor from his years in graduate school that he couldn't even afford to take her to a decent restaurant. We ate at a place just like this one on our first date. We went Dutch treat." He wasn't smiling now. "That's probably why I come here. I make my connections with her any way I can now."

He had remembered that first restaurant.

Gypsy sat quietly stirring the last inch of her coffee and trying to put everything Owen had said into perspective. It was tempting to believe he still loved Elisabeth. Tempting and poignantly satisfying. But how much was guilt and how much just sentimental memories that had no real meaning in the present?

"I'm sorry," he said.

She looked up. Owen did look sorry. Frustrated and sorry and altogether miserable. "Why?"

"I don't have the right to put you through this. I don't know why I have."

"Maybe you just needed to tell someone what you were feeling."

"There are no words for what I'm feeling."

They stared at each other a heartbeat too long. His brown eyes were still uncommonly beautiful, clear, long-lashed and soulful. She had fallen in love with those eyes the first time they had met hers. They were eyes in which she'd thought she could see a shared future. But in the last year of their marriage those remarkable eyes had been turned away from her far too often.

Owen looked away. Then, almost as an afterthought

he looked at his watch. "I have to get back to the nursing home."

"If you need somebody to talk to or just somebody to be quiet with . . ." She wondered where the words had come from and why.

"Surely you've had your fill of me and my problems?"

"We're connected in a very odd way, Owen." It was certainly the truth. She reached across the table and laid her fingertips against his sweater. She had bought the sweater for him. She remembered where and when. She desperately wished she could feel his pulse through the cable knit wool. "I haven't minded one second of tonight. I'm glad you talked to me."

For a moment he seemed incapable of words. Then he nodded. His voice was strangely husky. "Can I drop you somewhere?"

Reluctantly she withdrew her hand. He was leaving, and she might never see him again. "Don't worry about me. It's a nice night. I can walk to the station from here. I'd like the exercise."

"You're sure?"

"Absolutely. You go on."

"Thank you. For everything."

She nodded. She didn't trust herself to say anything else. He slid out of the booth and stood. He didn't move away immediately. He looked down at her and she, unable to control her own actions, looked up at him.

Another heartbeat passed, then two. He turned sharply on his heel and walked away.

She lingered over the last drops of coffee until she was sure he was gone. Her hands were trembling, and the room seemed infused with a fine gray mist. More than anything she wanted to cry, but not here. Not in this place, which was nearly a shrine to their past.

Owen had paid the bill, which was no surprise. She nodded good-bye to the owner and walked outside into the chilly evening air. On the sidewalk just beyond the restaurant parking lot she stopped to put on her coat and look for an evening paper for the train ride back to the city. A moment later she was bending over a vending machine when someone began to shout.

She straightened, but not quickly. She was still thinking about the dinner with Owen, and she was used to noise in the streets. So used to it that for a moment, she failed to detect the aggression in the man's voice. By the time she realized something crucial was happening, the man's shout had been eclipsed by a woman's piercing scream.

A siren sounded nearby, a police car or a fire engine. The noise confused Gypsy, and for a moment she didn't know which direction the screams were coming from. She whirled to search for the sound and found that she was standing in plain view of a hooded figure who was pointing a small revolver at an old woman. The woman, pink hair curlers bobbing with every shriek, was lost in the throes of hysteria.

Gypsy stared at the man whose face was partially obscured by a knotted red bandanna tucked into the hood of a dark green parka. She was fascinated and not one bit frightened. She hadn't been frightened when her throat closed after one succulent bite of Perry's shrimp creole, and she wasn't frightened now. Dying was familiar, an old friend with comfortable, welcoming arms.

The man swung the gun toward her and lifted it higher. There was a split-second opportunity to be glad that she had spent her last hour on earth with Owen before a bullet split the air in front of her and she fell to the sidewalk.

⌑ 19

Billy was stationed in Gypsy's hallway to screen all the co-op's comings and goings. Even Des reported thorough scrutiny when he'd stopped by for a few minutes to see for himself that Gypsy was all right. Now Casey stood guard just inside her apartment door with his arms folded across his chest like a *mafioso* enforcer.

"I wish you'd sit down. You're making me nervous." Gypsy paced the small living room. The hand-loomed rag rugs which had replaced the plethora of animal skins were getting their first real workout.

"You'd still be nervous if I sat down. Somebody tried to kill you a couple of hours ago."

Gypsy was becoming an expert on "almost dead." After the first shot outside the café two additional bullets had plowed into the tree lawn bordering the sidewalk where she'd flung herself. The third bullet had missed her brain by inches, grinding a well-seasoned pile of dog excrement into valuable compost.

She didn't know why the gunman had missed an easy shot three times, any more than she knew why he had chosen her as a target. She only knew she was alive. Again or still, depending on perspective.

"Look, I'll sit down if you will," Casey said.

"You first."

276

He smiled, just a brief crack in a face as stiff as a dram of Scotland's finest. He left the door and crossed the room to her new soft-as-a-pillow sofa. He lounged in the corner, but even in that position he looked like a man who could launch himself across the room at a moment's notice.

She perched on the edge of the sofa, two pillows away. "You didn't have to come. I'm all right."

"No, you're not."

"After it was all over I had the strangest desire to climb to the top of the World Trade Center and dive out a window, just to see what would happen."

"Three near-death experiences are a charm. I wouldn't try for four."

"The police are insisting that I just got in the way of a mugging."

"What do you think?"

"I think the mugging was a cover. I think that guy wanted me." For the last three hours Gypsy had gone over and over the scene in her mind. The man with the gun had ignored the commotion around him. The woman screaming. The panicked squealing of tires in the streets. The piercing siren of the squad car that had been cruising the area looking for a good place to grab some dinner. The man in the parka had pointed his gun directly at her and pulled the trigger. Not once, but three times. Then he had disappeared into the closest alley.

Casey slung his arm over the sofa cushions in a forced attempt to appear casual. "Next question. Do you think it's related to Mark's death?"

Gypsy contemplated the gauze adorning her shin. She had scrapes and bruises from her clash with the sidewalk, but they were nothing compared to what could have happened. "Casey, I don't remember the day Mark died. Nothing about it. I don't even remember Mark, and there's no chance I ever will. I'm not going to regain any of my memory."

"You sound sure of that."

"It's one of the few things in the universe that I am sure of."

He abandoned casual and pulled out a notebook from his inside jacket pocket. "Let's go on the assumption that the two shootings are related, even if you didn't recognize the guy with the gun."

"I didn't see enough of him to recognize. For all I know he could have been my brother." Actually, she wouldn't recognize her own brother, either, but she wasn't going to get into that. "He had a bandanna covering his forehead well past his eyebrows, and the hood of his parka covered the sides of his face. He was young, I think. Medium complected. About your height or a little taller. And that narrows it down to about a million men in a hundred-mile radius." She craned her neck to see what he was writing. "What are you doing?"

"Making a list."

"Of what?"

"People who might want you dead. Who would you put at the top?"

"Cripes, you make it sound like it's going to be a foot long."

"I think you'd better be creative and thorough, Gyps. I had my doubts all along that you were in danger. But I don't have any now. I think we've got our own personal news story here, and we'd better go after it like good little reporters."

"Or?"

"Don't make me say it."

"I don't know why anyone would want me dead. I can't remember anything."

"Let's start with your life since the car accident. If that's all you can remember, that's all we have to work with."

She closed her eyes and leaned back against the cushions. She was close to tears, and she wasn't even sure exactly why—there were too many good reasons to cry just to center on one. "The Reverend Bordmann still calls now and then to breathe heavily in my ear. Maybe he's some kind of psycho as well as a pervert. There's the guy who used to send me a rose—"

"You know it's a guy?"

"I'm guessing."

"Not a good idea under the circumstances."

She shrugged. "Nan. Julie. I had them both fired."

"Anyone else at the studio?"

"I don't know. There's a lot of competition. I've locked horns with Kevin and Loretta a time or two, but never with any apparent animosity."

"How about higher ups?"

"I'm the golden girl. Why would anyone want me out of the way? If the ratings were dropping, I might be persuaded to look closer. But they're not."

"How about your family?"

"My mother dislikes me, but she's a Ten Commandments kind of gal. And besides, she's softening up a little. She sent me the biography of Mother Teresa after my visit. I think she's hoping I'll move to India and do good works to atone for the rest of my life."

"No one else from home?"

"Not that I know of."

"Lives you've ruined on the air?"

"I've done this before, when Nan was splashing blood around at the studio. And if it's someone like that, it's connected to a story I did before the accident. I just can't help there."

Casey tapped his pen. "You've watched videotapes of past shows?"

"I've watched every single one of them."

"Maybe that's the key. Maybe we should go through them again, one by one. Make notes of any real exposés that you were responsible for. Then we can follow up. See how people have picked up the pieces of their lives. Where they are and what they're doing."

"In other words if someone's life was ruined, he

might want to ruin mine in return? I can buy that. But what would Mark have to do with it? He was only here for a short time. Would he have been involved in a story? Was that the reason he was murdered right in front of me?"

"Like I see it, there are three possibilities. One, you and Mark were both connected to some sad sack's woes, and whoever it was started a campaign of retribution with Mark. Two, the first gunman was a lousy shot. He meant to take you out and he took out Mark instead. And if it's the same guy, he missed this time because his aim hasn't improved. Three, Mark's death was a warning. Someone was hoping you'd back off a story the two of you had been working on together. Or maybe Mark had nothing to do with it, and he was killed just because he'd had lunch with you."

"If you ever plan to lunch with me again, we might consider takeout in a dark closet."

He stuffed his notebook back into his pocket. "We might as well talk about that now."

She opened her eyes. Casey's were absolutely serious. "Maybe not," she said. "I don't know if I can handle anything else tonight."

"Gyps . . ."

She sniffed back tears.

"Come here." He opened his arms.

She slid closer. Her voice trembled. "We tried this in Cleveland, remember?"

"Not this." He leaned over and pulled her against him. "Relax. You're safe. Nothing else is going to happen tonight."

He smelled good, felt good, and he always looked wonderful. The magical tug that had existed between them since the moment he'd walked into her hospital room was still in full force. She could feel her body warming in response to his. There was a loose wire deep inside her that connected and charged every time he touched her. She knew she could easily turn toward him, rest her fingers against his cheeks and guide his lips to hers. She had no doubt that in her current state of mind, sexual attraction and human warmth could double as love.

But tonight, after her dinner with Owen, she knew for certain that they weren't the same things at all.

He smoothed her hair back from her forehead with his palm. His hand wasn't quite steady. "I think we both know this isn't working anymore."

The "this" in question was absolutely clear. "Do we?" She sniffed.

"You're not the same since the accident, and I guess I'm not, either."

He was holding her, but Gypsy had never felt more alone. She suspected that if Casey had said almost anything else or even nothing at all, she might have succumbed to the potent urge to lose herself in his lovemaking. But he was too fine a man to play second fiddle to another man's memory, and she was not the woman he had loved. He had loved the former Gypsy Dugan. Perhaps the word had never surfaced in his thoughts. Perhaps he had repressed it because it was so impossible. But he had loved her. And the Gypsy he had loved was no more.

"I'm not the same. You're right." She turned in his arms and held out her hand. "Are we going to be friends?"

He linked fingers with her, his hand warm and comforting. "I'm leaving the show."

"No, Casey."

"I'm leaving. I'm tired of it. All of it. I don't know who or what I am anymore, but I know I'm better than what I do here. I've got enough money saved to live for a year, two if I'm frugal. I might try writing. I might even take a newspaper job, but not at one of Tito's rags. I want to be a serious journalist again, even if it's someplace in the middle of nowhere."

"When?"

"Once I know you're safe."

"But that's not fair. You shouldn't have to put your plans on hold for me."

"It'll give Des time to replace me. I'd like to leave in a cloud of goodwill. It's a small world, and I might need references."

She couldn't tell how much of his decision had to do with the job and how much with their relationship. But she knew that whatever that balance, he was doing what was best for them both.

"I'll miss you." Her voice trembled. Tears swam over her eyelashes and spilled to her cheeks.

For a moment he looked as if he wished he could cry, as well. "The strange thing is that I'll miss you, too. You. Exactly like you are now. Somewhere along the way we did become friends. Apparently we weren't meant to be lovers at the same time." His lips quirked into an infinitely sad smile. "Fate's played quite a trick on us."

She could only echo that. "Quite a trick."

He squeezed her hand, then he brought it to his lips. "I wish you the best, Gyps, and maybe love if that's what you want. But let's keep you alive in the meantime. Let's find out who wants you dead before the guy with the gun finds you again, and this time he's learned how to aim."

"You're sure I don't look like Shirley Temple with this hair?" Perry peered at her image in the mirror of Gypsy's dressing room.

Gypsy stood back and squinted at her. "Cuter. Much, much cuter."

"Sweet thing, you got me into this, you'd better look me over good or I might just embarrass you to pieces."

Gypsy grinned. "You look wonderful."

Perry had agreed to a makeover for her first day in front of the camera. She'd kept the dreadlocks, but they were shorter now and pinned back from her face.

She wore fuchsia linen pants, a turquoise wool jacket, and a yellow blouse that were bold enough in design to assure the viewers that the days of Nan's simpering pastels had ended. Perry looked sassy, intelligent, and ready for trouble, and all the test clips indicated she was a star in the making.

"Then I'm off to Staten Island." Perry adjusted her jacket. She was on her way to film a brief stand-up for a feature in the works about New York City's smallest borough and its desire to secede. Tomorrow she would be transformed into a Norman Carroll transfer student in tight faded jeans.

The one-day shoot at Norman Carroll had undergone a change. After careful negotiations, the show had decided to enroll one of their reporters as a student. Perry had been the obvious choice since she was new and her face was still unfamiliar. She would attend the school for two weeks, and at the beginning of the third, she would become the student whom a camera crew would tape for a week, both overtly and covertly. She had proved to everyone's satisfaction that she could look and act young enough to pull off the deception. And it was a great way to really introduce her to the viewers.

"Break a leg."

"Thanks, Gypsy. You didn't have to go to bat for me."

Gypsy put her hand over her heart. "You called me Gypsy. It's a first."

"Yeah, don't know how it slipped out."

"I appreciate the thanks, but I haven't done anything you didn't deserve. And I don't know how I would have gotten through these months since the accident without you."

"You're sure paying me back big time." Perry put her hand on Gypsy's arm. "All this and being your friend, too."

Gypsy felt the same strange sense of loss she had

felt after Casey's announcement that he would be leaving the show. Perry would still be around, but she was moving into her own sphere. They would still see each other frequently, but Perry would no longer be at Gypsy's beck and call. That was exactly the way it should be, but Gypsy already missed her.

She covered Perry's hand. "We're going to stay friends. Just don't get so successful that you don't save time for an occasional sandwich across the street with me."

After Perry left Gypsy finished doing her preliminary makeup for the day's taping. In the weeks since the shooting she had persuaded Des to let her take full control of the Norman Carroll segment, and her days had been busier than usual. She had wanted as little time for thinking as possible. When she wasn't working on the high school story, reworking the day's copy, or taping anchor spots she viewed videotapes of former shows and made notes. Des had assigned Kendra to discover what had happened to the subjects of particularly scandalous stories that Casey or Gypsy asked her to investigate. So far they had come up with no useful leads, although Des, ever the bureaucrat, planned to do a series entitled "Where Are They Now?" with the most bizarre information that Kendra uncovered.

Gypsy hadn't been back to see Elisabeth. Now that she was under constant surveillance again, the visit would have been difficult to explain. And she hadn't wanted to run into Owen. She'd had drinks at the Plaza a week ago with Marguerite, and they stayed in constant touch, but Gypsy had asked her not to discuss Owen, and Marguerite had obliged.

It didn't matter if she talked about Owen or not. Gypsy still dreamed of him at night. Sometimes she would wake up and expect to find him in the bed beside her. She would turn to her back and stare at the ceiling, wondering where he was at that moment. The resulting mixture of anger and sadness kept her awake until dawn.

She was lucky that Gypsy's metabolism allowed for very little sleep.

With her makeup finished she got up to change into the clothes she'd chosen for the taping. She was just buttoning the waistband of a scarlet Armani suit when someone knocked. She called an invitation to come in as she bustled to the closet and retrieved the matching jacket from a hook beside the door.

"I'm intruding. I knew I would be."

She turned. She would know the voice anywhere. "Grant . . ."

"Hi, Gypsy."

She stared at Grant and was reminded of evenings when he was a little boy. If she had been required to go to a party or out to dinner with Owen's clients before Grant's bedtime, she had always brought him into her room as she finished preparations to go out. He had perched on her bed and chattered about his day as she finished her makeup or chose jewelry. Sometimes he had hidden as she studiously pretended not to notice, then he'd leaped out at her from some perfectly visible corner as she gasped and pretended to be terrified.

Tears sprang to her eyes and threatened her make-up. "You're not intruding." He had never intruded. She had loved every second of raising him. While her friends had bemoaned their children's adolescence, she had only mourned the fact that he would soon depart for college.

"Are you all right?"

She forced a cough. "I think I'm getting a cold. Or I'm allergic to something. My eyes are watery."

"Vitamin C." He favored her with his Owen smile. "If it extends life expectancy, I'll live to be a thousand. My mother was unbelievably conscientious."

"I'll get some immediately." She turned back to the

closet and took her time removing the jacket from its hanger. "Nobody let me know you were here. I'm surprised to see you. And delighted."

"I met Perry in the lobby. She okayed having me sent up. You invited me to see a taping. Remember?"

She did remember. She just hadn't known he would take her up on it. "How'd you get out of your classes?"

"I took a personal day. They're finishing up placement tests today, and a substitute can handle that as well as I can."

"Well, I'm glad you came." She slipped on the jacket and adjusted the shoulder pads. "I don't think you'll find it very different from your television courses at Northwestern."

There was a brief silence. "How did you know that?" he asked.

She looked up. "Know what?"

"That I took television classes, or even that I went to Northwestern?"

She froze. Her mind went blank. The Gypsy Dugan part of her, that amoral and manipulative psyche-leftover that had so often helped her get out of jams seemed to have headed for higher ground. "You know, I really don't know." She shoved her hands in her jacket pockets. "How on earth did I know that?"

He cocked his head. She'd seen the same suspicious look on his face as a little boy when he'd asked where babies came from, and she'd told him the hospital. He'd known there was more to the story.

"Either you mentioned it, or we got it from background material for the Norman Carroll story," she went on. "You'd be surprised how much research our staff does."

"Why?"

But how do they get in the hospital, Mommy? Does the Daddy put them there?

"We have to be thorough," she said. "Background checks are routine. Imagine what would happen if we singled out particularly devoted teachers to interview on camera, and we found out later that they were all child pornographers."

"Then you'd have the kind of story you could air until the Apocalypse."

She dimpled. "Exactly."

He laughed. "Find out anything more interesting than where I went to school and what I studied?"

With the worst over she moved toward the door. "You are a surprisingly clean-cut and virtuous young man."

He put his hand on her arm as she started past him. "I might surprise you."

The air was sizzling. She looked up from Grant's hand to his eyes. The invitation in them was perfectly apparent. Even to his mother.

The emotional and sensual wallop almost knocked her to the floor. She could divorce herself from the situation just far enough to see what a startlingly attractive man she had raised. Grant, her polite, good-natured, unfailingly kind and totally beloved son, was a lady-killer. Had she been any other woman, the word "yes" would be forming on her lips.

But she wasn't anyone else. Not exactly.

She searched for Gypsy, screamed for her to come to her rescue. His hand inched a little higher up her arm. "Aren't I a little old for you?" Her voice sounded like it was coming from the depths of the subway.

"That's pretty retro, don't you think?"

"Aren't I a little wild?"

"I don't know." He smiled and the room was ten watts brighter. "Are you?"

She searched frantically for a way out of this. "Grant, I'm bad news. I'm the kind of woman your mother warned you about."

"You didn't know my mother. She was convinced that everyone could turn over a new leaf."

"But I don't want to."

He stepped a little closer. "Good."

She adored this Don-Juan-in-training. She would no more hurt him than she would take a rush hour stroll down the right lane of the George Washington Bridge. But she wasn't about to act out the New Age rewrite of *Oedipus Rex*.

Like a gift from above, an obvious out occurred to her. "I have a firm rule. I never date anybody I'm involved with on stories, no matter how tempted I am. I have to maintain a certain distance or my work suffers. And there has to be some journalistic integrity at 'The Whole Truth,' or this show would be a complete sham."

"Never?"

"No matter how tempted I am." She moved a little closer and her voice dropped half an octave. "And I am sorely tempted."

He didn't blink an eye. Her baby boy was no egotist, but he knew his effect on women. He wasn't embarrassed at her rejection; he wasn't uncomfortable. He was completely sure that she should be attracted to him, so he believed every word she'd said. "You're a lot more than you seem."

His father had said something similar at the café. This time the observation didn't throw her. Gypsy gave him a harlot's steamy smile and a mother's best advice. "Find yourself a nice girl, and make sure she knows just how lucky she is."

"Does the offer still stand to watch you tape?"

"You bet it does. There's nothing in my set of rules about not being friends."

In the studio he struck up a conversation with one of the new assistants, a recent UCLA graduate named Holly who aspired to television greatness. She was a slender blond who was probably prettier in person than she would ever be on camera. She reminded Gypsy of Elisabeth at the same age, gracious and womanly, intelligent as well as perceptive about people. But like Elisabeth she didn't have the hard edges she would need to head for the top. She was too polite, too considerate. Gypsy determined to take her aside one day soon and build a fire under her.

For old time's sake.

Holly and Grant left together after the taping, and Gypsy was left alone to take care of post-taping details. She felt empty inside, and today, despite a thousand things to be done, her job didn't fill the hole. She was living in another woman's body, but she had systematically destroyed that woman's personal life. She had halted her relationship with Casey, helped Perry get a promotion, and gracefully rejected Grant. She knew enough about her past to realize that there were a number of men she could call tonight who would take her to dinner or somewhere distinctively more intimate. But she had proved that sex for sex's sake was not her cup of tea, and she had no energy for fending off would-be lovers.

She wondered what she would do with the rest of her life. She loved her job, but the job wasn't enough. What had she planned before the accident? At the peak of their marriage Elisabeth and Owen had talked endlessly about what they would do when Grant was gone and Owen had enough talented architects in his firm to relieve him of the most burdensome projects. Owen was not a man who would ever retire; he loved what he did far too much. But Elisabeth had looked forward to a time when he would slow down, take only the challenges that really appealed to him, and find more time to travel for pleasure. They had talked about building a house on Martha's Vineyard for long, wicked weekends.

What had Gypsy planned?

Early in the evening she was still at her desk, elbows propped on the desktop and fingertips massaging her forehead. Somehow everything always came back to Owen. It had been easier when she believed that he didn't love Elisabeth at all. She still didn't know exactly what he felt, but she couldn't ignore his loyalty to his comatose wife. The word "devotion" came to mind. The word "guilt" did, as well. She wondered if his constant attendance at Elisabeth's bedside was one or the other or a murky combination that even he didn't understand.

"Gypsy?"

She looked up to find Kendra in the doorway. She straightened. "Got something interesting for me?"

Kendra shook her head. "I wish. I really wish. But that bootlegging Missouri sheriff is as happy as a clam living in the wilds of Idaho with a new wife, twin baby boys, and right-wing survivalists. He trains weekend warriors to live off the land."

"Corn liquor 101." Gypsy put her head in her hands again.

"And the bank president who was funding the cathouse in downtown Des Moines has a new job in California as the owner of a topless bar. He's making money hand over fist, and he just married his star dancer, who by all accounts has the biggest hooters on that side of the Mississippi."

"Well, it sounds like he's got his hands full."

Kendra rolled her eyes. "Jeez, you've been at your desk too long. Go home."

Gypsy stood. It was good advice. "I don't suppose you'd like to go somewhere for dinner?"

"Love to, but I'm meeting someone for drinks. I answered a singles ad. Nothing like a little danger to spice up a life, huh?"

"Any bets about what the guy looks like?"

"You know, I really don't care? I'll settle for fat, bald, and toothless if he treats me right. I'm sick of the come-on, the groping, the posturing. I want somebody who's still going to be there when I wake up the next morning. Somebody I can talk to."

"You deserve somebody like that." Gypsy smiled. "But preferably somebody with teeth."

"I hardly even notice anymore when you do that."

"Do what?"

"Get all warm and cuddly."

"It's a miracle. In the blink of an eye I was transformed into everybody's favorite maiden aunt."

Kendra clapped her on the back before heading for the door. "Go home, order Chinese, then get some sleep. Things will look better in the morning."

Gypsy gathered the notes she planned to work on at home that night and called downstairs to have security notify today's resident Billy Boy that she was on her way out.

"There's a guy here to see you," the security guard said. "No credentials on file. No appointment, and he's not on your list. Billy's talking to him now."

"Billy himself, huh? What's the guy's name?"

"Owen Whitfield."

She stood with the receiver in her hand and stared into the newsroom.

"Miss Dugan?"

She gripped the receiver tighter. "Ask him to wait. I'll be right down."

"Sure thing."

She hung up. Her hands were trembling.

Kendra poked her head back into the office. "You know, I could postpone this guy, Gypsy. If you'd like me to."

"It's okay. It looks like I've got plans after all."

"Hey, maybe your plan has teeth, too."

Gypsy smiled wanly. "He sure does. All of them except one lower back molar."

~ 20

SHE WASN'T DRESSED UP. SHE HAD CHANGED after the taping into black cuffed trousers and a sequined designer T-shirt that sported a picture of Chairman Mao with a bee stinging his nose. She had scrubbed her face, and now her street makeup consisted of lipstick, most of which she had chewed off halfway through the afternoon and a quick slash of eyeliner that only emphasized how tired her eyes were.

She took enough time to reapply the lipstick and comb her hair, but she knew Owen couldn't be trusted to wait. He wasn't particularly impatient, but like most creative people, his mind, and often his feet, would drift to another location if he was left alone too long. Elisabeth had often found him blocks from the place where she'd agreed to meet him, ogling rusticated stone joints or juggling Ionic and Corinthian columns in his head.

She took the elevator to the bottom floor and went in search of him. She found him in an animated conversation with Billy.

"Owen?" Her heels tapped an exuberant welcome on the polished marble floor as she covered the distance between them. He looked up, and his eyes warmed appreciably.

"I wondered if you would still be here," he said.

"I'm surprised to see you." She held out her hand.

"I'm surprised to be here."

"I'll bet."

Each regarded the other for a long moment. He looked tired, too, as if the whirlwind schedule that had once been his greatest joy was too much for him now. His wool suit—Brooks Brothers fall of 1995— hung from his once sturdier frame.

"Elisabeth?" she asked at last. "Is she . . . ?"

"Just the same. No changes."

"I don't know what to say."

"There's nothing you could. I got up early this morning and went in to be with her for a while. I knew I'd be too late getting back tonight." He realized he was still holding her hand. She could see it in his eyes. He dropped it immediately, almost rudely. "I didn't hear what had happened to you until this afternoon."

"Happened?" She was so busy drinking in the sight of him she was having trouble thinking logically.

"At the café. My God, Gypsy, you were almost killed."

"It's a familiar sensation."

"It's my fault. I should have taken you to the station. Hell, I should have driven you back to the city."

"Don't be ridiculous. I'm a big girl, and I told you I wanted to walk. I should have been perfectly safe. It didn't have anything to do with you. The guy probably would have gone after me on the train or—"

"Gone after you?" His eyes narrowed. "You mean you don't think this was a random mugging?"

She was silent. Trained newswoman or not, she had been indiscreet. The shooting was common knowledge, but the possible motivation behind it was not.

"This guy's protecting you?" Owen nodded his head toward Billy.

"And doing a very good job of it, too. You don't need to worry about me."

"Gypsy . . ."

He looked so tormented, her heart went out to him. "It's really okay. *I'm* okay. You don't have to worry about me. You have enough to worry about."

"I want to do something. What can I do?"

She started to repeat herself. There was nothing he could do. But she couldn't say the words. There was so much she wanted from him.

"Would you like to go somewhere and talk?" he asked.

She knew better than this. She knew what she should say.

"Miss Dugan, you'll need to go somewhere that I can secure," Billy said.

"I keep an apartment in the city, not too far away," Owen said. "It would be safe, and I was on my way over there before I stopped here."

She knew the apartment well, although it had been almost a year since she'd crossed the threshold. Owen kept it for the multitude of nights he worked too late to make the drive home, as well as for out-of-town guests and clients. She had decorated it herself. Many times since, she had wondered how Anna and Owen enjoyed her handiwork, particularly the beautifully crafted wedding ring quilt and pillow shams that graced the master bedroom.

She shook her head. "You don't have to—"

"Please come."

She didn't have the strength to say no. "Maybe for a little while."

"Good. I have friends stopping by later. You'll enjoy meeting them."

"Friends?"

"Just some friends of mine and Elisabeth's. They're coming by to check on me, I suppose. They worry." He shrugged.

"I'm glad. They should." Her palms began to sweat. She wondered who would be coming and how she would handle meeting people she had known forever.

"I'll have the doorman send out for something. Just tell me what you like."

She liked him, despite his infidelity during their marriage. She liked knowing that despite all the absurdities, all the incongruities and universal mysteries that had brought them to this point, they were going to spend the evening together. And she disliked herself for falling prey to all those feelings so easily.

"I'll need to run upstairs and get my coat and purse."

"I'll be happy to wait."

She nodded. Where were the words that should be rising to her tongue? Where were the excuses that would keep her from spending another evening with him?

She turned away and blindly headed for the elevators again. There were no words and no excuses. Because despite all the ways she had grown stronger from living Gypsy's life, she still could not refuse Owen Whitfield anything.

They ordered Indian food, one of the few cuisines Elisabeth hadn't enjoyed but Gypsy relished. Owen stripped off his jacket and tie and reheated the fragrant coconut soup, which they ate with parchment-thin papadoms. They swilled ice-cold beer and plates of basmati rice to offset the spiciest chicken vindaloo Gypsy had ever encountered and finished with raspberry ice he retrieved from the farthest depths of the freezer.

She had been starving. For a substantial meal instead of yogurt and corned beef sandwiches. For conversation instead of another episode of "The Whole Truth" plucked from the show's archives. For the sight of Owen Whitfield across the table from her, his gaze warm on her face and his laughter rumbling across the space between them.

"I've talked your ears off," she said, when the last

bite of raspberry ice was just a sweet memory. "And eaten everything in sight."

"How do you stay so thin?"

"Youth. When I'm thirty-five I'll start to gain weight. Then I'll have to watch everything I eat, join a gym." She smiled and lowered her eyes. "I'm well acquainted with the routine."

"Elisabeth was always absolutely sure she weighed too much. I loved every ounce she hated."

"Did you?"

"It made her a little less perfect, a little more approachable."

She looked up and cocked her head in question. "Approachable?"

"All those years together, and I'm not sure I ever lost all traces of awe."

"Is that really the way a woman wants her husband to feel about her? Did she nurture that?"

"Not at all. The fault was mine. I worshiped her. I was always trying to prove I was good enough to be her husband. She gave me my start, you know."

Gypsy, of all people, knew the story inside and out, but she cocked her head in question. "How's that?"

"Her mother's family had a large North Shore property, Brookshire, just outside Locust Valley, with seventy acres of land on the Sound, a thirty-room mansion of white granite that had been carried stone by stone from the hills of Vermont at the turn of the century, a Victorian stables that looked like the gingerbread house in 'Hansel and Gretel.' "

He turned up his hands in a what-can-you-do gesture. "Orchards, a poolhouse, clay tennis courts, a white frame gazebo larger than most Midtown apartments. The Brookshire wealth dwindled considerably over the years. Income and property taxes were the beginning of the end for most of those old estates. But somehow through it all the Brookshires managed to hold on to what was theirs."

"They don't call it the Gold Coast for nothing, do they?"

He smiled. "No one had lived in the mansion for years. No one could afford to. Elisabeth was raised in the gatehouse, a lovely old gray-shingled Colonial that's still standing. But we were married in the mansion. Her parents insisted. I'll never know what it cost them to open it for that one afternoon and evening. I suspect it cut Elisabeth's inheritance in half. But it was the party of a lifetime."

Owen had wanted to elope. By the time Elisabeth's wedding day was nearly over, she had wished fervently that she had agreed. "It sounds like something out of a fairy tale," Gypsy said.

"Not one with the standard ending," he said dryly. "We went from that house, that incredible house, falling down in stately grandeur all around us, to a shabby little Queens row house that was falling down, too, for our wedding night and another year after that. I had a job at a good firm, but I was paying off my student loans. We both knew it would be a long time before I got a chance to show what I was really worth. Then her parents died, one right after the other, and they left Elisabeth Brookshire."

When he didn't go on, Gypsy asked. "And?"

"Elisabeth came to me and asked me to develop the property for her. She knew she would never be able to hold on to it the way it was. By all practical standards the big house was beyond repair, and what little her parents had left her wouldn't have taken care of the taxes for a decade. So she asked me to develop the land, design seven one-of-a-kind homes that wouldn't look like a development at all and place them on ten-acre plots. She was sure there were a lot of very rich people who wanted to move to the North Shore and that there would be a tremendous demand for houses of the caliber she envisioned. I had ideas, of course, portfolios of sketches. I'd won a fellowship to Rome, and I spent that year designing the houses. When we got back to New York I presented six complete designs to the senior partners of my firm and told them that if they would let me oversee the entire project, that Elisabeth would sell the land to the developer of their choice at a very reasonable price."

She knew the rest of the story. Owen's ideas had been remarkable, the finished products even more so. The mansion had been dismantled at a great price and the original staircases, woodwork, doors, and door surrounds had reappeared in the houses Owen had built. The gazebo was now the centerpiece of tiny Brookshire Park, which had once been Brookshire's formal gardens. The stables and bridle paths were shared by several horse-mad families.

The white granite was used to build a Roman temple masterpiece on the choicest piece of land in the entire parcel.

Owen and Elisabeth's house.

"So that's how you got your start," Gypsy said.

"Elisabeth would have given me anything that was hers. And now when she finally needs me, there's not a damned thing I can do for her."

It was a touching story, a fairy tale in its own way. But Gypsy wondered how much of the story was about duty and gratitude, and how much about love. She couldn't help herself. She had to ask. "You know, I'm a reporter, and I make my living asking in-your-face kinds of questions. So forgive this one. But was your marriage really happy, Owen?"

He didn't seem startled or offended. They had fallen so naturally into talking about his feelings for Elisabeth that this probably seemed like the next logical step. "For a long time I was deliriously happy."

She waited. She *was* a reporter, and she knew that sometimes probing too hard destroyed the fragile bond between interviewer and subject. He looked beyond her, to a place she couldn't see. "How about some coffee to finish this off?"

Subject closed. She felt such a rush of disappointment she was afraid her voice would betray her. She managed a smile and a nod, and he left the small dining room before another word could be spoken.

The coffee took longer than it should. Even Owen, who was used to being served, knew how to make coffee. Gypsy wandered the apartment while the coffee and his self-control gathered strength in the kitchen.

Nothing much had changed. If Anna was routinely sharing this space with Owen, she hadn't yet made her mark. Familiar desert landscapes by a Taos artist Elisabeth and Owen had discovered on a business trip hung from the cream-colored walls. The walnut side tables and Haitian cotton sofas and chairs stood in the same groupings. She lifted a small granite statue of a cat that Elisabeth had discovered in an antique mall in Nyack. The cat had been a housewarming gift to Owen when he'd purchased the apartment. Elisabeth had told him he needed a pet when he stayed overnight in the city, and without missing a beat he had named the statue Jake. Jake had become a running joke between them; the cat's escapades were legendary.

She heard footsteps behind her, but she didn't turn. "This looks like the proverbial cat that ate the canary."

"And more besides."

"He has such personality."

"You can tell it's a he?"

"Definitely." Something wicked and dangerous overcame her good sense. "He needs a name. Something like Alfred. Or Jake. He's definitely a Jake."

Owen was silent. She turned and smiled into suddenly suspicious eyes. "Am I wrong?"

"How did you know that?"

She feigned surprise. "Don't tell me that's really his name?"

"Yes."

"Now that's funny. I guess he was so clearly a Jake we both picked up on it."

"What else have you picked up on?"

"Well, not a lot. I like the way you've done this room. It's not so Southwest that it will have to be redecorated when people get tired of cactus and sandstorms. It's subtle. The paintings will be treasures some day. The furniture is classical enough to be used in a number of interesting decors." She shrugged. "But what else should I expect from you?"

"What about your place?"

She thought about her apartment. With the help of a decorator that Elisabeth had used, Gypsy had transformed it into a cozy space. She had given in to a taste for flowers and whimsy, neither of which had fit into Owen's Roman temple by the Sound. She had covered the floor with large pastel rag rugs, painted the walls a soft yellow, used bright pottery, antique lace, and summer cottage furniture to enhance her spectacular view of Central Park. Now when she came home from work, she looked forward to opening the door and kicking off her shoes.

"I don't think you'd like what I've done," she said. "It's cluttered and kitschy. But it's mine."

"This isn't mine. Not really. I never really live here, it's just a place to stay until I can go home. It feels like a hotel, or a house that's been abandoned. No one suffers or loves here. Not really."

No one loves here. Was she reading what she wanted to hear in Owen's words? Hadn't he brought Anna here after all? Maybe Marguerite's observation that Owen didn't seem to be having any fun was true.

Gypsy was instantly angry with herself for grasping at straws. Scarlet A's were out of fashion. There was no way to know what Owen did and with whom when he wasn't sitting at his wife's bedside. And if he didn't bring Anna here, there were a thousand other places they could go, including and especially, Anna's apartment in the Village.

"I suspect you've suffered here," she said. "You probably suffer everywhere you go these days. Owen, you seem like a man eaten up with guilt and sorrow." She tried not to stress "guilt" too overtly, but she was unsuccessful.

"Guilt?"

"You've expressed it every time we've talked." She set Jake back on the table. She'd been clutching him like a good luck charm.

"How could I not feel guilty? Have you ever lost somebody you loved? Do you have any idea what it's like?"

"Yes." She had lost him.

"There are things I *should* feel guilty about. And now I'm stuck with them. Stuck forever."

A part of her wanted to shout "good." It was the natural response. Owen felt guilty, and he was going to have to live with it because Elisabeth was in no shape either to forgive or release him. But Gypsy felt no exaltation at his pain. He was not a demon, just a man who had given in to temptation. At the center of his heart he was a good man.

She moved closer and reached for his hand. "I guess you just have to make yourself move on."

"I can't move on. Elisabeth's alive, at least some part of her."

"Will it be better if she dies?"

His hand jerked spasmodically. "I can't even think about that."

She wanted to tell him he'd better think about it. She was no expert on miracles. In fact she, of all people, had become a true believer in the extraordinary. But Elisabeth's death seemed inevitable, and Owen wasn't prepared.

"I can't make myself believe she's going to die," he said, as if he could read her thoughts. "I expect to walk into her room some evening and find her sitting up in bed watching 'Masterpiece Theater.' I expect it every time I walk through the door."

"Owen . . ."

"I don't know how we got into this. I'm sorry."

"So am I. I'm not sure if you need to keep talking about this or if you need to let go of it."

"One doesn't help and the other isn't possible."

They were holding hands again. He was gripping hers like a drowning man hoping for rescue.

But there was more between them than a need for comfort. He let out a breath, as if he had been holding it tightly inside him. His eyes flicked down to their joined hands and then back to hers. Awareness caught, like parched wood touched by an errant falling ember.

"Let's talk about you." He didn't drop her hand. "And stop talking about me."

"We talked about me earlier. I told you all about my job."

"That's hardly the same thing."

"Maybe not, but it's close. I don't really have a life." She heard her own voice. Lower, sultrier than Elisabeth could have managed, a come-hither, play-at-your-own-risk invitation he couldn't ignore.

"Why not?"

"I guess I've been feeling my way since the accident. My priorities changed. *I* changed."

"How?"

"I guess I'm thinking more about the future and what I want. I suppose I used to be a one-day-at-a-time sort of gal."

That seemed to make sense to him, even without understanding exactly why. "And what is it you think you want now?"

"I haven't gotten that far."

"Home? Family? Kids?"

"Love, I think."

"I would think that was no problem at all."

"Would you?"

"You're beautiful, clever. Nice. That was the part I never expected. But you are. I can't understand why every man you meet doesn't fall in love immediately."

"Some do. But the only man I ever loved fell in love with someone else."

He was silent a moment. His gaze traveled over her. She could feel it like a warm caress. He was looking at her in the way that a man looks at a woman when he's contemplating taking her to bed. He had looked at Elisabeth the same way a long time ago. When his eyes met hers again, they were hooded, as if he was struggling not to show his thoughts. "He was a fool."

"I thought so."

"Then forget him."

"I've yet to make that happen."

His gaze dropped to their hands. He seemed surprised they were still touching, but he didn't pull away, as he had before. "It sounds as if we're both much too vulnerable right now."

"Yes."

He looked as if he wanted to lower his lips to hers. She wanted him to kiss her. She needed it as much as she needed air. She wanted to sink against him, forget that she was someone else now, forget the years when they'd drifted slowly apart and neither of them had tried to stop it.

"You're very young."

She smiled sadly, swaying slightly toward him as she did. "Inside I'm as old as you are, Owen. Every bit as old."

"Gypsy . . ." He put his hand on her shoulder, as if to steady her. He pulled her toward him instead.

The intercom buzzed.

She jerked backward; her heart skipped a beat, then slammed against her rib cage like a frightened bird. "Holy bejeepers."

"I told you I was having company." He stepped

backward, breaking all contact and checked his watch—an Anfiteatro from Bulgari's that Elisabeth had given him as an anniversary gift when she'd still felt they had something to celebrate.

She crossed her arms to ward off the sudden chill. "I could leave. I should, in fact."

"No." He answered so quickly, so impulsively, that she knew he didn't want her to go. "Stay. Please. At least meet my friends."

"Won't they find it odd that I'm here with you like this?"

"The only person I have to answer to is lying in a nursing home bed. She doesn't know where I am or what I'm doing." His eyes told her the rest. "And we have nothing to be ashamed of."

Not yet. He never would have added the last. She could see regret warring with desire. He had been as enraptured by her as she with him. If the intercom hadn't squawked . . .

It squawked again, and she was passionately grateful. She had almost made the most grandiose mistake of a mistaken-ridden life.

He left to speak to the doorman, then he went into the kitchen to check on the coffee. When a knock sounded he was ready.

And she was ready to go back to her apartment and have a double shot of Jameson's and a good hard cry.

Owen came back into the room and she got her first glimpse of his guests. Missy Adamson, her dark hair stiffened by spray into a Wagnerian helmet, was followed at a distance by Richard who was chatting with Marguerite and Seamus O'Keefe. Gypsy's eyes squeezed shut involuntarily. She would answer to Marguerite for this.

"Gypsy, meet my friends."

She stepped forward and struggled to remember who she was. Not Elisabeth, the woman who had counted these people among her closest friends. But Gypsy, who didn't know them at all.

She shook hands and murmured names, smiled and nodded until she came to Marguerite. Marguerite gripped Gypsy's hand with the same force that she gripped a tennis racket on a game point serve. It was all Gypsy could do not to screech in protest. "Miss Dugan," Marguerite said, lifting one aristocratic brow. "How interesting to find you here."

Gypsy retaliated. "How are you, Mrs. O'Keefe. It's good to see you again." Gypsy smiled her flirtatious anchorwoman smile.

"You two know each other?" Owen asked.

Gypsy continued to smile. In retaliation for the handshake she was going to let Marguerite get them both out of this one.

Marguerite lifted her chin and looked down her straight-as-a-Republican nose. "We ran into each other in the park one morning. We seem to share it."

"And other things," Gypsy said. "I was delighted to see we have common interests."

"You've been hobnobbing with celebrities, and you didn't even tell me?" Seamus shook his head at his wife. "You're hopeless, Marg."

"We've met, too," Richard Adamson said to Gypsy.

She couldn't remember, of course. But she did vaguely remember a conversation at the dinner party Elisabeth and Owen had given on the night before her miraculous transformation. Richard had said that he'd met Gypsy and despised her.

"Yes, I think I remember." She nodded politely. "A long time ago."

"You have a good memory, then. Because it has been a long time."

She wondered if that was true. She hoped to God it was because if there was more to the story, it very well might be that Richard Adamson and Gypsy Dugan had gone to bed together. She had no evidence that the former Gypsy was the tramp she'd led the world to think she was, but neither was there any to suggest she had indulged in one committed, long-term relationship at a time. She had liked men. And she had probably gone to bed with some very famous ones to get stories.

Richard Adamson might very well have been one of them.

She dimpled coquettishly, just to test the waters. "I never forget an important face. And you're becoming important in New York, Richard. It's too bad there's absolutely no scandal attached to your name. I would dearly love to do a story about you. We all would, but you seem so determinedly upright."

Missy took Richard's arm, like a bodyguard who smells danger. "Wouldn't that be a story in itself? A politician who doesn't lie, steal, or fornicate? I'd think that's all your show would need for a headline."

Gypsy wagged her finger playfully. "I'm afraid we'd just see that as a challenge and dig a lot deeper. Richard, you must have cheated on a test paper in prep school, or tortured tadpoles at summer camp. We'd find you out."

For just the briefest instant he looked dismayed. Gypsy had been teasing, and her aim had been at herself, not him. She'd been making fun of her show and what she did. She had no illusions that "The Whole Truth" was hard news, and she'd wanted everyone to relax and see that. Now she thought that she might well have uncovered a story, instead.

"He doesn't get near tadpoles for fear of the animal rights vote," Missy drawled. "If he did, he'd declare their puddle to be national wetlands and have it cordoned off."

Everyone laughed. Gypsy did, too, but she didn't take her eyes off Richard. He was fine now, nicely recovered. But when he looked back at her animosity flared briefly in his eyes.

"I've made coffee," Owen said. "I'll serve. Everyone make themselves comfortable."

"I should go." Gypsy looked at her watch, although

it didn't matter what time it said. She wasn't going to stay and risk giving herself away. She shook her head regretfully. "I've got a taping to do first thing in the morning, and I'd better get some sleep or they'll be looking for someone without circles under her eyes to replace me."

"Yes, it's all about how you look on camera, isn't it?" Richard said.

"No. You'd be surprised, but it's really about how well I do my job. And I do it very well."

"You don't mean you go after your own stories now? When you were covering the Capitol I heard that the only thing you did between the afternoon and evening news was your nails."

The room was so quiet Gypsy could hear a clock ticking somewhere in the distance. "Did you?" she asked when she could speak calmly again. "I'm afraid that was just one of those rumors I planted to throw people off my scent. But I'm very skilled at getting information. It's what I live for. Let me interview you and we'll see what I can come up with."

"Children!" Marguerite clapped her hands. "Stop circling this instant. You are making me dizzy."

Gypsy turned back to Owen. "It's been a nice evening. Just what I needed. Thanks for dinner. You'll call if there's anything I can do?"

He nodded.

She said polite good-byes to the others. Owen got her coat and walked her to the door before he called downstairs to have the doorman tell Billy that she was on her way.

"I'm sorry," she said when he'd finished. "I don't know what came over me."

"Richard did, as a matter of fact. I'll apologize for him. Maybe he's had a hard day."

"Maybe he has." And maybe she would just see if she could find out why.

"Gypsy . . ."

She put her hand on his arm. Touching him was the

greatest pleasure she could imagine. "Let it go. We had dinner. It was good for us both."

"Maybe we shouldn't see each other again."

She knew he was right and that they would, anyway. "You need all the friends you can get right now. Don't cut me off."

He looked as if he wanted to say more. He didn't. He took her coat and held it as she slipped into it. "Make sure Billy is doing his job."

"I'm as safe as I can be." She stood on tiptoe and kissed his cheek. She hadn't meant to, although it was perfectly appropriate. His skin was smooth against her lips, and his scent was so familiar and welcome she wanted to inhale it forever. She stepped away from him before she pitched her lovesick body into his arms. "Take care, Owen." She opened the door and left him standing in the hallway of his apartment as Billy stepped off the elevator to escort her downstairs.

✑ 21

MARGUERITE'S BLOND HAIR ESCAPED IN wisps from a bun secured with ivory chopsticks. She had paced the length of Gypsy's apartment twice, and she was just warming up. It was early morning after their meeting at Owen's apartment, and Marguerite was paying an unannounced social call. Her mother would have been appalled.

"What exactly did you think you would accomplish going to Owen's apartment like that?"

Gypsy snuggled back against a Laura Ashley slip-cover and watched as her friend barely skirted the coffee table. "I'm not playing games with Owen, if that's what you're afraid of."

"Maybe that's not your intent—"

"Come off it, Marg. You don't have any idea what this is like for me, no matter how hard you try to put yourself in my place."

Marguerite faced her, hands on hips. "You have a size five body, legs as long as Birch Haven's front drive, and skin that will not wrinkle if you spend the entire night submerged in a Hollywood hot tub. I'm supposed to feel sympathy?"

"Give it a try."

"You know, you really never are satisfied."

Gypsy didn't answer. There was no point. Marguerite was winding up, and there would be no stopping her.

"You were not happy as Elisabeth. Oh, you never complained, but the unhappiness was there. We could all see it."

"Owen didn't."

"Hogwash. He certainly did. And, of course, you never told him why you were unhappy, so the poor man could not do a thing about it. He was left to imagine the worst. And now you're not happy as Gypsy. You want what you had as Elisabeth. Maybe it's time you gave some thought to making up your mind."

"Whoa! Why don't you back up a bit. What do you mean Owen was left to imagine the worst? Has he said something to you?"

"I was your best friend. I had no choice but to watch you. Owen did not need to say a thing."

"Then why didn't you say something?"

"It was not my place to interfere—"

"That seems to have changed."

"Quite a lot has changed."

The sofa was no longer comfortable. Gypsy got up and went to the window. The city was waking up. Just across the street a group of school children in prison gray uniforms huddled together for warmth under the watchful eyes of a man who looked like a strip joint bouncer. "What did Owen imagine?"

"I would be guessing."

"Then guess."

"All right. I think he believed you had fallen out of love with him. He was never that certain of you, Elisabeth—"

"I'm not Elisabeth. Not anymore."

"Fine. He was never that certain of Elisabeth. I don't think it will matter how rich and successful Owen Whitfield becomes. There's still the tiniest part of him that's reduced to nothing more than the son of immigrants who were the children of Polish peasants.

It does not matter how egalitarian he is in theory, in his nightmares he still believes Elisabeth is the lady of the manor."

He had said something similar himself last night. Tears filled Gypsy's eyes. She wiped her cheeks with her fingertips. "Lord, I didn't cry this much when I was approaching menopause in another body."

"Maybe Gypsy was more comfortable with her feelings than Elisabeth was ever allowed to be."

"Oh, come on. Pop psych from you of all people?"

"I grew up with the same expectations that you did."

"Elisabeth still loved Owen. Right up until the day she realized she wasn't the only woman in his life. I don't know what I feel now. Maybe Elisabeth should have gone to him, tried to tell him how she felt right at the beginning. Maybe she should have demanded that he tell her the truth about Anna. But she was afraid that's exactly what he'd do."

"Elisabeth was always a bit of a coward."

Gypsy played with the satin sash of her bathrobe, tying and retying it. "Gypsy is, too. But only when it comes to Owen. Gypsy can do things Elisabeth only dreamed about. You can't imagine what it's like. I didn't know Elisabeth was bound by so many chains until someone unlocked them."

"Then why aren't you happy?"

"I don't know!"

"Do you love Owen?"

"He broke my heart."

"And you let it happen."

"Square one. It's getting familiar."

"No, square one is this: Why were you with Owen last night?"

Gypsy stuffed her hands in her pockets to keep from untying the robe one more time. "I don't know. But if the opportunity arises, I'll be with him again."

"You cannot go back. You really are not Elisabeth anymore. You were right about that."

"Then I'll be Gypsy."

"He's attracted to you."

Gypsy faced Marguerite. Marguerite no longer looked angry, but she was clearly worried. "Why do you say that?"

"It was perfectly obvious last night. He never once took his eyes off you."

"Didn't he?"

"Seamus noticed it, as well."

"Seamus told you that?"

"Seamus is worried, too. Of course he does not know what I do."

"Well, he has cause to worry. After all, if Owen had an affair with me, it wouldn't be his first, would it? It's becoming a habit. Next thing we know he'll be standing up in smoke-filled meeting halls saying, 'Hi, I'm Owen, and I'm a sex addict.' "

"It would be Owen's first affair while his wife is lying comatose in a nursing home bed."

"Maybe. But wouldn't that make it more forgivable?"

"Will it be forgivable to Owen? If you end up in bed with him, what will he think of himself?"

Gypsy raised her chin a notch and stood a little straighter. "I really don't know. I can't even imagine what he thinks of himself now. How could he come home at night and face his wife after sleeping with Anna? Not that he ever came home that damned often."

"Oh, grow up! Do you think you're the first woman whose husband has cheated on her?"

"*My* husband hasn't cheated on me. I don't have a husband."

"Tell me you are not going after Owen to prove something to yourself."

"What do you mean?"

"I can think of two possibilities. Either you are trying to prove that this new 'you' has what it takes to get Owen Whitfield in bed. Or you are trying to prove that he *is* capable of infidelity. You have never been a hundred percent certain, have you?"

"Ninety-nine point nine. I never had the opportunity to be in the same room while he and Anna were down to their skivvies engaging in foreplay!"

"Have you set out to make Owen go to bed with you?"

Gypsy almost wished she could say yes. If she were that sort of woman, her life might be easier and even more successful. But in the baggage she had toted from her life as Elisabeth had come a ton of scruples and another of compassion. "No, I haven't. I never bargained on the attraction we feel. He's twenty years older than I am. I was still hurt and angry. I never thought . . ."

"Lord, lord."

"What would be wrong with it? I'm the closest thing to a wife he has left."

"His *wife* is in a coma on Long Island."

"I'd love to see the courts take up that one, wouldn't you? Think of the headlines. Wife's soul in new and better body. Husband forced to choose . . ."

"I am going home."

Gypsy couldn't blame Marguerite. She sighed and the fight went out of her. "I'll walk you to the door."

Marguerite picked up her coat, which looked suspiciously like a sixties Nehru jacket. "Just think about the consequences. Please."

"I fumble through every minute just waiting for heaven to intervene again. How can I think about consequences?"

"If you can not think about consequences with Owen, then think about some with Richard."

They stopped in the foyer. Gypsy tried to read Marguerite's expression, but it was hopeless. She fished. "What on earth do you think all that hostility was about last night? I've never seen Richard like that."

"I don't know if I have anything to say that you want to hear."

"Try me."

"Are you listening with Gypsy's ears or Elisabeth's?"

"I can't separate us anymore."

"Well, Richard was never the goody-goody Elisabeth believed him to be. They had been friends too long for her to see him clearly."

"You've been friends with him every bit as long."

"But I see everyone clearly. Loyalty has never hindered my eyesight."

"What are you trying to say?"

"Richard is not above political shenanigans. I remember when he was at Yale and running for some student office or the other. He befriended this odd young man—Web, I think his name was—to help him run his campaign. They put together a frightfully schlocky platform that tied in the war, student protest, the draft. I can't remember it all. But the worst part was that he totally misrepresented his opponent, who was far more sincere about those issues than Richard himself. Richard won, of course. And he will keep on winning every election he enters unless someone exposes him for what he really is."

"And what is he?"

"A ruthless manipulator who only gets more so with age."

Gypsy opened the door. "Have you ever met a politician who wasn't a ruthless manipulator?"

"You have always been blinded by Richard's Democratic ideals."

"And you've always been disgusted he wasn't a Republican."

Marguerite stepped over the threshold. Someone was frying bacon and Marguerite wrinkled her nose. "Think about what I've said. Richard seemed very wary of Gypsy Dugan last night, and Richard has powerful friends."

"I'll think about it. In fact I'm planning to look into it." Gypsy watched as her friend started down the hall. "Marguerite . . ."

"Yes?" Marguerite turned.

"The friend's name was Web? For some reason I don't remember him."

"He was Richard's roommate during his senior year. An odd-looking young man with short legs and huge shoulders." She smiled a little. "He had strange hair, like a steel wool pad. He could have been a linebacker if those little legs had just moved faster."

Gypsy had an instant vision of another man who fit that description nearly thirty years later. "I still don't remember him."

"I think they became friends after you refused to go out with Richard anymore. Your friendship was rather strained for a while, wasn't it?"

"This Web . . . His real name wasn't Desmond, was it? Desmond Weber?"

"Well, yes. Actually I think that was it. I'd forgotten. You must have met him, after all."

"Yes, I met him."

"I wonder whatever happened to Web. He was a funny boy, but I rather liked him."

Gypsy wouldn't have put the facts together so quickly if she hadn't known that Des had gone to Yale. But the relative age and unusual description had fit like a suit from Savile Row. Des and Richard had been friends, close friends from the sound of things. And neither one of them had ever mentioned the other in her presence—or Elisabeth's.

"Kendra, got a minute?" Several days after her conversation with Marguerite Gypsy stood beside Kendra's desk and fiddled with the other woman's letter opener, which was shaped like a medieval dirk. It could do a fine job of drawing and quartering the competition.

"For you? Two." Kendra popped a wad of gum. "Nothing on Thad Lester."

"The gospel singer with all the illegitimate kids?"

Kendra popped in affirmation. "His wife divorced him and took up with a grunge rock star out in L.A. Thad's singing country and western in small-town bars and witnessing for Jesus on the side. He hasn't been anywhere near New York, and he claims he's a happier man now that he's repented. Sounds like he gives you and the show credit for saving his soul."

"This is a weird, weird job."

"He's even paying his child support."

"I've got someone I want you to investigate. Can you come in my office for a moment?"

Inside the office Gypsy closed the door behind them. "Kendra, do you know who Richard Adamson is?"

"Sure. I voted for him for congress. Cripes, Gypsy, don't tell me he's screwing elephants or shooting radiator fluid. I don't want to know."

"I don't know what he's doing." Briefly, and without mentioning Owen, she told Kendra about her encounter with Richard. Then she told her about Des. "Doesn't it seem odd that Des has never mentioned the connection?" she finished.

"I don't know. Maybe there's never been a reason. Adamson keeps his nose clean. I don't ever remember hearing a rumor of any kind about him."

"Then why was he so hostile toward me?"

"Maybe the two of you have a past. He hinted at one, didn't he?"

"Not that kind. And if we do, I don't remember it." Gypsy thought about that a moment. If she'd been to bed with Richard, she was just as glad she didn't remember.

"What do you want me to do?" Kendra asked.

"I want you to do some research on Adamson without mentioning it to Des. Do you mind?"

"No problem. I'm pretty autonomous. Of course if Des asks me point-blank . . ."

"He won't, and if he does, we'll know that Adamson's been talking to him. That will be interesting, too."

"I ever quit this job, I'm going to become a private dick. Pay's better."

"Think of this assignment as practice." Gypsy unlocked her desk drawer and took out her purse. "I'm going to the Bronx with my crew for some background shots of the Norman Carroll neighborhood."

"Perry's doing all right?"

Perry had been a Norman Carroll student now for two days. "Great. Last thing I heard two guys already asked her to have sex and one of the girl gangsters tried to trip her on the stairs. She made a C on her first algebra test, but the teacher was suspicious and demanded she take it again."

"I've got a lot of admiration for you for doing this story. It might really change some things."

There were a million students in the city's public school system and seventy thousand teachers, and this was only one television show. Gypsy didn't have any illusions. "You know, for the first time in a long, long time, the scores on standardized tests in the city's schools went up this year."

"Yeah?"

"And now they're talking about cutting the educational budget. Do you think what we're trying to do here might have an impact on funding?"

Kendra shrugged. "Maybe not. But you could talk to your friend Richard Adamson. Maybe if he's elected governor, that'll change, too."

"You're still here?"

Hours and a trip to the Bronx later Gypsy looked up to see Casey standing in her doorway. His hair was rumpled, as if he had been finger-combing it while he worked, and his five o'clock shadow had progressed to something darker and sexier. It was past nine o'clock, and apparently he hadn't thought about going home yet, either. "You, too?"

They stared at each other for a long moment before he spoke. "I thought maybe we ought to compare notes."

She knew he was referring to their search for her would-be assassin. All their conversations revolved around that now. "I'll warn you, I haven't eaten, and grouchy doesn't come close to what I'm feeling. Any chance we could grab some dinner while we talk?"

"Yeah. I think I wolfed down a hot dog from the stand at the corner about eight hours ago."

She stood and stacked the papers on her desk. "Your call where we go."

"Since when?"

"This is the new, reformed Gypsy, remember?"

"I'm in the mood for pasta."

"Sounds good. Let me comb my hair."

By the time she met him downstairs he had already given today's Billy Boy instructions. She was used to the rigmarole of entering and leaving the studio now. She scurried into the plain blue sedan while the young man stood guard, then Casey slid in behind her. They were moving slowly through the evening traffic before Casey spoke.

"I thought we'd go to that little place in the Village that you used to like so much."

"Sounds good to me."

"Still haven't regained any of your memory, have you?"

"Why? Was that a trick?"

"I just wondered . . ."

"I wish I could be more help. But I meant it when I said I wasn't going to get any better."

"So you don't remember the place we're going to in the Village. How about a certain taxi ride the night before the accident?"

"Did we get lost or something?"

He sighed heavily. "I've told Des I'll be leaving. He offered me more money. Then Tito offered me even more."

"Are you staying?"

"No."

She stared straight ahead. So many lives had changed in such a short time.

"What about you?" he asked after a while.

"I like my job."

"I think you like producing best of all."

She considered that. So far she had loved every minute of the Norman Carroll story. Not just because she had contact with Grant, but because she could shape the story herself. At least at this preliminary stage she worked well with her crew, and she'd discovered she had an instinct for background footage that might be valuable later when the story was edited. She could hardly wait to shoot the bulk of it, so that she could put everything together into a smooth finished product.

"I like being in front of the cameras," she admitted. "But I think I like what goes on behind them better."

"You could start your own production company when Tito gives you the ax."

"Have you heard something I haven't?"

"No. But he'll give you the ax eventually. That's the name of the game. You used to say you'd marry a rich man and live a life of leisure when Tito didn't want you anymore."

Elisabeth had married a rich man, or at least one who had become rich. The new Gypsy knew that wasn't all it was cracked up to be. "Were you rich enough to suit me?"

"You were thinking more along the lines of an oil-rich Texan."

"I was pretty short-sighted."

"You were scared to death of being nobody again. It haunted you."

Their Billy Boy driver turned on to a side street. With a stab, Gypsy recognized the neighborhood. Anna lived nearby, in an apartment above an art gallery that sold cast-iron fish skeletons and waffle sculptures made from discarded egg cartons. Elisabeth and Owen had come here for dinner when Anna had first begun to work for him, and about a month before the accident they had come for a party. Owen and Anna had stood in a corner talking to each other most of the evening while Elisabeth spritely entertained the rest of the guests. Her suspicions had caught fire that night.

The sedan pulled to a halt three doors down from the gallery. There was no way Gypsy could refuse to get out. What would she tell Casey? That in another life this was the block where her husband had become an adulterer? She walled off her memories and followed him inside.

The restaurant was brightly lit and overflowing with people. The smells were heavenly. They took a table in the back and Gypsy's bodyguard took one not too far away, where he could keep an eye on her and the door. She hardly noticed him. She had become used to having someone nearby all the time.

"What did I like here?" she asked.

"Nothing you'd admit to."

"Everything looks good." She ordered manicotti stuffed with chicken and spinach and handed the menu to the waiter.

"That's what you always ordered," Casey said.

"I'll have to remember not to rave about it."

They chatted about the show and shared a bottle of inexpensive burgundy until their salads arrived. She tore into hers ravenously.

He let her eat for a while, working on his salad, too. When she started to slow down a little he got out his notebook. "I've completed the list of people I was supposed to investigate."

"And?"

"Nothing interesting. I looked them over pretty good, too."

"Damn." She swallowed the last of her olives with regret.

"I gather you haven't had any better luck than I have."

"Neither has Kendra."

"Well, I'll go over what I've found and you can do the same. Maybe one of us will notice something the other one missed."

They were finishing dessert by the time they finished their respective lists. She had opted for assorted biscotti and cappuccino. Casey was working on amaretto cheesecake.

"I even delved into the Lucy McNeil story again," Casey said, closing his notebook. "No go there. McNeil doesn't strike me as the sort of woman who would seek revenge, anyway. Too classy. And if she did, it wouldn't be against you. You were new to the show, and you didn't have anything to do with it. Kevin was the one who exposed her."

Gypsy sipped the cappuccino, made just the way she liked it with a mountain of foam and espresso so dark and rich it was dangerous to leave the spoon in too long. Elisabeth had always finished a meal with Darjeeling tea and a slice of lemon. "Lucy McNeil. The congresswoman who was sleeping with a married man."

"Congresswoman who quickly became an ex-congresswoman."

She remembered a discussion about Lucy McNeil at the last dinner party she'd given as Elisabeth. "That was the biggest story of the season, wasn't it?"

"Our story. Our scoop. Lucy McNeil put us on the map."

"Our scoop? Is that right? I don't remember that part."

"Ours alone. We left the networks in the dust."

Elisabeth had been in Europe with Owen during the scandal and rarely able to watch television. Still, she was intimately acquainted with the events from watching hours of tape. Lucy McNeil, Democrat and feminist, had been caught with a married man, an associate of her attorney husband. She had lost her seat in the next congressional election by a landslide. Until that upset she had been the odds-on favorite to run for governor in the next election on the Democratic ticket.

Now Richard Adamson held that dubious honor.

"Let's talk about that a moment," she said carefully. "Tell me what you know."

"What do you mean?"

"How did we get the story?"

"I really don't remember. It was a little before my time. I was just starting to move up. Why?"

She debated telling him about her encounter with Richard at Owen's apartment. She improvised a little instead. "I met Richard Adamson at a party several nights ago. He was just short of hostile. I don't remember meeting him before." She tapped her spoon against her saucer until she was two stanzas into "Hey Jude." "Look, I'll level with you. I did a little digging. Richard is a friend of Des's from Yale. Has Des ever mentioned that to you?"

"Des?" Casey frowned. "No. Never. Are you sure?"

She nodded. "Here we have Des, who was Richard Adamson's former bosom buddy. There we have Lucy McNeil, who was conveniently caught on our cameras with her skirts up just before the election. Plus we have Richard, who suddenly has a clear shot at the governor's mansion. Do you think I've hit on something here? Are you going to run to Des with it?"

"Yes and no. And you should know better than to ask that last question."

"Thanks." She set her spoon back on the table

before she could launch into "Octopus's Garden."
"Where do you suppose we should go from here?"

"I'll look into Adamson's background."

"I know it inside and out." She smiled in answer to
Casey's cocked brow. "And not for the reasons you
think, oh ye of the small, narrow mind. I've followed
his career, that's all. But go ahead and check him
thoroughly. Maybe you'll find something I don't
know."

"What are you going to do?"

"I think I'll check out Des. I really don't know—at
least I don't remember—anything about his background."

"I don't know a whole lot that will help. He worked
for CBS for a while before Tito offered him the job
here. Before CBS he was in Hollywood working at one
of the studios. Before that your guess is as good as
mine."

"I know he went to Yale. I wonder if he graduated."

"I bet you'll find out."

"Bet I will, too."

Casey slipped his notebook inside his jacket. "I'll
ask around and see what I can come up with."

"Good." Casey glanced at his watch. "Going somewhere after this?" she asked.

"Flying to D.C. on the earliest shuttle in the morning. I've got to get home and see if I can grab a few
hours sleep."

She set down her cup. "We can go right now."

He put his hand on her arm. "You finish. I'll get a
cab. It'll be just as quick for me, and you can take
your time."

"I don't mind."

He stood and leaned over the table. She looked up
as he ducked his head to kiss her. His lips brushed
hers. A friend's lips. A friend's kiss. "I'll see you when
I get back in a day or two. I'll do some checking in the
meantime."

She smiled up at him. "Thanks for everything."

He stepped back, and she followed his retreat with her eyes. Her vision broadened, and suddenly she realized that Casey wasn't the only person in the restaurant that she knew. Standing right behind him, with Anna tucked in at his side like a shapely appendage, was Owen Whitfield.

⌒ 22

"**G**YPSY," OWEN SAID, INCLINING HIS head in what was almost a nod. His voice sounded oddly tight, like a baritone sax with a sticky valve. Her name was being forced through places it really wasn't meant to go.

Gypsy's throat wasn't performing well, either. Owen's name emerged like tires spinning on a gravel driveway. Casey's eyebrows drew closer together, a look he'd perfected when confronting serial killers and terrorists who maintained their innocence. "Gypsy?"

"Casey, this is Owen Whitfield and—" She stopped herself just in time. She wasn't supposed to know Anna Jacquard. She wasn't supposed to know that Owen had traded Elisabeth for this woman with the waterfall of mahogany hair, the tiny waist and ample breasts, the brain that could design entire housing developments and compute the costs down to a dollar between the soup and salad courses at a leisurely business luncheon.

"Anna Jacquard." For a professional woman, Anna's voice was soft, almost breathy. Marilyn Monroe had sounded more sure of herself.

"Anna." Gypsy wanted to choke off that altogether feminine wisp of sound. She wanted to wrap her long, strong fingers around the graceful column of Anna's neck and squeeze and squeeze . . .

"I'm Charles Casey." Casey held out his hand to Owen. Owen looked the way he had years before when Grant had presented him with earthworms or dying flies and crickets. He took Casey's hand with grim determination and he gave it back immediately.

Casey and Anna shook just as briefly. He turned to Gypsy. "I'll see you when I get back?"

She didn't know what possessed her, or at least which of a wide variety of emotions possessed her first and hardest. She turned on her smile and flashed dimples as deep as Donald Trump's pockets. "I certainly hope so." Had she whipped out a prenuptial agreement and a box of Trojans' finest, her intentions couldn't have been clearer.

Casey's brows were now a seamless, shaggy line, but he played along. "I can't wait."

There were few women who would have made him wait. Heat seemed to radiate from every pore of his body. His eyes alone raised the room temperature to something worthy of high summer. "Go—od." Gypsy trailed the tip of one scarlet nail along the back of his hand before she sat back in her seat and turned her gaze to Owen. "Is Elisabeth . . . Is your wife still holding her own, Owen?"

He nodded curtly. She turned her attention to Anna. "Take good care of Owen. He needs . . ." Her hesitation was brief enough to be deniable . . . "friends."

Anna's cheeks went from fashionably pale to ruddy. "He certainly does. Real friends, who've known him for a long time. Friends he can trust."

"Of course. And so does his wife."

Casey touched his fingertips to his forehead in silent salute, then he drifted toward the exit, his sexy amble followed by every pair of female eyes in the place.

The brass ceiling fans seemed to work harder to stir

the overheated air. Gypsy gazed down at a cappuccino that suddenly looked as appetizing as the bottom of the Hudson. "I have to be going, too. Why don't you two take this table? It's nice and private." She raised her hand to signal the waiter. Owen caught it firmly in his.

"That's not necessary—"

"It really isn't," Anna said, overriding whatever he'd intended to say. "I've got a lot of work to do tonight, and it's later than I thought." She didn't even glance at her watch to give the lie substance. "I'm going to fix something at home, I think."

"You're obviously committed to keeping your boss happy," Gypsy said pleasantly.

"You're sure?" Owen ignored Gypsy. He dropped her hand to take Anna's.

Anna nodded. "Have a good dinner. I'll see you Monday." She turned, her long skirt swishing against her calves, and followed Casey's path out the door.

Gypsy slid to the edge of the bench seat. "Looks like you're alone for dinner. Bad luck."

"What was that all about?"

She wrinkled her forehead in question and didn't reply.

"Why did you insult Anna that way?"

"Insult her? We were just making casual conversation."

"You were implying all sorts of things."

Her hands were shaking. Her body was familiar with the role of vixen, but her heart was contracting painfully. "There's nothing I'd have the right to imply, is there?"

"Is this Casey more than a friend?"

"That's something *you* have no right to imply. Why does it matter who either of us sleeps with, Owen? We don't sleep with each other."

He caught her arm as she stood and started past him. "You're direct, aren't you?"

"I make my living that way, remember? I pretend to

be something I'm not while I'm sneaking past all your defenses. Then I grab you by the balls till you scream for mercy." She touched his cheek the way she had touched Casey's hand. "And when you're done screaming I just leave you in an exhausted, used-up heap by the roadside."

"Who the hell are you?"

No one else could have heard his question, so softly was it voiced, but every cell in her body grabbed a companion for comfort. "I'm the woman who could have made you happy forever, if I'd just been given the chance."

His fingers clenched spasmodically, sending pain shooting through her arm. Then his hand fell to his side.

She slipped past him and didn't dare another glance at his face.

Hours later she was still furious with herself. Elisabeth, who'd had every reason to be jealous and vindictive, had held herself above either—except in her dreams. She had never confronted Owen about his relationship with Anna, not even by innuendo. Until the accident she had remained in rigid control, cool to his touch and aloof from him emotionally—at least on the surface. She had played the hand he'd dealt her with the calm precision of a master bridge player. They had built too much together to see it dismantled publicly and at great expense to them both. Owen could have his little fling, and if she didn't make a fuss about it, when he was finished, they could resume their life together as if nothing had ever happened.

Now she knew what a fool she'd been. That sort of self-restraint, bred into her by generations of upper-class women who endured infidelity with the same skill with which they played tennis or organized charity teas, was as abhorrent as Gypsy's dinner temper tantrum. As Elisabeth she had manipulated her world and her husband with a demented, repressed serenity. As Gypsy her manipulations were less subtle and just as destructive. She had learned so much from living Gypsy's life, but she still hadn't learned to be honest.

She was no closer to living the life she really wanted, the life she needed to make her feel whole, than she had been as Owen's wife. She had yearned for freedom, for the paths she hadn't taken, but all along she'd had what she needed at her fingertips. She had needed to take charge of her life. She had needed to go to Owen and tell him clearly, plainly what she wanted and needed from him. Then, she had needed to listen carefully to his responses and make her decisions based on that information.

Now she wondered what he would have told her if she had confronted him. Had her distance driven him away in the first place? Somewhere along the way had he looked to her for a reason to remain faithful? She knew she wasn't to blame for his adultery. She would not make the traditional mistake of believing that a woman was responsible for whatever her man did. But at some critical juncture in Owen's life, had she been so wrapped up in her own unhappiness that she had handed him a reason to follow his inclinations?

From somewhere above her, she heard music. Someone was playing one of Chopin's Preludes on a piano not completely in tune. The hum of traffic was a poignant background drone. Manhattan at midnight could be the saddest place in the world.

She didn't want to be here anymore. She couldn't bear to be here. She wanted to see Owen, to somehow explain to him all the things she had learned. She didn't know how such a thing could be accomplished. Owen was a man with a fertile imagination, but he would not believe her if she explained what had happened on the day of the accident. He had abandoned his religious roots long before she met him, and he cherished no hope of an afterlife. He did not believe in wandering spirits; he'd had no Spiritualist relatives, no childhood encounters with unseen dimensions. No matter how many details of their mutual past she recounted, he would believe it was a trick.

She had to talk to him anyway.

The unseen pianist took up a different prelude, one that was simpler but even sadder. Owen had played this one often. He was not technically skilled at the keyboard. His lessons had come late in life, when his fingers were stiff and clumsy. But what he hadn't mastered in agility he had made up for in emotion. She had shed unshared tears over Owen's preludes and polonaises. So many tears and so much laughter had been unshared.

She picked up the telephone, but she couldn't dial his number. Her number. Elisabeth's number. Everything was so mixed up in her head that she could hardly keep any of it straight. The only thing she knew for certain was that she couldn't talk about any of this on the telephone.

She dialed Billy instead. He wasn't asleep; he answered on the second ring and there was music playing in the background. She thought she heard a woman's sultry laughter.

"Billy?"

"Yes, ma'am."

She blessed his Southern Mama and the manners she'd drilled into him. "Billy, I'm sorry, but I need to go somewhere. Will you be able to take me?"

"Right now? Exactly right now?"

"I'm afraid so."

He groaned in distress.

"Maybe not right now," she said. "Maybe in a few minutes?"

"Well, ma'am, I'll be on my way directly."

"I'll be waiting."

She hung up and stared at the telephone. What would she say to Owen? How could she tell him the

things that she needed to without telling him who she
was?

And who was she, after all? The woman he'd been
married to? Not entirely. Not anymore. Gypsy
Dugan? Not that either. She was someone else, but so
was he. They had both moved through time to meet
again at this moment. She felt as drawn to him and to
a mutual shared destiny as Elisabeth had on their
wedding day.

The prelude finished with three somber minor
chords. "I'm on my way, Owen," she whispered.
"And for once, I'm going to make certain that we
understand each other before this night is over."

Elisabeth had never really loved the house Owen
had built for her. In reality, no matter what he'd said,
she had never really believed he had built it for her at
all. It was a showcase for his vast abilities, the grand
prizewinner of an architectural talent show. She had
viewed the plans with quiet good grace and the
finished product with wifely pride, but she had never
endeavored to add her signature to any of it. She had
let Owen and the house itself dictate the choice of
furnishings and decor.

Now, shivering in the moonlight and gazing over
the wide-terraced gardens that bordered the front
walk, Gypsy was silent with awe at the spectacle
before her. The house rose from the ground like a
ghostly apparition. Fog from the Sound danced in
luminous wisps around the foundation and crept and
twisted up pillars and doorframes.

She had never seen anything so magnificent—or
perhaps she had, but not with these eyes. The house
was simple, as only the very best things are. Her gaze
was directed to a window, a portico, a discreetly
arching roof, but nothing called out for attention. In
its silent elegance, its classic form, the house made no
demands.

Just as Elisabeth, for whom it had been built, had never made them.

It was clear to her now that Owen *had* been thinking of Elisabeth when preparing this design. He had built a temple for his own resident goddess, a woman who could be placed on a pedestal and worshiped from afar. And he had worshiped her until the needs of mortal man had intervened.

"Miss Dugan?" Billy's voice sounded behind her.

She held up one gloved hand without turning. "It's all right. I'm going up to the house."

"I can't just leave you here. The temperature's dropping."

"Please. Go find a bar. You'll have your choice in Bayville. I'll call you when I need you."

"I'll feel better when you're inside."

She knew he wouldn't leave until she was safe, yet she couldn't make herself take the final steps. She moved a little farther up the walkway. The annuals Elisabeth had planted in the spring were shivering in the cool mist. Silver dusty miller hovered over frost-tinged petunias, as if to protect them from the final destruction of winter.

She bent and plucked a thistle growing under the low-spreading branches of an azalea. The gardens had been Elisabeth's domain and joy, but she had never allowed herself to plant the vivid, erotic splash of flowers she craved. She had permitted Owen's vision to dominate here, too. The gardens she had yearned for, wildflowers and exotic creeping trumpet vine, tangles of wisteria and shrub roses so heavy with bloom they sagged in picturesque abandon, had seemed out of place against the austerity of the house.

"What was I thinking?" She spoke the question as if the thistle might answer. It had grown where it wasn't wanted, grown against the odds in darkness among a thick mat of shallow roots. And still it had survived to destroy the garden's perfection. There were others. She could see them now. Weeds she would never have tolerated. Wildflowers in training. On an impulse she squatted and scooped out a hole in the cold earth without removing her gloves. She dropped the thistle in and patted dirt carefully around it.

"Miss Dugan?"

She got to her feet and headed to the front door without a word. Door chimes sounded inside, hollow echoes in a house that seemed abandoned.

She didn't have to wait long. When he answered the door Owen had a drink in his hand. From the way he gazed at her she knew it wasn't his first.

He didn't say a word. He stepped aside and opened the door wider.

The white granite floor felt familiar under feet that had never stood there. She faced him without speaking. He was wearing gray flannel slacks, scuffed loafers, and a white shirt rolled at the wrists and unbuttoned halfway down his chest. He worked on his drink, measuring her with his eyes as he did. He looked exhausted or tipsy. Possibly both. He was definitely a man stretched to the limit, a man whose world had crashed around him. The aftershocks were threatening to destroy him.

"How did you know where I lived?" he asked at last.

She lied without blinking. "I did a story out here last year, and someone gave me a tour. Your house was on it."

"You have a remarkable memory."

"How I got here seems unimportant."

"Was that Billy at the end of the walk?"

"Yes. He'll come back for me when I call him."

She almost expected him to tell her that the time had come. Instead he turned away and started toward the library. She followed, but not on his heels. She stripped off her coat and gloves and surveyed the house as they moved through it. The dogs were probably shut up somewhere in the back or in their kennels behind the garage. She had missed their hulking golden bodies, their lolling pink tongues and generous affection. She wondered if they might have recognized her tonight.

The house was tidy and unchanged. Owen hadn't taken this opportunity to live out new interior fantasies, to banish whatever small personal touches had been solely Elisabeth's. Instead it was as if the house and all its contents had stood motionless in time.

Waiting for what? For whom?

There was a small fire in the fireplace and a stack of open books on the table in front of the leather sofa. An uncapped bottle of Stolichnaya Cristall stood watch on the mantel.

She was the first to speak. "The house is brilliant, but it's almost hard to believe anyone really lives here."

"No one does."

"Then you're spending your nights in the city?"

"I sleep here. I haven't lived anywhere since the accident."

"Would she want that?"

"I can't very well ask her, can I?"

"Are you going to ask me why I'm here?"

"I assume you'll tell me when you're ready. I haven't failed to notice that you speak your mind."

"I'm not even sure I remember why I came. It had something to do with straightening out what happened tonight."

"What did you mean when you said that you were the woman who could have made me happy forever?"

"We're caught in some godforsaken time warp, you and I. You feel it, too, don't you? Our destinies are intertwined."

"In some terrible destructive way." He reached in front of her to pour himself another inch of vodka, and he tossed it down as if it was the water it appeared to be.

"Perhaps," she said.

"I have a wife."

"And yet, you don't."

"I wake up most mornings and I fully expect to see her face beside mine. Though God knows why. We were only rarely sleeping together. Hope springs eternal, I suppose."

"Why weren't you sleeping together?"

"Do you always take what you want, Gypsy? Do you zero in on a target and go after it, no matter who it hurts?"

"Which Gypsy are we talking about?" She set down her coat and reached for the bottle, carrying it to a side table where gold-rimmed tumblers surrounded an ice bucket sporting romantic renditions of moose and mountains. She poured a healthy portion and fished for the last of several melting ice cubes.

"What do you mean?" he asked.

"The pre- or postaccident Gypsy? I can't tell you much about that other woman. I think she was confused about what she wanted. And I don't think she ever understood how to reach for what she really needed."

"And now?"

"She still finds it hard."

"What do you want?"

She wanted peace. She understood that much. She wanted an end to the turmoil, the cliff-walking, the sky-diving without a parachute. Elisabeth had yearned for excitement and challenge. She had needed those things, had deserved them, in fact. But she had deserved them as Elisabeth. Gypsy deserved peace.

"I want to know that whatever I am is enough." She straightened and faced him. "I don't need more or less. Just what I have, what I am."

"I don't understand."

She didn't understand completely, either. She tried to put her feelings into words. "We spend our whole lives wishing for the things we don't possess. Now I know that the things we really need are right in front of us, and most of the time we're just too scared to reach for them."

She doubted he understood or approved of those sentiments, and she couldn't blame him. Her explanation sounded like something from a New Age bestseller, facile and, at heart, just so many words. He set down his glass at the edge of the mantel. For a moment she thought it would crash to the floor as he crossed the room.

"I think you'd better call Billy now." He stopped right in front of her.

She leaned toward him. Inches separated them. Gypsy's voice emerged, low, sultry. But the words were Elisabeth's. "Do you really want me to go?"

He closed his eyes. He looked older and supremely tired. "Don't do this to me."

She touched his cheek with her fingertips. He needed a shave. Stubble rasped against her tender skin. "I've wanted you since the day I met you." It wasn't a lie.

He squeezed his eyelids tighter, as if looking at her would seal their fate. "I'm a married man."

"It doesn't matter tonight. Let me make up for what I've taken from you."

She didn't know where those words had come from, or which woman had spoken them. She only knew they were true. She hadn't come here to seduce Owen. At least she hadn't admitted it to herself, not even in the throes of revelations about honesty and reaching for happiness. But she had come to settle things with him, to somehow tie up the thousand threads of commitment, of caring and misunderstanding that were between them.

And this was the only way she knew.

She rested her forearms on his shoulders and buried her fingertips in his hair. Desire was like the fog outside, a twisting, rising wraith diffusing and filling the space inside her. Her skin tingled, her body temperature seemed to soar, to warm the space that was still between them. Her throat swelled, as if with tears, but none rose to her eyes. "Owen," she whispered. "Look at me. Please?"

He opened his eyes. They shone with resignation. "You're the picture of life. Of everything that's pulsing and moving and changing . . ."

She understood what he wasn't saying. That Elisabeth was none of those things.

She slanted her lips over his, kissing him softly, gently, turning her head to kiss him again. She stroked his hair as she kissed him and moved closer until her breasts were grazing his shirt.

He sighed, a defeated yet hungry sigh that filled her with sadness. "Oh, Owen."

"What do you want from me?"

His voice was barely audible. She wasn't certain he knew he had spoken out loud. "Just this. Just tonight," she said.

He rested his hands at her waist. Reluctantly. They were feather-light, as if he couldn't force them to bear the weight of his arms. When she kissed him again, his lips moved under hers.

She remembered a long-ago night when he had first begun his courtship of Elisabeth. He had not taken her to bed immediately, sensing, perhaps, her peculiar innocence. He had kissed her this way, hesitantly, as if he was waiting for something or someone to intervene, to snatch away a lifetime of potential happiness. Between each kiss he had given Elisabeth time to change her mind. She hadn't wanted time. She had known the moment his lips touched hers that this would be the man to take her virginity and her heart.

Now he wanted time for himself.

She didn't give it to him. She moved closer, pressing her breasts, her hips against him. He was already erect. He was easily aroused, and that hadn't diminshed with age. His response to Elisabeth had always made her feel supremely powerful. In their early years she had played with that power, discovering exactly

what turned him on. She had learned to brush her
hand casually against his hip or thigh, to unbutton her
skirts and let them sink like tropical blossoms to the
floor at her feet, to lift her hair off her neck and lower
her eyelashes like a nineteenth century Charleston
courtesan.

She had learned exactly how to sway against him
when they danced at the country club, how to moisten
her lips with the flick of her tongue while she was
gazing at his. And she had learned how to press her
hips against him just this way when she wanted to
arouse him quickly and tumble into bed for instant
passionate sex.

"You smell like her." His voice sounded strained,
like a man trying not to break in two.

She wasn't wearing perfume. Gypsy's vast collection had seemed too bold; Elisabeth's favorites had
seemed too sedate. But she always used the cosmetics,
the moisturizers and creams she had bought at Shu
Uemura. And she realized now that the subtle scents
would be familiar to him.

"I'm not her," she said. It was true. She wasn't
Elisabeth anymore. She would never be the same
woman who had sped toward Stony Brook on that
fateful afternoon.

"I want you to be."

"I know." She felt him relax against her. His hands
slid to her bottom and he pressed her closer. This
time he kissed her, a deep, draining kiss that took
desire to a new level. He was kissing Gypsy, but he
wanted Elisabeth. That knowledge was so heady, so
poignantly perfect, that she was boneless in his arms.

She slid her hands down his back to his belt and
grasped his shirt. With practiced ease he found the
zipper that snaked along her spine. She lowered her
arms and the dress bloomed in a scarlet circle on the
floor. She brushed her hands across his chest and
slipped buttons through buttonholes. His shirt joined
her dress at their feet.

She could undress this man with her eyes closed, so well did she know every inch of him. But she took her time unfastening his belt. Each moment seemed precious, one last chance to show him what he had meant to her—as she hadn't on her final night as Elisabeth. One last chance to say good-bye. She lingered over the clasp of his pants, the elastic of his boxers. His skin was cool and smooth beneath her hands and his erection strained against her palms when she touched him at last.

He groaned, a man beset by forces he would never vocalize. He stripped off her stockings and panties, which were Gypsy-flamboyant and brief. Her bra was such a simple affair that it took just the twist of his hand for it to join the growing pile of clothes beneath them. He clasped her hard against him, as if he could absorb all of her into his body, into his bloodstream and, possibly, his soul. She had reached the limit of her endurance. She stood on tiptoe and eased herself over him, letting him slowly fill her until there was nothing separating them except memories he didn't know they shared.

He groaned again, and she didn't know if it was with pleasure or shame. In this new incarnation she was tall enough to make love to him this way, to lift to her toes and lower herself again and again. The shattering pleasure of it erased everything else from her mind. She felt him clasp her tighter and begin to move with her. It was a dance, an erotic, explosive dance that could only lead to one thing, and quickly.

He lifted her high and she wrapped her legs around his hips. Carrying her he moved to the couch, just a few feet that seemed like miles. She wasn't aware exactly how he maneuvered them to their sides on the soft leather cushions. She could only feel the perfect friction of his body against hers, the warmth of his tongue as it moved in a flawless duet to the rhythm of their hips. She bore his weight with ease when he moved over her. She stared into his eyes as he thrust harder. There was pain there, and pleasure too intense to measure. She wanted to hold him this way forever, to resist the inevitable burst of ecstasy, to move into eternity in Owen's arms.

Resistance was impossible. She felt her response grow and turn inward, her pleasure intensify until there was nothing else but fulfillment. In that moment, when they were as close as two human beings could be, she closed her eyes and cried out. And she heard his cry at the same instant.

He sagged against her. She could feel every blessed inch and pound of him against her lithe young body. He was so familiar. His taste, his skin, the long, hard stretch of his legs along her own.

She could feel his breath against her neck and shoulder. She stroked his back and kissed his ear, rituals of past pleasures. At last he moved away, rolling to his side so not to hurt her, and turning his face so that she couldn't see his expression.

She had imagined making love to him again, but not what would come after. He moved to the sofa's edge, sat up and put his head in his hands.

She had to speak first. The silence was too ominous. "Owen?"

He didn't answer.

She knew his satisfaction had been as complete as hers. His orgasm had been as powerful, as prolonged as her own. She turned to her side and rubbed his back in silence.

"I wish you would go," he said at last.

Her hand stilled, then began its stroking again. "I'll go in a minute. Talk to me first."

"About what?" His voice was harsh.

"Owen, it's all right. We didn't hurt her." She could say that with conviction.

"You don't know what you're saying."

She felt the first prick of anger. "Don't I?"

"Elisabeth is the most ethical woman I've ever

known. She'd be devastated if she thought I'd been unfaithful."

"Oh, really?" Anger was more than a prick now. It was a jolt. The tender rush of feelings, the aching sweetness of unspoken farewells were fast dispersing. "You can't know. You couldn't."

"I know that you're putting me on." She sat up beside him, careful not to touch him. There was a telephone on the end table, and she dialed Billy's cellular phone number and told him to come for her. Then she stood and crossed the few feet to her clothing, angrily sorting hers from his and tossing her discards at his feet.

"What exactly do you mean?" He lifted his head and watched her dress.

"Come on, Owen. I'm not blind. I've seen the way your protégé looks at you, and the way you look right back. I saw it in Elisabeth's hospital room, and I saw it tonight. I'm surprised the sparks haven't ignited a fair piece of Long Island. Don't tell me you haven't slept with that Anna person."

"I haven't."

"Right." Her tone made it clear she didn't believe him.

"Is the attraction that obvious?"

"As plain as the nose on your face. I'll bet your wife had already discussed it with her attorney."

He stood and took her arm. "You don't know what you're talking about."

"We both know what I'm talking about!"

"I've never slept with Anna Jacquard." He spaced the words for emphasis. At the end, he dropped her arm. "There was a time when I wanted to. Once I came close. But I never have."

She stood, the top of her dress in her hands, one arm poking through a sleeve. "What's the point of lying? Do you think I'm in any position to judge?"

"There is no point. That's the point." He looked

past her, as if even the desire to have sex with another woman was something he should still be ashamed of, despite the fact that he was standing naked beside a woman he'd just filled with his sperm.

"You came close?"

"We'd both had too much to drink. We were celebrating a professional success. Anna's a tempting woman. I was growing old and Elisabeth had been growing more and more distant. I couldn't seem to breach the gap between us, and I was staying away from home as much as possible because I didn't know what else to do. Anna was just getting over another relationship, and she was vulnerable and available. She also had a bad case of hero worship, and I knew it. I almost took advantage of it. We got a room, went up the elevator together . . ." He looked back at Gypsy. "And then we talked about why sleeping together was a bad, bad idea. In the end I went home to spend the night."

There was no reason to lie. This was the moment when lesser men hauled out tales of their sexual exploits as extended proof of their manhood. His story had come out in a rush. It was a confession. "You never . . ."

He shook his head. "My wife is dying, and I'm here fucking you on a sofa she chose for me."

She couldn't think about his revelation. She couldn't think about everything it meant. She tried desperately to push it aside. "Tonight was a lot more than that."

He looked up at her. His voice was choked. "It can't be."

"No, it can be. It is and was." She touched his hand. "This was about her. About Elisabeth."

"I don't know what you mean!"

"There were things she didn't know how to say to you. I know there were." She held up her hand when he tried to interrupt, to tell her she was crazy. "Don't ask me how I know. Just believe me. She adored you.

You were everything to her. No matter what happens now, that part will always be true."

"You'd better go."

"Don't torture yourself over this, Owen."

"Please go. And don't come back."

She wouldn't come back. She knew that now. There was no way she could re-create what she'd lost, and there was no way he could survive the guilt of another encounter like this one.

She zipped her dress and slipped on her shoes. "If Elisabeth was half the woman you believe her to be, she wouldn't expect you to worship at an empty altar. You can't grieve forever. Find a way to make yourself happy. That's what she would want."

"You shared an accident and an ambulance with her. You never shared her heart!"

"For a few moments we shared eternity." She leaned over and kissed his cheek. Gently. Tenderly. "She wanted me to say good-bye to you. And now, I have."

She choked on the final word. He turned away from her, confused, distressed, and completely unaccepting of everything she had said. This hadn't been a farewell for him, but a test he had failed.

She let herself out the front door, but she couldn't wait for Billy on the front porch. She didn't care if half the hit men in New York were waiting in the shrubbery. She started down the drive on foot, putting distance between herself and the man she would never make love to again.

23

HE WOULD NOT DESTROY HIMSELF OVER ONE moral lapse. Gypsy knew Owen well enough to understand that. He was a sophisticated man whose expectations of himself were tempered by reality. But he would feel that he had deserted Elisabeth emotionally when she most needed him. He would retreat further into his pain.

Owen had not been unfaithful with Anna. He had not been unfaithful last night with Gypsy, either, though he could never know that. Despite their mutual alienation, despite the enduring silence that had characterized the final months of his marriage to Elisabeth, Owen Whitfield had remained faithful to his wife. Not because he was a saint. Not even because his ethical standards were higher than those of most men. But because he had loved her, and he had hoped, at the most primal level, that they could find their way back to each other before it was too late.

Gypsy watched the sky lighten over Central Park. She hadn't slept after the return trip from Long Island. She had tried desperately to sort out her feelings, to find a solution to this cosmic riddle which was now her life. There was no answer. When the intercom sounded and Marguerite was announced, she was almost grateful for the relief and the excuse to brew a new pot of coffee.

Marguerite was wearing overalls covered by a cashmere pullover of burnt orange. Her hair hung over one shoulder in an untidy braid and cotton gardening gloves hung from her hip pocket. She looked like a farmworker Seamus had commissioned to help him plant gardenias and camellias where lilacs and forsythia were meant to grow.

"A woman needs eight hours of uninterrupted sleep. Elisabeth's mother would not have approved," Marguerite said from the doorway, looking Gypsy over carefully.

"Elisabeth's mother would assume that women like me come out at night just to sink our bloodred nails into anything that can grow a beard."

"Is that what you did last night?"

Gypsy motioned for Marguerite to follow her into the kitchen, where the coffee was finishing its final drip. She kept her voice light. "Did you stop by for a blow-by-blow description of my close encounters?"

"No." Marguerite stepped from one side to the other as Gypsy reached around her for cups and saucers.

"Just to chat?" Gypsy glanced up at the clock. "It's not even seven."

"I know you leave for the studio early, and besides, I didn't sleep last night, either. Seamus dragged me to a party and I heard something there that I've been mulling over ever since."

"Oh?"

"It's about Richard and Missy."

"Oh . . . ?" Gypsy poured the coffee and set it on a tray. She went to the refrigerator for cream, one of Marguerite's vices. "Something to prove your theory that he's not the preppy do-gooder that Elisabeth believed him to be?"

"Just why did Elisabeth stop dating Richard? Do you happen to remember?"

"Because it was clear that he wanted a wife who

looked good on his arm at political rallies, and he thought he and Elisabeth made a stunning matched set."

"I rest my case."

"Okay. He's a politician through and through, and that means he's a conniving bastard."

"Do you remember Gloria Fields?"

Gypsy carried the tray into the living room and waved Marguerite toward a chair. "Is this some sort of test? Gloria and Elisabeth chained themselves to the same tree at the old Goldsborough mansion two summers ago to protest the developer's plans for the property. There were thirty upstanding North Shore women breaking the law and communing with tree trunks under your leadership. Of course I remember Gloria. There were hours to talk while the police went off looking for proper hacksaws and wire cutters. I know everything about her."

"She told me that Missy isn't happy with her marriage, and that for a while she considered leaving Richard."

The hair at Gypsy's nape prickled in good reporter style, but she kept her tone casual. "Try standing in chains with friend Gloria and see what a variety of gossip she comes up with."

"Do you suppose it's true?"

Gypsy poured the coffee. "Did she give any reasons?"

"No. She just indicated that Missy had lost faith in him."

"That's all?"

"She was purposely vague. She seemed to feel she'd said too much at that."

"Were you by any chance pumping people for information on Richard?"

"I did find Richard's reaction to you quite intriguing."

Gypsy debated telling Marguerite what she and

Casey had talked about. She couldn't think of a good reason not to. "Do you remember the Lucy McNeil debacle?"

"There is nothing a Republican likes better than a Democratic scandal."

"'The Whole Truth' scooped that story. I didn't realize we were the first to break it, but we were. And Desmond Weber, Richard's buddy at Yale, is our executive producer."

"So that's how you came up with his name so quickly."

"And now that Lucy is out of the way, Richard's chances of becoming the next Democratic nominee for governor seem assured. She would have been a formidable opponent," Gypsy said.

"Yes. And now, of course, she has no chance at all."

"Do you know what happened to her after she lost her seat in the House?"

"I believe she moved out of state."

"I'm going to find out where."

"There might be answers closer by. Mrs. McNeil still has children living here. A son who's a stockbroker on Wall Street. A daughter, too, I believe. I think the daughter married into some prominent Italian family in Brooklyn. Wasn't there quite a fuss about it? It guaranteed Mrs. McNeil the Italian vote. Some people thought she had engineered the romance."

"Some particularly suspicious WASP Republicans . . ." Gypsy hesitated. "Can you come up with the last name, Marguerite? The daughter's married name?"

Marguerite poured enough cream in her coffee to send her cholesterol level and Sealtest stock soaring. "I'm afraid not."

"Was it Santini?"

"I'm sorry. I really do not know."

"It doesn't matter. You've remembered enough."

"Well, perhaps not. I can't remember what I did with my time before you made a home for yourself in

Gypsy Dugan's body. I certainly don't remember life being quite this interesting."

"Definitely not Santini," Kendra said. "Romano. Patsy McNeil's husband's name is Vincent Romano and they don't call him Vinnie for short. He's known as Ducks. And don't ask me why."

"Ducks Romano. Sounds like the Wednesday night special at Villa Napoli." Gypsy shook her head. It wasn't even noon, and Kendra had already dug up a bushel load of information on Lucy McNeil and all her kin. She had come down to Gypsy's dressing room to make a full report.

Perry, who was sitting catty-corner from Kendra, did a few nearly perfect quacks.

"How long will it take to put together a family tree?" Gypsy asked Kendra.

"For a family like the Romanos? About a year, give or take a century. These Italian families are what's politely known as extended. They're large to start with, then on top of that they count everybody they ever shared pasta with. In-laws, distant cousins, godchildren, friends of great-godchildren's stepcousins." She shrugged.

"I want to know if Mark Santini had any relationship to Ducks Romano."

"That's a lot easier. Can I use the phone over there?" Kendra didn't wait for an answer. She crossed the room and started dialing.

Gypsy had already filled in the whole story for Perry. "You can't go talking to these people, sweet pea," Perry said. "No matter whether Romano had anything to do with Santini's death, he's not going to be real fond of you or anybody else on this show. We're the folks that ran his mama-in-law out of town."

"No, you're right. I'm too well-known. But not everyone who works on the show is."

Perry rolled her eyes. "Oh boy."

"Come on. Here's your chance to be a real reporter."

"I'm sitting through *King Lear*, Skinner's theories of behavior modification, and sex education trying to be a real reporter. You know that three girls in that sex-ed class thought douching with Coca-Cola would keep them from getting pregnant?"

"Diet or regular?"

Perry shook her head. "What do you want me to do?"

Kendra hung up the phone. "Mark Santini was Ducks Romano's first cousin. His mother and Ducks's father were sister and brother."

"Bingo." Gypsy's interior computer was overloading. She took a legal pad and began to diagram relationships.

"How'd you find that out so quick?" Perry asked Kendra.

"I grew up in Brooklyn, and I still go there to get my hair cut. The guy who does it is a regular Italian genealogy service. He's always talking about who married who in the old neighborhood and where they're living. I figured if he didn't know, he'd know somebody who did. Nailed it on the third call. Told 'em I was trying to find a long-lost godchild."

"So did this Ducks dude have something to do with Mark Santini's death?" Perry asked.

"There was talk at the time that the shooting met all the criteria for a Mafia hit," Kendra said. "I don't know if these Romanos have connections to the mob, but they've got more money than God. And some people think one thing means the other. I can do some checking."

"But that leaves out Richard Adamson entirely. And that's where we started." Gypsy leaned her head back against the sofa.

"You've got to get ready for your taping," Perry pointed out. She was out of school for the day. A water main had broken and flooded classrooms. She and Gypsy were going to spend the afternoon together working out bugs in the Norman Carroll story before the taping commenced.

"Yeah, I know." Gypsy closed her eyes. "Why would Ducks Romano want his own cousin dead? And what would it have to do with Richard, who had already taken care of Lucy McNeil . . ."

"Who happens to be Ducks Romano's mother-in-law in exile," Kendra finished.

The telephone rang. Perry answered it and brought it over to Gypsy.

"Hey, Gyps."

Gypsy recognized Casey's voice. "Hey . . ." She remembered the way they had parted. She had sunk to a new low by using him as a way to make Owen jealous. Her entire moral code had decayed beyond recognition.

"What was that all about last night?" he asked.

"Stupidity and manipulation. I'm really sorry."

"You're still obsessed with the Whitfields, aren't you?"

He couldn't know the half of it. She had spent the whole day trying not to think about Owen, but she hadn't succeeded. She suspected that was going to be the blueprint for the rest of her life. "I don't think it's something I'll have to worry about anymore. I'm just sorry I involved you."

"Look, I've got some information about Richard Adamson. I've talked to a few people since I got here. The story I came for didn't pan out, so I've had time to do some checking around. Seems that Adamson decided he was going to move to the executive mansion in Albany well before Lucy McNeil was out of the picture. One of my sources said old Richard did a little wheeling and dealing trying to convince some of Lucy's supporters on the Hill that she wasn't competent or upright enough to be New York's next governor. It's common knowledge that he and Lucy had a bit of a confrontation after that, and he came out the worse for wear. He's a gentleman, or he's supposed to be one, and he was hitting well below the belt, even for our nation's capital. Anyway, he went back to New York."

"And?"

"It wasn't too long afterward that McNeil was exposed, so to speak."

"What's the prevailing wisdom now?"

"Essentially that Adamson tried to warn people in the party, and no one paid enough attention. He comes off looking pretty good. Tough enough to take risks, savvy enough to see what nobody else was willing to, gentleman enough to let Lucy hang herself."

"What do you think?"

"I think there's more to the story."

Gypsy thought so, too. And the pieces were all falling together now. She hung up carefully and faced Perry and Kendra. "There's just a little more I have to know. You two willing?"

"I'm in," Kendra said.

"It could mean your job."

Kendra smirked. "Hey, there are a thousand places for a woman of my talents."

"Perry?"

Perry hunched her shoulders forward and hooked her thumbs in nonexistent belt loops. "Dese and doze and dem. I'ma riding over ta Brooklyn, see, and I'ma gonna find out what kinda friends dem two, Mark and Ducks was. You know what I'm saying?"

Gypsy knew exactly what she was saying. Lots of things might be wrong with her own life, but somewhere along the way, she had made wonderful friends.

The story wasn't pretty. In fact even in "The Whole Truth" Hall of Infamy, it stood out like a shining beacon of betrayal and greed.

At close to midnight Gypsy sat alone in her dressing room looking at the diagram that she'd made earlier in the day. Names were circled; arrows connected circles. Dates had been added. She had spent the evening going through her address book and dialing everyone with a Southern California area code, most of whom were complete strangers to her. In the six and a half months since the accident she had perfected the art of carrying on entire personal and indepth conversations with acquaintances who rarely caught on that she didn't remember one thing about them. That skill had served her well tonight.

She mulled over everything she had discovered. Now that she knew why Mark had been murdered, she wasn't sure exactly what to do with the information.

"Gypsy?" A knock coincided with her name, and the door swung open.

She had just enough time to turn the notepad over before Des walked in.

"What are you doing here so late? You're going to look like hell tomorrow. You looked like hell today."

She hadn't slept in more than thirty-six hours, but she wasn't a bit sleepy, just punchy. Her judgment was impaired. She was sure of that because she wanted nothing more than to stand up and take a swing at Des's Pekingese nose.

"What are you doing here?" she countered. "I thought you went home hours ago."

"Billy called and said you hadn't left yet, and he was worried about you."

"I didn't realize Billy reported to you."

"That's not reporting. That's concern. He's concerned, I'm concerned. You don't seem like yourself."

"Which self don't I seem like? This one? Or the one before the accident?"

"It's all the same to me."

"But it's not. We both know I'm not the same. There are things I don't remember. Or didn't . . ." She watched him carefully.

She got the desired response. For just a moment he

seemed flustered, then he grinned. "Your memories are coming back?"

"Some of them." She might be a little disoriented and loose-tongued, but she knew better than to go on. She stood up, casually slipping the notepad against her skirt. "Maybe if I go home and get some sleep, I'll remember more. Who knows?"

"What have you been working on there? The Norman Carroll thing? Another story idea?"

"Just some ideas. We'll have to schedule some time to go over them." *You, me, Richard Adamson, and the district attorney,* she added silently.

"Don't leave me in suspense. What kind of ideas?"

She started around him. "The kind that win prizes. What else? Trust me, Des."

"Now you've got my curiosity up." He reached for her notepad.

She held it tighter. "Whoa, boy. Hands off. My story. I'll let you in on it when I'm ready."

"This story got anything to do with your phone call to Sandy Ferguson at Alpha-Omega?"

Sandy Ferguson had been call number six. He had propositioned her after two sentences. "You know, that's the dumbest name for a movie studio," she said. "It sounds like a college sorority." She started to sing off-key. "We are the sisters of Alpha-Omega. Turn up the music and rent a keg-a." She moved a little farther around him, but his hand still held tightly to her notepad.

"Sandy called me. Said you sounded a little odd. He wanted to know why you were pumping him for information about my years there."

"It never hurts to understand the people you're working for."

"It might just hurt me."

"Don't be silly. Sandy Ferguson didn't have a thing to tell me that could hurt you." Not by itself, anyway.

"Give me the notepad, Gyps." He yanked and the notepad slid from her hand.

He turned it over and his eyes scanned the top page. She took a step backward. She was one step closer to the door.

She expected him to become furious. Instead he only looked tired. "So, what exactly do you think you know?"

"I don't want to talk about this here, and I don't want to talk about it now."

"You're going to anyway. And don't try to get any closer to the door because you won't make it."

Resignation, not threat, sounded in his voice. But Gypsy wasn't going to test him. Des was a short man, but his shoulders were nearly as wide as his legs were long. And his hands were powerful enough to finish her off quickly.

As if he knew what she was thinking he shook her head. "Put that out of your mind. You don't have to worry. I'm not going to hurt you. I don't hurt people."

"No? Too bad Mark Santini's not around to ask about that."

"I didn't kill Mark. I didn't hire anybody to kill him, either. His death was as much a surprise to me as it was to you."

"I doubt that. I was standing right next to him at the time, and I suspect it was mighty surprising to me."

"You don't remember?"

She shook her head.

"What do you know, Gyps?"

She didn't have any reason to believe he wouldn't hurt her except for the expression in his eyes. "What are you going to do to me if I tell you?"

He smiled. Not an evil smile, just an exhausted one. She hadn't slept in thirty-six hours, but from Desmond's smile Gypsy knew he hadn't slept in months. Not a real night's sleep.

"I'm going to listen," he said. "And then I'm going to tell you if you're right."

"And then?" It was the question of the year, the question of her life—or what was left of it.

"And then we're going to sit down together and figure out exactly what we should do about it." He handed back the notepad.

"Do?"

He smiled the same sad smile. "You're looking at the biggest story of your career, Gyps. Don't blow it. Sit down with me, and let's make sure you win the show an Emmy."

∽ 24

THE FINAL FRAMES DISAPPEARED FROM THE television screen and there was an appreciative silence. Then Kendra began to applaud, and the others who were gathered in Gypsy's apartment to preview the Norman Carroll story took it up. Gypsy flicked off the VCR. "So you like it?"

"You did a really great job, Gyps. It works. It's not maudlin, but I felt a couple of moments right here." Casey touched his chest.

"A big, tough guy like you?" She shot him a grateful smile. She had struggled hard not to play to the lowest common denominator. She had let the violence, the pathos of the kids' lives speak for themselves. The most significant scene was a fight on the school grounds during the lunch period. Her favorite camera man had realized that the faces of the observers were as poignant as the fight itself. In the editing Gypsy had interspersed that footage with interviews of some of the same kids, who had insisted in macho monotones that nothing that happened at the school upset or frightened them. The television audience could make their own decision.

"Perry, you're sure you're not sixteen?" Kendra asked.

Perry tossed her head. She had proved herself to be a real trouper. She had sized up story potential like a seasoned reporter, and during the taping she had made sure that she was always where the important action was taking place. "Baby doll, I'm never going to see sixteen again. Wouldn't, if somebody gave it to me as a gift."

Grant cleared his throat. "Speaking of gifts, I've brought a little Christmas present for Perry."

Gypsy knew her cue. She crossed the room and pulled the package from the inside of an old steamer trunk. Grant had given her the gift to hide. As a little boy he had liked nothing better than wrapping found items and giving them away. It was still his delight.

Perry tore off the green foil and began to chuckle. "I knew you had it in for me." She passed the gift around the room for everyone to admire. Grant had carefully framed Perry's essay on the theme of betrayal in *King Lear,* complete with his red-penciled corrections and helpful suggestions—and her hard-won A minus.

"You've got a future in academics," he said.

"Nope, she's got a future on television." Gypsy was still basking in the warm glow of a job well-done. Norman Carroll segments would run all next week. She had put together the promos herself, and already considerable interest had been generated. Her first full-fledged project as producer was going to be a success.

It might also be her last.

"What about you?" Casey asked Gypsy. "Are you ever going to be content just reading copy again?"

She shrugged. "That's a bridge I'll cross later." Or not at all.

"We could start our own production company," Kendra said.

"Yeah, we could call it 'Some Part of the Truth As Near As We Can Figure It.' Be more honest," Perry said.

"'The Truth or a Bunch of Damned Vicious Lies,'" Kendra suggested. "Or how about 'Whatever Sells'?"

"I'll have to put someone else in charge of promotion," Gypsy said. "You two are a washout."

In reality, the idea of a production company was immensely appealing. It was something Elisabeth could have done if she'd just used her imagination. She'd had the capital, the contacts, and at least some of the experience she would have needed to get started. All she had been missing was the conviction that she had the right to pursue her own dreams. Owen wouldn't have stood in her way. He had loved her, and she could have made him understand.

Before the alienation had set in. The doubts. The fears.

Grant and the two colleagues he'd brought with him got to their feet. "We've got a faculty-senior basketball game this afternoon. The last one before Christmas break, so we've got to get going. Thanks for giving us a preview. We'll tell the rest of the staff they don't have to skip town before this airs."

Gypsy walked the Norman Carroll contingent to the door and got their coats while "The Whole Truth" crew dug into the food she'd ordered from the corner deli. "Grant, may I speak to you for just a moment?" The other teachers said their good-byes and left to wait for him downstairs.

"I just wanted to say thanks for everything." She really wanted to say a final good-bye, but none of the reasons for it would make sense to him.

He shrugged, a self-deprecating lift of his wide, young shoulders under his wool overcoat. "I didn't do anything. I'm glad you decided to film us. Maybe now more people will understand what's happening to these kids."

"Just keep doing what you're doing. The show will be forgotten in a matter of weeks, but you can make a real difference."

He smiled his perfect Owen smile. "You'll find this strange, but sometimes you sound like my mother. That's exactly what she would have said."

Gypsy swallowed, determined not to cry. "I'm glad you can still hear her voice."

He held out his hand. "Good-bye."

She took it in hers, a wider, stronger hand than the tiny one Elisabeth had held for walks along their private beach. "Good-bye, Grant."

"I don't suppose now that the story's completed and we're not working together . . ."

She leaned forward and kissed his cheek. "Go find some nice young woman who really deserves you."

He grinned, not at all humiliated. "Your loss, you know."

"Oh, I know."

She watched him walk away. She was still staring at the same spot, empty now, when Casey came over to put his arm around her shoulders. "You okay?"

She leaned against him and took a deep breath. "I'm fine."

"I still don't think you should go to that party tonight."

"I know you don't."

"I don't think you realize how dangerous this could be."

"I do."

"I can't believe Des sanctioned this. I really can't."

Casey only knew a part of the Richard Adamson story. He didn't know how thoroughly Des was mixed up in it. If Casey knew the "whole truth," he would have moved heaven and earth to keep her from going to Marguerite's Christmas party. And if Marguerite had known everything, she could not have been persuaded to give the party at all.

At least Owen wasn't going to be at the party to witness the biggest scoop of Gypsy's career. Marguerite pointedly had not invited him. It had been a month since Gypsy had seen him.

"Nothing's going to stop me from going tonight." She turned so she could see Casey's face. "You really don't have to go with me."

"I'll be there. I'm not letting you do this alone."

"You're a pal."

"Yeah. And don't think I like it that way . . ." But he smiled, to let her know he understood that things between them were the way they had to be.

She made arrangements to meet him in the early evening at Birch Haven. He was going to visit Connecticut relatives first, then leave from there for Marguerite and Seamus's estate. Billy would be driving Gypsy.

"We've got to go," Perry said, coming up behind them with Kendra trailing her. "We don't have the whole day off like some people."

Gypsy held out her hands to both of them. They had come into her life when she desperately needed friends, and neither of them had ever wavered in their loyalty to her.

"Hey, sweet patootie, we're just going across town. You'll see us tomorrow . . ." Perry cocked her head and searched Gypsy's face for the source of her tears.

Gypsy smiled a watery smile. She had hoped to stay in control. "You're both terrific, you know that? I can't say thank you enough. For everything."

Kendra looked suspicious. "Hey, is something going on?"

"Nope. Just letting you know how much I appreciated your help on this. Both of you."

Neither woman looked convinced, but Perry hugged her and Kendra kissed her cheek. Then they were gone, too.

"Gyps, you really aren't as blasé about this confrontation with Adamson tonight as you've been letting on, are you?" Casey asked.

"One thing dying—nearly dying—teaches you is not to hedge your bets."

"You're not going to die tonight, Gyps. I'm not going to let you."

"Of course you're not."

He was silent for a long time, staring at the same

empty patch of hallway. "You called your folks recently?"

"Last night. I wanted to wish them a merry Christmas."

"They have anything good to say?"

"My mother's still praying for my soul."

"What did you say to that?"

She managed to smile a little. "I told her to pray a little harder."

She had died once—or something closely approximating it—without any warning at all. No angels had visited since, no heavenly jazz quartets had sounded, and no technicolor dreams with Dolby Surround Sound and a Cecil B. DeMille cast of thousands had warned her of her inevitable ending.

But Gypsy had known, since waking from the accident, that the rules by which she had always played were temporarily suspended. The former Gypsy Dugan existed somewhere else; this Gypsy Dugan wasn't making any bets where her predecessor was or in what form.

And out on Long Island, Elisabeth Whitfield lay in a nursing home bed, her heart beating steadily while her soul wandered increasingly dangerous paths.

The old saying that the only things for certain were death and taxes didn't even apply. Death was far more relative than she had ever expected.

So what was she doing standing in a doorway across from Owen's office building, waiting for him to leave work for the day? She knew he was expected at the nursing home about seven. She had called the home, passing herself off as his secretary. Then she had passed herself off as the nursing home bookkeeper in a conversation with Owen's real secretary, in order to discover that he would be leaving his office about four for an early business dinner.

It was 3:56, and she had been standing there for fifteen minutes listening to a Salvation Army Santa on the corner shaking a handbell. The most she could hope for was a glimpse of Owen. The glimpse would settle nothing, prove nothing, accomplish nothing. But still she waited. Because if she had learned one thing in the past months, it was that the heart had an agenda all its own.

He exited precisely at four, unheard of punctuality for a creative genius who only rarely was certain what day of the week it was. His Burberry cashmere overcoat was unbuttoned, the belt flapping as he strode toward the parking garage where he would pick up his car. He carried a large briefcase—no one in Manhattan walked the streets with their hands empty. She supposed it was filled with work to keep him busy during the long, lonely night after his visit with Elisabeth ended.

She wondered if he would read Elisabeth poetry tonight or if he would just talk softly to her. Had he confessed to his sleeping wife that he had made love to another woman on their library sofa? That he was consumed with guilt, overcome with shame? She hoped he hadn't, that somehow he had accepted their joining for what it was. A release. A reunion.

But she really didn't think he had.

She stepped out of the doorway when she could no longer see him. She watched him turn the corner, his bright, silver hair and charcoal gray coat disappearing among the crush of people exiting nearby buildings.

Gone.

"I love you," she said out loud. "Goddamn it, I love you, Owen Whitfield!"

No one seemed to find that unusual. Midtown Manhattan moved around her as she continued to stand there, and no one said a rude word or seemed to think that her weeping was strange.

Birch Haven had been in Marguerite's family for six generations, and little had changed since those first Warringtons had planted orchards of plums and cherries and hired master craftsmen to hew shingles and fire bricks—both of which had weathered artfully and without complaint through two eventful centuries. The succeeding generation had designed the drive and flanked it with birch trees to give the property its name. The generation after that one had enlarged the house to its present twenty rooms. But the spirit of staid tranquillity, of old money and older values had probably remained much the same from the beginning.

The young Elisabeth had loved Birch Haven. She and Marguerite had ridden every inch of its fifty-five acres on high-spirited ponies. They had climbed the magnificent old trees to pelt each other with sour green plums and cherry pits, adorned their young bodies and flaunted what little they had to impress the boy-heirs of neighboring estates.

Autumn at Birch Haven had been Elisabeth's favorite season. The leaves had turned pumpkin orange and Lucifer red, and there were fragrant bonfires and Jonathan and Winesap apples to press for cider. The house had been perfect for Halloween parties, with household staff dressed as skeletons and ghosts, and room after room draped with angel hair cobwebs.

There were no cobwebs tonight. The leaves had already performed their flamboyant salute to death, and Halloween was just a memory. But the ghosts that Gypsy was interested in were no respecter of seasons. They were Richard Adamson's ghosts, and they had lived with him for some time, waiting for exposure.

"Yes, your men were here, and they did their dirty work," Marguerite said. "I still can't believe I agreed to let this happen at Birch Haven."

Gypsy wandered the old library, smoothing her palm along the walnut panels and over the cracked wine leather sofas that had resided in this room as long as anyone could remember. "Good. Nothing looks out of place. And you did it because you want to see justice done and because you're becoming addicted to excitement."

Marguerite, in black velvet and a rope of pink pearls, made a noise not unlike a snort. "Whatever else he is, Richard has been part of my circle of friends for years."

"And you've seen through him that long. You know, with your insights about people, you could have had a career in television news, too. Or you could have been an important asset to the production company I never thought to start."

"What are you talking about?"

"Just one of the ways dear Elisabeth screwed up."

"Please remember there were many more ways that she did not."

"I know that, too."

"You are just full of little gems of wisdom from this experience, aren't you? I hope if this body-hopping phenomenon ever happens to me, I will come back as a horse, so I don't have to think incessantly about all my failures."

Gypsy looked up. "I'd watch what I wished for. You could end up as a drop of Superglue."

Marguerite gave one of her rare smiles. "I have to leave you now. I have a dozen things to see to."

"I know. Everyone should be arriving soon."

"Seamus is probably off somewhere repotting bougainvillea or trimming mounds of jasmine into pirate ships and mermaids."

Gypsy had been amazed to find that Seamus's bizarre experiments in hybridizing and adapting tropical plant life were beginning to pay off. Among other oddities Birch Haven now sported a magnolia tree of the type that grew so prolifically and sweetly in the land of cotton. It was only three years old, but so far it had survived Connecticut's harsh winters. "He really has done extraordinary things with the grounds."

"Seamus is no different from the rest of us, though

he's more vigilant about it. He wants to master his own little world. And he's proving that he can, at least occasionally."

"Go master yours. I'll get a shot at my own when Richard arrives."

"Just promise me you will be careful."

Gypsy didn't quite meet Marguerite's eyes. "I'm becoming a great believer in fate. Whatever happens here tonight is exactly what's supposed to. You have nothing to worry about."

By the time Gypsy emerged from the library there were sounds from outside that indicated the party was beginning. Marguerite had gone over the guest list with her. It was a medium-sized dinner party with about forty guests, most of whom Elisabeth knew but Gypsy didn't. She got her coat and wandered down the snow-dusted front steps to Seamus's expansive conservatory, which sat in glassy splendor some distance from the house. She took a martini from a bartender wearing a white jacket, and oysters en brochette from a young woman who was tempting the expanding crowd with the contents of a silver tray.

Gypsy knew the evening's plan. The guests would mingle and sip cocktails for the first hour in the conservatory, as well as out on the lawn where an old-fashioned horse-drawn sleigh offered rides for the nostalgic. Then they would adjourn to the snug barn built of ancient chestnut logs, where pot-bellied woodstoves warmed the air and twinkling Christmas lights strung from the rafters illuminated a hardy buffet. A harp and flute would entertain, and, later, when the meal had ended, everyone would move inside, where a small dance band was set up in what was still a functioning ballroom.

Gypsy planned to make her move inside with Richard, before the crowd led the way.

She was still working on her first martini and deeply immersed in a conversation with a dotty old dowager who had been a friend of Elisabeth's mother when she saw Richard strolling through the crowd. Missy wasn't at his side, which surprised her, but Richard and Missy often went to separate parties. That way, if there was more than one important social event in an evening, they could cover them both and be certain that the advancement of Richard Adamson's political career was among the topics of conversation.

Missy's absence was a bonus. Richard would be easier to corner. And to trap.

Gypsy avoided him neatly, skirting the crowd and choosing conversations in remote corners hidden by palm trees and hibiscus. As the evening progressed she took walks around the grounds just to maintain her distance, and when the guests were neatly herded to the barn and the buffet, she trailed behind with a young married couple who were fascinated by every story that she told them about "The Whole Truth."

"Charles Casey has not arrived," Marguerite said, pulling Gypsy to one side when she approached the buffet.

"I know. I can't understand why he's not here." Gypsy understood perfectly well, of course. She had been the one to painstakingly map out directions to the wrong side of Litchfield County. She hoped Casey wouldn't find his way here at all. She knew of no maps to the estates and farmhouses of the rich and famous. He could wander the winding roads of rural Connecticut for the entire evening and never expose himself to the dangers that waited for him here. Likewise, Billy had been dismissed for the evening on her instructions. She had known she wouldn't find out anything with either man hovering over her all evening.

"Well, if he doesn't come, I do not want you to go through with confronting Richard. You cannot do it alone."

"I won't be alone. You know I won't." Gypsy unobtrusively tapped her chest. Under the red knit dress with the hemline that drew attention to her long slender legs was a transmitting microphone, a professional wire straight out of "NYPD Blue." And somewhere down below, in the plum grove that had been her childhood delight, was "The Whole Truth" sound crew, who were going to record every word that Richard Adamson spoke.

Marguerite was called away before she could issue more ultimatums, and from that moment on, Gypsy made a point of avoiding her as well as Richard. She filled her plate, although she couldn't eat a bite, and went to sit beside several friends of Owen's who willingly played the Tarleton twins to her Scarlett O'Hara.

Dessert was circulating by the time she started toward Richard. She had done such a thorough job of staying away from him that she wasn't sure he realized she was there. She was sure of it when his expression changed at the sight of her. The same flash of animosity that she'd noted the last time they'd met burst like poorly timed fireworks across his face.

"Miss Dugan." He inclined his head in greeting.

"Richard." She nearly cooed his name, and the three women surrounding him moved a little farther back to make room for what was obviously going to be an interesting exchange.

"Did you just arrive?"

"No, I've been here." She dimpled deeply. "I've been admiring you from afar." Her long eyelashes fanned her cheek.

He frowned. Her message was so clear that no one standing in ear shot could fail to miss it. Gypsy Dugan and Richard Adamson were old friends . . . or more.

"Have you had dessert?" he asked.

"Not yet. Could I . . . tempt you?"

He took her elbow and said his good-byes to the others. They strolled out of the barn and toward the house. They were out of immediate earshot of anyone before he spoke. "What was that all about?"

"About? I was just saying hello."

"You were coming on to me. It's a little late for that, don't you think?"

"I can't imagine what you mean." She actually could imagine, but she needed some direct clarification. Richard's relationship to the former occupant of this body was still a mystery.

"I think we tried this some years ago, and it went nowhere."

She tried a shot in the dark. "You mean *you* tried this. As I recall I wasn't available."

"Not to me. Just to half the men in Washington."

Bingo. She scored a point for the former Gypsy Dugan, who'd obviously had more class than she had let on. "Richard, you absolutely do exaggerate."

"I have no intention of starting anything now. I have a career and a wife."

"And the rumor is that the wife isn't terribly happy with you." Gypsy touched her fingertip to his chest. "There are other rumors, as well."

He looked as if he might like to strangle her, and not because she had refused his advances many years ago. "A politician's life is rife with rumor. And people like you are the reason."

"Well, not this time. Unfortunately for you, this rumor seems to be too, too real."

"I don't deal in rumors. If you have proof of something, the first amendment is still in effect," he said stiffly.

She nodded. "And this will make a wonderful story for our treasured free press. I have my calls in to Lucy McNeil right now. As soon as she gives me some verification . . ."

He hadn't dropped her elbow. Now he squeezed it hard. She jumped and jerked her arm from his grip. "Quite a response," she said, rubbing the injury with her fingertips. "As good as a lie detector."

"What are you trying to pull?" He was no longer stiff or pompous. Anger sparked in his eyes.

"Pull?"

This time he took her arm. He turned his head, as if looking for a place out of traffic where they could go.

"I've got what I came for," she said. "So you did have something to do with Lucy McNeil's fall from grace."

"I had nothing to do with anything. We're going inside and you're going to tell me exactly what you're trying to do and why."

"Desmond said you would behave this way."

He drew in an audible breath. She decided that like all politicians, his lung capacity must be enormous. Just when she thought he would explode, all the air came back out again in a jagged rush. "We're going inside."

"Fine." She dropped her classic sex-among-the-vocal-cords routine. Now she sounded as calculating as an Eleventh Avenue hooker. "And while we're walking, you might try thinking about what you can do for me. Because my silence is going to cost you, Richard. It's going to cost you big time."

She and Marguerite had carefully chosen the old library for the scene of this confrontation. The problem now was to be sure that Richard chose it, too. Marguerite had stationed staff in the other obvious downstairs rooms so that Richard wouldn't take her there. There were several empty rooms in the front of the house, but they would obviously be too public. And to keep Richard from dragging her upstairs, Marguerite had simply asked Seamus to pry up several of the ancient oak steps leading to the second floor. A warning sign made it clear that the stairs were in the midst of repair.

Richard knew the house. He made his way to the back, where the old library was the final room on the left of the main hall. The library had been Marguerite's father's retreat, the last male bastion in a house ruled by his wife and daughter. When Marguerite had brought friends home from prep school or college, the girls had enjoyed the run of most of the house, but the boys, and the boys alone, had been invited into Curtis Warrington's library. Richard had been one of them.

After her father's death Marguerite had left the library as a veritable shrine to his life, and Richard knew that, too. The library was the most obvious place to avoid interruption. To Gypsy's great relief he herded her there now. He had no reason to suspect that she even knew of the library's existence, much less that her camera crew had been busy there this afternoon installing equipment of the kind they had used to tape parts of the Norman Carroll story. The old paneling, the rows and rows of moldering first editions, had been perfect props.

Richard pushed open the door and flipped on the desk light, a banker's lamp with the traditional green shade. The room glowed with seasick brilliance.

"How quaint. I can almost smell cigars." Gypsy fanned the air in front of her.

Richard hadn't released her arm. Now he did, so that he could cross to the door again and close it. He leaned against it and folded his arms across his chest. "Let's have what you know, or think you do."

"Does that mean you're willing to pay to keep me from going public? You know, a story like this could make my reputation as a newswoman. It's worth a lot to me."

"I'm not going to pay you a cent. I don't believe you know anything that could hurt me. There's nothing to know. I'm scandal free."

"None of us is scandal free. Look at poor Des."

To Richard's credit he didn't pretend that he had never known Desmond Weber. "How long have you known that Web and I were roommates at Yale?"

"Awhile. But I didn't know the rest until recently."

"Rest?"

"You know, at first it was hard to imagine Des filming X-rated movies. And as a way to work his way through college." She shook her head. "Of course being a working-class gal myself, I know how desperate he must have felt sometimes, trying to compete with you silver-spoon-in-the-mouth prep school boys. I just never figured Des for that kind of flexibility. Then I started thinking . . . Some of the stories we do at 'The Whole Truth' aren't that different from pornography."

"This sounds like a conversation you should be having with Web, not me."

"Oh, I did. And that's how I found out the way you went to bat for him in your junior year when a fraternity brother discovered what he was doing. He would have been expelled, of course, and probably arrested if the dean of students had gotten involved. I mean, using girls from the surrounding colleges in starring roles . . ."

"Web was an excellent student. Intelligent, creative. When I discovered what was going on and how close he was to exposure, I pulled a few strings. I did nothing illegal or immoral. I helped a friend."

"Pornography, Richard?"

"I shut down the operation, and Web turned over a new leaf. Hardly indictable offenses." He straightened and pushed away from the door.

She gauged their distance and decided she was still perfectly safe. "You're right. Everything you did was admirable, even using your connections to get him his first legitimate job with Sandy Ferguson at Alpha-Omega studios after graduation. All admirable until the day two years ago when you went to Des and told him it was payback time."

"I don't know what you mean."

"I'll be happy to jog your memory. You went to Des and asked him to help you frame Lucy McNeil. You wanted to discredit her so that you would have a clear field when it came time for the gubernatorial primary. You had already secured the help of a law partner of Lucy's husband. You had something on him, too, I suppose, although I'll confess I don't know what it was. Not yet. But I do know the favor you asked of Des. You asked him to get the encounter between Lucy and her husband's colleague on tape, then make it public. You told him it could only benefit both of you. 'The Whole Truth' ratings would soar, you would have a good shot at the governor's mansion. Lucy McNeil, without a shred of proof that she'd been set up, would disappear from politics and the state of New York."

Richard was silent.

"Not a pretty story, Richard. Just exactly the kind America and 'The Whole Truth' love the most."

"If any of this was true, and, of course, it's all preposterous, what proof would you have? McNeil's word that she was a virtuous lady after all? I've seen those tapes you aired. Good old Lucy was having the time of her life."

"No, you chose the man for her downfall like the pro you are. Her marriage was foundering; her husband's partner was attentive and attractive, and she was absolutely sure he would be discreet. Lucy was guilty, but not half as guilty as you."

Richard started toward her. "What do you want me to say, Gypsy? That I'm guilty? We both know it would be my word against yours . . ." He stopped in front of her and rested his hands on her shoulders. "Unless you happen to be recording this?"

Her heart was beating double time. She had maintained an outward appearance of calm, but with every word she had grown more anxious. "How could I do that?"

Before she could stop him, he hooked his thumbs under her collar and wrenched his hands apart. Six tiny pearl buttons left six button loops at the same moment. And the device taped to her chest was visible.

He ripped it off in one easy motion, although she doubted he'd had this experience before. She gave a soft cry and tried to push him away. He threw the microphone to the floor and crunched it under his heel. "I suppose you could tell someone about this," he said, "but since it makes you look even more like the sleazebag reporter you are, I doubt you will. And you have nothing on tape to incriminate me. Nothing but some harebrained theories."

"That's where you're wrong. I've got Des, and he's with the police right now giving his statement. You made a big mistake when you had Mark Santini killed. Des would have stood by you on the Lucy McNeil story. She *was* guilty, after all, even if she was set up. But when you realized the link between Mark and Ducks Romano, and Ducks and Lucy, you lost your cool. When you discovered that Mark was working with Ducks to try and find some evidence to incriminate you, you decided the easy way out was to have him murdered. And I was supposed to be a target, too, wasn't I? You were afraid that Mark had talked to me because we were becoming good friends. But the crowd closed in too quickly, and your hit man couldn't get off another shot in time."

Richard didn't bother to deny it. Obviously he felt safe now that she could no longer tape his every word. He had no idea that sandwiched between leather bound volumes of Shakespeare and the Transcendentalists were cameras recording every move and sound he made.

No one could sneer as chillingly as someone of Richard's impeccable breeding. He proved it now. "You're absolutely right. Then, later, you conveniently lost your memory, and since you'd never had any scruples to begin with, I was sure I was safe again. Until I started hearing that you were making changes in the show, that you were pushing Des to do socially relevant material, that you were digging deeper and deeper and talking about Mark's death . . ."

"Des told you that?"

He shook his head. "Des is a wuss. I had other

sources. Kevin O'Flynn will do anything if the price is right."

Gypsy didn't wince, though the temptation was there. "So you tried to have me killed again, even though you'd promised Des I would be safe. You hire bozos. If they were running your campaign, you couldn't get elected dogcatcher."

"I'm truly surprised you had the brainpower to put all of this together."

"You underestimate your enemies. What happened to you, Richard? You've always been a manipulator. When did you become a killer, too?"

He went from sneer to Boy Scout poster smile. "You can't prove a thing."

Her own responses had been flawless until that moment. She had maintained bravado and faced him down without giving away any of her emotions. But now her facade slipped. Triumph, or something close to it, must have shown in her eyes. Because Richard's smile faltered.

Then recognition dawned. "You bitch!"

"Now, now . . ."

"There's a tape in here, too. Or a camera."

"Don't be ridiculous. How did I know you were going to drag me in here? And Marg's not the kind of person who would—"

"Marg?" Rage contorted his face. "Marg? Jesus, you've become a good friend of Marguerite's, haven't you?" He slapped her across the face so hard that she stumbled back against the desk. "Who do you think you are to come after me?"

There were people watching this, and people who knew she was here. Help was only seconds away. But somehow Gypsy had known that tonight would be the end for her. Some instinct developed by too many brushes with death had warned her. She had said her good-byes. She had even sent Casey away so that he wouldn't be here to witness the end. She was sorry that Marguerite and Seamus had to be party to it.

But she was glad, so very, very glad, that Owen Whitfield was miles away at Elisabeth's bedside.

She pushed Richard with all her strength, but her strength was nothing compared to his. And Richard had gone mad.

"Bitch!" He grabbed a glass paperweight from Curtis Warrington's desk and lifted it high. The door flew open and with surprise Gypsy saw Casey flying across the room toward them. For just an instant she thought her instincts had been wrong after all. She even smiled at Casey, or thought she did.

Then there was a shattering pain in her right temple and eternity shimmered somewhere in the distance.

"Gypsy!" She heard Casey's voice. She wanted to tell him that it was all right. She had borrowed this life. It wasn't hers to live or leave. Her sadness was as great as her pain, but eclipsed by both was simple blessed relief.

There was a light in the distance. A familiar welcoming light. She relaxed and let herself drift toward it.

～ 25

SOMEONE WAS MURMURING IN A FOREIGN language. The words were mellifluous, and even though she couldn't understand them, they were somehow familiar and comforting.

Her head hurt, and her body felt stiff and rusty, like the Tin Woodman after a night in a thunderstorm. Her eyes were shut, but she wanted to shut them tighter, because she knew when she opened them that life was going to begin again. And she wasn't sure she was ready for it.

She couldn't remember anything clearly. A party. A car accident. A rugged, dark-haired man with a deep voice and cynical grin.

Owen.

The voice faltered. She heard a rustling, as if someone was getting out of a chair. Change clanking, fabric sliding against a harder surface. She felt something cool against her cheek.

A kiss.

She considered not opening her eyes. It hurt to remember, and she knew that as soon as she began to stir, it was going to hurt more. But curiosity was victorious over the instinct to protect herself.

She opened her eyes. Her pupils weren't used to the light, and the harsh glare was a stabbing pain. For a moment she remembered another light, one brighter than the sun, and she wondered why she was no longer moving toward it. Then the light began to fade. A man was bending over her. She couldn't adjust her vision quickly enough to see who it was. He was there, and then he wasn't.

"Sleep well," he said.

The man wasn't looking at her. She could tell that much. As her vision sharpened she could see him turning away.

Then she knew.

He was moving toward the door, a door adorned with a colorful wreath of holly and red velvet bows. She couldn't push herself upright because her muscles seemed too weak and out of practice to respond that quickly. She opened her mouth to say his name, but nothing came out except air.

He was almost to the door. Tears spilled over her eyelids to gently wash her cheeks. She lifted her head and tried once more.

"Ow—en."

He paused, but he didn't turn.

"Get back . . . here!"

The command was pure Gypsy Dugan, but the voice that emerged was Elisabeth's.

The voice that emerged was *Elisabeth's*.

She was home again.

Owen turned slowly, as if he fully expected to see her lying there with her eyes closed and her hands limp at her side.

She lifted one of those hands in a slight wave. And she managed something like a smile.

His face contorted. His shoulders began to shake. Hers were shaking, too, and that seemed like a very promising sign.

He was at her side in heartbeats, tears streaming down his cheeks. "Are you really . . ."

She would never waste another moment of this chance. This precious chance, this unfathomable gift. "I . . . I love you. I kept forgetting . . . to tell you."

"Elisabeth." He grabbed her hand and held it to his cheek.

Her arm moved slowly. Her fingers extended. She touched his hair. "Owen . . . I have to know . . . Is Gypsy Dugan . . ."

He smothered her palm with kisses. He was crying harder. His head was bent, his words muffled. "Don't worry about her now."

"Is she . . . dead?"

"No one died in the accident. You weren't responsible . . ."

But Gypsy was dead, and Owen knew. Elisabeth could feel the truth. She knew the truth at the very center of her soul. Someone had called Owen to tell him what had happened at Marguerite's party.

She hadn't dreamed Gypsy's life. None of what she had experienced in Gypsy's life was a dream. . . .

She formed her words and pushed them out. "Gypsy was a good woman . . . no matter what anyone thinks. . . ."

Owen crawled up next to her on the narrow bed and wrapped his arms around her. Elisabeth buried her face against his neck.

It would have been hard to say who was holding whom.

Discover Contemporary Romances at Their Sizzling Hot Best from Avon Books

THE LOVES OF RUBY DEE
by Curtiss Ann Matlock

78106-9/$5.99 US/$7.99 Can

JONATHAN'S WIFE
by Dee Holmes

78368-1/$5.99 US/$7.99 Can

DANIEL'S GIFT
by Barbara Freethy

78189-1/$5.99 US/$7.99 Can

FAIRYTALE
by Maggie Shayne

78300-2/$5.99 US/$7.99 Can

Coming Soon

WISHES COME TRUE
by Patti Berg

78338-X/$5.99 US/$7.99 Can